FRIENDS AND ENEMIES

FRIENDS AND ENEMIES

David Field

ATHENA PRESS
LONDON

FRIENDS AND ENEMIES
Copyright © David Field 2005

All Rights Reserved

ISBN 1 84401 460 6

First Published 2005 by
ATHENA PRESS
Queen's House, 2 Holly Road
Twickenham TW1 4EG
United Kingdom

Printed for Athena Press

To Louisa, Camilla and Helle

Contents

One: The House Swap

ommy was on holiday with his parents. Tommy was fifteen years old, but he still liked going with his mum and dad, because, basically, they were crazy and you did not know what was going to happen from one moment to the next. And some pretty funny things did happen from time to time. At any rate, Mum and Dad had decided that they would have a lot of holidays, and last year they had been in South America, and were off to China soon, but in between they were going to France.

What had happened was that Great-aunt Jemima had died at the age of ninety-three and had left all this money to Mummy, but the will stated that Mummy had to spend all the money by three years after Great-aunt Jemima died, because Great-aunt Jemima believed, and this was in the will, that the world would end three years after she died, so what was the point in not spending it all? Great-aunt Jemima was only one of the rather curious relatives to be found in Tommy's family – but that's another matter!

So Tommy was on holiday in France. What had been arranged was a house swap. The idea was that some people in France wanted to go on holiday in England and some people in England wanted to go to France. So they just swapped houses. This was all arranged by a very clever holiday company in England (Daddy tried it on the Internet, but lost his temper in five minutes, although Tommy could have done it easily enough, or so he thought). This company had the names of all sorts of people in lots of countries who wanted to go on house-swapping holidays. Of course you swapped your house with the same kind of house in the other country.

Anyway, Tommy's house was just a little house by the sea, quite an ordinary little house. His mum had made it look very neat before they left, and had bought new knives and forks, because they knew that French people were very keen on eating. Dad said that they wouldn't be very keen on eating English food, but Mum had said that appearances help even English food. Anyway, Dad had gone to France and bought a tiny little Renault, a 'Twinkle', he said, or a Twingo, as it turned out to be, because they drive on the wrong side of the road in France and it was very nice to have the steering wheel on the other side. Also, it used up a bit more of Aunt Jemima's money – more even than all the ice creams that Tommy was going to eat, or so Tommy hoped.

The Twingo was very small indeed and Daddy said he was worried that a large dog might come and do something through the window when they were stopped at traffic lights, it was so near the ground. But it hadn't happened yet. Tommy sat in the back and they whizzed along the *autoroutes*, which is what they call motorways in France. They were going to 'two louse'.

'To rhyme with *mouse*,' said Tommy.

'No!' said Mummy, '*two loos.*'

'Like as if you were saying two toilets,' said Daddy, 'like in the painter Toulouse-Lautrec.'

Mummy sighed. Apart from the fact that she had heard the joke twenty times before, it was hardly the thing to tell Tommy. He would be sure to say it at the wrong time – not that there was a right time, anyway. In fact they were going to a little place called Ellie-la-Forêt, just about twenty kilometres outside Toulouse. A kilometre, by the way, is a kind of devalued mile and it is how they measure distance on French roads, something Tommy knew. They still had a very large number of kilometres to go before Toulouse, so Tommy went to sleep in the back seat of the Twingo.

Mummy and Daddy had bought a Michelin map, number three thousand, seven hundred and sixty-six, Tommy had seen, and this showed where Ellie-la-Forêt was, as a little blob. Somewhere in the village they would have to find their house. Funnily enough, it did not seem to have an address, just 'Ellie-la-Forêt', but the holiday company had said that there was no problem, they would find it alright.

'Wake up, Tommy,' said Mummy, as they drove through the suburbs of Toulouse, 'we'll soon be there.'

'I need a toilet,' said Tommy. 'Now,' he added.

'Well, we're in Two-loos,' said Daddy.

'Oh, shut up!' said Mummy.

'Now!' said Tommy again.

'Can you wait five minutes?'

Tommy made no reply. It was not a question that he found very easy to answer. The next bad bit of road surface settled it, though.

'No,' said Tommy, 'I can't!'

Daddy managed to pull off the road by some little bushes, just enough to preserve English decency, perhaps.

While they were waiting, Mum and Dad consulted map number three thousand, seven hundred and sixty-six.

'We're very nearly there,' said Daddy, 'look out for the sign. There's a little village coming up on the D996372 called Romolue les Bains Romains de Saint Etienne-Just. Do you notice that the longer the name, the smaller the village?' he asked Mummy.

'How big is Ellie-la-Forêt?' asked Tommy returning to the car.

'Actually,' said Mummy, 'we don't know.'

'It's just beyond Romolue les Bains Romains de Saint Etienne-Just,' chimed in Daddy.

'Who was St Etienne?' asked Tommy.

'He's the patron saint of circuses,' said Daddy, 'he was martyred by being fired from a cannon into the jaws of the circus hippopotamus, which, by the way, was called Humphrey.'

'Oh, stop it!' said Mummy. 'We'll miss Ellie-la-Forêt, if you go on with all that rubbish. It's just round the bend here.'

'Who's round the bend? Same to you. Anyway, it's not rubbish,' said Daddy. 'Have you no faith? Why, after the smoke had cleared, all they could find was little bits of feathers and a blue...'

Tommy never found out what was blue, for as they came around the next bend there was a sign saying *Romolue les Bains Romains de Saint Etienne-Just*. He saw a couple of houses, and a faded yellow sign on the side of a house saying *oily Prat*, which was a bit odd. But before Tommy could wonder about that, there was Romolue les Bains Romains de Saint Etienne-Just again, but all crossed out.

Tommy had noticed that before. When you came out of a town, they showed the name crossed out and he thought that it wasn't really very nice. He wouldn't like to see the name of their little place all crossed out. Who would, really?

Just after the crossed-out sign, there were some big ornate wrought-iron gates on the right-hand side and a glimpse of a broad gravel path and the top of some high gables in the far distance. Then a little further on, the next village sign appeared: *Abbaye des Oursiniers-Seiche-Capucins*.

'There must be an old abbey around here somewhere,' said Daddy.

'That's a bit odd,' said Mummy. 'Ellie-la-Forêt should be in between Romolue les Bains Romains de Saint Etienne-Just and Abbaye des Oursiniers-Seiche-Capucins,' rolling all the French vowel sounds around the Twingo. (Mummy was very proud of her French vowel sounds; she'd been told by a French friend that they were better than Daddy's.)

'Between Romolue and Abbaye blah-blah,' said Daddy. 'Blast! We missed it somehow.'

Daddy pulled into the side of the road just beside a sign that said 'BAR 100 m'. 'Let's go and ask in the bar,' he said, 'we must be close to the road somewhere...' and off he went.

The bar was full, but there wasn't much conversation. The TV was on: the Tour de France!

I've come at a bad time, thought Daddy. A groan went up from the crowd in front of the TV. A *very* bad time, thought Daddy. Just then the man at the bar noticed the English stranger standing in the doorway.

'*Viens, viens!* Come in, come in. What can I do you for, Monsieur? Never mind them,' the barman said, gesturing towards the crowd glued to the TV. 'They are all *les fanatiques!*'

'Well,' said Daddy, 'we are looking for Ellie-la-Forêt. Could you tell me how I can get to it from here, *s'il vous plaît?*'

"'Ow to get to Ellie-la-Forêt...? It iz eazzsy!'

'Great! Good,' said Daddy.

'Which way did you come from? Which direction?' asked the barman.

'From Romolue les something.'

'Ah! Romolue, then you went right past it, right past.'

'Ah!' said Daddy, 'so there's a turn-off to the right – or to the left…'

'To the left from here,' replied the barman. 'You can't miss it. Great big iron gates. You must be the English Milords who have rented it? Yes?'

'Well, we swapped it, actually,' said Daddy, wondering about the iron gates but assuming the 'Milords' was something out of an old film, an expression that the barman must have picked up.

'Will you have a trink – on the 'ouse, as you say in England?'

'Well, er… my family… well, okay then, thanks! Just a little one!'

'A Pernod?'

Dad hated Pernod – it tastes of liquorice – but he said yes anyway, and watched as the barman poured a large Pernod and then added water, making it go all milky and cloudy. Taking a deep breath, Dad took a gulp.

'This Tour de France,' said the barman, gesturing towards the TV. 'I never talk to anyone for a week. They are *les fanatiques*,' he repeated. 'It goes past quite close to here. It is a bedlam, a mad 'ouse!' He turned to the hissing coffee machine behind him and asked, 'Where are you from?'

'We're from—' But the reply remained unfinished as Mummy marched into the bar.

'You beast, boozing away in here! We're waiting in the car and—'

'No, look here, the barman offered…'

'Yes, but what about…?'

'It seemed a bit rude not to have just a…'

'Gosh, Pernod! I like that. You hate it…'

'Sssh! The barman gave it me,' whispered Daddy. 'Do you want a sip?'

'No, I don't. We can't both of us turn up at Ellie-la-Forêt half gone. Who's going to drive?'

'Gosh, that's a point. Can you drive? I'll tell you where to go.'

'Do you know where to go?'

All the while, the barman was watching this scene with a trace of a smile on his lips.

'*Madame, enchanté*,' he broke in. 'Madame, would you like also a trink, on the 'ouse? You must be Milady, who has taken Ellie-la-Forêt? It is a *grand plaisir* to meet you. A Pernod?'

Mummy had the good sense to say, 'No, thank you, but a coffee would be lovely, thank you.'

Almost instantly a tiny cup of steaming black gunpowder was placed on the table beside her, and the barman, all beaming smiles, retired behind the bar and began to wash glasses, in the way that barmen always do and must do to be real barmen.

'Well, do you know the way?'

'Well, yes, it's just back the way we came and on the left, or the right, one or the other!' said Daddy, the Pernod already beginning to take effect. 'It's very close. We just turn off by some big iron gates.'

'I'm not sure that I saw them.'

'I did!' said Tommy, who had got fed up waiting in the car and was disgruntled to see his father boozing away and his mother sipping coffee.

'You beasts, boozing away in here! I'm waiting in the car and...'

'No, look here, the barman offered...'

'Yes, but what about...?'

'It seemed a bit rude not to have just a...'

'Perhaps the boy would like a trink also?' said the kind barman. 'A Coke, an Orangina, a Red Devil?'

'A what?' said Tommy. 'I mean, oh, thank you. I'll have the Red Devil, please.'

If you're abroad then you might as well try something new. The barman whisked onto the table a large glass of something that looked like one of the solutions in the chemistry lab at school, cobalt something, but with bubbles.

'*Pétillant*,' said the barman. 'How do you say it in Engleesh? Ah, yes, *farting*.'

Dad snorted with laughter.

'What?' said Tommy. 'F-f-f – oh gosh, I asked for it, and I got it!'

Actually it tasted quite nice. 'Thank you,' said Tommy, and added in a whisper, 'for the farting drink.'

'What's that about the iron gates, then?' said Mummy. 'You saw them on the way here between Romolue les…'

'Yes,' said Tommy.

'Well, that's where we turn off,' said Daddy.

'But there wasn't anywhere to turn… I mean, there was just the gates,' added Tommy.

'Oh, well, perhaps there was a little road you didn't notice, or something,' said Mummy.

'Yes, let's go and have a look,' said Daddy.

They all said goodbye politely, and the barman said, 'Too soon' – which seemed a bit odd, but must have meant 'please come back soon'.

'We will,' said Daddy, as he glanced over his shoulder at the crowd huddled around the TV set showing the Tour de France, 'and perhaps we'll meet some more of the locals. The barman's a nice chap, anyway!'

Mummy took the steering wheel, and back they drove towards Romolue.

'There're the gates!' shouted Tommy, and as they slowed Tommy could get a better view of the long and broad gravel path, with beautifully clipped bushes on each side, and behind high trees in the distance, the roof of an enormous house.

'Ooh, that looks fun,' said Mummy. 'A real château! I wonder if we could get a peek inside. Mind you, I've heard that these French nobility are a bit reluctant to mix with the plebs.'

'The hoi polloi, don't you mean?' said Tommy.

What the heck, thought Dad, who taught him that? Mummy looked a bit surprised too, but she was concentrating on the château as she slowed down to a walking pace past the gates.

'Ooh gosh, fancy what it would be like living in a place like that!' said Tommy.

'Fat chance,' said Daddy. 'Now where is that blooming turning?'

The road stretched straight in both directions. A few plane trees stood in the middle distance, but otherwise there was a ditch, the wall along the side of the grounds of the château, lots of long grass, grass-hoppers buzzing away in the warm afternoon air, and a sense of sleepiness, caused not only by the Pernod, for

Tommy felt it too. There was a kind of magic in the air, which Tommy had felt briefly as they passed earlier, but he could not quite describe it. It slipped around his mind like a goldfish in a bowl, glittering in the sunshine... a kind of magic in the air.

There was in fact no turning to be seen. However, wobbling along towards them on an ancient bicycle was a postman, with his peaked cap on and his sack full of letters.

'Bit late for the post,' said Daddy, 'but if anyone knows where Ellie-la-Forêt is, it'll be the postman.'

Mummy stopped the car just beyond the gates, and they watched as the postman trundled slowly, meandering towards them, the peaked cap shading his face. Daddy got out of the car, and waited as the postman pedalled slowly past.

'Excuse me,' said Daddy, and the postman wobbled to a stop and lifted his hat, revealing a weather-beaten face and what is more, a dog collar. It wasn't the postman at all, it was the village priest, out delivering the church news, from door to door. Between the two, Daddy and the priest had consumed a fair proportion of a bottle of Pernod, and as Daddy stuttered, 'Er, er, umm, umm...' he wondered why the priest was wearing the postman's hat. The priest glanced at the car number plate and said, 'English?'

'Yes,' said Daddy.

'Lost?' said the priest, clearly a man of few words: perhaps he saved them for sermons.

'Well, not exactly lost...' began Daddy.

'Well, that is okay, then,' said the priest, and started to cycle off again.

'But wait a second,' said Daddy. 'We are a bit lost, really. We are trying to find Ellie-la-Forêt. Is it near here, please?'

'Eh!' said the priest. 'No, it's not near here, it *is* here!' and laughed, a strange snorting noise, with a whistle at the end of it.

Tommy got out of the car too, to hear what was going on. Much to his consternation the priest leant over, and Pernod breath all over him, chucked him under the chin, as if he was a little child. At fifteen years old, he hadn't been chucked under the chin so very much recently.

'It's just here,' repeated the priest or postman or whatever he was, 'just here.' He pointed a long bony finger at the big iron gates, which Tommy now noticed had a coat of arms fixed to them, all painted black, but he could make out a sort of lion thing. He walked over to the gates and peered through.

'That is Ellie-la-Forêt?' said Daddy incredulously.

'Of course,' said the priest. 'The Comte and the Comtesse are in England for the summer. You must be the English who are coming to stay, no?'

'Oh my gosh!' said Daddy, and Mummy rolled the car window down.

'Where is it then?' she asked. 'Ellie-la-Forêt?'

'Here,' said Daddy, pointing at the gates, with Tommy peering through them. 'The Comte and Comtesse are not in residence to receive us, apparently, but the liveried servants will be here any moment.'

'Oh, do stop it and make sense!' snapped Mummy. 'Where the devil is this blooming Ellie-la-Forêt?'

Just then she noticed the dog collar, put her hand over her mouth, and the priest grinned, showing several yellow teeth, but more gaps than fangs.

'Madame does not believe me? Ah, it is the fate of priests not to be believed!'

Dad wasn't interested in alcoholic philosophy just at that moment. He was much more taken with the idea of the château.

'Well, I don't know,' he said, interrupting the priest, 'but it seems like this is really Ellie-la-Forêt, behind these gates. I suppose that there will be a little caretaker's house where we will be put up. Or something like that. Anyway, it's pretty exciting to be so close to the château. You may well get a look inside it, hoi polloi or no hoi polloi!' he added, winking at Tommy.

The priest was listening to the conversation, rubbing the cycle bell with his worn old jacket sleeve and grinning to himself.

'The Comte and Comtesse have swapped their house with some English people. It is you, is it not? You must have a castle in England. Is it very old too, like the château here, built in 1580?' asked the priest inquisitively, his long, thin, none-too-straight nose wrinkling like a rat smelling its way to some cheese.

Tommy noticed that the priest had pimples on his nose, and watery eyes.

'1580?' said Daddy, 'no, more like 1950, actually,' but then thought better of this revelation. 'Well, *refurbished* in 1950.' Try not to let the cat out of the bag just yet. It would be round the village like wildfire, that was for sure.

Mummy got out of the car and joined them.

'How do you do,' she said, and extended her hand to the priest; and Daddy, who had quite forgotten his manners, did the same.

'*Enchanté*,' said the priest.

A second person enchanted with her today already, she thought. This looks like being a holiday full of enchantment. And as this came into her mind, a strange air of enchantment did seem to fill the space around the gates where Tommy was standing.

Mummy stepped towards Tommy, with just a shade of protective instinct, and began, 'The priest says that this is Ellie-la-Forêt and we are going to…' Then she tailed off, because she was not sure what they were going to do.

Tommy simply said, 'So, how do we get through these gates, eh?'

Then he noticed a little grill at the side and some bells to press. 'That's what we should do, press the bell,' he said, pointing at the metal grill.

'Shall I help?' asked the priest, and, before he received a reply, pressed the bell marked *Le Château*. They waited and the warm air flowed around them and, as they waited, it lulled them almost into a trance. This was interrupted suddenly by a squawking from the little metal grill.

'No ice cream today,' wheezed a voice, then, *click* – the phone was off. The priest said a word that priests shouldn't say and pressed the bell again.

'*Quoi?*' came the wheezy voice a second time.

'Your English guests are here!' said the priest,

'Oh! It's you. I thought that the ice cream van was there.'

Oh, good, thought Tommy. An ice cream van. Let's hope it comes past once a day, at least.

'No, it's not the ice cream van, it's the English Milords.'

Then he added something that Daddy couldn't hear very well but sounded like something about 'not a Rolls-Royce', but Daddy was not sure. Anyway, the conversation ended in another sharp click and the great wrought iron gates swung open, as Tommy retreated rapidly out of the way.

'Gosh!' said Mummy and Daddy simultaneously.

'Gosh!' said Tommy. 'This looks posh.'

'More than posh,' said Daddy, 'we're joining the aristocracy from now on!'

'Get your aristocratic backside in here, then,' said Mummy, opening the passenger door, and saying thank you to the priest, who waved and pedalled gently away, grinning again to himself – not a very nice grin, Tommy thought.

Mummy ushered Daddy and Tommy into the car, reversed, swung round and drove through the gates, the tyres crunching on the gravel. The grand entrance way was framed with plane trees, which waved gently in the breeze, as if to greet the English Milords and Lady. The drive wound around a corner and as they turned they saw the full view of the château, face-on. What a superb building it was! Rising high from the ground, grey-white stone, patterned with red brick in oval forms, with wonderful little turrets at each corner, and a forward facing wing on the right, great chimneys dominating the smoothly tiled black slate roof, which curled and rolled over the upper reaches of the building. There were large white windows with shutters, some wide open, some ajar, and two large lanterns hanging outside the front door, with, Tommy saw, chains and pulleys to draw them up and down.

For lighting the noble guests in and out of their carriages, I suppose, thought Tommy.

'My gosh, what a place!' exclaimed Mummy.

Daddy just let out his breath in a great sigh.

To the left of the château flowed a fast-moving river, with a broad flight of steps leading down to it. The remains of a bridge, just a few stones, could also be seen peeping through the long grass. The château had a moat! As it basked in the sun, reflecting the bright afternoon rays from the lighter stones and absorbing the red colour, painting the air, Mummy and Daddy and Tommy felt that they had never seen such a wonderful building in their lives before. Anything more different from their little house by the sea could not be imagined.

'You don't think that the Comte and Comtesse swapped this for our house, do you?' whispered Daddy.

'Surely not…' said Mummy.

'I bet they did,' said Tommy.

'Let's see – I expect we'll be in the converted henhouse or something,' said Daddy.

They drove slowly up to the main front door, parking at a respectful distance. As Mummy turned the engine off, the side door to the kitchen opened and out hobbled a strange old creature, moving with a surprising agility and clearly dressed in his best outfit – which did not fit too well.

'The wrinkled old retainer,' muttered Daddy.

'*What?*' said Mummy and Tommy together, but their interest was concentrated rather on the remarkable little figure before them.

'*Bienvenues à Ellie-la-Forêt,*' it was saying, '*bienvenues*. Welcome to Ellie-la-Forêt, Milord, Milady, sir.'

Heavens, they must all have been seeing the same old films, thought Daddy – unless, and a brief notion crossed his mind – it is linked with that business with the priest about a castle in England? Oh well, let's see what's going to happen.

'Welcome to the Château of Ellie-la-Forêt,' repeated the figure.

Well, that's it, thought Tommy, we are really going to be staying in the château, not in the converted henhouse.

'I am Jasper, your 'umble servant,' said the old man, his wrinkled eyes twinkling a bit.

I think that I am going to like him, said Mummy to herself.

'Well, we can't stand here speechless,' muttered Daddy, and he walked forward and shook the papery old hand of Jasper, a handshake returned with a surprisingly strong grip, and then Mummy and then Tommy shook hands too.

'Thank you,' said Mummy. And then she added, 'How lovely it is. Are you all alone here?'

'Well, yes, apart from the housekeeper, the housemaid, the

first, second and third under-housemaids, the gardener, the first and second under-gardeners, and the odd-job man. All alone, yes, as you say, all alone. The Comte and Comtesse are of course not in residence, but must now be close to your ancestral home, indeed yes! They are so looking forward to a peaceful holiday overlooking the sea. Indeed yes!'

Mummy and Daddy exchanged glances. Well, it certainly would be peaceful for them. The third under-housemaid, and the first or second, would not be causing them any trouble, for sure; nor would the gardeners. Because, of course, there were none. My gosh, what a mess this holiday company had made! Let's make the best of it till we get turfed out, anyway, thought Daddy, smiling at Monsieur Jasper.

'Shall we go on a tour of the house, so that you can know your way around immediately?' asked Monsieur Jasper. 'I will ask the second under-housemaid to take your luggage to your rooms,' he added.

He led the way up a few steps to the great wooden panels of the double front doors. These opened directly onto a hall, paved with heavy flagstones in a diamond pattern, some quite worn with centuries of use. A deep-stained wooden staircase rose in front of them, forming a massive axis to the château. Standing in the stairwell, Tommy stared upwards into the dark reaches of the upper part of the house, admiring the strangely carved wooden pillars that curved and twisted like boiled sweet wrappers, holding up the banister rail.

'This is the drawing room,' said Jasper, leading the way to the left.

They entered an enormous room, big enough for a basketball game, hung with pictures, and painted a delicate light bluish-green, like Aunt Jemima's best tea set, but without the pink violets. Somehow, standing in the room was really like being in a giant delicate porcelain tea set. *Egg shell* was how Tommy thought of it, egg shell like that blackbird's egg he found broken on the ground, just as they were getting into the Twingo to leave from home.

How can it be so massive and yet so delicate? Tommy asked himself. Mummy moved closer to Daddy, took his hand and looked around in wonder.

Gilt furniture, with curvy carved legs and pale green upholstery, surrounded a fireplace at the far end of the room. A mantelpiece above held a wonderful ormolu clock, with naked ladies draped over it all covered in gold and, strangely enough, a stork, with one wing partly outstretched, and beside that a marble vase, with golden grapes, and above that – ah, this really caught Tommy's eye! – a portrait, *the* portrait, the portrait of portraits, of the most beautiful lady that Tommy had ever seen, ever imagined. He fell instantly in love, and just gazed and gazed at the little smile playing on the lady's lips, whilst the others walked around the room, being shown the family trinkets, priceless objects rather unlike Mummy's sewing basket or the ashtray, inscribed 'Minehead', or the little mermaid from Copenhagen, which is what the Comte and Comtesse were going to find in their home.

One thing that caught Tommy's eye, when he was able to drag himself away from the painting, was an alabaster inkstand, with quill pen, but beside it a PC, with cordless mouse and flat screen – a big one too, Tommy noted, a top spec job. Fine… Are they on the Internet?… Must be with that machine. All this was on an ancient leather-covered desk.

On each side of the fireplace, French windows (real French windows, thought Tommy) looked out on the fast-flowing river, glittering in the sunshine. A concealed door to one side, looking just like the panelling, opened into a tiny room, part of the turret tower. Really cool, thought Tommy. And on the shelf in the little tower room, the complete adventures of Tintin. Or they looked complete, anyway, as there were so many of them. But all in French. Now Tommy felt for the first time the full force of his French teacher's argument about learning French. Ah well, I could try 'em, I suppose. The pictures should help. He gingerly pulled a volume a little way out and glanced at the front cover:

Les Bijoux… Castafiore… later. All the time, however, Tommy's eyes strayed back to the portrait of the lovely lady. Who could she be? Would Monsieur Jasper know?

While Mummy and Daddy surveyed the view of the river and Monsieur Jasper strolled, hands behind his back, around the drawing room, Tommy began to explore a bit. A piano – a grand piano, of course – stood in one corner of the room. A Pleyel, it said. It was very long and sitting on the piano stool you looked down the length of it like looking down the bonnet of a vintage Rolls, like the one Dad had shown him in that museum in the harbour in... in wherever it was.

'Tommy, Tommy, come here a moment!' His mother was pointing out of the window. 'Look, a black swan.'

'Gosh, I thought they were only in Australia,' said Tommy, and as he said 'Australia', so a beautiful white swan came sailing out of the moat and joined the black swan on the river.

'This place really is enchanted,' said Mummy, and Tommy felt a shimmer in the air as she said this. Mummy put her arm around him as if she too was aware of something unknown lingering in the room.

After the drawing room, they saw the dining room, with a great, beamed ceiling, and an enormous fireplace; then the cavernous kitchen, with brass pots and pans hanging twenty feet up in the air... I wonder how they get them down, thought Tommy; the pantry, the back staircase (for the servants, Monsieur Jasper explained); the library, full of bookcases with glass doors and ancient encyclopaedias; and upstairs they found a bathroom – their bathroom – with enormous brass taps, and lions' feet on the bath with bronze claws.

'The hot water can show temperament,' said Monsieur Jasper, 'and not always temperature,' he said, giggling at his little joke.

Just then the telephone rang. Monsieur Jasper left the bathroom, walked twenty metres down the corridor outside, and began, 'Ellie-la-Forêt, the residence of Monsieur le Comte de... Oh! Yes, of course, Monsieur le Comte, yes, they're here. You would like to speak to them? Yes, of course. Er... Monsieur,' he called out, 'Er... Monsieur le Comte would like to speak to you!'

'Oh, gosh! Now we're for it,' said Daddy to Mummy. 'It was nice while it lasted,' he added walking towards the outstretched phone.

'Monsieur le Comte? Ah! yes, you have just arrived at... Yes, so have we. What a beautiful house, and the sun is... What's that? Ours too? No, I mean, yes. What? Oh! Crikey,' said Dad, putting his hand over the phone, 'They've just... Er, what was that? Sorry the phone reception was a bit... What? You think the lake is

beautiful. And how do we keep the lawn so perfect? The, the...
What, and such, eh! What's that? The chocolates in the bedroom,
such a nice touch and the... the four-poster bed, from Queen
Anne. Yes, of course, I mean, be our guest – or somebody's!...
No, nothing, sorry, nothing.' There was a short pause, and
Tommy and his mother waited expectantly.

'The summerhouse will be wonderful for picnics, you think!'
resumed Daddy. 'Ha, ha! Yes, of course it will. Well, well, I hope
you like it as much as we like your wonderful home, I mean, we
have never been in a real French... castle? You think our castle is
simply marvellous. Yes, of course... Well, have a good holiday. If
there is anything... The staff know best, of course. Eh? The
chauffeur wants to know if the Jaguar or the Rolls would be best
for... Oh! The Rolls, I should say. Yes, definitely. Er... Yes...
Madeleine... Ah! Yes, your wife, la Comtesse, of course. My
Countess too, I mean... Au revoir, au revoir.'

Daddy replaced the receiver as if he were handling a
poisonous snake. 'Phew, gosh! I dunno, I mean, there's some sort
of merry-go-round...'

Mummy frowned and put her finger to her lips, with her back
to where Monsieur Jasper stood at a respectful distance, and
Daddy shook his head briefly, as if to clear his thoughts.

'Greetings from Monsieur le Comte,' he said suddenly, and
Jasper looked up, a little surprised, but nodded in thanks with his
little smile.

Tommy had listened in fascination to the telephone call and it
did not take much to realise that the merry-go-round Dad had
incautiously mentioned was simply this: all the house swaps had
got muddled up. The Comte and Comtesse were at a lovely castle
in England somewhere, and the people who were normally at that
castle were no doubt in France (or Germany, or goodness knows
which country), maybe at another nice castle, or maybe not;
maybe in a converted henhouse somewhere. On the other hand,
when you thought about it, it was possible that each swap just
went downhill a little bit, so that people did not really notice
much. Then at the end of the chain were Tommy and his mum
and dad, and that was where the thing went a bit haywire...
Anyway here they were, and they were going to enjoy it until the

business came crashing down around them – if it was going to at all. As long as they never actually have to meet the Comte and Comtesse, things should be okay. I wonder, though, thought Tommy, who is staying in our house?

No time for wondering now, however: next stop was the bedrooms, enormous bulky beds, heaped with eiderdowns and flounces and pillows, and their luggage waiting, unpacked. *Unpacked*! Gosh, no! Tommy was certain that there must have been something to be very embarrassed about in his suitcase, though he couldn't think just at that moment what it was. His mother had gone a bit pale too. Had she packed those underpants that Dad got last Christmas, the ones that were just a kind of sumo wrestling outfit, but with Mickey Mouse on them, or had she decided to leave them out?

Up another flight of stairs, and a few steps off to the left, then a small door to the right, and into – how strange – a small chapel. Why, the château had its own chapel!

'This is where all the family have been married for centuries,' said Monsieur Jasper. 'That lady, whose portrait is downstairs,' – Tommy felt his heart give a great lurch – 'that lady was married here, you know. She married an Englishman, but nobody seems to know much about him. A love marriage. Unusual in her class.'

An *Englishman*. I wish that it had been me, thought Tommy and he went a little bit red, and he saw his mother steal a glance at him. She too had sensed again that same little waft of magic that had come into the air before the château gates. It was a little stronger this time, beckoning Tommy, beckoning him on to some strange adventure which he could not name.

Down the main staircase they came.

'Mind, the steps are a bit worn in places,' said Monsieur Jasper. 'We have been thinking about replacing them, but somehow it is part of the *patine* – 'ow do you say, "patina"?' he looked inquiringly at Tommy's father.

'Yes,' mumbled Dad. He had not really recovered from the telephone conversation with Monsieur le Comte quite yet. 'Yes, we do.'

'The patina of age,' continued Monsieur Jasper, 'the patina of age,' he repeated.

Monsieur Jasper seemed to like the phrase, and Tommy repeated it to himself. It was a good phrase, the patina of... but just then he passed a painting hanging on the wall of the stairway. Well, not really a painting, it was black and white and a little bit smudgy.

'A picture of the château as it was in 1599,' said Monsieur Jasper, and as he said this the feeling of magic became so strong that Tommy had to suppress a cry of fright. No, perhaps not fright, but of shock, surprise at meeting the unknown.

Tommy stood before the etching, for that was what it was, and saw that it showed not a view of the château at all, but rather a view *from* the château, over the river into a magnificent garden, all in geometrical shapes, with figures here and there, and a stone bench, inscribed *in Arcadia*, he could see – or 'something *in Arcadia ego*'... or something.

The magic grew as he looked deeper into the view and then Tommy felt his mother's arm around him, pulling, tugging him away from the picture, breathlessly pulling almost in panic, as the ancient view from the château beckoned him further inwards, pulling away from the twenty-first century into the end of the sixteenth. As Mummy tugged on his arm, Tommy felt the tentacles of the past slowly relax from around him and he moved a step down the staircase, then another, and his head began to clear.

Dad looked back. 'Are you okay, Tommy?'

'I thought that he was going to faint,' said Mummy.

She looked pretty white too, or grey, Tommy thought. She feels it too. It's not just me. But she's stronger than me. She fought it off alone. Gosh, I'm going crazy: fought what off? With each step Tommy took down the staircase the pull weakened, and the sunshine brightened. Monsieur Jasper did not notice, or pretended not to notice. Tommy tried to take the next two steps quickly, and then ran helter-skelter down the rest, and as he did so, he saw just the flash of a glance from Monsieur Jasper, a flash fast, but not so fast. It was enough to show that Monsieur Jasper knew exactly what had happened on the staircase.

Dinner in style; the family silver was out, emblazoned with the crest of Monsieur le Comte and la Comtesse.

'Gosh,' said Daddy, when briefly they were alone, 'I feel like My Fair Lady, but with no Professor Higgins to put me right!'

'Some fair lady you are!' retorted Mummy.

'Mummy's the fair lady,' broke in Tommy, dutifully, though he had no idea what they were talking about.

'At least I know that white wine goes with fish,' said Daddy.

'Why's it called white when it's just nearly colourless?' asked Tommy.

'That, I don't know,' said Daddy.

Tommy had been feeling a bit odd after the encounter with the etching on the staircase. Somehow, however, it did not seem that a bad thing had happened to him. The magic was not there to hurt him. It was almost as if it were reminding him of some duty that he had and that he had forgotten, and it was a painful reminder. Some duty he had. That was it; some duty, something that he had to do.

That night in his enormous bed, enclosed by billowing duvets, and pillows like cumulonimbus clouds, which Tommy had learnt about in his geography lessons, he lay half awake, half asleep, perhaps dreaming, and in his dream believing himself awake, Tommy saw the etching on the staircase in brilliant detail. Each outline was clear, and the tones seemed to hover between black and white and colour, flickering in and out, as though the scenes were coming to life and then dying again many times. He could see the stone bench again, the figures, some women, some men, and among them a girl, about his age, about fourteen or fifteen, but it was hard to tell in those funny clothes they wore in 1599. Again there came the feeling of a beckoning past, seeking to envelop him in its soft arms; no harm would come, though there was the smell of danger there too. And so he slept.

Tommy woke to sunlight filtering through the shutters. He was in France, in an ancient château, he was on holiday and he leapt out of bed, threw on his clothes, rushed out of the room, thundered down the great staircase, out of the main door, down the steps, across the gravel, whipped off his clothes again, and sprang into the river. Well, as he lay in bed, he thought that this might be fun, and then he turned over and began to wonder what they had for breakfast in France.

'Tommy, Tommy, come and have a swim!' It was his mother, in her single-piece swimsuit, not to offend Monsieur Jasper or whoever with a display of too much flesh.

She was standing at the door, waving his trunks at him. The steps to the river ended way above the waterline and the water, when they managed to haul themselves down into it – it is always much more difficult to get into a river than it looks at first – it had a tremendous current. But it was a good way to start the day, even if later on he found that eggs and bacon were not on the menu, but rather, some flaky kind of pastry things, that you might like for tea, but were a bit odd for breakfast; though Tommy actually quite liked them really. Anyway, four of them filled him up pretty well, and he went dashing off into the woods nearby to explore.

'Be back at one o'clock for lunch, not later!' called Mummy after him.

Tommy had his mobile with him so he set the alarm for a quarter to one, to make sure that he would not be too late. Tommy was too old to pretend to be a Red Indian – at least when anyone else was around. But he could pretend to be a hunter. What he did not realise was that there was quite a lot to hunt around here – deer, and best of all, wild boar. In fact they had eaten some last night, just like in *Asterix*, though they did not get one each, of course. Tommy found tracks of boar; they weren't difficult to see, since they root around and make a terrific mess often enough. And in the distance he even caught sight of a small one trotting off along a forest path. That was something to tell his friends. He was tempted to ring Harry, his best friend, and tell him about seeing the wild boar. But then the cost of the call would bankrupt him, and he wouldn't be able to buy that three-foot-high Eiffel Tower with the thermometer on the side that he had seen on the ferry.

Lunch was over. It was pretty scrumptious, mind you, with a luscious creamy sweet encrusted with brown sugar to end it all, and the afternoon turned sleepier and sleepier. The warm sunlight lulled everything into a stupor, and Tommy decided to go on his own private exploration of the château. There were lots of rooms on the top floor that they hadn't seen at all. No one was around and he was sure that all the people in the house were having an afternoon nap, a siesta. Tommy wanted to go into the rooms at the very top of the towers. So up he went, up and up the back staircase, till he came to the very top. It seemed as though it was not much used up here and the sunlight coming through little dormer windows shimmered through the dust that he stirred up. He dared not open any doors that he found shut, in case the second under-housemaid was sleeping in there, or putting on her make-up or whatever second under-housemaids do at the top of châteaux in the south-west of France. In fact, Tommy came to a sort of dead end, and found a couple of rooms filled with old furniture, which would have set an antique dealer drooling, and old magazines stacked on shelves. Tommy turned up the corner of one. *Marie-Claire, 1955*, it was called, and had a picture of a cheerful fresh-faced girl advertising deodorant, it looked like. Boring. Tommy decided to go back down the main staircase, and it was half in his mind to see what would happen as he passed the etching on the stairs.

Two: The Château, Now and Then

he stairs were dark after the bright sunlight along the top floor. Tommy had to look carefully to avoid slipping on the old stone steps, and he held on to the banister as he went down. Concentrating on not tripping over, Tommy arrived at the etching almost without knowing it, dark as it was. But he could feel it rather suddenly, gripping him, calling him, beckoning him inwards towards the wonderful geometrical garden, whispering his name, *Thomas, Thomas…* Someone was gently shaking his shoulder. He woke with a start, feeling the hard surface of a stone bench on which he was half lying, half sitting.

'What – where am I, what's this?' he exclaimed, and he held out his hands and looked at his wrists encased in frilly lace cuffs, and then at deep red velvet sleeves, shiny pointed shoes, brass buckles and black satin trousers. Then he looked up at the face above him. It was Monsieur Jasper.

'I thought that I should follow you through to make sure that you had a safe landing, Monsieur,' he said; then he grinned, his little old eyes twinkled and he began to fade.

'No, no! Wait!' cried Tommy. 'Where am I? Where did you come from? Where are you going?' he shouted confusedly. 'How do I find my way home?'

'It will happen when it will happen,' said the quiet voice of Monsieur Jasper, who faded completely from view as the last words were spoken.

So there was Tommy all alone, on the stone bench. Why! The stone bench – it was the bench in the etching. He bent down: *Et in Arcadia ego* was carved on it. He had entered the world shown in the etching and the world of the château as it was in 1599. He was in a world four hundred years in the past! People were the same then, Tommy reminded himself. Yes, but they hadn't had our history. He knew millions of things they did not, but they knew millions of things and believed millions more that he had no idea of. He had to think. He wished that he knew more French history. Who was King of France in 1599? Louis the sŏmethingth, for sure. What was he to do? He felt like an actor thrust onto a stage with a great audience before him – but an actor who had never been told his lines, for whom no lines had even been written. He did not even know his name, his age, his parents, his friends. But Tommy felt knowledge flowing into him. He knew that when he saw his... sister, yes, he had a sister – he would recognise her: Madeleine. That was his sister's name, and he was Thomas. Gently now, let it slowly flow in. His father, no his *adopted* father, was the Count and his adopted mother was the Countess of... of... the name was... *Romolue*. And there was Eloise. Who was she? he wondered, and putting his hand to his face, he felt himself blushing. He allowed his thoughts to flow on. His old nurse, Marie. Ah, yes, Eloise was his cousin, adopted cousin. He was fifteen and so was she. His little sister was only eleven. He had gone to sleep on the bench after eating too much at lunchtime.

He could remember what they had eaten. Yes: lark's tongue pâté, cold pie made of minced and roasted boar, with cranberries, marzipan sweets... what else? Oh yes, pastries filled with nuts and honey, and cloves. Yes, cloves, that was rather odd, but of course, it keeps all illness away. He could remember, someone – Dad, no! Monsieur le Comte de Romolue – saying so. Yes, cloves keep away illness. So that was something that everyone knew, here, or rather now, or then, or whatever. I had better decide to be part of 'now', thought Tommy to himself. If I can just be allowed to sit here a little longer I may be ready to face this world, as more facts flowed in. Like where his room was in the château, his mother's face, his dagger, the kitchen, that rather pretty housemaid, who used to giggle when she delivered his hot water in the morning; and again he blushed at this memory. His horse, of course he had a horse, and his groom, the name of his horse, just on the outskirts of his mind: Penelope, a mare; and more and more, the floodgates opened and all his life formed as a clear landscape in front of him. Tommy, or rather Monsieur Thomas, felt almost ready to face the world of 1599!

Tommy began to examine his clothes more carefully, running

his hands down his velvet jacket, over his trousers, and as he did so, he felt a small hard object in his pocket. No, never! It was his mobile. He pulled it out and gazed at it in wonder. Could he ring up the twenty-first century with it? My gosh, the battery! They didn't have electricity four hundred years ago. Electricity was Faraday's idea, he had learnt, in the nineteenth century. Tommy remembered that he had charged the battery fully just the day before, so he had a couple of hours, maybe, if it would work. He could ring his mum and dad and tell them where he was. They would think that he had gone cuckoo. Never mind. He was about to try, when just round the corner came skipping along a little girl, all done up in the most wonderful frilly things. My little sister, Madeleine.

'Hello, Maddy,' he said using her pet name without thinking, hurriedly pushing the mobile phone back in his trouser pocket.

'What's that you've got there?' asked Maddy.

Blast, she had seen it!

'Oh! Nothing...'

'Yes, it was. Why were you hiding it, if it was nothing, then?'

Little sisters had not changed in four hundred years, that was clear. Why not just show it to her? No, that was too risky. He felt as if he knew her well, but yet, did not know her at all. So he just ignored her question and looked sleepily around as if he had just woken up that moment.

'Hadn't you better go and get your proper clothes on?' said Maddy. 'We've got to be in church soon, sleepyhead,' she giggled.

Of course, it was Sunday. It was absolutely essential that the Comte, the Comtesse, all the children, cousins, uncles, aunts, all the household servants and everyone else should appear in church. Eloise would be there. Why did this interest him so much? He could not picture Eloise – Ellie, as he called her, or used to call her when they were much smaller – anyway. He just could not put a face to her name. That would come, he hoped.

Still, he must go and change into church clothes, more sombre, less colourful than these, and very uncomfortable, he remembered, if 'remembered' were the right word to describe something that he had never experienced really, but only remembered that he had. But was that right? All the people,

Maddy at first, but then lots more, seemed to know him, as he walked hand in hand with her out of the garden across the bridge, the one which was just a trace of a few stones four hundred years later, across the bridge and towards the French windows of the drawing room – the 'salon' as he knew it was called. A nod here, a curtsey there. Yes, they knew who he was, so he must have been here last Sunday in his Sunday clothes, and that was why he knew they were uncomfortable. Tommy felt his head begin to swim. I can't figure it all out in one go, he thought. Let's just live from one moment to the next...

As he walked towards the château, he could feel the mobile phone bulging in his pocket. He hoped no one had noticed it. Did people have things bulging out of their pockets in 1599? He was a young nobleman, or adopted at least as a young nobleman. Perhaps he should not have a bulge in his pockets. Perhaps servants carried everything around that you wanted handy? It was lucky he knew his way around the château and up to his room on the first floor. He had sort of hoped that he might have had one of the tower rooms, but now as he glanced up, just before entering the salon, he saw that there were no little towers on the château.

Without thinking he began, 'Where's the...?' and then he quickly hid his surprise.

'You're a bit funny this afternoon,' said Maddy, as Tommy tripped over the entrance to the French windows.

'Only a bit sleepy still,' he said.

'Then you had better wake up for the sermon,' replied Maddy, 'Daddy said you'd be horsewhipped if you fell asleep and snored again like last week, in the middle of it all.' Then she ran off laughing.

Was that serious? thought Tommy. Would I be horsewhipped? Or was that just a sort of exaggerated threat, just like you would say in the twenty-first century, 'We'll beat you to death if you don't drink up your milk' – or something?

Musing in this manner, Tommy made his way up to his room, a large room overlooking the moat. He went over to the window and looked out. No black swans, of course. Australia had not been discovered yet... or had it? He wasn't quite sure. Anyway, he had to think, he needed peace and quiet. First of all, since they all knew him there had to be a second Thomas. Was he locked up somewhere in the château? Tommy leaned out of the window, his elbows on the window ledge, his hands on his cheeks.

What about his Mum and Dad back in Ellie-la-Forêt? They would miss him and get really worried... call the police... drain the moat, in case he had fallen in and drowned. 'Oh, gosh! I'd better ring them,' he muttered to himself.

He pulled out the mobile. No, first, there was a catch on the door. He went over and locked it. No matter if he didn't normally do that. He mustn't get caught trying to use the phone. He had a suspicion that magic – and they would be bound to think that it was magic – was dangerous in this society. The Church did not approve. He knew this, somehow. Something that he had learned from this life of 1599. Sitting on his bed, (gosh, it was hard!) he selected the phonebook and his mother's number, pressed and waited. It was ringing! There was an answer!

'Hello, Tommy,' said his mother's voice. He could have cried, but there was no time for that.

'Mum, this is Tommy. I'm...' But just then to his horror, a panel in the bedroom wall opened – a hidden door – and in walked his... *mother*, the Comtesse de Romolue!

Tommy stuffed the phone in his pocket.

'What's that, Thomas?' she asked, in a low sweet voice, 'that thing you had up by your ear?'

'Nothing, Mother.'

Fancy having to tell a fib, the very first time you ever speak to your mother!

'Well, that's funny... it was a sort of purple thing.' For Tommy had bought one of those extra covers you can put on top – an absolutely essential extra. 'You seemed to be listening to it!'

'Well, it's a secret,' Tommy risked this reply, hoping that he had a nice mother.

And indeed he did. She just smiled. Thomas liked secrets, and she always found out in the end with a bit of patience. So all was well, at least for the moment.

'Church is soon,' said his new mother.

'What time?' said Tommy without thinking, and the Countess gave him a startled look.

'Well, just an hour before sunset, of course. I'll go and change now myself.'

But as she walked over to the secret door, Tommy's mobile started to ring. This was such an alien sound in the château of 1599, that the Comtesse de Romolue simply froze in her step, with a look of panic on her face.

'What,' she whispered, '*is that?*'

Tommy was furiously groping in his pocket trying to find the off button. Instead, he pressed connect and the tiny voice of his mother could be heard, saying, 'Tommy, Tommy, are you—'

Click! At last he'd found it. The Comtesse de Romolue stood stock-still, eyes wide in astonishment.

'What – what…?' she gasped.

'No, nothing really, Mother, really. Just a little toy I got down the village from Monsieur Rabelais. He's clever with things, you know,' Tommy gabbled, furiously improvising still more lies.

'But I heard a strange voice – crying "Tommy, Tommy", it sounded like. Do you have a homunculus in your trousers?'

'Oh! No, that was probably me muttering to myself. I don't know.'

His mother took a step towards him, then changed her mind, gave him a very peculiar look, and left the room without another word.

What on earth is a 'homunculus'? wondered Tommy. 'Gosh,' he said to himself, 'I must get back to Mum double quick and warn her not to ring me up, whatever she does.' He pulled the phone out of his pocket, put in the pincode – thank heavens he could remember it, 3142, easy as pie, heh, heh! – and instantly his mother picked it up.

'Bit of a problem with the connection?' she asked.

'Yes, well, I'm…'

'It's okay, I can see where you are. I'm on the second floor of the château and I can see you down the drive from here. Why, you are looking straight at me, though I can't see the phone in your hand. It's a bit far, though, to see.'

'What?' said Tommy. 'You can see me? I'm where?'

'What do you mean, where are you? Don't be daft! You're standing in the drive. I can see you. Stop playing silly games and come in and have some tea. The second under-housemaid has just brought all sorts of little cakes in. It's laid out in the salon, the drawing room, you know. See you in a mo.' And she rang off.

'Blast and blast and blast it!' said Tommy rather loudly, and then to himself, 'This is super-frustrating. I'm going bonkers. What on earth is Tommy, I mean *me*, doing there then, when I am here, now, or then, or, *blast it!*'

Tommy sat miserably on the bed and sighed deeply. What was going on? Suddenly a thought struck him.

Gosh, I've got it. Of course that's why they know me here. The Tommy from here and now has gone to where I come from, and I've replaced him. Of course, Mum thinks that that Tommy is me, and they think, here and then and now, that I am their Tommy! We must be identical twins. Or at least, so close that if you are not looking for a difference, you don't see one. That's why the Countess didn't say anything, of course! Oh my gosh! Also, I didn't get a chance to tell Mum not to ring me. I'd better turn the phone off. She can SMS me – I'll turn the sound off. Imagine that going off *peep*, *peep* in the middle of the church service!

Just then the phone rang again. '*Blast!*' said Tommy loudly, and then, 'Ssshhhh!' to himself. Then he grabbed the phone, which was lying on the bed.

'Why haven't you come to tea?' said Mum, rather annoyed.

Tommy did not know how to begin, so he just said, 'Mum, look, the most important thing is that you don't ring me. Don't ask me why. Just don't ring me. Send an SMS – and I'll send SMSs to you too, and explain the whole situation. I've got to go now. Bye!'

Click. Quick as that. No time for arguing. Heavens knows what his mother was thinking. He turned the phone off completely: no point in risking anything more.

Just then there was a sharp knock at the door, and the handle was rattled.

'Thomas, have you locked the door?'

Blimey, it must be my dad, the Count! What's he going to be like? Tommy raced over and released the catch. A tall grey-haired man of about fifty surged into the room, brimming with authority, and demanded, in a deep bass voice, 'Why was your door locked, Thomas?'

Tommy thought rapidly. Tell the same fib as you did to your mother. They are bound to exchange stories.

'I've got a new thing that old Rabelais made. I was trying to keep it a secret, so while I was looking at it, I locked my door.'

Now what Tommy had not bargained for was that Monsieur le Comte de Romolue was, inside his quite considerable self, a little boy too, who loved new toys and gadgets. He and Tommy often looked at them together. In fact Tommy remembered this just as he replied to his father – or adopted father, or whatever he was. Gosh, what a blunder he'd made! His father was bound to ask to see it. He could hardly refuse to let him. What sort of half-baked story could he invent? Lost it down the bed, it was broken, half-finished only. Actually, why not just let him look at it? It was turned off, no lights were flashing, anyway. Yes, that was the best thing.

'Here, have a look,' he said and took the mobile from his pocket and handed it to his father.

The Comte de Romolue took the mobile in his hand and ran his fingers over it.

'What strange stuff,' he said, 'smooth and cool. Is it wood?'

'I think so,' lied Tommy.

'And what are these little things with numbers on, 1, 2, 3 all the way to 9 – and zero also?' asked the Count.

Oh! gosh, he wasn't going to press the buttons. He just could start the blooming thing going…

'Let me see,' said Tommy, and his father handed the mobile back. 'I'm not sure. I think if you push on them there's maybe a little bellows inside that makes noises,' he went on, seizing inspiration from thin air, lying madly and thinking that if it did make a noise, then he had explained why beforehand.

'Little bellows?' said his father. 'Well, Monsieur Rabelais is getting very clever. I shall ask him to make me one too.' Suddenly, the light on the screen blinked on: <SMS for you> it said. Thank heavens he had switched the sound off – no little bellows would explain the first few bars of 'Für Elise'! Anyway it was two hundred years before it was written! Tommy quickly covered the screen over with his hand and held it away from his father. Fortunately it was daylight. If it had been dark, the green glow from the screen would have been easily visible. I must remember that, thought Tommy.

'We can have a closer look later,' said his father. 'You'd better get your clothes on for church. I'll get Jacques to send your maid up. Put the darker waistcoat on today. You're reading the lesson, you remember, I'm sure. I hope that you've been practising it well.'

With that bombshell, the Count left the room. Tommy collapsed on the bed. Reading the lesson, reading the lesson. Oh, no! The other bloomin' Tommy had no doubt been practising it but this Tommy had not! I wonder how he's getting on though, thought Tommy. But Tommy had no time to reflect on how it would be to be catapulted from 1599 into the twenty-first century, except to realise that it would be terrifying. The first plane that went overhead would probably require a clean pair of trousers to be issued immediately. Gosh!

There was a tap at the door. A pretty young girl came in carrying a bundle of clothes. Well, at least that hasn't changed, thought Tommy. Pretty girls are still, and were still, pretty girls – even in 1599. However this pretty girl plonked the clothes on the bed and said, 'Please remove your trousers, Monsieur Thomas.'

What, what? Not likely! For one thing, he was not sure what he had on underneath. Maybe not much. That would be embarrassing, to say the least. What was he to do? Take off his pants – what else? So very shyly, looking at the floor, he started to undo the buckle.

'Not there,' said the young girl (she was called Flore, he remembered suddenly). 'Undo the buckle at the back. Look, I'll help you.'

He felt her fingers crawling around his waist and he blushed furiously. Flore did not seem to notice, and his pants were round his knees in no time. It seemed that he had something like ballet dancer's tights on underneath. No wonder he had felt a bit hot out in the garden when he first woke up. Flore handed him his church trousers and in no time he was properly dressed for his ordeal of reading the lesson. Flore departed with a little grin (perhaps she had noticed his confusion!) and then he remembered that not only had he to read the lesson but he had to read the lesson in Greek. *Greek*! He couldn't read Greek, not even the letters. Panic. It was the Gospel thing, er… Luke, according to Luke: 'In the time of the Emperor Augustus, blah, blah,' so he did know it a bit. He would just have to trust to luck, fate or whatever came his way.

'Thomas, are you ready?' It was the voice of the Comtesse de Romolue.

Tommy remembered the SMS that had flashed on before. No time to look at it now. How were they going to get to the church? Just relax your mind, and the information will come. That's it. Tommy was learning how to tap into the mind of the real Thomas, now stranded in the twenty-first century. By coach? By coach it was then.

The family was assembled by the main entrance. Suddenly Tommy was thrust among people whom he had known, but not known, all his life. The experience was a strange blur, a brain overload. Aunts, uncles, cousins, a very much younger brother (gosh, I did not know about him. What's his name. Ah yes, Jasper. Jasper? That's odd). There were three coaches. Thomas went in the first one, the son of the household. It was tiny inside, a kind of Twingo-coach, thought Tommy. No one to share that idea with – unless that old servant holding the door, Jasper, gosh, it was Monsieur Jasper, gosh! But too late, with a great jolt they were off. All he got was a flicker of an eyelid from Monsieur Jasper and he was gone. Best not to leap from the coach and rush back. Anyway, he was wedged between his mother and father.

'I hope the boy will make a good shot at the lesson,' said the Comte de Romolue over his head to the Countess.

Tommy kept his eyes on the floor, trying to remember the Greek he had been practising, or the real Thomas had been practising, at any rate. At first, keeping his eyes down was okay, but then the motion of the coach made him feel a bit queasy. He raised his head a little and glanced towards the three occupants opposite. His sister, Maddy, on one side; his little brother, Jasper, on the other; and in the middle, in the middle, the most beautiful girl he had ever seen in his life. This was Eloise, of course, Eloise.

He fell violently in love on the spot. That little smile playing on her lips, it reminded him so much of something that he knew from his own time. It would come to him. But he must not stare like that. Eloise would blush and turn away any second now.

His father and mother were talking about some boring matter about pigs running wild in the village. Maddy was fiddling with her lace cuffs, Jasper was staring out of the window, and it seemed that it was just the two of them in the carriage. Eloise raised and lowered her lovely long eyelashes, smiled and seemed about to say something. Tommy shook his head ever so slightly and Eloise opened her eyes just a little wider. This was not her normal Thomas. He never looked at her with such adoration. He usually sulked and bit his lip if she so much as glanced at him, though she was sure that he was secretly in love with her. Here was a Thomas who boldly stared at her, would not take his eyes off her. Ah! What bliss! Love returned at last. What had changed? How was it that the sulky, shy boy of this morning had become the strong and bold lover of the afternoon – well, the late afternoon? How could it be the same person? Though he looked identical. Identical? Just about identical, anyway.

Now Eloise was the only person who had really studied Thomas's face in detail, really in detail. Just above his left eyebrow there was the trace of a scar, just a very small trace, where an arrow had grazed his forehead when he was five years old, a careless shot in a boar hunt as he sat on horseback, held in front of his father. Eloise studied his face, for she had a sudden feeling that there was something not quite familiar about the Thomas opposite her. That was it! The scar. It was missing! That faint trace of white skin was missing. Eloise felt a moment of panic, of fear. Was this an assassin sent by Robert de Toulouse, the leader of the rival family? What was the meaning of this substitution? Had Thomas somehow erased the scar? Had it unaccountably faded, and she had not noticed? Who was this person, whom everyone took for Thomas, sitting opposite her, squeezed between parents who surely would see a difference – if difference there was!

Tommy noticed the many emotions flitting across Eloise's face. Love, panic, a look of thought, fear, doubt, suspicion and then love again. Beware this girl, an inner voice told him, beware this girl, for she alone suspects! I love her and I will tell her all, swore Tommy to himself. She will think you mad, replied the inner voice, and you will lose her love. Never, said Tommy, never will that happen, and just went on gazing at her, and Eloise, despite herself and her doubts, gazed back. The other four people in the carriage seemed totally unaware of the unfolding of this great drama, of the emotional turmoil roiling around them. Jasper picked his nose and the Countess gave him a black look; the Count waffled on about the intelligence of pigs, comparing them favourably to his footmen; Maddy scratched herself – flea bites probably – whilst Tommy and Eloise continued to gaze and gaze.

The short journey came to an end. The noble party emerged from their carriages, entered the church and took their special places at the very front, in the pew reserved for the family. The Count sat in the place of honour, his Countess beside him, then Tommy, Maddy, Jasper and Eloise in the front row, and the aunts, uncles and other cousins dispersed about behind. All was silent, the church was full and the last rays of sunlight shone through the west door. Just then, a flickering shadow disturbed the peace of the building and darkened into a massive and threatening form, which stretched and lengthened over the central aisle, as the stooping figure of a black-robed priest entered and moved slowly towards the altar.

From the corner of his eye, Tommy glimpsed a lined and wrinkled face, a thin nose, with pink and hairy pimples and watery eyes. Disgust welled up inside him, half-hidden memories came unasked of the rough flagstones of the chapel in the château, on his knees, raw and cold. Tommy cringed and so did the entire congregation. Fear was this priest's weapon, fear of stepping out of the orthodox line, fear of some heresy, of mixing with witchcraft, of using your mobile phone, thought Tommy – not as a joke, either. Keep your distance, said the voice inside him, this man has power to make and break, to judge and condemn, to condemn and kill.

'*In nomine Patris, et Filii...*' The church service droned on in Latin. Tommy understood very little and the villagers not a word of it. All that kept Tommy wakeful was that at any moment he might be called up to recite the passage in Greek from St Luke. Tap in to Thomas, hidden away four hundred years in the future; let it flow in…

I hope to heaven that the real Thomas did know it, said Tommy to himself, or I will stand no chance. His father glanced at him and gave an encouraging smile. It was now! The priest motioned him with a glittering eye and a slight tilt of the head on his scrawny neck, and Thomas got to his feet. He tottered towards the lectern. He was thankful for this lectern, since only by gripping it firmly could he stand straight on his wobbling legs. The words of the Gospel were spread out in front of him, in the great Bible which rested on the lectern. Why did it have to be Greek? The text swam before his eyes, the little letters crawling over the page like demented beetles. What sense could he make of them? He could only recognise alpha, beta and omega anyway, and only omega because Aunt Jemima had given him an Omega watch for Christmas last year.

But the little letters seemed all at once to arrange themselves into a pattern, and then, without warning, he was off. Have you ever imagined the steering wheel coming off in the driver's hand? That was what it was like, reciting this Greek text. Out of any control, his tongue wound around his mouth as he made strange sounds, perhaps Greek, perhaps not, vowel sounds flying, consonants cracking until just as abruptly as he had started, he stopped. There was silence in the church, until suddenly the Comte de Romolue let out an audible breath which he appeared to have been holding throughout the entire performance, and then the entire congregation moved as one body to relax. For almost none of the people in the church knew if it was Greek or gabble, or either, or both.

'Good,' whispered the Count, as Tommy returned to his place.

'Good,' whispered his mother, and smiled sweetly.

A glance, which said much, fell from Eloise, a glance of happiness, but also of doubt.

Did I do it too well? thought Tommy. Was it out of character? Why that strange look on the lovely face of Eloise?

Outside the church, the Count was being congratulated on his son's successful debut at reading the lesson.

Ah! thought Tommy. So it was the first time that I have done that – yes, of course, so it was. Tommy had to ask the question, before the answer came. He'd noticed this and it was clearly going to make things a bit difficult for him, even more difficult than they already were.

The priest approached him, like a crow with a broken wing, in his black cassock.

'Well done, young sir. Well done! I could not have got through it better myself. The old traditions must be kept up, of course, of course.' Here he laughed, a kind of strangled snort, ending in a whistling sound from between his teeth. That sound brought back a sharp memory of the priest outside the gates of Ellie-la-Forêt.

Yes, thought Tommy, it's the priest from Romolue. All he's missing is his bicycle and the bag of church notices. It's him. Has he 'come through' as well, like Monsieur Jasper? Or is he the original version from 1599? Is he another copy, or nearly a copy, of someone living in the twenty-first century? Because neither the priest, nor Jasper for that matter, could be absent from their time without it being noticed; at least they could not be absent for long.

Tommy's heart sank at this last thought. He was dying to get back to the château and find Monsieur Jasper, whom he was sure had been the little old man holding the carriage door as they set off for church. Now he realised that probably Monsieur Jasper just nipped in and out of 1599, just to – just to what? Also, how did he do it? Tommy would dearly love to know. Tommy was sure that in some way Monsieur Jasper was a friend – perhaps a dangerous friend, but a friend.

He was even more sure that the priest was not. Maybe he was a dangerous enemy. Fleeting thoughts belonging to the other Thomas passed through his mind. He had always been wary of… Drogo – the name came to him suddenly. Drogo had treated him cruelly as a child; he'd always feared him. And Drogo was certainly powerful in this community. His brother was, after all, the Bishop; this came to Tommy as a vivid image of a taller version of the priest, all got up in gorgeous robes, holding a mitre and wearing a cleft hat, like the bit at the top of the bishop in the chess set at home. A wave of homesickness overcame him at this thought, and he put his hand in his pocket for the reassuring feel of the mobile. Oh no – it was gone! His heart leapt. Ah! Of course, he had put it under the pillow on his bed at the château. Tommy was suddenly terribly anxious about it. For all he knew the third, or fourteenth, under-housemaid might come in and make the bed three times a day. But surely no one would have dared to touch it. But when would they return to the château, so that he could write a great long SMS to his mum and dad, explaining everything?

Suddenly he felt a papery hand grasp his and heard a whisper in his ear. 'In your pocket – and never let it out of your sight again!'

And he felt the mobile in his hand, and slipping it as fast as he could into his pocket, he turned to see the back of Monsieur Jasper disappearing into the crowd.

'Monsieur Jasper!' he called but dropped his voice as he realised the foolishness of his action.

He could not plough through the crowd. Who was Monsieur Jasper anyway? Obviously an ally after this, but an ally in what battle, in what struggle, against whom, for what purpose?

Monsieur Jasper had chosen his moment well, for the priest had turned his attention once more to Tommy and was asking him if any mention had been made of a betrothal.

What's that? thought Tommy. What is a betrothal?

Seeing the puzzled look on Tommy's face, the priest repeated the question. 'Has Monsieur le Comte raised the subject of the marriage of Thomas?'

Good gosh, the old crow, he's asking me if my marriage has been organised! At my age…' But then Tommy realised, drawing on the memory of the true Thomas, that arranged marriages, betrothals, promises of marriage, were often made at a very early age among noble families. Why, his father had been betrothed when he was only twelve years old; not to his mother, mind you, but to some other, now forgotten, young noblewoman. It fell through for political reasons, he – or rather, Thomas – had been told. Well, anyway, it was only done in the first place for political reasons.

The priest was talking again. 'Would it not be a wonderful

match for you to be joined to the family of Toulouse? This would end the terrible quarrel between the families of Romolue and Toulouse, which has caused so much death and destruction,' said the priest. 'Death and destruction,' he repeated, drawing out the words as if he relished them, which Tommy had no doubt at all that he did. 'I will talk to your father and my brother the Bishop about this.' Then he smiled a sickly smile at Tommy, who smelt a trace of foul breath and gained a view of yellow fangs, with more gaps than fangs.

He's got the same teeth, too, as the priest of Romolue, thought Tommy. Somehow, in reply to the priest's last remark, Tommy knew how to blurt out, 'That is very gracious of you, Father Drogo, but am I not too young for such things?'

'Oh no,' said Father Drogo, 'tradition is that when the eldest son of the house of Romolue successfully gives his first lesson in the church – in Greek, of course – the tradition is that then we must start thinking of your betrothal. Have you not been told this?'

'Yes, Father,' answered Tommy. Talking with Father Drogo was like circling around a dangerous animal, waiting for it to strike, to grip you in its horrid jaws. 'Yes, Father,' repeated Tommy, 'but I have not had time to reflect on it.'

'Do not reflect, my boy,' said Father Drogo, putting his arm around him, and then he struck. 'For you will do as you are told, with no question of course, my boy, won't you?' Tommy noticed how Father Drogo clenched his fist as he said this, making the boniest knuckles that Tommy had ever seen.

And if I do not, if I do not do what I am told, what then? Tommy asked himself, as Father Drogo withdrew his arm. Even in 1599 you couldn't be burnt at the stake for turning down a bride, could you? I suppose I might end up in a monastery, he reflected. But Tommy looked the priest straight in his watery eye.

'I will do what is best for my family and my title,' he said proudly, 'of that you can be certain.'

Drogo gave a grunt of assent, but Tommy could see that he had not been as servile as the priest expected. Tommy was beginning to get the impression that the real Thomas was a bit of a wet fish, or at least, well, anyway, not so extrovert and outgoing as he was. He felt really like saying straight out, 'Look, I am going to marry Eloise, and no one else,' but he knew, from the part of his mind that belonged to the real Thomas de Romolue, he knew that this would be a great error in front of the priest. Father Drogo, he was sure, would be violently opposed to a match between Tommy and Eloise. But why was he so sure? There was something that neither he nor Thomas de Romolue knew, but something that he needed very badly to know, something between Eloise and Father Drogo. There was some secret buried in the breast of Father Drogo, that, once out, would destroy him, remove him from his position as the priest of Romolue, cause him to be shunned by his rich and powerful brother, and bring great shame to his family throughout the province. This idea of some secret shame was hidden in the dark corners of the memories of the real Thomas de Romolue – but what this shame was he had no clear idea at all.

Tommy felt that he must find this secret and use it to protect himself from the dangerous clutches of Drogo. This priest wanted to make Tommy a pawn in his game of power, to hold the balance between Toulouse and Romolue. That was the priest's goal, something that Thomas de Romolue knew and Tommy could understand with sudden clarity. That was it! Marry off Tommy to Clarice, the daughter of Robert de Toulouse, control them both, build a wall around them, grasp them and squeeze them in his bony fingers, until their very pips squeaked. Between this ambition and the priest came the figure of Eloise. Father Drogo would try to dispose of her somehow, to destroy her.

Tommy was also sure that this secret of Father Drogo – surely some dreadful fall from grace – was bound up in some way with Eloise. Destroy Eloise, and Drogo would kill two birds with one stone, removing the witness or memory of some sin and pushing forward his plans for Thomas and Clarice. These thoughts hung like dark clouds in Tommy's head and he frowned to himself. The priest studied him carefully for a further moment and then turned thoughtfully away.

He's plotting already, said Tommy to himself. I must not let him get ahead of me. What move do I make? Go straight to the Count? Go to my mother? Does she have much influence with my father? Would she be on my side? Will anyone be on my side, when the future of the family is at stake? Whom should I make a friend of, whom can I trust? Perhaps someone among the servants. What do they know of this Father Drogo? Do they trust me, do they like me?

Something told him that they did not like the old Thomas too much, but that they might like the new a bit better. I can only trust to my instincts in this alien place, said Tommy to himself.

All this musing took place with Tommy studying the cobblestones, his eyes cast down, ignoring all the people around him.

'Is the ground so very interesting?' asked a sweet and melodious voice.

Tommy started and looked up into the lovely shining eyes of Eloise. In this, his very first conversation with his beloved Eloise, under the eyes of Father Drogo, he must act foolish, sullen, shy and silly, thought Tommy quickly, at the risk of hurting her. He felt the priest's gaze on them. He must not betray his true feelings under the evil surveillance of the priest.

At the same instant, Eloise also seemed to notice that they were observed. She backed away with a little cry. Tommy pretended to ignore this; he scowled, looked back at the ground, curled his lip and answered gruffly, 'What's that to you, then?'

He also made a little sneering face. It was hard to do so to a face so beautiful as that of Eloise, and Tommy moved away as rapidly as he could. A swift glance told him that the ruse had worked. The priest had given a little sigh of relief at this closely observed encounter between Thomas and Eloise, as if he needed reassuring that there was nothing there to foil his plans. With a small inclination of his head, Father Drogo summoned Eloise to his side.

'Never approach Thomas in that way,' he commanded, as Tommy strained to hear his words. 'He is not yours, nor will he ever be.'

With that, Father Drogo turned on his heel and walked away from the crowd. Eloise stood with a look of fear and anguish on her face: fear of Drogo, and anguish that the Thomas of earlier in the carriage, who had looked her so full in the eyes, with such love and adoration, had turned back into the silly, sulky Thomas whom she knew of old. And then she thought again of the scar, how it was missing from Thomas's face, and a spasm of fright passed through her. Who was he?

Three: The Banquet

ack in the château, Tommy crept unobserved up to his room. The whole party was assembled in the salon. There was to be a sumptuous banquet that evening, in his honour. He would have to make a speech, he had been told. Father Drogo would sit by his side, or very close by, he was sure. Perhaps Drogo would use the occasion to further his plans for a marriage between Thomas and Clarice. He might even announce the idea; no, he'd prepare the ground like any clever politician, sow the seed, to be reaped later. Tommy needed urgently to know more of the history of Eloise, of Clarice – perhaps she had her own ideas too about whom she wished to marry – and especially of the history of Drogo, to find his weakness, the spot where he could be attacked, the secret that the real Thomas de Romolue hinted at. Tommy also needed desperately to talk with Eloise alone. This was dangerous, but it was necessary. They needed to know each other's hearts and purposes.

But most of all, Tommy had to send an SMS to his Mum and Dad. Putting the catch back on the door, he opened up his mobile. <Message for you> blinked at him. The first was from Harry. They won the football… Oh, gosh, normally he would have been so pleased, but now, he turned rapidly to the second SMS, from Mummy.

<What is going on??> it read. <You've been ringing me up and now you say that you've lost your mobile, five minutes later!! EXPLAIN, wherever you are.>

Tommy put his hand to his brow and vigorously scratched his forehead. *Explain, I like that. I wish that I could explain. 'Wherever you are…' What did that mean? I mean, I know what it means, but what did it mean really? Maybe if I sent a message to Harry, and then Harry were to tell Mum and Dad – would they believe it from him? Would Harry believe it? No, he'd think it was just a complicated joke or something.* Tommy didn't think that Harry would risk making a really big idiot out of himself in front of his

Mum and Dad. No, he would have to tell them straight out. After all, Mum had noticed the strange magic pull of the etching, and the odd feeling around the gate of the château, just as he'd done. She might already have a suspicion that something funny was going on. Tommy turned back to the mobile. 'Wherever you are' should read 'Whenever you are' really!

Just as Tommy was about to start typing in a message to Mum and Dad, he was interrupted by a gentle tapping at the door, and a whispered, 'Thomas, Thomas.'

Gosh! It was Eloise. What a risk she was taking! Didn't she realise the danger? More tapping... 'Thomas, Thomas!'

Tommy raced over to the door. Through the crack in the door, he whispered urgently, 'Go away, go away!' And then, without thinking, he whispered, 'I love you.'

'Oh! I love you too,' whispered Eloise in return, with a little sob, 'but I have something very, very important to talk to you about! Though that's the most important thing really, isn't it, I love you, I mean?'

'Yes,' said Tommy, 'but this is terribly dangerous. Don't you realise the danger that you are in – we are both in – if Drogo were to find us together?'

'Oh! Thomas, can we meet tonight, after everyone has gone to bed? I do so need to speak to you! You're—'

'Where can we meet?' interrupted Tommy.

'In the pantry, behind the kitchen,' replied Eloise, 'there's another little room, on the left, where we could probably be safe. When the moon just passes through—'

'No!' interrupted Tommy again. They must all be amateur astronomers here! 'When the church clock strikes twelve. Meet me there, where you said. Now go, go and do not be seen!'

A small patter of feet and she was gone.

I hope that no one saw her talking through the crack in the door! thought Tommy. What a way to make a declaration of love! Everything is wrong here. The first words I speak to my mother and to my father are fibs, I tell the girl I love that I love her, without even being able to see her – through a crack in a door! Tommy made his way over to the bed, retrieved the mobile and began to type in his message.

<Do you remember the etching on the second flight of steps on the main staircase? Go and look at it, please. Stand in front of it...> But Tommy got no further. The door handle rattled and he heard his father's voice.

'Heh, Thomas! Locked in again, are you? Playing with the new toy, eh! Well, your place is downstairs, my man. You're going to have to be a grown-up person tonight. Everyone's asking after you. Come on out now!'

Tommy sighed. Of course, he should be down with the guests. It was his duty. *Duty...* that word again; his duty.

Hiding the mobile away deep in his pocket, Tommy unlocked the door, and came out into the corridor. His father put his hand on his shoulder,

'We need to talk about what you are going to say in your little speech tonight, you know, Thomas, my son.'

'Yes, Father.'

His father seemed a kind man, but how far could he trust him? I'll risk something, he thought.

'You know, Father, today after the church service, Father Drogo was talking to me.'

'Mmmm,' said the Count, 'and what was it about?'

'Well, he seemed to be suggesting that we – I mean, you – and him and his brother, the Bishop of Toulouse, might, well, want to be thinking about whom I might be betrothed to!' There, he had said it.

'Yes, yes,' said the Count. 'Actually, he brought it up with me as well, you know.'

Ah! thought Tommy. Straight on the attack. 'Oh. Well,' he added aloud, 'what did he say? Or perhaps I should not be so inquisitive?' Tommy was trying to use all his diplomatic skills, for he had no idea how he was meant to behave. Was it agreement in everything, unthinking obedience, that was expected of him? Or could he express his own wishes?

'Well, of course, in these matters, the family must come first, and any personal feelings second, yes!' said the Count.

Tommy's heart sank.

'Yes, of course, Father. What did Father Drogo say, though?'

'Well, he said that we should be thinking of a peaceful and

prosperous future for everyone. He did not suggest anyone specific, of course. But I think that he may have been hinting at an alliance with…' Tommy held his breath, this is it… 'Er, er,' continued the Count, 'with an *English* family, you know. Our English estates should be closer to the centre, closer to the centre.' The last remark the Count made was almost to himself.

Anyway, Tommy breathed a great sigh of relief. Obviously the idea of a marriage with the Toulouse family was far too sensitive a subject just to bring up like that! Very interesting. Clearly the Count would need a good deal of preparation, and Drogo would no doubt have his plans about that. Obviously they'd be all worked out with his powerful brother, the Bishop of Toulouse, Bishop Henri, and maybe also the Abbot, in the Capucin monastery nearby, a very fat and friendly abbot, Tommy could recall. Someone who would do what Drogo told him. More fond of good food than using good sense, the Abbot, Charles de Montfort, was a cousin of Drogo, Drogo de Montfort, and his brother the Bishop, Henri de Montfort. A powerful family and difficult enemies to deal with, thought Tommy. The family of de Montfort lived on power like vampires live on blood.

'Thomas, Thomas, there you are!' It was the Countess, embracing him gently. She did everything gently, as though the world was made of delicate china, and, if it was roughly handled, it would break. Indeed it would break… or maybe it had broken, and let him in, thought Tommy, this outcast from the twenty-first century, who could cause chaos in the world of 1599.

'You did so well in the church. I was proud of you. You must have worked so hard to read that Greek so well!'

'Yes, Mother, thank you. I did work hard, yes.' More fibs; he seemed to leading a life of unending lies.

'Wine, sir,' said a footman, and handed him a brimming glass.

Tommy had never really drunk wine before, apart from a sip here and there at weddings and Christmas, and with Aunt Jemima once, when she had made him swig it out of the bottle – just for fun, she said. It was a bit sour but felt nice afterwards, he remembered. The problem now was that he had to remain absolutely sober. His speech had to be prepared, he had to give it without making a fool of himself… or maybe a bit of a fool of himself? And most important of all, he was under the watchful eye of Father Drogo, and the strong, oh so strong temptation of talking to Eloise, just to be in her presence, hold her hand... Gosh, he might just forget himself enough to do that, if he drank more than a sip of wine. No, wine was a bad idea. So he simply handed his glass to a passing servant saying, 'Here, take this.'

'Good boy,' said the servant, 'keep on your toes tonight. Watch that Drogo like a hawk!' Then the little old stooping servant was gone.

Tommy gasped. Monsieur Jasper again! But he had disappeared, deftly making his way rapidly out of the salon, and then a brief glimpse of him again as he later turned to the left, Tommy saw. To the left! But that only led out to the moat – or up the staircase. But no, he had gone beyond the staircase.

'What are you staring at, my boy?' asked the sickly voice of Father Drogo, who had slithered up beside him, approaching unseen from behind.

Tommy jumped. 'Sorry,' he said, 'I'm a bit nervous, you see. I have to give this speech. Perhaps you could help me?' It struck Tommy that the priest would want to put words into his mouth, which might help Tommy find out how the priest was plotting to control the two most important figures in the province, Toulouse and Romolue. The thoughts spilling up from the real Thomas de Romolue convinced him that this was the priest's purpose.

'Ah!' said the priest, for he too could see his advantage in helping Thomas de Romolue with his speech. But he made an error in underestimating Tommy. 'Yes, I should very much like to be of help. It would be an honour to aid you in this.'

Hooked, thought Tommy.

'Now, you remember of course the little conversation we had after the service today?' began Drogo. 'Well, do you think that it would be a good idea to mention the old tradition that after your reading of the lesson for the first time...?'

'Yes, yes,' said Tommy, 'the thing about betrothal. Who I should be marrying, you mean.' He said this quite loudly, on purpose, and one or two of the family close by stopped in mid-sentence and turned their heads to hear more.

'*Sshh* – not so loud!' muttered the priest, beginning to wonder if this had been such a good idea after all.

'Well, it's not a secret that I must soon be betrothed, is it? And I know that you are very interested in this,' Tommy added, almost as loudly as before. A good number of people were listening now. Father Drogo took Tommy's arm and led him into a corner of the salon.

'Now, my boy,' he said, not suspecting that he was in fact being fooled with, rather than dealing with a fool. 'Now, my boy,' he repeated, 'we have to learn to be a little bit diplomatic, you know. We only want a *hint* about betrothals. Just a hint, and certainly it would be quite wrong to mention anyone by name.'

'You mean Clarice!' said Tommy, quite loudly again, really playing the fool, and several more heads turned.

'Ma foi, Thomas!' said Father Drogo, getting a little angry. (Play this more gently from now on, Tommy boy!) 'That's just exactly what you must *not* say!' The priest wished he hadn't said so much to this dreadfully indiscreet child. Good Lord, he might repeat it to his father! That at least must be prevented. 'Let's say that all this business about betrothal is a little secret between us. All you might do in your speech is to let out a little hint... mention the old tradition, you know, and perhaps just talk about how marriages between families can lead to new and happy alliances, can even heal old wounds. But no more than that, please! It would not be seemly, at all!'

'Of course, Father,' replied Tommy, all obedience. 'I am most anxious to please you,' he added sweetly, lying through his teeth. 'I could say something like this: There is an old tradition, blah, blah. Then, I could add that this means that...' He went on, giving every impression of being a rather silly boy, whom Drogo could more or less do as he liked with. 'There is one thing, though. When are we going to see your brother, the Bishop of Toulouse, I mean?'

Drogo was off his guard. 'Oh! I intended to see him next Sunday, at the great mass in Toulouse. Your father will attend too, I believe, with you, of course, and many of the Toulouse family will also be present. Robert de Toulouse himself, I expect; in fact I am sure of it.'

That's a useful piece of information, thought Tommy. The game is going to get quite hot quite quickly. The Count must be warned. How can I build confidence between the Count and me in just a few days, so that he'll take seriously what I say, and I can let him in on Drogo's plotting?

'Dinner is served!' announced a footman.

'When should I make my speech, please?' Tommy asked his father, as they moved in the throng along the passage, past the library and into the brightly lit dining room.

'Ah! We have not discussed yet what you were to say. I was so taken up with Madame de Seiche on the subject of the pigs running wild in the village... they plough everything up, you know. I... erm, well, let's see.'

'Actually, I did talk it over a bit with Father Drogo,' hazarded Tommy. He wanted to see the Count's reaction.

An eyebrow was raised just slightly, a short intake of breath. These were useful signs that showed that the Count was at least wary of the good Father Drogo.

'Yes,' continued Tommy, 'he was very keen on my going on about how I should be betrothed now that I had read the lesson in church today. Though he did not say whom he thought.'

'Whom he thought?' asked the Count.

'Yes, no, I mean, who he thought I should be betrothed to. Just something about healing old wounds, perhaps someone we are not so very friendly with...' Tommy trailed off. He wanted to plant a suspicion in his father's mind, not enough for him to confront Drogo, but enough that he might start some manoeuvres of his own, to counter the priest. These conversations were like a fencing match, thought Tommy. Tickle the ends of the swords together, lunge a bit, but not really make a hit, tickle a bit more, and so on.

'Mmmm,' said his father.

Tommy reckoned that this probably meant that his father was thinking. At least, he hoped so.

Anyway, Monsieur le Comte and Madame la Comtesse and also he himself had now to be good hosts. There were fifty or more people being shown their places around the table. A glittering company, with diamonds dancing in the bright lights of hundreds of candles, astonishing hair-does, piled up high, with more diamonds glinting in them, flounces and ruffs, and shining satin, both on the men and on the women. In fact the men were perhaps even greater peacocks than the women, thought Tommy. Suits embroidered with flowers, powdered hair: peacocks, thought Tommy again.

Tommy had been so absorbed with his own thoughts and with Eloise, and with his strange predicament, that he had somehow hardly noticed the other people in the salon. Now he realised that the place looked like the Victoria and Albert Museum come to life. If he went in the next room perhaps there would be a mighty stuffed blue whale! No, Tommy, pull yourself together. This is the real world of 1599. Immediately he was brought sharply back to earth by Father Drogo, who took his arm and led him to a seat at the centre of the table. Drogo wanted Tommy firmly in his sights, and he took the place beside him, his father on the other side. Where was Eloise? Tommy hoped that he would be able to see her, but then again, it was better not. If Drogo caught them exchanging loving looks, disaster might follow. But where was she? Ah! There she was… Oh gosh, opposite me, nearly! And my mother? She was beside my father, but too far away to talk with. I must make the Countess my ally, gentle but maybe strong, perhaps.

The banquet began. Strangely enough, the first thing served was little marzipan sweets with pine kernels. Then it went into top gear. Miniature pastries filled with bone marrow and cods' livers, a creamy brown soup, made with truffles, goose liver pâté and mushrooms, a purée of artichokes, carrots and radishes, venison in cinnamon sauce, a fish soup, with mussels and garlic, boiled eels in a thick vegetable purée spiced with cloves, crayfish fried in butter and stuffed with parsley and mint, a great roast joint of venison, brought in steaming and carved at the table. Honeyed fritters, jellies, poached fish. As far as Tommy could see, all the courses were mixed up: sweets, starters, soup, main course. Tommy was hungry and he tucked in. He was always one to try new things, and when pike fish balls were served he was straight for them. Delicious.

I wonder if I can get them in the twenty-first century, thought Tommy, hoping he could. The truffle soup was lovely too, and the venison. Actually there were practically no vegetables, the bit of purée, yes, but none of the 'eat up your greens or there's no pudding for you' type of thing. 1599 might be a downer for lots of things, like falling in love with the wrong people, but it was certainly okay for food. Gobbling a honey fritter, Tommy had almost forgotten his troubles, although he had managed to remember to keep off the wine.

The conversation was loud and boisterous and he could not make out much of it. Beside him, Drogo was silent, fiddling with little bits of one dish or another on his plate and continually calling a footman for a cloth to wipe his hands, his nose... His bum next, thought Tommy, and nearly swallowed a fish bone trying not to giggle. His father was a good host and spent all the time ordering this or that dish to be given to the Comtesse of this, or the Comte of that, and there was in fact no time for conversation with his father.

But what about my speech, thought Tommy? Won't it be coming up soon? They can't go on pigging themselves like this much longer. They'll all be ill, or drunk, or both. It was a regular orgy. A braised goose appeared and an enormous round of veal in a great tureen, swimming in creamy sauce; and then, to crown it all, a massive boar's head was carried in by two footmen, surrounded, on an enormous platter, by a dozen or more little roasted larks, swimming in melted anchovy butter. Tommy's stomach began to turn over. Poor little birds. He had heard somewhere, at school probably, that people used to eat larks' tongues to improve their voices, especially if they were singers, of course. Well, here they were, anyway.

Amidst the applause – for this last dish was greeted with applause by the guests – his father turned to Tommy and said, 'Thomas, traditionally you make your speech over the boar's head, as you know, of course. Off you go then.'

Just like that. Tommy gulped and rose to his feet, and footmen scrambled to pull his chair back. He had scribbled on his napkin a few ideas and he glanced down, only to find that a footman had just removed his napkin and replaced it with a nice clean fresh one. The company began to quieten down as they waited for Tommy to begin.

Peep-ee-ee-ee-ee-ee-pee-ee-or rang out, and for the first and last time for two centuries the opening bars of 'Für Elise' pierced the air. *Blast and blast it*! An SMS. In his rush he had forgotten to switch the mobile off. He made a grab for it, fumbling in his pocket, and thank heavens found the off button immediately. Had anyone noticed? Drogo, his ear right beside Tommy's trouser pocket, looked very startled indeed. His mouth flew open and his hand clasped his ear. He put his other hand to his brow and rubbed his forehead as if to erase the memory of the strange alien sound. Occasionally he got the most terrible singing sounds in his head. Was it some forewarning of hell? He shuddered. It must have been an attack of that kind he had had before. He had been known to faint in horror. With a shake of his head, Drogo did his best to dismiss it. Tommy noticed Drogo's terror with satisfaction. But who else had heard it?

'You've got that toy with you, you silly boy,' grunted his father. 'Now is not the time to play with it.'

'Sorry, it just went off by mistake.'

His father gave him a strange look. Tommy's eyes moved around the guests. Some were looking startled at this twenty-first century intrusion into their lives, others just grinned, and a small servant in a darker corner of the room rolled his eyes to heaven, as if to say 'You twit!' – and then was gone.

Monsieur Jasper again. Gosh! He must think that I'm a fool. And so I was, thought Tommy. Well, I'd better start…

'My Lords and Ladies,' he began, 'today I read you the lesson at church. I hope that you all enjoyed it.' A murmur which showed that they were listening, anyway. 'The Greek is not so easy to read – at least not for me.' *Be modest*, thought Tommy, they may like me for that, and I need friends. 'So I hope that you could all follow it.'

Some titters here. Hardly a single person there knew a word of the language. Their Latin was pretty ropey, for that matter. But some people at least were flattered that Tommy thought that they knew some Greek.

'Well anyway, I did my best to try and tell you of the ancient times.' *My gosh!* What waffle… could he keep this up? How long was he meant to go on for anyway? 'And the love of God.' Better stick that in, can't do any harm. Drogo threw him a look as he said this.

'The love of God,' he repeated, 'which is so important to our everyday lives.' More titters, and a scowl from Drogo. 'Well, anyway, it is a kind of growing up in our family to read the lesson, as you know. And this means that I should be thinking of finding a bride to be betrothed to.' This sally was greeted by some startled looks and a general shuffling of feet, so Tommy added, 'As Father Drogo has told me.'

'*That's enough!*' hissed Drogo, so only Tommy could hear.

Tommy nodded. 'Father Drogo says that I should not talk about that, really.' Several people laughed at this and Drogo made as if to rise himself, but then thought better of it.

Tommy looked down at the boar's head and regarded its beady eyes – in fact they'd put in imitation glass eyes – how horrid! The open mouth with the tongue hanging out was also repulsive and Tommy could find no inspiration there. He looked across the table. Eloise! She must be finding this quite painful. Did she realise that he was making a bit of a fool of himself on purpose? Drogo and the others (he surely has allies here, too) must not suspect that he was anything more than a silly child.

'Marriage,' he continued, and he noticed that Eloise's glance fell to the table as he said the word, 'marriage is very important, of course. What would we do without it?' A suppressed guffaw came from old Great-uncle Jacques, and several other people were heard to murmur comments to their neighbours, of which Tommy only caught, 'Poor boy!'

'So,' continued Tommy, looking very serious, 'this has been a very important day for me. This you can see from the boar's head,' here he gestured at it, and all the guests followed his gaze, 'which is served only on this occasion – at least with all the larks round it!' he concluded.

At this, his father rose to his feet. 'Thank you Thomas, thank you. That's enough for now. Thank you!'

Everyone politely clapped. Tommy sat down feeling both ashamed and elated. He had managed to embarrass Drogo, so that everyone knew that he was mixing in with Thomas's betrothal, pushing Drogo on to his next move, perhaps before the ground was well prepared. Also he had projected himself as a foolish little boy, which was necessary. Still, there was some damage to undo there. He needed a serious talk with his father, and his mother, as soon as possible.

What do I really want to achieve? Tommy asked himself. He had to have this clear in his mind. First, neutralise Drogo, find his ugly secret, which he somehow knew existed from memories of the real Thomas; second, marry Eloise, or at least, be betrothed to her; third, return to his own time, bearing Eloise with him... if she would come, if she *could* come. And he frowned to himself. What were the means to these ends? Push Drogo on to rash acts, try and keep some control of the power struggle, take the initiative when possible. Make friends with the servants. Find out if they have information on Drogo's past, and corner Monsieur Jasper to enlist his help. Get the Comte and Comtesse in on the act. Perhaps contact Clarice (though how?); but first find out something about her. Maybe he would see her at Toulouse Cathedral next Sunday. Why not press Drogo to introduce them then? That would be a rash act for Drogo, under the eyes of the Count of Romolue, but maybe Drogo would be fool enough to try it.

Another and very different thought struck Tommy. He seemed not to know anything of Eloise's parents. As he searched his memory, his artificial shared memory, he could find nothing to guide him, save that her mother had died when she was a tiny baby, perhaps died in childbirth, and her father, her father... he could not squeeze from his mind any information about her father. Some of the older servants might help him. Perhaps the key to Drogo's secret lay there?

As a practical start, could he not send down some present to the kitchen and the staff for the wonderful feast which they had made in his honour? He had no time except to bribe them in this way – or even more directly. Did he have any money? How did one deal with things like money in 1599? Did a nobleman need money, or use money directly? No, he had no money – ah! – except a few golden coins in a purse in a drawer in his room. These he had always had and they were valuable. Each one was worth a year's wages for a footman. There was no time like the present for action.

'Father,' he said, turning towards the Count, 'might I express my gratitude to the servants for this great feast by presenting them with... um?'

'Good heavens, child,' replied the Count, 'think of the leftovers they are munching in the kitchen this minute. They've done pretty well, as it is!'

Seeing the look of disappointment on Tommy's face, the Count added, 'I'll have a word with your mother and see what she says. Anyway, what were you thinking of giving them? What have they not got which they need?'

Tommy felt like saying, 'Television in the servants' parlour,' but restrained himself, although keeping up this whole tissue of lies was starting to tell on him. He needed to be alone.

'My dear,' said the Count, addressing his wife, 'our young son here wishes to express his gratitude to the servants by presenting them with a gift of some kind. Do you think that this is something that we should do?'

'My dear Thomas,' said the Countess, 'it is a kind thought, and shows that you have a good heart. But what do they lack?'

The same thought as the Count, said Tommy to himself. What indeed did they lack? Did they use money at all? An extra week's pay, maybe. A barrel of wine. Knives for the men, shawls for the women. The real Thomas had apparently no clue about the needs and deeds of the lower classes, the servants, and Tommy had nothing to draw on. So instead he said, quite truthfully, 'Mother, I really do not know. What would they appreciate? Goods, wine, money?'

Sadly, though it came as no surprise, it seemed that the Count and Countess themselves had little knowledge of their servants' lives. They lived a world apart, and had done for many centuries, and would do so for two or three more centuries, as Tommy knew from his history lessons at school.

'Couldn't we ask the chief butler?' suggested Tommy.

The Count turned to the footman standing behind his chair. 'Could you tell Jacques that I should like to talk to him.' The footman bowed and walked rapidly away on his errand.

Just a few moments elapsed before Jacques stood before them. Tommy's heart came into his mouth. It was Monsieur Jasper!

And the true Monsieur Thomas had not even really seemed to know it! Monsieur Jasper gave not the tiniest sign of recognition and Tommy was wise enough to follow his example. Father Drogo, though engrossed in deep discussion with his other neighbour, was only a few feet away, and he surely had spies everywhere – among the servants, perhaps, Tommy realised.

'My son, Thomas,' the Count was saying, 'wishes to recognise the hard work of the servants in preparing this magnificent feast, which was in his honour. We seek your advice how best to do this. What reward would the servants like the most? We rely on your advice.'

'Ah, Monsieur, that is so gracious! It is without precedent.' Oh dear, thought Tommy. Perhaps I have overdone it! 'Though perhaps not quite,' continued Monsieur Jasper, or Jacques. Jacques here, or 'now', I suppose, thought Tommy. 'I remember that your father, Monsieur, rewarded us when we helped to fight off the forces of Toulouse, when they tried to storm the château some twenty-five years ago.' Tommy felt Drogo's eye flicker over them for an instant as these words were said. 'The ancient château, of course!' continued Jacques. 'You must remember only too well yourself, Monsieur, for you fought very bravely, and you were wounded in the arm.'

'Yes, and you bound it for me! Do you think that I have forgotten that!' cried the Count, and a gleam of great affection for the frail little man before him came into his eye.

Tommy, via Thomas, had heard of this story, naturally enough. It was recent family history, of course. But much had remained unsaid. Another clue, perhaps, certainly about the hatred that existed between Toulouse and Romolue.

'True, yes, you were all rewarded – generously too, I remember. This is not quite the same thing, of course!'

'Hardly, Monsieur,' replied Jacques with a smile, 'hardly.'

'Anyway, remind me, what was that reward?'

'Two gold coins a head to the men who fought, Monsieur, and one to each of those behind the lines. The women each received, as I remember, a shawl. I am sure that Marie has hers yet.'

Jacques looked Tommy full in the face for the first time as he mentioned Marie, as if to say, 'There's someone for you.'

Marie? Of course, *Marie*, Tommy thought; Marie, my old nurse. Tommy's childhood came flooding back. Marie was constantly with him until he was more than ten years old; she had loved him and adored him as her own child, still did. She is a contact for me. She may know many secrets. Marie has been in the heart of the family for years untold.

'Why not send Monsieur Thomas to ask Marie what the serving-women might like, while we discuss something for the men?' suggested Jacques.

He's setting me up with the perfect excuse to go and see her and pump her for information! Tommy realised.

'Tomorrow, I think,' said the Count. 'Marie will be in bed asleep by now. Go and see her tomorrow.'

Tommy was elated that he had the direct advice of the Count to go to Marie. Just how important his visit to Marie would be, he little realised.

In the distance, the village clock began to strike, ringing out ten mellow tones. Ten o'clock! Gosh, he had only two hours before he had to meet Eloise, thought Tommy. The Count rose to his feet, and all the company followed suit. Grace was said by Father Drogo, and everyone dispersed, some to their rooms, others to waiting carriages. The house became quiet.

'We will, you know, have to start thinking about Thomas's betrothal, as he mentioned in his little speech,' remarked the Countess to her husband, as they parted in the corridor outside Tommy's room.

'The less I hear about that speech, the better,' said the Count. 'What a little twerp!'

Tommy had heard his mother's comment through the door, and now his ear was pressed hard against the wood, and he smiled at his father's reaction. He could hear his mother's whispered reply.

'Ah! I think that he may have done that deliberately, you know, made a bit of a fool of himself – on purpose.'

'Eh, really? The boy's always been a bit of a twit, you know. Anyway, come to my room and let's discuss this further,' said the Count, and the two walked off together.

It seems that my mother is pretty clever, thought Tommy.

She's got me partly worked out. I think that I may go to her first when the time comes.

It would come sooner than he expected.

Tommy put the catch on the door, extracted his mobile and opened the latest SMS from his mother. Things were starting to get serious. Obviously Thomas had been having a good talk with his mum and dad.

<Tommy darling, we are frightened for you. You say that you have lost your mobile but you send me messages. Why are you doing this? It might have been a funny idea, but it is beyond that now. And you tell us the most crazy stories. You seem to be both here and not here, according to you. If you can only tell us things through messages, tell us the truth. Maybe you need some help. If you can only tell us crazy things face to face, then try to write to us and explain what you are really thinking and doing. Please. Love Mummy and Daddy.>

Okay, here goes. <Dear Mum and Dad, in simple words I am trapped in the year 1599. The Tommy that you have looks the same as me, perhaps identical, but he was living in 1599 before, and now he lives with you in our time. Of course the trouble is that this is the story that Thomas – as he is called here – has been telling you, and you think of course that he is me. We have a kind of shared memory, which is a bit imperfect, because for one thing we only remember things on the spot, when we ask about things, if you see what I mean. This transfer in time happened yesterday afternoon when I walked down the main staircase, and was simply sucked into the etching of the garden of the château as it was in 1599. You remember the very strange pull that the picture had as we passed it earlier. You know what I mean, Mummy, though Dad did not feel it. After I was sucked in, I found myself on the bench in the picture. Jasper came with me and then faded out. I will find a way to come home. Question Jasper closely. See how he reacts to the name 'Jacques', which is his name here. I cannot risk being found with my mobile, so that is all for now. I'll find a way back. I must! Love from Tommy. PS: Be kind to your present Tommy. He must be having a living nightmare> Send.

Tommy had about an hour before he was to meet Eloise. He absolutely must not snooze off. So he spent the time searching through his room, discovering his memories, filling his mind with his past life, so that he would have it ready when he needed it, instead of the few seconds' delay that had come close to costing him dearly once or twice already. Now he knew when his brother Jasper was born, the date of Maddy's birthday, he knew that his mother came from Narbonne. In 1599 this was a great distance to the east of Toulouse, though it's just an hour or two down the autoroute in the twenty-first century. There was nothing more of Father Drogo or of Eloise to be unearthed from his memory, though, try as he might. He found the little purse with the gold coins, and then, under the purse, a little miniature painting of Eloise – good heavens – Thomas was maybe in love with her too! Of course, how silly I have been, she was continuing with him, Tommy, where she had left off the day before, maybe just a few hours before, with the real Thomas. What then does love mean, he wondered? Can she be so mistaken, and yet still be in love? Maybe it is this that she wants so urgently to talk to me about. The clock struck the first note of twelve. Tommy felt a prickle of anticipation pass through him.

Four: Meeting at Midnight

reeping and feeling his way along the dark corridor in bare feet, Tommy came to the head of the back staircase, the servants' staircase. The silence was so strong, so powerful a sense of quietness, that he felt that it would almost overwhelm him. The atmosphere was made still more oppressive by the striking of the church bell. Silence of this quality was unknown in his world of the twenty-first century. There was no murmur of distant traffic, no hum from a nearby town, no lights in the sky, except the full glory of the moon and stars, which, glancing out of the window, Tommy now saw for the first time in his life, or so he felt. The moon cast sharp shadows of the building on the ground, a tree rustled, and Tommy shivered. Were there guards around the château at night? he wondered. What was that dark shape half obscured by the lower branches of an oak tree. Did I see it move? thought Tommy. Or is it a statue? There were many of them to be found in the grounds of the château. Tommy watched for a few seconds. He could see no movement. He stood hesitating at the top of the stairs. The bell struck for the twelfth time. A faint sound of snoring, from behind a closed door, reassured him that he was not alone in this world, and then a brief grunt, as someone turned over in their sleep.

'Let's go,' said Tommy to himself, 'let's go!' Cautiously, he made his way down the curling narrow staircase. A floorboard squeaked, and there was a faint scuttling as mice, or rats, made off. Tommy paused for a moment as an owl whistled its lonely and ominous song, and another replied in the far distance. Turning to the left at the bottom of the stairs, into the kitchen, he was met by silence again; there was no one there. Left again into the pantry, left again into the little room, and there, holding her breath, was the beautiful form of Eloise, her face palely lit in the moonlight, which was coming through a small window set in the angled ceiling.

'Oh!' She made this little exclamation and then put her finger to her lips, and gestured to Tommy to close the door. He was standing there, just gazing at her, forgetting the danger of discovery, just swimming in her lovely eyes.

Close the door, she mouthed at him, and he came to life and, as gently as he could, he shut the door. There was a hook on the inside, so he fastened that too. With no thought for any other purpose, Tommy walked towards Eloise and simply enclosed her in his arms, and kissed her. After a moment, a long moment, she broke away from him, trembling and shaking her head.

'*No!*' she whispered. 'No! it was not for this I asked you to come here!' And her eyes shone with tears. 'Who are you?' she whispered urgently. '*Who are you?*'

'I... I,' Tommy began. Then, changing his mind about a simple statement which she would not be able to believe, though it would be true, he simply said, 'You know who I am – I am Thomas. Why do you ask?'

Again a lie! Maybe the truth would have been better, especially as she suspected. 'But I am a little changed,' he added, leading her gently towards the truth.

'A little changed!' replied Eloise and then looked down at her hands, which were clenched together in nervous doubt.

'Stay still,' she said and moved towards him. She reached up and her hand travelled gently over his forehead, and he felt her sweet breath on his face. He put his hand on her arm, but she gave a small shake of her head and he let his arm fall again. She moved aside the hair that had fallen over his forehead and ran the tips of her fingers over his brow, tilting his head so that his face was fully lit by the moonlight.

'It's gone, it's not there!' she whispered, with fear in her voice, abruptly removing her hand from Tommy's forehead.

'Who are you?' she asked again.

Suddenly the powerful memory of the hunting accident flooded back into Tommy's mind. He could feel the arrow, the pain, the yell of rage from his father, the bucking of the horse... and then the memory faded. Of course, of course, in a boar hunt, a careless shot had grazed him, when he was a child, and left a small scar on his right forehead just above his eye, just a small whitening of the skin. Tommy of the twenty-first century did not have such a scar. He hadn't thought of that difference! There were no boar hunts for him as a child. Eloise, who knew his face so well, was searching for the scar, and of course it was not there. She must have noticed this already in the carriage on the way to the church earlier. Yes, she had! That explains the strange expression on her face, almost of panic, blended with love and doubt, that he remembered so well from the brief ride. No wonder she needed to talk to him urgently!

'Ah! You mean my scar, Eloise,' said Tommy, trying to sound casual.

'Yes, where is it? How can it be gone?' asked Eloise.

So intensely were they concentrating on each other that they failed to hear the kitchen door open, creaking gently on its hinges. Far better if they had been listening more carefully!

'Who are you?' she asked insistently.

'I am a little changed from the Thomas you have known. Perhaps more than a little,' answered Tommy.

Eloise replaced her hand on Tommy's brow, her face still close to his and the impulse to kiss each other again was too strong to overcome. As their lips met, a creak from outside the door caused them suddenly to freeze in fright and draw away from each other. Tommy put his finger to his lips.

Someone was outside! He could hear the heavy breathing of an older man. This was a rat-trap they were in. There was no way to escape, unless they could squeeze through that little window. But what then? The alarm would be sounded. They would be picked out in the brilliant light of the full moon immediately. Tommy cursed the moon, having gloried in its beauty just a few minutes before. Perhaps the man outside the door would just leave. Had he heard them whispering? Did he suspect that there were thieves in the house? Eloise stood with a look of simple terror on her face. Tommy raised a finger and pointed towards the small window above their heads. Eloise's eyes opened still wider with fear. Suddenly, the door was rattled. Blast it and blast it! thought Tommy. Now they know there's someone inside! A voice growled at them through the door.

'Who's there? I'll have you whipped if you're stealing the jam, my boy. I know it's you, Ralph, you rascal! You'll be whipped before the whole household at sunrise tomorrow. Open the door, or worse will come to you! Answer me, you little rat!'

Eloise gave a little whimper of fear, and Tommy put his finger to his lips, and grinned at her.

'It's Thomas, my man,' he said, 'and I'll not open the door. I've a little assignation here, and she's getting very frightened by you. Be off now, and a reward will come your way tomorrow, I promise you that!'

'Ho, ho!' replied the guard, 'keeping up the family tradition, are you? Very well, my Lord, I'll be off. I can keep a secret. But who is it, eh? Flore, I bet. She fancies you and she's a pretty girl. When you've had enough of her, just pass her on, will you, there's a good boy!' And with this coarse demand, Tommy and Eloise could hear his footsteps departing.

A great sigh of relief escaped them both. But only for an instant. For just then they heard a much more feared voice.

'Who was that you were talking with, my man?' It was the voice of Father Drogo. Tommy and Eloise exchanged an anguished glance.

'Ah, good Father, are you sleepless again tonight?' replied the guard; for Drogo often wandered the corridors at night, unable to sleep, consumed by his schemes and his hatreds.

'Answer me!' demanded Drogo.

The guard was a man of few wits, and he was unable to make up any story that would convince the wily Father Drogo.

'Quick, break the window open,' said Eloise, and Tommy was already reaching for it to unlatch it, if he could. They could hear the conversation outside quite clearly now.

'Well,' said the guard, 'I promised not to tell!'

'I'll have you whipped,' said the priest in a fierce whisper, and the guard knew that he would, as well.

'Your name!' demanded Drogo,

'Jean, Father,' whispered the guard, 'and I have served this household long and well...' he dared to add.

'Who were you talking to, Jean, for the last time!' said Father Drogo, beginning to lose control of his voice, which rasped through the air like a rusty blade against metal. There were stirrings from the floor above. They would wake the entire household! Before this happened, Tommy and Eloise had to be out and away. Tommy found the latch on the window jammed solid – it had not been opened for many years – so he took a log of wood, that was lying in a corner, and smashed it against the window pane, knocking out the jagged pieces remaining as best he could. The sound would be sure to bring Father Drogo and half the château running, but there was no help for it.

Tommy lifted Eloise to the window and pushed her though, her dress catching and ripping on the sharp pieces of glass which still remained. She crawled out onto the roof. This sloped down towards the moat, beyond a small chimney, and she had to steady herself, with one arm around the chimney, from rolling straight down into the water. Tommy's head appeared, and an outstretched arm. She hauled on Tommy's arm and he pulled himself through. Both of them were breathing hard. Tommy had cut his hand open on the broken glass, heaving himself up, and telltale drops of blood, shining in the moonlight, were dripping on the slates of the roof.

They could hear Drogo rattling the door of the room, cursing and yelling for them to open up. The sound of other feet running from all directions could also be heard. The alarm was raised. Suddenly the door of their little room burst open under the constant rattling and pushing, and Drogo and the guard rushed in, Drogo with a dagger in his hand.

'Stop, sir!' shouted the guard. 'It is only the young master with a serving girl!'

For an instant Drogo stood bewildered. The room was empty. But then he saw the broken window.

'A servant girl?' he muttered. For he smelt the rich scent used by ladies, not by servant girls, and he saw the shreds of a silk dress hanging from the fragments of glass in the window frame.

'Silk dresses are not worn by servant girls, nor do they use that scent,' he continued to himself.

Drogo reached up and removed a fragment of material and held it in his hand. Was this not the material of the dress which he had seen Eloise wear at the banquet? Had she dared to meet Thomas here, at night? What was the meaning of this, acting in direct disobedience to his command to her! They must be up on the roof, through the broken window. Father Drogo put one hand on the window frame and called for the guard, who was hanging back fearfully, to help him up.

The instant that Tommy saw the hand appear, without much thought he stamped upon it furiously, stamped with as much force as he could, jamming the priest's palm hard against shards of broken glass.

Drogo gave a great scream of pain and dropped back into the room, hugging his hand, and yelling to the guard, 'After them, you fool! After them!' Blood poured from a great gash in his hand and wrist, giving Tommy and Eloise a short respite.

'Quick!' said Tommy. 'Into the moat!'

Eloise gasped with fright.

'Now listen,' he said, 'do as I say. Take a very deep breath, just before we go in. We are going to swim along the moat underwater and out into the river, where they will not find us. All you must do is to hold your clothes around you with one hand, and my shoulder with the other hand, and let your breath out slowly, bubble by bubble. Keep your eyes shut. Be a brave girl!'

'We'll drown. You're mad!'

'No,' said Tommy. 'There's no time for talking. We're going in now. Take a deep breath now, hold your nose and we're jumping – *now*!'

He grabbed her hand and in they went. Tommy duck-dived, dragging Eloise down with him. Her eyes were closed and she was quite limp with fear. Her dress billowed around her, and Tommy grabbed it and shoved it into her free hand.

Tommy was an excellent swimmer and he had learnt to swim underwater an entire length of an Olympic pool. So they made good progress, despite the burden of Eloise, with Tommy's strong breaststroke pulling them rapidly along the moat. Tommy could hear shouts and yells from the château, muffled as they were by the water. He glanced up, and could see the distorted rippling image of the full moon shining down upon them. When they turned the corner into the main river they would rapidly disappear into the dark shadow of the château, and there they would be safe. All at once there was a commotion above him and a scrabbling of webbed feet. The swans slept in the moat at night and he had swum straight into them, like a fool.

Gosh! I hope that they do not give the game away... Tommy was counting on his pursuers not realising that he could swim underwater, and that they would be vainly looking for them somewhere on the roof of the château, at least for a short while. The swans meanwhile settled down again. Tommy just prayed that no one would look at the moat, or notice the commotion that the swans had made. Surely he and Eloise would be visible as dark shapes under the water? Not far now... He could hear the hue and cry more clearly, as guards and servants ran out of the château, down the drive, up on the roof of the kitchen; but no one thought to look in the water. His guess had been correct. To jump in the moat would be suicide. These people were no swimmers and were terrified of water. How he got Eloise in, he did not know. She was a brave girl – or she had fainted. At all events bubbles were coming slowly out of her mouth, and she was not drowning yet, he could see, as he glanced at her. He doubted, however, that she could hold out much longer. They had been the best part of half a minute in the water. Not far to go.

Tommy glanced upwards again. My gosh! A guard was standing on the bridge over the moat, as it entered the river. Surely he would see them! But the strongly reflected dappled moonlight on the choppy surface made it difficult to see into the water, and the guard wasn't looking in that direction. Rather, he was trying to see along the wall of the château, thinking perhaps that the two fugitives might be clambering up there, making maybe for Tommy's bedroom.

Tommy and Eloise passed under the bridge unobserved, and were immediately picked up by the swift current of the river. He could feel Eloise's grip on his shoulder slowly relaxing, and he knew if they did not surface soon he would be bearing not a lovely living girl but a drowned corpse. The transition into the shadow of the château was sudden and startling. The blackness overwhelmed Tommy for an instant, before he realised that they had made it. Up they came, Tommy holding Eloise's head up for air. Then he turned on his back, and in the life-saver's style kicked as hard as could for the opposite shore, away from the château. The far bank was quite steep, but after dragging the half-conscious form of Eloise out of the water, smeared in mud, Tommy sat her up, and pushed her head forward as she vomited muddy water from the moat. Then he leant her back and gave her the kiss of life, as he had been taught, breathing deeply into her mouth; for luckily enough, he had done a life-saving course just a few months ago. Suddenly, Eloise struggled in his arms, gasped, opened and shut her eyes rapidly, and looked up at Tommy in astonishment. Then, rolling on her side, she burst into tears. Tommy pulled her rather roughly against him to muffle the sounds of her sobbing.

'Ssshhh,' he said, 'or you will give us away!'

At once she quietened, 'Sorry,' she murmured. 'Sorry. I had forgotten where we were!'

I hardly know this girl, thought Tommy, and here I am sitting dripping wet, covered with mud, a bedraggled mess, my best church clothes a ruin, her embroidered best silk dress in tatters, sitting together on a river bank, in terrible danger – of what exactly? Eloise has broken all the bounds of behaviour expected of a young lady, in any day and age, certainly of 1599. I have stamped on the hand of one of the most powerful priests in the land, wounding him badly (I hope)… As well as running off with a noblewoman and nearly drowning her in the moat. To what purpose? Only so that she could tell me what I already know, that I am not Thomas, but Tommy from… No, it is more than that; much more. But no matter now. How do we escape from this? How can we get back into the château without being seen?

He looked at the pale and exhausted form of Eloise. He could think of only one way of re-entering the château without capture. Could she manage it? He held her gently in his arms and she pressed her head against his shoulder. He placed his hand around her head and gently rocked her, trying to soothe her, to stop her trembling. Little by little she became more relaxed, her trembling coming and going, and then she lay quite still. He smoothed her hair. Her crazy hair-do had come completely undone, and he saw that she had lovely long deep brown hair, almost to her waist.

'Eloise,' said Tommy, 'Eloise.'

'Oh, Thomas, what have we done? Where can we go now?'

'Back into the château,' replied Tommy.

'Back to them?' exclaimed Eloise.

'Yes,' said Tommy, 'that is our only hope. I shall invent a story, some story, that will at least keep off the worst of the anger of the Count and Countess.'

'Your parents, you mean,' said Eloise, looking at him in surprise.

'Yes,' said Tommy, 'my parents.'

This was not the time for further explanations, and Eloise did not raise the question of the scar again. The din around the château was beginning to die down. They expect to find us in the morning, thought Tommy. They will have posted guards around the château, and there is no escape for us across country. Anyway, we could survive only a few days without being recognised and caught. There would probably be a reward on our heads. Just think of that! Gosh, Harry would be really envious: a reward on his head! Just like the three musketeers! Stop it now! This is no childish adventure. Think, think!

Eloise raised her head to study him more closely. She kissed him on the cheek, and left her cheek resting against his.

'Eloise,' he said, 'are you strong?' She nodded, rubbing her cheek against his, but then dropping her head in exhaustion. 'Are you?' asked Tommy, taking her shoulders, and she raised her head a little, and smiled and nodded again. 'Well,' he said, 'what we are going to do is this…' And he explained his plan to her.

The look of dismay as she found that she was expected to take another dip in the moat was replaced by horror at the thought of scaling the wall of the château into Tommy's bedroom.

'Let's just wait a little longer until the château is quite quiet again,' said Tommy.

The night was warm, but their soaking clothes felt very uncomfortable. They were completely wet through.

My gosh, my mobile! thought Tommy suddenly. It would be soaked. His hand dived into the recesses of his pocket and he fished out the mobile. Too bad if Eloise sees it, he thought. Luckily it was still dry. The thick cloth had protected it and it would survive another dipping, he was sure. Another SMS. Eloise had closed her eyes, and lay with her head in his lap.

Open message 1. <The next match will be on Wednesday. Wish us luck. Why haven't I heard from you? Rotten, rotten, Tommy rotten. Lots of worst wishes, Harry. PS: best wishes, I meant.>

Wish you luck! thought Tommy. Harry, wish me luck, please! Nothing more from Mum and Dad. They are probably off with Thomas consulting a head case doctor, I expect! Poor Mum and Dad. If they could see me now, they would probably need the head case doctor themselves. Tommy simply did not have the heart to write a message to Harry. He would have to wait and think that Tommy really was rotten, rotten, Tommy rotten. He stroked Eloise's cheek, gently running his fingers through her hair. The moon was moving to place the moat more and more in shadow.

Good, thought Tommy. We'll wait until the wall up to my window is in shadow too. That should be just a few minutes.

'Time to go,' he whispered, leaning over Eloise's ear. She shuddered. 'What we'll do is to go a bit upstream, so that we can float down and get into the moat.'

So Tommy and Eloise, crouching, made their way behind the bushes which formed the outer part of the geometrical garden, and crept along, hunched down out of sight, scurrying between gaps in the hedge until they were well upstream from where the moat joined the river.

'Let's slip in just here,' said Tommy, and holding Eloise's hand, they waded in up to their waists.

Just then a guard appeared, patrolling the bridge across the river. Without a word, they ducked below the surface, Tommy grabbing Eloise's dress as it billowed up. We should have taken that off, he thought. Too late now. But no; if we take it off here, it'll float down the river and be found somewhere further downstream. People will think that she has drowned. That might put them off the scent. I can hide her in my room for a bit, perhaps...

The guard turned and walked back towards the château and Tommy and Eloise broke the surface, gasping for air. For neither had had the time for a good breath when the guard appeared.

'Eloise,' whispered Tommy, and he explained his little

diversion to her. If the light had been better, he would have seen that Eloise was blushing violently at the idea of removing her dress and her petticoats, and indeed Tommy had no idea of what she was wearing underneath. Perhaps not much; that might be a bit of a problem. He remembered his surprise at his own tights, earlier on that day. Perhaps Eloise had something similar? Thomas, naturally enough, had nothing to offer by way of memory on this subject, and he hardly liked to ask! They stood in the river in indecision.

'Oh! Thomas,' whispered Eloise, pulling sharply at the buttons of her dress, 'help me out of it.'

Following her orders, Tommy fumbled furiously with laces, and buttons, and more laces and more buttons.

'You would make a terrible lady's maid,' giggled Eloise, and Tommy grinned.

She was a girl of spirit, and by gosh she was going to need it! What an image though, undressing his girlfriend in the middle of the night in the middle of a river! When I get back home, no one is going to believe this bit, thought Tommy; especially not Harry. Thank heavens, she did have something like tights on under it all! The dress and petticoats floated off down the river, shining as they caught the moonlight.

God! If anyone sees them, thought Tommy; but there were no shouts from the château. He hoped they wouldn't catch too soon on any branches. But the sides of the river were well kept, and they were whisked out of sight around a bend, to his relief.

'Deep breath,' said Tommy, 'hold your nose as we go in.'

And down they went together, Tommy breaststroking strongly for the other side and Eloise hanging on with all her might. They made it easily into the moat, and Tommy swam straight over to the wall directly under his window. The swans were nowhere to be seen. He grabbed some pebbles and a heavy waterlogged stick from the bottom, thinking a bit of ammo might be useful, just in case, and then they emerged with only their heads above the water, right up against the lower stonework of the château. A faint light was burning in his father's window, he could see. Probably his poor parents would not sleep until he was found, for he was sure that they were fond of him – or Thomas, anyway. Now I have upset my parents, both in the twenty-first century and in 1599, he thought. What a bad boy!

The wall up to his window provided many footholds, and was not a difficult climb, at least for him alone. It turned out though that Eloise, once out of her dress and petticoats, was quite a bit of a tomboy – she had been climbing trees from an early age. So they shinned up the wall without difficulty and, in the dark shadow of the château, without detection. No guard returned to the bridge, but that was only a matter of time. They had to move fast. Tommy's window stood slightly open, on this warm summer night. Gingerly, Tommy eased his head over the window sill. It was lucky that he did, for there inside his room facing the door stood a guard, with his back to Tommy!

So they were not so stupid, thought Tommy. The idea that he might make his way back into the château had not eluded them. They too realised that really he had nowhere else to go! He turned to Eloise, who looked up at him questioningly, hanging on by her fingertips and a single foothold to the wall, just below him. He shook his head, as if to indicate, 'Don't move until I say.' Then, after reflecting for a moment, he motioned her to move to one side, if she could, out of easy sight of the window. He nodded, whispering, 'That's far enough.' Then, taking a pebble from his pocket, he pushed the window a fraction further open, and threw the pebble, hitting the guard on the backside. Not hard, but enough to thoroughly wake him up from the snooze which he was well on the way to falling into. With a jerk he stood bolt upright, put a hand to his backside, and turning with a puzzled look, walked over to the window, and thrust his head out. This was the mistake that Tommy had been counting on. He had moved to one side, and raised the heavy water-logged stick in readiness. He brought it crashing down on the guard's head, and the man collapsed with just a low grunt, his head lolling over the window ledge and a very silly expression on his face. Slowly he slid inwards, and Tommy grabbed his arm, which served both to soften the noise of his fall, and, since the guard was much heavier than Tommy, to drag Tommy very nicely through the window and into his room. Immediately his arm went out to Eloise, whom he lifted quickly through the window, shutting it after her.

'First, we must get rid of this character,' whispered Tommy. 'He won't stay out cold forever.'

The best place for him would be outside the door in the corridor. But maybe there were more guards out there.

'I'll just check the corridor,' he whispered to Eloise, and he walked as quietly as he could across his room and very carefully cracked open the door.

The corridor was moonlit, but there was not a soul in sight. Tommy could hear the murmur of voices from his father's bedroom, just next door, unfortunately. They were still up, waiting for news of him and Eloise, he supposed. Or maybe his father was out with a search party. Anyway, they would have to be quite soundless in removing the unconscious guard.

He looked back at Eloise, standing shivering in her underclothes. A tiny groan came from the guard. Surely he was not already waking! He was loath to whack him again, in cold blood. He shut the door very gently, and as he turned, to his astonishment he saw Eloise grab his stick, as the guard stirred again, and crack him hard over the head. This was some girl! The guard was really out cold now, maybe for good and all. Perhaps they'd killed him. Tommy shuddered.

'Quick, let's get him out,' Eloise whispered. 'Take his sword and things off first,' she added, 'or they'll clatter along the floor.'

Tommy unbuckled everything that he could, and he took the head end and Eloise the legs, and they carried him over to the door easily enough. But now came the tricky bit! Tommy pushed the door very gently with his foot. It squeaked! Blast it! thought Tommy. They held their breaths for a moment. There was no sound of running feet, no reaction from his father's room. Tommy nudged the door a bit further open. *Over there*, Tommy indicated with a vigorous motion of his head. *In that dark corner.* He mouthed the words to Eloise. She nodded, and slowly they carried the limp body of the guard just a few yards along the corridor and dumped him on the ground.

Quick as they could they regained the refuge of Tommy's room, closing the door and putting on the catch. At some stage they would be changing the guard... or perhaps not? Better not to be caught completely unawares, at any rate. Now, the problem was, how to keep Eloise safe from detection. There was a tiny closet beside the window, he knew. This was used for, well, yes, the château did not of course have any plumbing, and people had the same needs in 1599 as in the twenty-first century. Was there room for the poor girl to lie down in there? He would take the china bucket and put it out of sight behind his bed. It was so strange that he visualised all this without ever having entered his 'lavabo', as they called it! At least he hadn't used the bucket itself. How often did they empty it, he wondered?

Holding Eloise's hand, he walked over to the door of the closet. How romantic, he thought, leading his lady-love to the bog... He opened the door. The smell was not the freshest, and Eloise wrinkled her nose slightly. Not the time to be squeamish! He lifted the china contraption, and a brush fell down from behind it. Blast! His mother's room was just on the other side of the wooden panelling! Tommy looked at the brush. The brush was... not very nice. Gingerly, he picked it up and placed in inside the china bowl, which at least was empty. Then, taking hold of the bowl, practically embracing it, trying to keep his nose away from the rim, he began to stumble across the room. The bowl was surprisingly heavy. Eloise helped him by putting her hands under it, to take some of the weight.

'Behind the bed,' he whispered. God! he thought, what if Eloise wants to use it? I mean, it wasn't so easy always to be dead silent, was it! On the other hand, people would presumably think it was just him. After all, the noises were not especially male or female, were they?

They lowered the bowl gently down behind the bed. It was quite out of sight, because the wooden sides of the bed went all the way down to the floor. A good place to hide, thought Tommy, if you can get the sides off. Perhaps he should loosen them, for an emergency, like someone coming in while Eloise was sitting on the pot, for example. Yes, he'd do that, loosen the sides of the bed, at least on the pot side.

Tommy pulled a rug off the bed and went to lay it on the floor in the lavabo. He made up a little bed for Eloise, as she watched with a mixture of both love and dismay on her face. She too felt that this was far from the romantic ideal, her lover putting her to bed in the bog. The danger of discovery was acute. She would not be staying there long, that was clear. Completing his little love nest, Tommy motioned Eloise over to him. They needed to sit and talk a bit, discuss plans, but it had to be out of sight of the door. The only place really out of sight was behind the bed, in the company of the bog bowl! So they edged it a bit out of the way and crept in to the space that they had made. Tommy remembered now that you could slide the lower part of the bed sideways on some wooden runners. So he very slowly and carefully moved it, whispering to Eloise that this would be a hiding place of last resort, if she were really cornered. She nodded and tried to look braver than she felt.

'Now,' whispered Tommy, 'we need to make plans. We have to get you out of here to a safe place. Where can you go? Drogo knows it was you in the little room with me.'

He paused a moment. A wizard scheme was sorting itself out in his mind. What if... but, could he bluff it out? Perhaps if he made out it was not Eloise at all but some other girl who... Well, that could wait. First, how to get Eloise to safety. Marie! Marie, his old nurse, she was the answer, she would be on his side through thick and thin. Eloise's head rested on his shoulder and he put his arm around her. Really they must get out of these wet clothes, damp and smelly from the moat. He could feel Eloise gently breathing, snuggled up against him. Turning his head, he could see that her eyes were half closed, her lids dipping up and down and her lovely eyelashes fluttering gently. As he watched, her eyes closed fully and he kissed her very gently. A small sigh, and she was fast asleep. He cradled her softly and they both slept soundly in each other's arms.

Five: A Room Full of Secrets

ommy and Eloise woke with a start to the sunlight striking them through the half-open shutters.

'I'll change my clothes and then go and see Marie,' whispered Tommy.

'Marie?' murmured Eloise sleepily. 'Why Marie?'

'Because Marie is my best friend here in the château. We have to get you out of here undetected. Marie'll help us, for sure. Also, she'll have some good ideas about where you may be sheltered until I have dealt with that devil, Father Drogo.'

A look of fright passed over Eloise's face as he mentioned the name of the priest, and Tommy pressed her hand reassuringly and planted a gentle kiss on her cheek.

'I wonder what time it is?' he said, and Eloise gave him a strange look.

Tommy really had to remember that people just did not have watches on them in 1599! Every time he mentioned the time, he got a funny look. Brushing this aside, he tiptoed over to a cupboard and scrabbled around for some clothes, pulling off all his damp things as he did so, but being careful that his mobile came to no harm.

'Gosh! Another SMS!' he said as he glanced at it. No time for that. His underwear clung damply to him and felt horrid. As he peeled it off, standing eventually with nothing on at all, he wondered if Eloise could see him, maybe just taking a little peek – he was sure that he might, if she were standing there with nothing on – and he blushed at this thought. He glanced in her direction. All he could see was the bog pot. Just as well, really. Eloise was well hidden. Did they care much about things like that, like seeing people standing around with no clothes on, in 1599? Flore and his trousers, he remembered, and felt his face redden still more, as he thought of her fingers crawling round his waist.

All sorts of strange things were hanging in the cupboard, some

81

of which he could not see how he could possibly wear on any part of him. Long strips of highly patterned material, with tassels and frilly bits, unattached sleeves with lace cuffs, and pieces of richly woven material with buttons in odd places. He searched through this heap of things and found some tights. He pulled these on and then a vest, a shirt, some red velvet trousers, with buttons instead of a zip (fly buttons, he thought that he had heard them called), a jacket with little flowers embroidered on it... 'Sissy stuff,' he could just hear Harry saying. That's enough clothes, thought Tommy. Shoes! He had to have shoes. There they were, where he had left them last night when he went out to meet Eloise. If only there was a mirror! Running his hands over his trousers, Tommy tried to smooth out the wrinkles and he tugged at his jacket, which did not seem to fit too well about the shoulders. It had always been a bit tight, he remembered.

'Eloise,' he whispered, 'do I look like a scarecrow?' He walked over so that she could see him.

She smiled and shook her head. *I love you*, she mouthed.

Tommy grinned and whispered, 'I'm off now. If anyone knocks or comes in, just slip under the bed. I'm going to make sure that they can hear that I am in my room, so don't be alarmed by the noise I'll be making in a moment!'

Eloise nodded and blew him a kiss with her hand. Tommy smiled. It was good to see such a familiar gesture, but it made him feel homesick, and a little lump came to his throat. He blew a kiss back and then, quite noisily as he said that he would, Tommy opened the door and shut it loudly. Immediately, as he had supposed would happen, there was a commotion from his father's room. His father's door was flung open and the Count rushed out and grabbed hold of Tommy's arm.

'*Thomas!*' He was angry, very angry. 'Thomas,' he repeated, shaking him. Tommy realised that perhaps the deception which he planned would not be so easy as he had hoped. He'd do his best, though. The Count took both his arms now and held them in an iron grip, and bending him backwards, hissed in his face, 'You little idiot! Where have you been? Where – have – you – been?' He emphasised every word with a powerful shake. 'You fool! Running off with...'

Using all his strength, Tommy pulled his arms free and boldly faced his father, interrupting him.

'Father! Listen to me. You are not fair with me. I know I was silly, I know that I was wrong! I know that I should not accept offers like this. But I am only human. She was such a pretty girl. And she did ask me.'

'*What*?' roared his father, astonishment crossing his face and still angrier than before. He thrust Tommy hard against the wall of the corridor. '*What*! What did she ask you? You are talking about your cousin, Eloise, not just some pretty girl! Do you not understand what you have done? Have you gone mad?'

Perhaps I have, thought Tommy, perhaps that's it. I'm in a lunatic asylum, where the lunatics have taken over the management. The Count glared at him, and clenching his fists, seemed about to strike him.

'*Eloise? Eloise*? No, Father, no!' cried Tommy. 'Who told you that? It's not true! Who said that the girl I was with was Eloise?' He was shouting now. He had to be sure that Eloise would hear what he said. She could surely hear every word!

'So you don't deny it, then? You were in the cupboard room with Eloise? Where is the little minx? In your bedroom, maybe?' shouted the Count, paying no attention to what Tommy was saying.

'No, no! Not Eloise, I said. Listen, listen!' yelled Tommy. 'It's just not true. There was a girl, of course. But not Eloise. Who is spreading such a story? Who told you this rubbish?'

'Who told me this?' said the Count, more quietly now, but with cold irony. 'Do you really need to ask? Who told me that you and Eloise were in the pantry cupboard room at twelve o'clock last night? Why, Father Drogo, you little liar, Father Drogo of course. He saw you there!'

Ah! thought Tommy. He did *not* see us there, though. Bluff it out, bluff it out!

'Well, that's odd,' said Tommy, 'because I did not see him. I heard him, though, breaking down the door and yelling at us, me and the girl.'

'He's got some shreds of cloth that he says is Eloise's dress, caught on the jagged glass of the broken window. The place stank of the scent that Eloise uses, too!' retorted his father, a little calmer now. 'We have been worried silly for you, you foolish child.'

'Now look, Father,' said Tommy, 'that girl was not Eloise. When I met her, and it was only for two minutes before we were discovered... a pity, perhaps...' Here he grinned. Try to make a bit light of it, make out it's not a serious matter, that's a good idea...

'Don't grin at me, boy!' yelled his father.

'But listen, Father, please. I saw at once that she was wearing Eloise's clothes and wearing her scent. Straightaway I asked her how that was. The little monster only giggled. She must have lifted it from Eloise's room. I was pretty angry and she could see that. That was the moment that the guard arrived. I thought that I had to protect the girl, though. No gentleman would ever give a girl up like that, surely.'

His father nodded.

'And I have no idea who she was,' added Tommy.

'What were you doing there, then, at dead of night?' demanded his father. 'You didn't just meet by chance! Don't tell me that.'

'No, it was just after the party broke up. This girl sort of brushed against me, perhaps an extra servant hired for the banquet – Jasper, er, Jacques will know – and she whispered, "Meet me in the little room at midnight." What would you have done, Father?'

His father could not suppress a grin, because he had done exactly the same kind of thing as a young lad, several, no, many times. But the results had never been so disastrous.

'My God!' said the Count. 'You little fool! Tell me what happened after that, then.'

'Well, Father, when she realised that she was going to be caught, she panicked, smashed the window, hauled herself out through it onto the roof – with a bit of help from me, I must admit. I couldn't just leave her there. I mean, I had got her into this to some extent, hadn't I? So I pulled myself out after her. Here, you can see where I cut my hand open on the glass.' Tommy stretched out his hand to show a nasty cut cross the palm.

'Anyway,' he continued, 'the girl was pale and shaking with fear and, when Father Drogo burst into the room below, she lost control completely and stamped with all her might on his hand when he put it through to haul himself up. I couldn't stop her, she did it so quick, and then she ran off madly and threw herself in the moat – to try and drown herself, I suppose.'

His father was nodding vigorously. He much preferred this version of events to Father Drogo's, which had been given him in rage and pain late on the previous night.

Where was Drogo? Tommy wondered, but he continued, 'What could I do, Father? I couldn't let her drown. So I jumped in after her. You know I can swim a bit.' His father did not know, but he let it pass. 'But she had already drifted out of my reach, and then the blooming swans attacked me! They sleep at night in the moat. It was awful, Father. Suddenly she was caught by the current of the river. I could not catch her. She was carried rapidly away, half submerged. She seemed to make no effort to save herself. She drowned, Father, she drowned!' Tommy, madly acting, covered his face with his hands.

'Calm yourself, my boy,' said his father. 'It's a sad story. Very sad. She was a wicked girl, but she did not deserve an end such as that. My poor boy, what an awful thing to happen to you,' he added, putting his arm around his son, and then, 'Not Eloise!' he muttered to himself, '…not Eloise!' holding his son more tightly.

Things were going well, so far, thought Tommy. There were some pretty loose ends here and there, though. Would Drogo buy any of this? Probably not. He'd soon catch me out, realised Tommy. His thoughts were interrupted by his mother's sudden appearance at the end of the corridor.

'I thought that I heard your voice!' she cried. 'Oh, Thomas, Thomas! I thought that you were drowned as well!' She threw her arms around her son, clasping him hard against her.

What was that? thought Tommy, half smothered by the musty satin ruffles of his mother's dress. Drowned as well? he said to himself. Ah! They must have found the dress. That's a bit of luck.

'No, Mother. I'm alive and well,' he said, as she released him, trying to sound cheerful.

'Oh, Thomas!' said his mother, holding him away from her,

and then clasping him against her again, rather awkwardly this time, for Tommy had turned away his head, to avoid another face full of stale ruffles. From his position, jammed against his mother's bosom, Tommy had a view out of the window and along the drive. To his dismay, he could see the black cassock of Drogo, one arm heavily bandaged, with his back to him. Just at that moment, Drogo turned and glancing up at the window, and seeing Tommy, cast him a most malevolent stare, before looking away and walking firmly towards the main door of the château. Gosh! He's coming after me, thought Tommy.

'Thomas,' said his father, 'how did you get back into the château, without being seen? No one saw you come back in. That's why we have been so worried.' Then he added, turning to the Countess, 'Eloise wasn't the girl!'

The Countess caught hold of his arm. 'Oh thank God!' she exclaimed with a long sigh. 'It wasn't Eloise. Thank God!' she exclaimed again.

'But how did you get back into the château?' repeated the Count.

'Well, Father, I was very upset and terribly embarrassed by this thing with the girl. I wasn't really thinking very straight. I just did not want to be seen by anyone. So I just climbed up to my room, from the moat. Before that I had spent quite some time seeing if I could find the poor drowned girl,' Tommy added, trying to cover his tracks.

The guard with his head bashed in! What was he going to say about that? Better say something before he's asked – he could hardly have forgotten the guard, after all. 'I looked all bedraggled and covered in mud, and I just did not want anyone to see me! It was silly, I know, but it was just my pride, silly pride!'

His father nodded. He would have done the same thing. He was beginning to think quite highly of this new daredevil son of his. The best, however was still to come.

'I took a stick with me, from the bottom of the moat, to kind of help me up the wall, and heave myself up,' explained Tommy. 'And when I put my head over my window sill this stupid fellow came running at me, drawing his sword. He must have thought I was a robber, I don't know. So really without thinking I cracked him over the head with the stick and knocked him clean out!'

'Bravo!' cried his father, and his mother smiled. Thomas had never shown much guts before, but he was obviously growing up rapidly.

'I just hauled him out the door and stuck him in the corridor, put the catch on the door and went straight to sleep against a cushion on the floor.'

'In all your wet clothes!' gasped his mother.

'Yes, well, I did,' said Tommy. 'But I was exhausted. I've only just woken up and changed now.'

It was lucky that at that moment Tommy managed to finish his version of the adventures of the previous night, for just as he said these last few words, Father Drogo appeared, advancing rapidly toward the group in the corridor, his black cassock billowing out behind, bandaged arm trailing on one side, with a look of thunder on his face. For he knew very well whose foot – bare foot, that was no girl's foot! – it was that crushed his hand and wrist against the shards of broken glass, and he knew well who was the girl with Thomas in the cupboard room behind the pantry. He had the proof in his pocket, the shreds of Eloise's dress.

But Tommy saw his chance to divert Drogo from his purpose of denouncing him to the Count and Countess. With his arms outstretched, Tommy rushed towards Father Drogo, all sympathy.

'Oh, Father! I was so worried about you,' he cried. 'That terrible girl. Your poor hand! I could do nothing to stop her, though I tried to pull her away. She did it so fast, I couldn't prevent her.' And rather too roughly he took Drogo's bandaged hand in his as if to comfort him.

Drogo let out a yell of pain and anger, and Tommy, begging his pardon many times, released his damaged arm.

'Oh, Father, Father,' continued Tommy, 'wounded on my account! Can you forgive me? I beg you, please, please forgive me. I did not mean any harm. It all got out of control. The girl, she is beyond punishment. She is dead. Drowned…' Here, Tommy put his face in his hands again.

'Yes, so I've heard,' said Father Drogo, trying to keep his voice cold and steady, but with a strange note of anguish.

Tommy looked up and for an instant stared at Drogo through his fingers.

'Father,' said the Count, 'Thomas has told me that it was not Eloise with him last night. We must thank God for that, for it is not Eloise who drowned.'

Drogo drew in a short quick breath as these words were spoken.

'It seems a serving girl,' continued the Count, 'the girl who was with Thomas, was drowned, however, as Thomas says. But Eloise is safe and has no knowledge of all that's happened!'

This of course posed a bit of a problem for Tommy, who was furiously thinking about how he could explain Eloise's absence, which they were bound to discover pretty soon. Could she perhaps have departed with one of the visiting guests at the banquet, to spend a few days away?

'The girl was not Eloise?' said Drogo, sarcasm tingeing his voice. 'Then who was it that was wearing her clothes and her scent, may I ask?' He raised his voice dangerously.

Tommy continued to hold his face in his hands, and just moaned gently, as if the memory of it all coming back to him was too much. His mother put her hand on his arm.

'My poor boy has been through so much, Father Drogo, let the Count tell you the story. Why don't we make that call on Marie,' she said, addressing herself to Tommy, and began to lead him away along the corridor.

But before they could go more than one or two steps, Drogo had put out his hand to stop them.

'One moment, Countess,' said the priest, 'if you would. I should be so thankful if what you tell me is indeed the truth, that Eloise is not involved, that she is alive and well.' His voice rose. 'And it was just some foolish business with a serving girl. But, as you can see, I have received the worst of this.' He paused a moment as a little groan of pain escaped him. (I hope he's not faking that, thought Tommy.) 'And,' continued Drogo, 'I should be deeply grateful to you if perhaps we could just go and talk a few moments with Eloise herself, to hear what she has to say. When did she miss her dress, for example?'

As Drogo was finishing his request, Tommy saw, at the end of the corridor, out of the corner of his eye, the little bent form of Jacques – or Jasper. Jacques was walking towards them with his hobbling but rapid footsteps tapping on the flagstones.

'I could not help overhearing your last remark, good Father,' he said. 'How is your arm, by the way? Not throbbing any more, I hope. Has the pain subsided a bit?'

'It's a little better, thank you, Jacques, but it will be many weeks before I have my full strength back, thanks to that… thanks to the…'

Here he trailed off, unable to accuse Monsieur Thomas directly of a lie to his face, in the presence of the Count and Countess. Better to wait until they failed to find Eloise and then grill Master Thomas alone, until he caught the stupid little boy out in an obvious lie. For Father Drogo believed, of course, that he was dealing with the Thomas that he knew, a bit of a wet fish, as Tommy had thought, not terribly bright or resourceful; or at least hadn't showed it yet, and certainly unable to withstand a grilling by Drogo.

'But, as I said,' Jacques went on, 'I heard your last remark, good Father, about Mad'moiselle Eloise. I think that you will not find her in the château at present, Father.'

'*What?*' cried Drogo. 'Where is she, then?'

'Ah, you see, sir,' continued Jacques, 'last night after the banquet ended, there were many people milling about, carriages everywhere, Count this and Countess that' – Jacques, being an old and trusted family servant, was allowed a bit of familiarity when talking of the noble friends of the family – 'a good number of footmen running this way and the other, hailing carriages and so on. In the middle of all this comes Mad'moiselle Eloise, changed out of her beautiful dress…' (Oh, good stuff, thought Tommy, good stuff, Jasper! Drogo just glowered.) …'She had a rather plain one on, in fact, as I remember, and she told me that she was off to stay a few days with… with, well, that's a problem, in fact, I do apologise, there was such a lot of noise and I was so busy overseeing everything, that I am afraid that the name did not come across to me very clearly; but anyway, of course with one of your noble friends.

'I asked her, "Have you asked Madame la Comtesse, and Monsieur le Comte?"' Jacques had now turned towards the Count and Countess. 'She said that no, she hadn't, but that you were so busy, she did not want to interrupt, and the carriage was waiting outside the door… And I glanced out, and indeed, there was the coachman, whip in hand, sitting impatiently, the door of the carriage open, just outside the main door, where we were standing. I was a bit surprised, but I said that I would tell you,' said Jacques.

'There, you see!' cried the Count, triumphantly, 'just as Thomas said, it was not Eloise in the pantry cupboard room.'

At this, Drogo stamped his foot in frustration, turning away so that the look of fury on his face would not be apparent to all. He was unused to being hoodwinked in this way. Revenge would come, and he would be sure that it would take a particularly hideous form, even if he had to destroy the whole household of Romolue in the process.

'I do apologise,' continued Jacques, 'that I did not tell you before now. But there has been such turmoil in the château, and you have not been much out of your room, Monsieur.' He turned to the Count, who was now smiling broadly, and had placed his arm again around his son's shoulder.

'No, no, Jacques,' said the Count, 'no, that's nothing. Good that you came just at the right moment to tell us now.'

Drogo's eyes narrowed as the Count said this. How is it that they are all in league against me? he thought. The right moment it was indeed. Once inside Eloise's empty room, Master Thomas would not have been able to explain things away so neatly, of that he was sure. Perhaps he could continue his investigations there, thought Drogo. Perhaps some vital evidence would emerge with which he could confront them all.

As if he was reading Drogo's mind, Jacques now added, 'While Mad'moiselle Eloise is absent, sir, I have locked her room. After the theft of her dress, we must watch out that there are no other thieves about.'

'What? Do you suspect anyone of our staff of being a thief, Jacques?' exclaimed the Count.

'No, Monsieur, not anyone specially, sir. But just as a precaution, sir, you know.'

'Very well, very well,' muttered the Count, and shook his head.

Drogo ground his teeth in rage. They would not make such a fool of him, however. He would break into Eloise's room if necessary. He had controlled that girl all her short life, and she would not slip away at this critical moment. He would see Thomas betrothed to Clarice, daughter of Robert de Toulouse, and he would see Eloise into a nunnery, or married off in England perhaps – that was an idea! He needed to be away from these people and think of plans to make this happen. It had seemed that Thomas had played right into his hands, but now the prize was slipping through his fingers.

'I will trouble you no longer,' he said, 'but I will be in the chapel of the château, praying for the soul of the poor departed, drowned girl, whoever she was. Suicide is a crime against Christ, but my poor prayers may save her a few years of burning in hell!' And with that he moved off down the corridor.

It is amazing, thought Tommy, that not one word of truth has been said for the last ten minutes. The least truth of all was in the last remark of Father Drogo. He was wishing the girl *in* hell, not out of it, or rather he was wishing Eloise in hell, or he was wishing them all in hell. A good priest, thought Tommy: 'Good Father Drogo.' And he incautiously emitted a little, 'Huh!'

'Yes, well…' began the Countess.

'You go along to Marie, now,' said the Count, interrupting. 'And now, Jacques, perhaps I could have a little word with you about the pigs running wild around…'

Tommy could not hear any more of the sentence, as he and his mother turned the corner and mounted the main staircase and made their way up to the second floor. When they were well out of sight of anyone, his mother took his hand and squeezed it.

'Thomas,' she whispered, 'we need to have a little talk.'

'But I thought…' He paused. 'Marie. Shouldn't we…?'

'No, Thomas, you can stop the acting now,' she interrupted, whispering still more quietly but more urgently.

Tommy thought of Eloise, huddled behind his bed in his room, terrified every minute of capture. What was he to do? Put his trust in his mother? Tell her everything? But everything would be exactly what she could not accept, something that no one could accept. He had even steered away from telling Eloise about his strange – no, more than strange – crazy journey into their history. Who would believe it? Yet he felt very much the need to tell someone. Was the Countess, his mother, the right person? He would have to feel his way. Whatever happened, quick action was needed, or Eloise would be discovered and the whole thing would blow up in his face! For one thing, the servants would soon be in his room.

'In here,' whispered his mother, drawing him through a small door on the left, and then into an inner room, through another small secret door, disguised like the one in his bedroom, this further room padded with satin. Thomas – and Tommy, of course – had never been here before. A secret room, he thought, specially made so that no conversations could be overheard, with padded walls. He noticed also that his mother had put a catch on each door as that they had passed through. That explains why she was whispering, thought Tommy. She too must suspect that Drogo was plotting against them and that he might have spies everywhere. Okay, he thought, let's start with Drogo.

'Now, Thomas,' began his mother, but to her surprise, he held up his hand

'No, Mother, forgive me! But before anything, we must clear things up. First, you do realise, don't you, that Father Drogo is an evil man, plotting the destruction of the house of Romolue.'

The Countess gasped. Her Thomas had had his eyes and ears open much wider than anyone had ever imagined. Was this the same – what did the Count call him? – 'twerp' (or was it 'twit'?) who talked about the boar's head and the larks only last night, in that foolish way that made all the guests giggle? She did think, though, as she had told the Count, that last night he was making a fool of himself on purpose, at least partly. She and the Count had talked about it afterwards, but not to much advantage really. They had just agreed to watch him a bit more closely in future. Well, the future had come more quickly than she supposed it would. And what was she to say now? Take him completely into her confidence?

'An evil man, Thomas? Well, perhaps not a very nice man, but—'

'But nothing, Mother!' interrupted Tommy, rather rudely. ' If you cannot agree with me on that, then we have nothing to discuss.' Tommy realised that he should have tried to be more patient, especially with a Countess, and one who thought that she was his mother! In fact, he blushed as he spoke, and the Countess gave him a startled look.

'Very well,' she said, collecting herself. 'You are not far off the mark.' Now she'd done it! Tommy took her hand and pressed it.

'Why is he here in this household, then?' he asked, still holding her hand tightly. 'Can't you turn him out?'

'Thomas... Thomas! His brother, the Bishop, asked us to take him as the family chaplain, to be the priest at the village church. Bishop Henri is strong, with many connections among the most powerful men of France, my son. Father Drogo is also very well connected, as the brother of the Bishop of Toulouse, if nothing else. I know that Drogo is a Trojan horse, planted among us to plot our destruction, or at least to suppress our influence and to reduce us in time to nothing. The Church is very powerful, Thomas. Do you know how many witches they burnt just last year in the province of Toulouse alone? One hundred witches, all innocent of any crime. The Church runs a reign of terror in this land, ruling the people with fear. It is hard to resist them openly.'

Tommy had read about some of this in school history books. They were always going on about burning witches and things, but he had never thought of it as a way of holding on to power, as a political thing. But it was clear: that was how it was. A reign of terror. Yes, that described it well. Why were religions so horrible? he wondered. In his own time, terrible crimes were still committed in the name of faith, though really in the name of some kind of destructive madness, he thought. What would the Church of the sixteenth century have done if they had had modern weapons? Jet fighters, bombers. Much as we do in the twenty-first century, he realised. At least we don't burn witches. We burn little children instead... Oh, blast it all!

His mother was watching his face closely, trying to understand the many emotions which she could see passing across it. Thomas has a lot to learn, she thought, but if I have got his measure, he may well turn out to be a match for Drogo in his wicked plotting. Not like the Count, she said to herself. He's just too kind to think that anyone can be as scheming as Drogo. He always thinks the best of everyone until he is absolutely forced to change his mind. Then, of course, there is no stopping him. If once the Count could be convinced of Drogo's purpose, I would not give two sous for Drogo's life, bishop or no bishop!

'Mother, Mother, there is something I have to tell you,' Tommy blurted out. 'Mother, I am not your son!' He said this so abruptly and wildly that a look of fear came into the Countess's face.

'Calm yourself, Thomas,' she said. 'Be calm and let's discuss this carefully. For one thing, I know Jacques well enough that he was lying in every word he said…'

'No, Mother!' said Tommy, almost shouting. 'Listen to me. This is bigger than that! This is…' Then he stopped, for what was he to say? So he just repeated, 'Mother, I am not your son!' urgently stressing the words, drawing out the phrase. *'I am not your son,'* he said again.

'Nonsense, Thomas,' said the Countess, thinking that somehow Thomas must have heard some absurd rumour about his birth. It was true that he had been adopted; that was no secret. But he was their son and heir. What did this mean – 'I am not your son'? No one knew how he came to be found in the château, in the salon, before the fireplace on that cold December evening, fifteen years ago. But no one cared much either. Was there some strange new rumour about, that she had not heard. Was this the work of Drogo?

'Mother, please,' said Tommy, and he took her hand and raised it towards his forehead. But in mid-air, he stopped. Why am I doing this? he suddenly thought. What is the purpose of this confession? His main concern was to get Eloise safely out of the château, to somewhere secure, somehow, and he did not know how. This wasn't going to help. But it was too late to stop now. The Countess was gazing at him in surprise, her hand limply in his, poised in front of his face. Almost without his intending it, he guided her hand to his forehead, to just above his right eyebrow, and she rubbed her fingers softly over the skin of his forehead.

'God help us, Thomas,' she whispered, 'it's gone. It's disappeared! Is this some sort of witchcraft?' And her hand stiffened and she pulled it suddenly away.

'Witchcraft!' exclaimed Tommy in surprise, and at just that instant, his mobile went off! This time it was Mozart's 40th symphony that pierced the air, only about 190 years before its time in this case. Blast and blast, it's Harry! I must have pressed something in my hurry to get my clothes on. Blast it! He fumbled around in his trouser pockets for the 'off' button, but pressed the 'on' button instead.

'We won, Tommy. Is that you, Tommy?' said Harry's voice loudly. Oh! In for a penny, in for a pound, thought Tommy.

'Hello, Harry!' he said, drawing the mobile out of his pocket.

The Countess gave a little shriek and drew back in horror from this little squeaking monster, with its eerie green light visible in the darkened room.

'What was that?' said Harry, 'that shriek? Are you with a girl, then?' He stressed the word 'girl' strongly, and giggled. 'Is she frightened of my voice?'

'Yes, I mean… no. It's my mother, I mean the Countess of Romolue. And yes, she is frightened of your voice, if you really want to know!'

'The Countess of…' began Harry.

'Anyway, look, I don't want to sound unfriendly,' Tommy went on, completely ignoring the interruption, 'but this will be costing you and me the earth. Congratulations on winning the football, I'm four hundred years in the past and I've really got to go now!' *Click*. Phew!

The Countess was gazing at Tommy with her mouth slightly open, her eyes wide and her face the colour of blancmange.

'Now look, Mother, now look!' said Tommy.

The Countess half raised herself up and backed away from Tommy as he put his hand out to touch hers.

'You're a monster. You were sent by the devil!' she said. 'Don't touch me with your fiery hands. Don't come near me! Oh, God help me!' Then she collapsed into her chair again, still staring wildly, casting her eyes between Tommy's face and the mobile which he held in his hand.

'No, Mother, don't say that, please. Look, I am as frightened as you. Let me just say this to you straight. I am from four hundred years in the future. I did not come here on purpose. I cannot explain it, and I want to go home.'

Just then the mobile rang a second time. Not Harry, please, no, it wasn't Mozart's 40th. In fact it was the standard *bleep, bleep*.

'Look, Mother, I am going to talk to it again. Listen!' The Countess watched him petrified.

'Tommy, it's Mummy. I know you said not to ring you. I am beginning to understand why that might be, though it all sounds quite incredible. You poor thing! I'm going crazy with worry, and so is Daddy. But the key to getting you back may well be Jasper, as you said. But he's pretty evasive at the moment. Keeps disappearing – into the past, I suppose. We've got to find out how he does it! Dad's mouthing hello to you! Look, I've got Thomas here. He says he wants to talk to his mother. I think he really has to! Can you arrange this? Get the Countess there and ring me, would you?'

'Mum! Oh, God, it's good to hear you. Look, by good luck, the Countess is right in front of me!'

'Right there?' asked his mum.

'Yes, here, right here. We're in a secret room, discussing things. I've just told her about who I am. It's a tremendous shock for her. I don't think that she has taken it in at all. People here, then, now, you know what I mean, they just aren't really able...' He paused. 'Never mind. You can see what I mean. We can worry about that later. Put Thomas on the line!'

'Right you are. Here he is.'

'Tommy?' a querulous little voice emerged from the mobile.

The Countess jumped and she shut her eyes, taking a deep breath. I think that she's starting to pray, thought Tommy!

'Thomas?' said Tommy, into the phone. 'Yeah, right, I'm giving your mother the phone.'

Tommy took the Countess's hand – she seemed quite passive now, in the clutches of the devil or something – and Tommy placed the mobile in her hand, lifting it to her ear and holding it there, for fear she might drop it.

'Mother,' said Thomas. 'Mother, say something! We may not get another chance to talk for ages! Say something, please.'

'T-T-T-Thomas!' she managed. 'What... where... how can you be in this... *thing!*'

'Mother, never mind how it works. I don't know either. No idea. Anyway, it's called a telephone. Just accept that we can talk through it, please. It's me, your son. You can hear that. I can hear that it's you.'

'Then, who is this in front of me here, if you're Thomas?' demanded the Countess. She had come alive again! Then she raised her finger. 'Now look, I've got a question for you. Put your hand on your forehead, just above your right eyebrow. What do you feel there?'

'Well, my forehead, of course, Mother!'

'Nothing more than that?' she said.

'Well, yes, that little tiny scar from the boar hunt, when I was five or something!' The Countess let out her breath in a gasp and a sigh.

'My God! Thomas, it is you! Where are you?'

'Oh, Mother!' Funny snuffly noises came from the phone.

Oh gosh, thought Tommy, he's blubbing down the phone. That won't do any good.

'Could I have him a moment, please,' said Tommy, and took the phone from the Countess.

'Thomas, it's me, Tommy. Could you tell your mum that everybody, where you are, has phones like the one I've got. It's important she understands that it is not witchcraft or magic or anything like that.'

'Yes,' sobbed Thomas.

'Here she is again,' said Tommy.

'Oh! Darling, darling Thomas!' said the Countess. 'What does Thomas want you to tell me?'

'Just that everyone, where I am, has mobile phones like the one that you've got in your hand. You're simply not cool if you haven't,' said Thomas. Gosh, he's picked up the slang quick, thought Tommy. 'It's not magic, not the devil, as we would maybe think,' continued Thomas. 'It's just something that they've got here, that we haven't got. There's lots of other things, too.

Like great shining houses, flying roaring through the air, and everything is so noisy and...'

'Look, my little darling, I can't understand a word you are saying. I just want you back, instead of this other Thomas here. Alright, this tel-e-phone thing is not the work of the devil. I believe you.'

Suddenly the screen on the mobile began to flash. SMS – from Harry, probably. Oh gosh, thought Tommy. The Countess took fright at the flickering light and almost dropped the mobile, but Tommy retrieved it in time.

'Tommy, it's Mummy again! I'm worried about the battery. Try and see if you can get Jasper to bring it back and recharge it! You might use that as a way of finding out how he gets back and forth.'

'Cool, Mum! Yeah, right on! I'll find out Jasper's secret. Say hi to Dad from me. See you soon. Bye!'

A quick look at the SMS, whilst the Countess recovered and collected her thoughts. Tommy sent her a glance and a little grin, but she seemed lost in her own world and ignored him. The SMS was from Harry, of course. It was a shopping list of things he wanted from what he called the 'Middle Ages'. Should pay more attention in history lessons, that's all I can say, thought Tommy. He certainly would in future. A pair of stocks, for the school playground; a mediaeval bra (huh!), Henry the Eighth's autograph and night socks. Oh, gosh, shut up, Harry! This is serious! <Give the Countess a kiss from me, he, he!> it concluded. Maybe he would, thought Tommy, maybe he would...

As it was, his mother, or the Countess, as he alternately thought of her, was sitting looking at him with an expression of anguish on her face. Half-dead with fear, paralysed by the knowledge that her true son was lost in some strange land, in some unknown corner of the earth, as she framed it in her mind, she sat motionless, and tears began to trickle down her cheeks. It runs in the family, thought Tommy. Perhaps blubbing was the thing in 1599. A bit out of style in the twenty-first century! Let's start some action, he decided. Let's face something that we can do something about. Getting Eloise out of the château, out of Drogo's clutches. The Countess is an ally. I'll just have to get her going, get her out of her funk. Blue funk! With her authority and the run of the château, we stand a chance.

'Okay,' said Tommy, pretending to ignore the tears and the deathly pale face of the Countess. 'We've got to do something. We've got two problems. The most important is to get me back home, and your Thomas back here. Right? But the most urgent is to stop Drogo from getting us all killed before we can do it.'

The Countess began to gather her senses. Her eyes flickered back to life, almost as though she was coming out of a hypnotic trance.

'You are right,' she said in a weak voice.

Now that she knew that Thomas was not her son, though more or less his double, it would be easier to deal with him, to treat him as an equal – which is what he seemed to be, when it came to action! He might as well have come from another planet as far as she was concerned, but if he could get her real Thomas back, then she didn't care if he'd grown up on the sun, or in the seventh pit of hell, or wherever he came from.

'You're right,' she said again.

'Okay, look, I'll come completely clean,' said Tommy. And he quickly told the whole story of Eloise, the guard and Drogo. Of how he had stamped on Drogo's hand, and of how he would do it again given half a chance, and of how Eloise had noticed the absence of the scar, but did not know about where he came from or anything about that; and that at this moment, Eloise was sitting in her underclothes, hiding between the bog pot and the bed in Tommy's room. 'How do we get her out of the château?'

'One moment, Thomas,' said the Countess. 'What about Jacques? He seems to play a key part in this! He saved us when Drogo was there, just before. What part in this has Jacques?'

'I'm not sure,' said Tommy. 'He is obviously a friend. But he is also something else, somehow the cause of all this. He has some purpose, his own purpose. I feel that he is using me and everyone – you too – for his own will, in some way which we do not understand. He exists, you know, also in our world. He has the same position as in your world, the old trusted butler in the château. More important, he flits between our two worlds. That is the secret which we need to fathom. I don't know how he moves between the two worlds at will. This must be the key to my return home and you getting your real Thomas back here! But, I don't think that we can include him in our plans. Yes, he may save us in a tight corner, but we can't rely on it, or we had better not, anyway.'

'Yes,' said the Countess, nodding. 'We could get him to tell with torture, of course,' she coolly added, to Tommy's horror. 'But we can put that off to another day. I think that now it would be a good idea to go and see old Marie. We'll need the servants' help to get Eloise out of the château, and Marie knows everything that goes on, one way or another. Let's agree that we will tell her nothing about your not being Thomas, nothing about tel-e-phones, nothing about those devilish things,' – Tommy raised his eyebrows – 'no, alright, those strange things. From now on, as you did before, I think that you had better call me "mother",' added the Countess, smiling for the first time since the phone had gone off.

They came into the corridor which overlooked the front drive of the château. As they walked along this upper corridor towards Marie's room, they saw a single horseman galloping away from the château.

'I'll bet that's Drogo, sending a message to his brother,' whispered Tommy.

The Countess nodded. They were both wondering what Drogo's next move would be, and when and how he would strike. Tommy had not mentioned his ideas about Drogo harbouring a horrible secret in his heart. But he would bring it up when he could and he'd have to start his detective work soon. Today was Monday. Something told Tommy that the next Sunday in the cathedral of Toulouse would be crucial. Things had to be ready by then.

Six: Old Marie

ommy and the Countess came to Marie's door, and knocking quietly, entered to find an old lady asleep in an armchair. She was half turned towards them, with the sun streaming through the gap in the shuttered window, just ajar, lighting up her wrinkled, kindly old face. There was a little smile on her mouth and her white hair formed a kind of wispy halo around her head, caught in the rays of the sun. She stirred a little at their entrance, sighed gently and opened her bright blue eyes. Such surprising eyes, thought Tommy, in an old lady. So lively, shining as the light glanced from them.

'Marie,' he said, feeling a rush of affection for her. He ran towards her chair and cuddled her, planting a kiss on her freckled cheek. She smelled of powder and lavender, reminding him a bit of the old wardrobe in his gran's flat in London.

'Thomas, my boy,' she said, blinking her blue eyes awake. Her voice was pure and high. 'I've been hearing stories about you, Thomas. Tell me that they are not true!'

Tommy pulled up a stool, and sat at her feet. The Countess pulled up another chair and sat close by.

'Well, Marie,' said Tommy, 'I'm afraid that the stories are partly true, but the point is not what happened but why it happened. Let me tell you the whole story.'

And Tommy related the whole saga, except the part about the scar, but including of course everything about Eloise. Marie nodded and tut-tutted and drew in her breath in shock and disapproval many times.

But as he finished, she smiled and said, 'Why, Thomas, you have been a really wicked boy, haven't you?' But he could see that she rather approved than disapproved. 'Eloise is really very naughty, but young love cannot be stopped, no, no!'

'Why?' asked Thomas earnestly. 'Did you ever…?' And the Countess could not help but laugh.

'Never you mind what I ever,' replied Marie. 'And you want me to get Eloise out of the château before Drogo finds her, I suppose!'

'Yes, oh, yes!' said Tommy, and he threw himself into her arms.

'Gently, gently, Thomas. You'll crush me to death. You're a big lad now. Look at that guard you laid out!' she said, and chuckled. 'Big oaf, Louis is.'

'Oh! You know his name, then!'

'There's not too much that gets past me, my lad! Begging your pardon, Countess.'

'You don't have to beg my pardon,' said the Countess. 'We know that between the two of you, Jacques and you, you run the place!'

'Is he alright?' asked Tommy

'Who? Oh – Louis, the guard? Oh yes! He woke up and didn't know what hit him. Still doesn't, never will. Got a skull as thick as a short plank! Not too much between the ears, that lad. He'll do fine! Don't you worry about him, Thomas. He'll serve you well one day, mark my words!'

'Eloise,' said Tommy.

'Yes, let's see now,' said Marie. 'Let me think a moment.' Then she fell silent. Well, not completely silent, for she started humming to herself: '*Sous le pont d'Avignon, mm, mmm, mm, mmm, um, um, um, um…*'

Then the room fell truly completely silent, with just the sunlight streaming in between the shutters. Tommy gazed into her old face. I wish that I had had a Marie, he thought, one like this. She had a rare quality about her. She was a kind of centre, a fixed point around which others rushed but always held on tight. She had shown no surprise at Tommy calling Drogo an evil man, that he wanted to control and destroy the house of Romolue. In fact she had shown no surprise at any of the story, dramatic as it was – at least to Tommy. He wondered how she might react to the mobile phone. Just blink, probably. Could she help him in finding the secret to destroy Drogo? What did she know? he wondered.

His train of thought was broken by Marie, who said, 'Every few days there's a delivery of things, vegetables and things, you know, to the nunnery, Seiche-Capucins, you know just up the road past Romolue. There's a delivery later on this afternoon. We could smuggle Eloise out with this and get her into the nunnery. She would be safe there for a bit. I know one of the gardeners there. He could keep her in a little shed where he spends the summer months. He knows how to keep his mouth shut. He's done things for me before,' she added mysteriously, turning towards the Countess with the flicker of a grin.

'Yes, but how…?'

'I'll see to it,' said Marie. 'What you have got to do is to make sure that no one sees you getting Eloise out of your room. No, better: we'll take the disguise in to her and put it on in there. We'll have to cut her hair off.'

'No!' moaned Tommy

'We'll see,' said Marie. 'Could you wait here, Madame, while I go down to the storeroom and fish out something suitable? Then we'll make it torn and dirty, suitable for a farming girl. Thomas, could you go and get some mud. We'll need to plaster her feet a bit, and… I don't know, let's see how it works out.'

With that, Marie rose from her chair, saying, 'Thomas, why not use that jar for the mud?' She pointed towards a large jar standing beside the door and disappeared into the corridor.

Tommy followed with the jar and the Countess was left alone with her thoughts. And what thoughts they were! Her son was not her son. Her real son was somewhere else, and she had no understanding of where this somewhere was, or how he could ever return. Only Jacques held out some hope for that. Other things were still more pressing. From what Thomas had said, Drogo was going to try to push things very hard next Sunday at mass in the cathedral of Toulouse. Was Thomas's betrothal to Clarice such a bad idea, in fact? Never mind about Eloise, and Thomas obviously being in love with her. Anyway, that was a passing thing. When she got her Thomas back – and at the thought there was great lurch in her breast – when she got him back, she repeated to herself, he would do as he was told. Marry as he was told to marry. At least he was not in love with Eloise – or was he?

'She's a dangerous little thing, Eloise, with her great beauty,' muttered the Countess to herself. Anyone could fall in love with her… Drogo, perhaps? The thought was disgusting, but who could tell what made these violent, evil men act the way they did? It wasn't a bad idea to get her out of the way for a few days. And what should she tell the Count? He had to know the truth, at least about Eloise, pretty soon. How can I persuade him of the ill intentions of Father Drogo? she wondered.

Her thoughts were interrupted by the return of Marie, carrying some old and ragged clothes, a large plain bonnet, some wooden clogs and other bits and bobs that peasant girls might favour.

'Too good for a peasant girl, but she'll have to wear 'em anyway,' said Marie, holding up the clogs, for Eloise's pretty soft feet would give her away in no time.

'D'you know who I met on the back stairs, Countess?' added Marie. 'Father Drogo talking to Christian. They shut up the minute they saw me. But I heard something like "drown her if you find her…" before they realised I was close by. Never trusted that Christian. Nasty snotty little child, with big ears sticking out like a little devil. Seems like he's one of Drogo's men. Not surprised. They're out to commit murder, those two.'

'And there may be others, too, Drogo's spies. We had better be very careful. There could be one outside the door even now!' said the Countess.

At that, Marie dropped the bundle of clothes on the floor, marched over to the door and pulled it open, to reveal the surprised face of Tommy, carrying the jar of mud.

'You didn't waste much time then, Master Thomas,' said Marie, recovering from her own surprise. 'Now we've got to get this lot down to your room, quick,' she said, indicating the bundle of clothes on the floor.

'Madame, could you perhaps go along in front, and tell us if the coast is clear? Then Thomas and I will follow with the clothes and mud.'

She started gathering up the things from the floor. The Countess nodded and walked past them, along the corridor, and began to descend the main staircase. Just then they heard footfalls on the staircase, coming up. It was Father Drogo! The Countess waved them back into Marie's room, furiously flapping her hand. *Drogo* she mouthed to them. Drogo had seen her now, so she composed herself and, smiling sweetly, asked after his damaged hand.

'Better, Madame, better. The throbbing has stopped. The Almighty is mending my body, and we should see that he also mends the soul of your son, Madame, if you forgive me for saying so. His wickedness must not remain unpunished!'

'Father Drogo, do you not think that seeing the girl drown before his eyes was punishment enough?'

'Ah yes, but as the guardian of his soul, since I am the chaplain of the family, I would advise that he does penance.'

The Countess could not object. She felt the dead weight of the authority of the Church about her neck. She could not make an open enemy of Father Drogo.

'What would you suggest?' she asked

'That he should kneel before the altar in the family chapel, this evening, without his dinner, and pray for his soul, reciting the Lord's Prayer one hundred times.'

'Very well,' said the Countess, 'I will send him to you.'

'Perhaps I can find him myself,' said Drogo. 'Have you seen him this afternoon? I need to give him spiritual advice before his penance.'

'Where should I say you are, if I see him?' answered the Countess.

'I shall be in the library, Countess, resting my arm and reading texts.' With this he made his way into the chapel.

At least we know where he will be, thought the Countess, but what of his spies – Christian, for a start? She made her way back up the staircase, and knocked on Marie's door. Tommy opened the door an inch, and then fully, seeing who it was.

'Drogo's in the chapel,' said the Countess, 'but he'll be going down to the library shortly. He wants to see you there, to give you spiritual advice, he said, but of course in fact to grill you. Beware of him, Thomas. He is a subtle man. He does not doubt his version of the story of last night, and he will try to catch you out. Say as little as you can and act the foolish boy. I've seen you do it

105

well enough! Boar's head and larks!' Here she laughed her little melodious laugh.

Tommy put his finger to his lips and then replied, 'I shall be as careful as I can, Mother. I don't underestimate the intelligence of Drogo, nor his vicious nature. I did not say this to you before, but somehow I am sure that he hides some shameful, nasty secret. I must find it out. Do either of you know anything?'

To Tommy's disappointment, both the Countess and Marie shook their heads.

'There was something strange about the death of Eloise's mother,' said Marie. 'We never were allowed to see her after she died, and her death was shrouded in mystery.'

'Yes, even as her own sister, I was forbade to see her body,' whispered the Countess, a tear coming to her eye. 'She was the most beautiful woman of her time, you know. Her daughter, Eloise, takes after her.'

'Yes,' said Tommy, and blushed.

'Whether not being able to see her had anything to do with Father Drogo, I don't know,' said Marie. 'Drogo was of course in charge of all the funeral preparations. Eloise, as a little baby, just two months old, he took from the dead arms of her mother, you know. Drogo found her lying stone dead on the cold floor of the cathedral of Toulouse.'

Tommy shuddered to think of his Eloise cradled in the arms of the priest. 'What about Eloise's father?' he asked. 'Who was he?' He knew that he had not been seen or heard of for many years.

'Eloise's father!' exclaimed the Countess. 'Oh! It's too long a story for now,' and she paused and sighed, adding 'We've not heard tell of him since Eloise was born. Except that he's said to have been heard of a few years later, as a pirate in the Spanish possessions, along with a frightful English pirate, called Drake, I think.'

'Drake's not a pirate!' Tommy blurted out without thinking, 'he's a national hero!' Then he added, 'In England, I mean,' dropping his voice.

The Countess looked at the floor and Marie looked at him in surprise.

'Where d'you hear that?' she asked. 'Never mind, we've got

more important things to think about. We must take these things down to Eloise!'

'We've got to wait until Drogo's left the chapel, then, and gone down to the library. Let me just have a look,' said the Countess, and she tiptoed out of the door and along the corridor. Just peering around the corner she saw the door of the chapel creak open, and the dark figure of Father Drogo emerge. He was carrying a parchment in his hand. Suddenly he stopped, glanced around him and turned back into the chapel. The Countess stood, quiet as a spider, as she heard a rustling sound and then a grunting noise from Drogo, as if he were moving something heavy. Then a scraping sound. Something was being pushed over the rough flagstone floor of the chapel. Then she could hear his heavy breathing, as he emerged from the chapel again, without the parchment, but with a look on his face of despair and hatred, which made his already ugly features look more than ever like the devil himself. The Countess withdrew silently, as she heard Drogo making his way down the main staircase towards the library.

Quickly, she told the others that Drogo was gone. Then she recollected another little plan which she had made just before.

'I'm going to order Christian over to the village to collect some, er... some leeks, let's say! That'll get him out of the house. Have you seen Jacques?' For the Countess would not herself address such a humble servant as Christian, but would pass her orders on through Jacques.

'Did I hear my name?' said Jacques, as he rounded the corner of the corridor just beyond Marie's door.

'Oh good, Jacques!' exclaimed the Countess. 'Could I ask you to send Christian to the village for leeks, the normal place you know, of course.'

'Ah! Well, Ma'am, I would do so, but er...' replied Jacques, hesitating a moment, 'I've already sent him on an errand, just a few moments ago, to take various shoes to the village cobbler, Ma'am. I am most sorry. Perhaps his brother, Marc, could fetch the leeks?'

'Leeks?' said the Countess, quite distracted. 'Oh! I mean, yes, of course. Oh well, never mind the leeks, Jacques. The shoes are more important!' Did she see his eyes twinkle just very slightly at this reply?

'Well, then,' said Marie, 'we can't stand here all day!'

Jacques took this as his cue to leave, and he went off humming to himself along the corridor – the first few bars of 'Für Elise', Tommy noted. 'The rotten fellow,' Tommy added to himself. Ah! No, maybe this is a sign he wants the mobile, to recharge it, perhaps?'

Marie picked up the bundle of clothes again, Tommy the jar of mud, and as rapidly as they could, followed by the Countess, they made their way down the stairs towards Tommy's room, along the corridor. Just as they were about to enter the room, their hearts came into their mouths, as footsteps came rapidly up the stairs. It was Jacques returning.

'Just one moment, Monsieur Thomas,' he said, completely ignoring the fact that Tommy was carrying a large jar of rather foul stinking mud, and Marie was standing gaping with her arms full of old clothes, and the Countess had her hand on the door handle to Tommy's room.

'A quick word, if I may,' said Jacques, and he gently guided Tommy to one side. Then he whispered, 'Give me the mobile, I'll get it charged.' Tommy fished it out of his pocket and handed it to Jacques.

'I'll give it you back this evening at dinner,' said Jacques, and departed as quickly as he had come.

Marie let out a great sigh of relief, and the Countess quickly opened the door and burst into Tommy's room. They were greeted by a little gasp of fright and a rummaging from behind the bed.

That's pretty useless, thought Tommy! Thank God, though, that she is still there and safe.

'Eloise, Eloise, it's me. Marie and my mother, they know all about what's going on. Now listen – put the door on the catch, Mother, please – you're going to get disguised as a peasant girl and smuggled out of the château on the vegetable cart going to the nunnery of Seiche-Capucins.'

In reply Eloise just gave a little gasp of fright and disgust.

'Come on out, now,' said Marie, 'we haven't got much time. I'll have to go down to the kitchen in a few minutes to set it up with the vegetable people. Come on out!'

Carefully skirting around the bog pot, Eloise emerged – in her underclothes.

'Those'll have to come off,' said Marie. 'Not peasant clothes.' Eloise and Tommy blushed. 'There's no time for that,' said Marie. 'Thomas, you go in there,' she said, pointing to the lavabo. 'And you, Mad'moiselle Eloise, strip your things off quick!'

Tommy rushed in confusion over to the lavabo, stumbling over the bed that he had prepared for Eloise, but she had never used. Sitting on the ground, he remembered his thoughts of earlier when he stood with nothing on changing his clothes. He was sure that Eloise had taken a peek at him, or at least she might have done, and so he would take a peek at her too, the naughty boy! So he pushed the door a tiny bit so that just a crack appeared and he could see Marie fussing about shaking the peasant clothes out, and then Eloise, quite naked, passed across his view. Oh, gosh, thought Tommy, and he felt his face get terribly hot, and he shut his eyes. Oh gosh! And kept his eyes shut in case he was tempted to look again.

'You can come out, now,' said the Countess, and there stood Eloise in peasant clothes, with a tight bonnet around her head, which held in her hair. They had not cut it off. Thank heavens for that, thought Tommy.

'Do you want to apply the mud?' asked Marie. 'Or shall I?'

'Thomas and I will do it,' said the Countess. 'Marie, why don't you go on down to the kitchen and get things sorted out!'

'Yes, Madame. I'll be off now. Let her come down to the kitchen alone. Make sure that no one sees you leaving Tommy's room, Eloise.'

So Tommy and the Countess put their fingers in the smelly bucket of mud and began to paint Eloise, to make her look like a dirty and smelly little peasant girl, who had not had a bath for a week. A bit went on the legs, a smear on her arms, and Tommy planted a swift kiss on her cheek, while the Countess was bending down for a refill over the bucket. Eloise's lips moved as if she wanted to respond, but there was no time for it! Tommy's kiss on the cheek was accompanied by a daub on her chin, and little bit up by her left ear. He would have giggled if it all had not been so terribly serious. He wanted to crush her in his arms, not put stinking mud on her beautiful face. Also she did not seem to look any the less beautiful for all the mud!

'That'll do,' said the Countess, standing back to admire the general effect. 'You must not walk like a lady either. Be timid, let your arms hang down. Look at the ground. Yes, sag, that's right,' Eloise tried to take up a peasant girl pose. 'Don't tilt your chin up!' And in response, Eloise sagged a bit more.

'Mumble in reply if anyone speaks to you,' said the Countess. 'Fidget a bit if necessary. Don't look anyone in the eye.'

'Yes, Mother,' said Eloise, for Eloise always called her 'mother', since she had never known her own.

'Walk around the room,' ordered the Countess. 'Would that take you in, Thomas?' she demanded. 'Walk as if you did not want to be seen, as if you wanted to fade into the background. Yes, that's it,' said the Countess, as Eloise tried to cringe and creep into the ground.

'These clogs, they hurt!' she protested.

'Oh, Eloise, I don't know when I shall see you again. But let us hope it is only a few days!' said Tommy, taking her hand.

'I'd better check the corridor,' he added, and put his head out. 'It's clear,' he said, and he could not resist kissing her cheek as she passed, but was rewarded with a mouthful of stinking mud. Tommy spluttered and tried to wipe his lips clean with the back of his hand. The Countess put her hand to her mouth to suppress her laugh, but tears came to the eyes of Eloise.

'No,' said Thomas, as Eloise choked to control her sobbing.

Pausing to collect herself, Eloise emerged into the corridor and hastily made her way to the head of the servants' stairs and down from there to the kitchen. Unknown to any of the three however, Eloise's passage out of Tommy's room did not go unseen by another of Drogo's spies. Christian's elder brother, Marc, a lout of twenty-five, with the same sticking-out ears, was also in Drogo's pay. He was standing by one of the trees looking up at the château, just as Eloise came out of Tommy's room in her disguise. His orders were to look out for any movement in the corridors, and he stepped quickly in the kitchen door and then to the library, to report to Drogo.

'A young peasant girl, you say,' said Drogo. 'Good boy! Well spotted.' And he smiled, a horrid sight, from which even the uncouth Marc recoiled.

'That's Eloise,' continued Drogo, 'or I'll be damned! Go to the kitchen and find her, keep close to her and come back and report to me where she goes. Ask your brother to come here as well, for instructions.'

Now Marie had lost no time in talking with her friend the gardener, who was piling his cart high with radishes, onions, spinach and carrots, brought earlier from the village that day. Eloise was helping him, and, just as Marc appeared at the back door of the kitchen, Eloise jumped on to the cart with the vegetables, the gardener whipped the mangy old horse which pulled it, and they were off. The gardener walked beside as they made their way slowly by the muddy path along a ditch, over a rough stone bridge and through the ruins of the old château, destroyed twenty years earlier by the soldiers of Toulouse.

Marc noted where Eloise had gone, and called out, 'Anyone seen my brother, Christian?'

'Yeah,' yelled another lad. 'He's gone off grumbling to the village with a load of shoes to be repaired. Jacques sent him. He'll be back quite soon.'

Marc went straight back to report to Drogo.

'You'd better follow them,' said Drogo, meaning Eloise and the gardener with his vegetables. 'Come back and tell me where they go. Go all the way. Never mind how late it gets or duties here. I'll see you right on those, if there's a problem.' And with that he put a small silver coin in Marc's hand, patted his arm and sent him off.

Meanwhile, Tommy and the Countess were tidying up Tommy's room, putting the bog pot back in the lavabo, and taking the bedding back to Tommy's bed.

'Y'know,' said Tommy, 'Jacques took the mobile to get it charged just when he knew that I could not possibly follow him.' The Countess looked at him very puzzled.

'Ah! I haven't really explained. That telephone. It will only work for a short time. It needs – it needs stuff putting into it,' said Tommy lamely. How can I explain electricity to the Countess? he thought. Anyway he didn't understand it himself! 'The stuff it needs, you can only get in my world. And that is where Jacques is gone! I had been hoping to see how he did it, I mean, going from here to my world.' The Countess was looking still more puzzled by Tommy's attempt to explain what he meant. 'Never mind. But the point is that if he can get from here to my world, so can I, and so can Thomas get back here!'

In reply to this, the Countess sighed and she felt her eyes began to fill with tears.

'No!' she said. 'Action, not tears! Look, Thomas, it's time that you went to see Father Drogo in the library. Be careful, be very careful! In the meanwhile, I am going to send an escort along with Eloise. I must be sure that she is safe, safely delivered to the nunnery!'

'Oh, Countess, thank you,' said Tommy and kissed her cheek.

They looked at each other, perplexed. He was not her son, but he had just done what only a son would do. He was like a son to her, and she could not help herself but clasped him in her arms and stroked his hair lovingly.

'Yes, yes,' she said, as they broke the embrace. 'Now go down to Drogo, and act the fool!' Then she turned her back on him so that he could not see the tears again in her eyes.

Tommy hurried out of his room, down the stairs, just in time to see the departing back of Marc turning the corner into the kitchen. Ah! he thought, another spy, perhaps. He'd remember the ears sticking out to identify him. Then with his heart in his mouth, Tommy entered the library.

Drogo sat up suddenly on seeing Thomas enter and snapped closed the heavy book that he was reading. He had decided not to show anger but to wheedle his way into the silly boy's confidence, get him to give away Eloise, and use the evidence to destroy her reputation and keep Thomas in his power. This plan was contained in the message sent to his brother, the Bishop, by horseback earlier in the day. This was the messenger that Tommy and the Countess had seen riding from the château.

'Ah! Thomas, my boy,' said Drogo, in a voice of poisoned honey.

'Yes, Father,' said Tommy, looking at the ground.

'We need, don't we, to talk a little about what happened last night.'

'Yes, Father,' said Tommy, eyes still on the ground.

'Look at me, Thomas,' said Drogo, and Tommy raised his eyes unwillingly, to confront the watery gaze, the long thin nose and flaccid lips of the good Father.

'That's better' said Drogo. 'You know, Thomas, that I am your friend.' Good God! thought Thomas, he knows that I know that he knows that I stamped on his hand last night!

'Yes, Father,' said Tommy, looking back at the ground. Drogo rose from his chair and walked towards him. Extending his undamaged arm, Drogo held Tommy under the chin and moved his face up to meet his direct gaze.

'Do you regret what happened last night, Thomas?' he asked, his putrid breath causing Tommy to wince and try to turn his head away. At this movement, Drogo held his chin a little harder. 'Do you regret it?' he asked again.

'Yes, Father,' said Tommy, and tried to will tears to his eyes. This was difficult because all he really felt was a nearly irresistible desire to strike the vile priest right on his ugly nose and bend it so that it was never straight again. Not that it was particularly straight at the moment, Tommy noticed.

As if Drogo sensed the violence almost boiling over in Tommy, he dropped his hand and said, 'Good, Thomas, good. Now tell me more about this girl who you were with. Who I thought was Eloise, but obviously was not, despite the dress and the scent.'

'Oh, Father. There is nothing to tell!'

'Thomas, come now!' said Drogo. 'Describe her to me! Was she tall, was she thin, fat, dark or fair? I know that she is gone from us, but we would like to know who she was. Someone will be asking after her eventually, you know. Her mother' – here he unaccountably ground his teeth – 'or maybe her father. They will want to know what happened!'

'Peasants,' said Tommy. 'They have no right.' He stamped his foot like a little boy.

'Still, describe her to me, Thomas,' insisted Drogo.

Okay, thought Tommy, and immediately an image of Harry's little sister came into his head.

'If you wish, Father Drogo, of course. She was fair, with some browner streaks in her hair, here and there, and quite small.

Eloise's dress was too big for her. And she had put on far too much of Eloise's scent,' he added for good measure.

Drogo was thrown by this, because his next question was to have been about how it was that Eloise's dress could fit her. But this sly Thomas had forestalled him! He'd try a different approach.

'I found some long strands of hair along with the dress.'

'Oh?' said Tommy.

'They were dark brown, not fair,' said Drogo, 'like Eloise's hair!'

'Maybe, then,' said Tommy, 'maybe they were Eloise's hair. Perhaps they had come off on her dress. And when this girl stole it from her room, then maybe that's how... Or, maybe they were just some of the darker hair from... from, whatever her name was. I never knew her name, even!' added Tommy.

'Tell me how you met her,' said Drogo.

'Well, it was after the banquet, you see. There were lots of people rushing back and forth. Footmen, carriages being called.'

'Where were you?' asked Drogo.

Ha! Thought Tommy, he's trying to trick me into being where I should have been able to see Eloise talking to Jacques!

'I was standing in the dining room, by the sideboard.'

'So you could not see along the corridor?' asked Drogo.

'No,' said Tommy, 'I mean, not unless I was specially trying to, I mean.'

'No, and why should you be?' said Drogo.

'What? Why should I? Sorry, Father, but what do you mean, why I should I be what, Father?'

'Tell me what happened next,' said Drogo, ignoring Tommy's question.

'She – this serving girl – just sort of rubbed against me.' At this Drogo winced. 'And whispered, very quickly,' continued Tommy, '"By the pantry at midnight" – and then she was gone. I did not even say "yes" or anything! I looked around for her a bit afterwards but I simply couldn't see her. I suppose that she was a kitchen girl, really.'

Drogo felt his anger begin to rise. This boy was lying through his teeth, he knew it! But he couldn't catch him in a direct lie. He wanted him blubbing on the carpet, crying for mercy, begging forgiveness for standing on his hand and wrist, cutting him against the glass, lying about Eloise. He had not seen Eloise in the cupboard room, but he knew, he *knew* it was her! It fitted too well with his plans to catch them in this way. He could not let this advantage go!

'And what did Eloise say about this?' asked Drogo, hoping to catch Thomas out without such an unexpected demand.

But all he got in return was, 'I didn't see Eloise anywhere. Anyway, why should I tell her such a thing? It is hardly for the ears of a young noblewoman! Father, why do you ask me such a question? Would you have asked Eloise about it? Should I have asked her?' said Tommy plaintively, beginning to play the fool properly. Drogo had given him a good opening!

'No, Thomas, you should not!' said Drogo in a strangled voice, placing his face right up against Tommy's and holding him by the shoulder with his one good arm. Drogo held this pose for an age, or so it seemed to Tommy. The hairy pimples on Drogo's nose were right in his line of vision. Tommy was sure he would wake up at night with nightmares about them. *Hairy pimples.* At last Drogo relaxed his stare, and turning his back on Tommy dropped back into the chair in which he been sitting reading.

'Monsieur Thomas, I am the guardian of your soul. Do you wish to be forever damned in hell?' he asked, raising his voice and sitting upright suddenly. Hellfire might frighten Thomas, Drogo thought, into a confession. He had made many grown men fall to the floor with fear, for Drogo was good at inspiring terror and fear, especially if there were a hint of the threat of torture in his words. Unfortunately, that was missing here.

Of course, to a modern boy, a boy of the twenty-first century, Drogo's words were nothing more than a farce, but Tommy did his best to look very frightened, cowering back and looking fixedly at the ground.

'Raise your eyes to me!' commanded Drogo, and Tommy instantly obeyed. 'Women… girls,' said Drogo, 'are instruments of the devil. Even a girl like Eloise, a noble girl, so beautiful.' And Drogo sighed, despite himself. 'Noble girls,' said Drogo again, trying to collect his thoughts, 'even they are a terrible danger.'

Getting back into top gear, the priest continued, 'You will

burn in hell, your liver will roast, while imps remove your toenails one by one, if you cannot put them to one side.'

What? My toenails, thought Tommy, and almost without thinking he said it aloud. 'My toenails?' And his eyes were wide with pretended fear.

'*Your toenails!*' yelled Drogo, finally losing his temper. He stood up again, advancing on Thomas. 'You will be damned, boy, damned to eternal hell,' he bellowed, his voice rising still higher. 'If you do not roast first on this earth, then you will roast in the next!'

Tommy blinked. My God, he thought, this man should be in a mental home. He really meant it! Drogo was shaking so with the power of his vision of Tommy roasting in the eternal fires of hell, that he forgot what he was doing and brought both arms crashing down on Tommy's shoulders. Tommy reeled a little, for he did not expect such force from the sickly and seemingly feeble priest.

Drogo let out a great roar of pain, and the bandage around his hand and wrist began to redden as blood began to pour from his reopened wound. Drogo sank to the floor, but Tommy just stood stupidly gazing down at him and let him howl. Let him suffer a bit, he thought, the foolish, perverted monster!

'Get... some... help!' croaked Drogo from the floor. And Tommy ran out of the room, into the kitchen, almost crashing into Jacques.

'Drogo, Father Drogo – his wound is bleeding again!' he said. 'Come quick with some clean bandages, in the library!'

Several people came running and, gathering Father Drogo up, placed him in his chair, and bound his hand again. Drogo cried out as Jacques yanked hard on the cloth and then he shouted, pointing his other hand at Tommy, 'It is Thomas who is guilty of this. It is Thomas!' And then he fainted, his face pale and set in a mask of hate and agony.

'No, Father Drogo,' said Thomas, 'it's not me. You just brought your hands down too hard on my shoulders because you were—'

'Enough!' said Jacques. It was good that the other servants had heard Thomas's explanation, but it was enough.

Into all this commotion came the Count and Countess. The Countess was just returned from ordering Louis, the one of the thick skull, to follow the vegetable cart carrying Eloise to the nunnery of Seiche-Capucins. The sight of Father Drogo lying in a faint, with blood dripping from his wrist, was not at all what she had expected from the interview between Thomas and Father Drogo. Had Thomas attacked him? That would have been very foolish! No, what was Jacques saying?

'Father Drogo was describing the terrors of hell to Monsieur Thomas, and became so excited in the service of Christ that he quite forgot his wounds and caused them to bleed again!'

The Count rushed forward to Father Drogo's side.

'Father Drogo,' he said, 'wake up! Return to us! Do not die! Give me that bottle of brandy, yes, there,' he said, pointing with his free hand, the other placed under Drogo's head. Pulling out the stopper, he splashed some brandy in the priest's face.

'Mind his eyes!' said the Countess; but too late, and it was probably the terrible stinging sensation that caused Drogo to come around so quickly. He woke with a scream, his hands flying to his eyes.

'Water, quickly, water!' shouted Jacques, and Father Drogo groaned.

Water was poured over him; then, stinking of good brandy, soaked with water and dripping blood, the good Father emerged from his stupor to a sea of faces gaping down at him. He summoned all his strength and raising himself up, supported by the Count, he shouted, 'Go – away – all of you!' Then he collapsed again, and the faces withdrew, one by one.

'You, Thomas!' said Father Drogo. 'In penance for your sins, you will say the Lord's Prayer one hundred, no, *five hundred* times.' Then he shouted it again, 'Five hundred times. You will not be at supper. You will be in the chapel, on your knees before the altar. You will not stir from the altar until you have done this. The fires of hell will burn—'

'Enough!' the Count cut in. 'I will see that Thomas does as you command him to! You need some rest, good Father. Take him carefully to his room,' he commanded the servants standing around him in the library. 'And you, Thomas, you had better start now, if you are going to finish before midnight!'

'I'll go with him,' said the Countess, and Tommy gave her a

grateful look. Tommy and the Countess left together, and as they mounted the main staircase the Countess asked him, 'What on earth did you do to Father Drogo?'

'Nothing, honestly,' replied Tommy. 'He got incredibly worked up about hell and damnation and then totally forgot himself, bringing his arms crashing down on my shoulders. It was all completely self-inflicted.' He nearly added, 'I couldn't have done it better myself,' but reckoned that this was perhaps too much of a twenty-first century thought for the Countess.

'Hmmm,' muttered the Countess. 'Well, look, there's something that I should tell you. In the chapel, I mean when I went looking earlier to see if Drogo had come out of the chapel, so we could go down to Eloise...' Then she described the parchment in Drogo's hand, the strange look on his face, his pushing around of things inside the chapel, and finally coming out without the parchment.

'You said something about a secret that Drogo might have,' continued the Countess. 'Well, you have a few hours in the chapel alone. Have a good look around, would be my advice! I'll get the Count to post a guard over the chapel door. To stop you getting out early – but actually to stop anyone coming in!'

'Gosh, yes, right on, mum. I mean, we make a good team, don't we? Can't we just pretend that you are my mother, while I'm here, I mean.'

The Countess stroked his cheek and said, 'Yes, Thomas.'

'Call me Tommy, when no one's around, if you like. It's what I'm called where I come from. A sort of pet name!'

'Yes, if you like,' said the Countess. 'Tommy...' the name coming out hesitantly. 'Now, in you go,' she continued. 'Put the catch on the door, and keep up some sort of murmuring, so that it sounds like you're reciting the Lord's Prayer, at least!'

Tommy didn't tell her that he probably couldn't remember the Lord's Prayer, off by heart anyway. But what the heck!

'I'll get a guard sent up immediately. Don't start moving things about until you hear him around. I'll tell him to ignore noises that you might be making. All part of your penance!'

Seven: The Confession

S o there was Tommy, locking himself into the chapel, to recite his penance.

'Let's see if I can remember the Lord's Prayer,' he muttered to himself. 'There's not much else to do, after all, until the guard turns up.'

'Our Lord... no! Father, which art in Heaven, give us this day our daily bread, forgive our sins as we forgive trespassers against us... No, wait a moment, that was wrong. Trespasses against us. That's better. Start again. Blah, blah. Oh, yes, and lead us not into temptation, forgive us our sins... No, already done that bit, or perhaps it comes afterwards. Oh, well... forgive us our sins as we forgive trespassers... no, trespasses against us, in the name of the Father, the Son and the Holy Ghost. Oh gosh, it maybe alright in the middle of the afternoon here, but by about twelve o'clock tonight, it might get a bit spooky! I wish that bit wasn't there, about the ghost, and then it's just, amen, I think. Heavens, let's try again. Our Father, which art... blah, blah...'

Ah! Here comes the guard. Great! thought Tommy. Keep it going. He began muttering away: 'Our Father, which art, blah, um-tiddle-um-dum in heaven-dum-titty-dum, trespassers will be prosecuted, de-dum-de-dum-de.' I wonder where I should start, he thought. Ah! wait a sec, let's use the old brains. The Countess said she'd heard scraping. Can I find any scraping marks on the floor? 'Our Father which are in Heaven, dum-de-dum, de-dum-de-dum, forgive us our sins,' Tommy mumbled on. Let's start here...

Raising the altar cloth, Tommy could see that the entire altar looked as though it had been moved quite recently. Uh-oh! this is a give-away, thought Tommy. 'In the name of the Father, the Son and the Holy Geese,' he intoned; he was done with ghosts. Anyway the Romans had holy geese, he seemed to remember. 'Tum-dum-tum-dum,' he droned.

Blast! it won't budge. Perhaps it's just marks where Drogo's feet have been scraping on the ground. I'll have to have a methodical search. 'Dum-te-dum, blah, forgive us our sins...' Now what heavy things are there in here? There's the altar itself, there's that great wardrobe affair on the left, there's a chest. Ah! That's been moved recently, surely!

'Gosh!' said Tommy out loud. 'It goes, "Our Father, which art in Heaven, hallowed be thy name, blah blah..." How could I forget that? But never mind the Lord's Prayer. I want to find that parchment.'

Tommy looked at the ground around the chest. It certainly looked as if the chest had been slid sideways recently.

'It's blooming heavy,' he muttered as he tried to push the chest over the scratch marks that he could now see quite clearly on the bare flagstones of the chapel floor. A small window overlooking the moat cast an oblique light on the floor, making the marks stand out in the late afternoon sun.

Drogo may well have a hiding place under there, he thought. I've got to move it, got to move it! I wish I could lever it in some way.

Tommy glanced around the chapel. It was very small. Just enough for a bride and bridegroom, best man and a couple of bridesmaids. Tommy slipped into a daydream and imagined himself marrying Eloise in the chapel. Oh, if only he could! But suddenly something dawned on him. Eloise *did* get married in the chapel, surely. That's what Monsieur Jasper – Jacques – Jasper had said. That painting he had seen in the salon, in the twenty-first century salon: that was surely Eloise when she was grown-up! And Jasper had said that she had been married in the chapel. Surely, surely, surely! Tommy was getting quite excited. That smile, those lips, that beautiful face, surely that was Eloise. Then Tommy paused in his thoughts for a moment. Ah, unless it was her mother, of course! Mmm, yes, it might have been Eloise's mother. Yes, it might. We'll see, said Tommy to himself and snapped out of his daydream and back to the heavy chest.

It was quite clear to him that there was nothing to lever the chest with in the chapel. A glance around the tiny space showed nothing except a broom with a rough wooden handle resting against a wall in the corner and the wardrobe, when he looked inside, was completely empty. But then Tommy's eye alighted on the massive bronze and gold crucifix, which was the centrepiece of the altar, with candlesticks on either side. Now, he could probably use the crucifix to lever the chest along the floor. So long as he was careful, he shouldn't damage it. He'd better be very careful, for if Father Drogo saw that he had used it for something, especially levering the chest along, and it was damaged, he would have to spend the rest of his life reciting the Lord's Prayer – forwards, backwards and sideways.

Oh gosh! I've forgotten about muttering on with the Lord's Prayer, thought Tommy. Oh well, it's too late now. And Tommy listened carefully to see if he could hear the guard moving about outside. Instead he heard a gentle snoring, a few little grunts, and more snoring.

'Good,' said Tommy under his breath. 'Now I need something to wrap around the crucifix, so that it won't be damaged. Yeah! I'll use the altar cloth, on the inside. Won't be able to see any marks when I put it back.'

Tommy did have some qualms about using an object like the crucifix for levering things about. He had, after all, some idea that it was really a sacred object, not a tool for moving heavy chests. But, he reasoned to himself, why not use Christ's image to do Christ's good works? This was surely a good deed he was doing, unmasking the evil priest!

So, carefully, Tommy lifted the heavy crucifix off the altar, put the candlesticks on the floor, and taking the altar cloth, wrapped it around figure of Christ on the cross, so that it was well protected, and also so that the pretty embroidery on the altar cloth was hidden away. Then, holding it by its massive base, Tommy wedged the crucifix, Christ downwards, under the end of the chest, prised it up off the floor by pushing forwards, got his foot a bit underneath and pushed as hard as he could with his lower leg. The chest moved a little, then a little more as he pushed again with his leg, and levered a bit more with the crucifix. It was working! He let the chest gently down, and started the same manoeuvre again. It was easier this time and he began to be able to push the chest quite readily, wiggling the crucifix under it. As he did so, he saw that emerging from under the chest was a block of wood, covering what must be a hiding place in the ground. One more shove and, and – oh God! – he felt something give on the crucifix. Perhaps it was not as strong as it looked? But he was not going to take any notice of that at the moment, though, for Drogo's parchment was surely under that bit of wood, and Drogo's secret might soon be his!

Placing the crucifix on the ground beside him, Tommy knelt down and managed to get his fingernails around the outside of the piece of wood, which fitted snugly into a carefully carved hole in the flagstone floor. Gritting his teeth, Tommy pulled the block slowly out of its hole. It was several inches thick, and was difficult to remove, especially with the impatience that Tommy felt. At last he got it out, and Tommy peered into the little hole. He could see at once that it was too small to hold a proper-sized piece of parchment. In fact, the hole was really only the same size as the block of wood, not only in width but also in depth. There was practically no gap underneath. And, since there was little light shining into the hole, it seemed to him at first, to his great disappointment, that the hiding place was empty! Then suddenly he could see a faint glint of light, and putting his hand in he could feel the outline of a key. Pulling it out, he examined the key carefully. It was large by the standards of the twenty-first century, about the length of his thumb and chunkily made.

'This key is surely the key to the chest, where the parchment must be hidden,' Tommy said quietly to himself. 'Yeah. Right!' He immediately started running his hands over the chest, along the sides where, among the wrinkled old iron bands which bound it, he would expect to find a keyhole. There was none. He crouched down beside it to get a better look. There really was no keyhole anywhere on it. He tried to lift the lid. It wasn't locked! He did not even bother to look if the parchment was in there. Obviously Drogo must have locked it up somewhere safe.

Okay, not the chest. What about the altar itself? He knelt down again and examined it. The altar was carved out of stone. It had no doors, or drawers or anything that could be locked. It was the same on the other side of the altar. It was just a solid block of stone. Tommy was getting frantic. The parchment must be in here somewhere, but there did not seem to be anywhere else it could be. Drogo had not had a chance to remove it since the Countess saw it in his hand, saw him take it out of the chapel, and then return to the chapel and reappear without it. It had to be in the chapel! He'd just have to look absolutely everywhere!

Tommy searched each dark corner, high and low. Was there a loose panel anywhere? He examined every section of every wall carefully. He even began to wonder if he could stand on the altar to examine the ceiling, in case it had a hollow part, or something like that. He was almost crying with frustration. To calm himself a bit, before he made another and still more methodical and thorough search, he thought that he had better have a look at the crucifix. At the thought of it, Tommy's heart came into his mouth. He had forgotten in his frenzy of seeking for the parchment, that he might have damaged the crucifix. Gosh, I hope not, he thought.

Tommy crouched down and picked up the heavy object from the floor where he had left it earlier. Oh no! He could feel something was wobbly underneath the cloth. He placed it, still in the altar cloth, on the altar and began carefully to unwrap it. As the last bit of the altar cloth was removed, Tommy could see to his horror, that Christ's head had come loose from the cross, and was attached by only a small and flimsy piece of wire to his neck. The metal around the base of the head had fractured when Tommy had been a bit over-enthusiastic in levering up the chest.

I can't possibly repair that, he thought, and jiggled around with the head a bit. 'Well, I can sort of get it to stay, if I just turn it upright.'

It was heavy enough so that Tommy's half-whispered voice sounded a bit strained as he said this. He just let the crucifix rest at an angle on its side for one moment, placing his hand under the base to support it better. As he did so, he could suddenly feel with his finger that there was a large depression cut deep into the base. How had he missed that before? At the bottom of this depression, he could feel a keyhole. It must be *the* keyhole! Completely forgetting the damage he had done to the crucifix, Tommy almost let it drop on the stone of the altar, as he turned to grab the key which he had placed on the floor beside where the crucifix had lain. Crouching a bit, Tommy could now see the keyhole. It must fit, it had to fit – it did fit! Tommy turned the key, holding his breath. A whole chunk of metal came out, and Tommy withdrew it. It was about half a metre long, fitting inside the crucifix. And there, wrapped around this long rod of metal, was the parchment that he had been seeking!

Tommy seated himself on the step, to one side of the altar, and carefully unwound the parchment from the metal rod. The parchment was quite dog-eared and had obviously been rolled and unrolled, read and reread many times. Tommy's hands shook with excitement as he looked at the opening lines and he had to be careful not to tear the fragile document.

And this is what Tommy saw.

Written the 15th August, in the year 1585, at the command of my brother, Henri de Montfort, secretary to the Cardinal of Ferrara, Piero Vincenzo di Colonna, at the Palace of the Vatican, Rome, in my brother's apartments.

Drogo de Montfort

Written in a different ink, below this opening statement, was a short note:

This is a copy of a document in the hands of my brother. He keeps his copy to force me to his will through blackmail and to hold me true to his policy of the ruin of the House of Romolue and the glorification of Toulouse.

And then the document continued:

Whosoever may see this document, be he of this time, of a time decades in the future or even of centuries to come, I ask that you should give me some little fragment of sympathy for the terrible torments which I have lived through, the agony which I have suffered. My crimes cannot be forgiven on this Earth, of that I am sure, but I seek forgiveness elsewhere, though I may have to pass through many further torments before I can receive the blessing of Almighty God! Read on, therefore, but do not condemn me utterly, as you read of my terrible deed.

In order to understand my story, I must lead you back a short time, just three years into that past and happier period before I first came to the Château of Romolue, to a time when I was still studying diligently to be a priest. I lived then in Toulouse, in the Bishop's palace. He was a good man, Bishop Ghislain de Toulouse, but he did me an evil turn when, one day of July in the year 1582, he suggested that I visit the Château of Romolue to pay my respects to the noble family of the same name.

My coming was announced and, of course, as a member of an illustrious family, a friend of the Bishop and brother of the secretary to a Cardinal at Rome, I was welcomed warmly by the family of Romolue. I was 20 years old at the time, and I am 23 as I write. But even at this age, nature has not favoured me. I am built like a scarecrow, misshapen, with bowed shoulders, with a long, thin and none-too-straight nose and pale, rheumy eyes. I was a miserable fellow, and remain one, only interested in my books, and shunning all the pleasures of life – most of all the company of girls, of course, since I was training to be a celibate priest.

I had only passed across the threshold of the newly built Château of Romolue for a brief time when, wandering among the rooms, I saw at the end of the long first floor corridor the form of a young woman, hardly more than a girl, walking in my direction. Her purpose seemed to be to greet me, so I waited as she came towards me. Oh, that I had not! That I had fled down the stairs, out of the main door, and left the Château of Romolue, never to return! As she approached I began to make out a face of such beauty that I felt it painful to look at her. I felt that I blushed, and I wished to run away, but I was rooted to the cold flagstones on which I stood. I knew that terrible temptation was advancing upon me. Oh, Eleonora, did you understand what you were doing as you smiled, parting your sweet lips (God forgive me!), and took my hand? Your very touch made me shiver. A slight frown passed over your face as you greeted me. Did you foresee your awful destiny in my face, in my thin and ugly body?

From that time on, my life was a continual torture. This beautiful girl aroused in me a feeling that no other girl had ever aroused or ever could arouse again. I knew that it was love – hopeless, bitter love. How could she ever look at me, a forbidden, ugly thing?

Forbidden as a priest, too ugly to think of, how could she ever consider me as a lover?

With her astonishing beauty, she had many suitors who paraded about her, like peacocks, as I described them to myself. To my satisfaction – for I watched her every move avidly – she seemed to favour none of them, any more than she seemed to favour me. This did not stop me feeling the most acute jealousy if she even smiled at any man. And she smiled often, since she had a lovely manner, which enchanted all who knew her, doubly enchanted by her beauty and her nature. When she entered the room, it was as if the sunshine had entered with her. When she left, darkness descended again.

I could think of nothing else but her. My studies suffered. As I read the holy texts, images of Eleonora came floating upon the page. I prayed on my knees before the Holy Virgin, and the Virgin took on the face and form of Eleonora. Her very perfume seemed to fill the air. I was distracted. Confession to my priest was useless. I knew myself what answer I would receive, for I had learnt what answer should be given to an infatuated student: give up my vocation in hopeless pursuit of Eleonora. No! That was something I could not do. So I toiled on, learning what I could. My memory was good, very good in fact. I had only to read something and I could remember it. So I could satisfy the Bishop that I was progressing in my studies, for he used to test me often, in a friendly way. But there was no depth in my studying. Eleonora filled my thoughts when I was absent from the Château of Romolue, and when I was present there, which was very often, all I could do was to remain in her presence for as long as I was able. I was nervous even to talk to her, unless I should betray what I felt for her. I lived in eternal anguish that others might see my infatuation, and laugh at me and taunt me as a foolish priest. Looking back, I am sure that I must have been detected; but if it was so, I never saw any clear sign.

Each time I left the Château of Romolue, I vowed, or pretended to vow, never to return. I rode slowly away, but galloped rapidly on my return, sometimes just the next day, on some pretext or other. Once I found Eleonora alone in the library. Her needlework was put on one side, and she was reading! Strange, I thought, as I watched her lovely head, bowed over a book, it was strange to see her reading. Women do not read, do they? I had never seen it before. I gathered my courage, I approached her, and asked what book it was that she was reading. She was startled at my sudden appearance, for she had been so deeply absorbed in her reading that she had not seen me enter. She blushed slightly and, in answer to my question gave me the book, open at the page where she was reading. It was a book describing travels in strange lands. She smiled shyly as I read the text. I myself had read only holy books, and never a book just for the pleasure of reading. It was immoral to read for pleasure. Books were given by God for the study of the Scriptures, and all books which were not religious books should be burnt, or locked away – or so I had learnt.

But what was written in this book was interesting! I sat on a broad couch opposite her and began to look more closely. There were illustrations, of strange creatures with humps on their backs on the page that she had open. I grew bold, very bold, and addressed her. 'Eleonora, come and sit beside me so that we can look at this book together!' We sat on the couch together, and for the next hour, the happiest of my life, I felt her warm body beside me, leaning over me, her breath on me, as she looked at the pictures, and we read the text together. Oh, that I could relive those moments, that time could have stood still, that I had not been a priest, that I had been a handsome man! But what nonsense! The world is a place of evil, a hateful place, and nothing suits as it should.

After that short time with her in the library, I began to see reminders of her more and more in every aspect of my daily life. The pattern on the altar cloth reminded me of the dress that she had been wearing the day before, the stem of the cup of Holy Communion seemed entwined in her graceful fingers, the smell of incense became the smell of her perfume, she appeared before my eyes in every shaft of sunlight that fell through the stained glass onto the floor of the church. And then came her voice inside my head, talking sweetly to me as she had that afternoon we sat together looking at the book. Her lilting voice was mixed in with the voice of the Bishop as he intoned the ritual prayers of Holy Mass. I could only wait out the time that I did not spend at the Château of Romolue.

I was obsessed with her. She had cast a spell on me. I began to suspect her of witchcraft. I could see her so clearly before me, hear her voice, and I would feel faint as these apparitions formed and faded away. If she had been a peasant girl, I should have had her burnt at the stake, and I should have been saved from torment. But noblewomen cannot be accused of witchcraft, at least not because of a witless foolish young priest, who has fallen hopelessly in love... For that is what I am, what I was, a man mad with love, with no way to find an outlet for this love. Ah, pity me!

Then a great disaster struck me. A cousin, a distant cousin, visited the Château of Romolue. If only I had had a poisoned dagger, I would have thrust it in his side, thrust it till it reached his vital parts, and killed him. This man was young and handsome, laughing and friendly to all. He had seen the world, fighting in Italy, and had sailed the Mediterranean Sea. Like all men who met her, he paid homage to Eleonora. At first, she treated him as she treated all her other suitors, holding him at a distance and not favouring him over any other. But after a short time, it was not more than a week, I began to see that there were more smiles in the direction of this cousin, Monsieur Richard de la Courtablaise, than there were for other men.

My jealous rage ate at me. I could not eat, I could not sleep. She still appeared in visions before me, but now she did not smile as before. Her voice was still inside my head, but the words were not so kind, although I could not make them out clearly, my thoughts were such a jumble. But my visits to the Château of Romolue did not cease. Indeed, they did not lessen. I would torture myself with frequent trips, watching Eleonora talking with Monsieur Richard, Eleonora riding with Monsieur Richard, Eleonora walking with Monsieur Richard, Eleonora sitting with Monsieur Richard, looking in the same book as we had looked at together. What heartless treachery!

They were betrothed, after only two months. I was beside myself with anguish and jealousy. I was a powerless onlooker at my own death, for that was how I felt it. Eleonora would be borne away, to live in some distant castle, where I would never visit, where I would never see her again. I felt that I should die if I could not see her, despite the burning jealous rage that possessed me when I saw Eleonora and Richard together. Richard – how I hate the name!

The date was set for their wedding. This was to take place at the Château of Romolue, in the private chapel. The Bishop was to marry them. Then, from one day to the next, the Bishop took ill and died. My brother was recalled from Rome to take his place. Almost his first action was to ask if I, instead of he, Henri, who hardly knew the family, if I could act as the priest at the wedding of Eleonora de Narbonne and Richard de la Courtablaise. This request sent me into a further frenzy of despair. I would rather have chopped off my own hand than be the vehicle of their marriage. But then the cleverer side of me prevailed. If I married them, then I would be able to have some influence over their future lives, perhaps. Give spiritual advice, and slide snake-like into their lives... into Eleonora's bed! Such were my thoughts, for I had by then lost all shame. So marry them, I did, hateful as it was to me to see their happiness, their hands joined, the ring slipped over her finger, the kiss of acceptance. It was I who should have had that kiss! *It was I!*

They were given a set of rooms on the top floor of the Château of Romolue and there they stayed for several months. About this time, it became clear that Eleonora was pregnant. Another cause for happiness, and another blow to me! Richard was to sail north and collect his old nurse, a skilled midwife, for delivery of the child. I did not see him leave, but when next I visited the château, Eleonora was not to be seen. She was confined in her room, I was told, awaiting the return of her beloved husband, and was rarely visible. Occasionally she went for a walk in the château grounds.

Perhaps, as the priest who married them, I might be allowed a visit, to comfort her? Indeed, she could not refuse me and I was able to gaze upon her lovely face once more. I returned two days later and gained a second visit to her. I was foolish enough to bring with me the book from the library which we had looked at together. When she saw this book, she burst into tears, and through her weeping explained that this was the book that she and Richard had read together and sworn never to touch until they were together again! She had quite forgotten, it was clear, that we had sat together and read it! My happiest moments were as nothing to her. My love began to turn to hatred from that time. She was a witch, of that I am now sure. Soon after this, I was about to leave, for I was afraid that the strong emotions that I felt might spill out and cause me to lose her forever, for now I loved and hated her, both at once.

As I turned to go, there was a commotion outside the door and the sounds of a loud discussion. Without warning or a knock on the door, the Count and Countess burst in. 'Eleonora,' said the Count, 'there is some terrible news.' Eleonora paled and the Countess knelt down and, putting her hands on Eleonora's shoulders, said, 'Richard's ship has been attacked by pirates. It seems that he was taken prisoner. They were close to the shore, and one of Richard's crew jumped overboard and escaped. We have just received the news!' Tears came to Eleonora's eyes and she let her head drop into her hands. 'No,' she moaned, 'no!' I left them attempting to comfort her, departing silently, rejoicing in my heart. There was still hope then for me, I thought, fool that I was.

I returned the next day to the Château of Romolue. I discovered that when the pirates found that they had captured a rich nobleman, they had sent word that they would ransom him. *Damn them all to hell*! I thought. Richard may return unharmed. I managed to find out many details of this ransom, for I was intent to foil the plans for Richard's release. The money was to be delivered, by no more than two men, at the stroke of midnight, Sunday next, at the cove of Labeyrie, north of the great sand dunes where the river Garonne reaches the sea. If the money did not come, they would cut Richard's throat and leave him on the shore; that, so I was told, was the threat.

I had a trusted servant, Roland. But I had told him nothing of Eleonora or of Richard. He remained always in Toulouse. Did he know of silent men who would commit a dangerous and secret act for the Church? I asked him. He found them, four in all. I never met them. Their duty was to kill the messengers carrying the ransom money, and share it between themselves and Roland. I needed to be sure that this was properly done, so that next Sunday evening I also rode out and kept just within sight of these murderers and watched them as they waited in ambush for the unsuspecting bearers of the ransom. Heavy clouds moved rapidly across the sky and the full moon cast a wavering and a ghostly light over the scene, and I can remember the sound of the gorse bushes rattling in the wind. As the messengers passed, the four men leapt out, silently slit their throats, left them lying in the path and rode noiselessly away, carrying the ransom money with them. They were never seen again. The sum which they had taken made them rich for life. Roland never received his share. But I compensated him with a good reward. This shows, I think, that I am a fair man.

I waited another day before visiting the Château of Romolue again. It was painful for me to keep away from Eleonora, now that I knew that she could be mine. But it was sensible not to show too much interest in the affair of Richard and the pirates. When I did visit, the château seemed unnaturally quiet and sombre. Of course, I had Roland drag the messengers' bodies in among the gorse bushes; they were never found. The pirates had sailed away empty-handed. I was hoping, naturally, to see the corpse of Richard, laid out in the château! But there was no corpse. The pirates must have spared him, for he had not been found dead on the seashore in the cove of Labeyrie, as they had threatened. I cursed my luck. But the months passed and nothing was heard. I saw as much of Eleonora as I dared. As her belly grew, my hatred seemed to grow with it. My hatred and my love were blended into one, and I could not tell them apart, now or then.

Eventually the baby was born, a girl, Eloise. The mother mourned the father but some joy did seem to come to her with the child. She would smile in greeting when I visited her and this would encourage me to come more often. My feelings for her seemed to become stronger with every day that passed. The visions returned and her voice inside my head became still louder. I saw her in every corner of the cathedral of Toulouse and in every shadow, I heard her voice in every prayer offered by my brother, the Bishop, I saw her form in every statue of every saint in the church. One day I had a very powerful vision. She stood before me and asked, 'Would you kill me if I cannot love you?' and then the image faded. After that, I must have fainted, for the next thing I remember is being shaken awake, lying stretched out on a pew in the cathedral.

I learned that Eleonora would be visiting the cathedral on the next Sunday, to offer special prayers for the safe return of her husband, Richard. She would arrive late in the afternoon, talk with my brother, and stay the night in the cathedral, praying. The days leading up to this fateful Sunday are blank for me. My memory, which as I said before is so strong, fails me completely. I know that I became consumed by a great rage and hatred against this woman, this witch, who had destroyed my life. I know that I entered the cathedral late on Sunday evening. I know that I took, from a little side chapel, the great crucifix, which now stands in the chapel here in the Château of Romolue, and I know that, creeping stealthily out from behind a column, I killed her with it. If it was not I who did it, who could it have been? I was found by my brother in the morning lying senseless by the altar, holding a sleeping baby in my arms, her baby, Eloise, just two months old. She, Eleonora, lay dead in the central aisle. I know no more and I can write no more. My courage, such as it is, my courage fails me.

There the terrible document ended. Tommy was shaking with disgust and rage. 'This very crucifix was used for murder,' he said aloud, eyeing it with horror. And then his eye fell on an extra note, at the very bottom of the page, which had been added in another ink, but clearly by the same hand. *The child grows so like her mother, that I may have to kill her too.*' Just that. No more.

Sitting motionless on the cold altar step, Tommy shuddered to himself.

This man should be in a mental home for insane criminals, thought Tommy. How was it that the Catholic Church could have such people in it? Tommy thought of the Spanish Inquisition, that he had been told about in school. Wasn't it going strong in 1599? Probably, he thought. Maybe that was why the Countess seemed so frightened of the Church. Drogo would fit perfectly in the Inquisition!

Tommy read again that last chilling note about coldly killing the child, and he shuddered once more. Well, he had not done it – yet. But Eloise must be getting to look very like her mother, he supposed, probably driving Drogo even madder than he was already. It was clear that Drogo would stop at nothing. Eloise's life was in danger, especially now. Drogo knew of course that Tommy and Eloise had been together in the little cupboard room behind the pantry. He knew that she had escaped his clutches, that his influence over her was slipping away. Drogo had dangerous men at his command. Christian for one, and also that other spy whose back he had seen retreating down the corridor, when he went to see Drogo earlier – people like the murderers described in the parchment that he had just read. Eloise's life could be in danger right now!

'I must get out of here,' said Tommy, 'and warn her.' First everything had to look as if it had not been touched. 'I've had time to say the Lord's Prayer five hundred times over. Well, I better have had the time. I'm not waiting for that!'

Tommy replaced the piece of wood in the floor, putting the key under it. 'If Drogo looks for it, he'll find it there. I'll keep the parchment, though.' Then he stuffed it down his tights, inside his velvet trousers.

Next he managed to push the chest back over the wooden block, using all his strength and without having to use the crucifix again. He replaced the altar cloth and the candlesticks, but then came the problem of the crucifix, with Christ's head broken as it was. Tommy took the head between two fingers and a thumb, and pressed it down as hard as he could on the brittle metal of the neck, where it had broken. By twisting a bit, he managed to get it to stay in place. So long as you did not look too hard, or move it, you probably would not notice. 'If Drogo picks it up, well, he'll be more worried about his manuscript missing than anything else,' said Tommy to himself.

Releasing the catch on the chapel door, Tommy pushed gently on it to let himself out without waking the guard. But something was obstructing the door. As Tommy pushed a little harder and the door edged slightly open, he peered through the crack and could see that the guard had gone to sleep slumped against the door.

What the heck! thought Tommy, and gave the door a good shove. The guard rolled over to one side, breaking his fall on the hard floor half in his sleep, and muttering, 'Leave me alone!' Then he gave a yawning snort and promptly fell asleep again.

Tommy shut the door of the chapel, giving it a sharp pull to get it to stay properly closed. He stepped over the sleeping guard, who was now stretched across the threshold. As quietly as possible, he crept down the stairs. He had to find the Countess and tell her what he had discovered. Then he would saddle his horse and be off to the nunnery of Seiche-Capucins to warn Eloise of the danger which she was in. He must find her a safer hiding place, until he could unmask Drogo. But as he was turning these thoughts over in his mind, he heard footsteps coming up the stairs, and the heavy breathing of a person in pain. It was too late to run away, and he knew that it was Drogo making his way onto the landing below him. Drogo lifted his eyes to Tommy and a look of hatred filled the priest's haggard face, matched only by the loathing which Tommy could not conceal on his own face.

You criminal murderer! thought Tommy, and pain and disgust almost overflowed from him. He wanted to shout and rage, and smash Drogo to the ground – this monster who had deprived Eloise of a mother, and a father, for all her life. He shook with the effort of self-control that he needed to stop himself from flying at Drogo and throttling him with his bare hands. He clenched and unclenched his fists, shaking still more as he stood his ground looking down at Drogo.

'Ah! you shake with fear when you see me, do you?' said Drogo, his mouth forming a foul grin. 'Well you might, my boy, well you might!'

Fool! thought Tommy. If you knew my real feelings and the truth that I know about you, you would be flying down that staircase and riding as hard as you could to the protection of your Bishop brother...

'Have you said the Lord's Prayer five hundred times?' asked Drogo, as he slowly mounted the staircase towards where Tommy stood.

Tommy stood mute, unable to address a word in a normal voice to this murderous priest. They eyed each other for a moment, each boiling with anger.

'Don't just stand there!' shouted Drogo. 'Answer me! Have you said the Lord's Prayer?'

'Do not forget yourself, Father Drogo,' answered Tommy icily. 'Remember to whom you are talking.' There was only so much that Tommy could take from this man, now that he knew the terrible truth of his crimes.

'You insolent boy!' snapped Drogo, with an air of menace. 'Remember that I am the guardian of your soul!'

The pain in Drogo's arm had redoubled after he lost control of himself in his interview with Tommy, and the wounds in his hand and wrist had reopened. The throbbing had returned and a spasm of pain shot up his arm as he climbed each step of the staircase. But Drogo had forced himself from his bed, for it had crossed his mind that leaving Thomas alone in the chapel for many hours was a dangerous thing to do, even given the boy's stupidity. His confession was locked away in the chapel, beyond the reach of Thomas, of course, but some accident might happen; the crucifix, that hateful crucifix, might fall from the altar…

Of course it could not! he said to himself. It has stood there for many years! But anxiety drove him on, and though his reason told him to stay in his room, his anxiety overcame his reason.

'Let us go and pray together for your soul,' said Drogo, with an attempt at a smile, placing his good hand on Tommy's shoulder.

Tommy recoiled, despite himself, but Drogo ignored him. He had seen the guard.

'What is this?' Drogo demanded, looking at the snoring form on the ground before the chapel door, and Drogo kicked the guard hard in the ribs, grimacing at the pain that this caused in his own arm. The guard clutched at his side, and half awake, stumbled to his feet, gasping with surprise.

'Father Drogo! I am sorry, sir, good Father. I must have drifted off, I…' His voice trailed off as fright crossed his face as he tried to find the words to wriggle out of his predicament. Looking from Drogo to Thomas and back again, noticing the grim expressions on both their faces, the tight lip on Monsieur Thomas, the evil glint in the eye of Father Drogo, he could sense the tension between them. He knew that some unpleasant drama was about to unfold, which it might be dangerous to witness. He should be gone as soon as he could, and with that thought – and wisely, not another word – he ran off down the staircase with as great haste as he could. The Countess had told him to report to her should Drogo, or indeed anyone, try to enter the chapel. So he was off to inform her, with the greatest speed, that Drogo had arrived.

'What was the guard doing here?' demanded Drogo of Tommy.

'I've no idea, Father Drogo,' replied Tommy, adopting a more respectful tone. The encounter between Drogo and the guard had given Tommy time to get some control over his emotions. 'Perhaps my father wanted to be sure that I fulfilled my penance in the chapel and did not try to leave before I had finished. Which

I did not, good Father,' he added hastily. 'I have realised that I have sinned and I have been bad,' he went on, falling back into the role of the silly harmless little boy as best he could. 'I shall try to be better in the future.'

Drogo dismissed the guard from his mind and, placing his hand again on Tommy's shoulder, feeling once more in control, said, 'Sins must be atoned for, young man. Your error was grave, and time will show if you have done enough to be forgiven. Let us now go and pray together in the chapel.'

Tommy opened the chapel door and allowed Drogo to enter before him. Tommy followed and immediately looked at the crucifix. To his horror, Tommy saw that the head of Christ on the crucifix was tilted to one side. When he had pulled the door closed earlier, he must have made a draft of air or enough vibration to displace it.

Oh, please, Drogo, don't notice it! thought Tommy, and hung back, still holding the door-handle limply in his hand. At that instant, someone must have opened the main door to the Château, for a strong draught of wind came sweeping up the staircase, pulling the chapel door from Tommy's loose grasp and swinging it shut with a loud bang behind him. The head of Christ sprang from his shoulders and dangled, lolling to one side, shaking back and forth, like a crazy puppet on a spring.

'No!' roared Drogo, and clutching at the altar, fell to the ground before it in a faint, striking his head hard against the stone as he did so.

Drogo's guilt had overpowered him. The sight of the head of Christ springing from his shoulders on the crucifix, this crucifix with which he had killed an innocent, beautiful girl whom he loved, this Christ's head falling from the cross, the cross where he had hidden the confession of his crimes, this seemed a miraculous damnation, a proof that terrible torments awaited him in the next world...

Tommy stood there astonished for a moment, looking back and forth from Drogo spread-eagled on the floor to Christ's wobbling head. But only for a moment, for he turned as he heard voices coming up the stairs.

'Father Drogo and Monsieur Thomas will be in the chapel,

Countess,' the guard was saying, as they turned the corner at the landing below, 'and…' But he got no further.

Tommy was standing at the head of the small flight of stairs to the chapel, with a grim smile on his face.

This is a bit of luck, thought Tommy. A narrow escape. He beckoned the Countess urgently towards him, but put up his hand as the guard advanced also.

The Countess entered the chapel and gave a little shriek, and her hand flew to her mouth. In this unguarded moment, she blurted out, 'My God! Tommy, did you kill him?' as she gazed at Father Drogo, lying on the floor, blood flowing from a cut on his head, and the wound on his wrist and hand reopened, also dripping blood onto the flagstone floor.

Tommy raised his finger to his lips. And then replied quietly, 'No, of course not, though he richly deserves to die.' The Countess gasped again at this. 'You will see why,' said Tommy, patting the place in his tights where he had hidden the parchment.

'Look,' said Tommy, pointing at the crucifix, and the Countess's eyes widened as she gazed at the head of Christ, still wobbling, held only by a thin strip of bronze. 'When Drogo saw this, he fainted. And you will soon find out why.'

There was a faint moan from the floor.

'Quick,' whispered Tommy, 'take the crucifix. Mind, it's heavy.' He grabbed it from the altar and thrust it into the startled hands of the Countess. *Hide it*, he mouthed, and ushered her out of the chapel.

There was another louder moan from the floor and Father Drogo stirred. Tommy put his head out of the door and said to the guard, 'Father Drogo has fallen and injured himself. Go quickly and fetch water and bandages, and ask Jacques to come, if you can find him!'

The guard was only too pleased to be able to leave. He scuttled down the staircase and was gone as if the imps of hell were after him.

Eight: Death on the Road

hilst these extraordinary events, so important to Eloise, were taking place in the château, Eloise herself was making her way slowly towards the nunnery of Seiche-Capucins. In her peasant outfit, and smelling unpleasantly of mud, she attracted little attention as she sat among the vegetables. It was a common enough sight, to see a peasant girl riding a cart, while her father, as passers-by supposed he was, took vegetables to the nunnery or wherever he was headed. A few of the younger men looked harder at her, noticed that she was extraordinarily pretty and wondered who she might be. Some called and asked her name.

'Who's that luscious young girl, then? She's worth more than the vegetables, that's for sure!' shouted one young man after them. He got short change from the gardener, who had been told by Marie to be careful not to say anything about the girl to anyone.

'Not anybody, mind you,' she had said, wagging her finger in his face. He promised and he was a man of his word, a man to be trusted, as Marie had said to the Countess and to Tommy.

Unknown, of course, to the gardener and Eloise, they were being followed by Drogo's spy, Marc. He walked some way behind, keeping out of their sight as best he could. And behind him followed Louis, of the thick skull, who had been set to follow Eloise by the Countess. Louis was armed with a sword, as a trusted servant at the Château of Romolue. In fact he was wearing the sword which he had retrieved from Tommy's room, where it was taken from him, after his humiliating crack on the head the previous night. Still, he wore it with pride, swaggering a bit, like the foolish boy that he was. Marc however possessed only a short dagger. He was not so well trusted or liked at the château. But no one would travel even a brief distance without some weapon of protection. Even the gardener had a dagger tucked in his belt.

Passing through the village of Romolue, the gardener took a narrow but well-worn road between the fields, with high bushes on each side. Louis, in the distance, had seen Marc walking some way behind the vegetable cart, but had taken little notice. Marc, whom he knew of course by sight, especially from his sticking-out ears, was just on some errand from the château, no doubt. But when Marc followed the vegetable cart beyond the village, and turned off towards the nunnery, Louis began to get suspicious. What business could Marc have at the nunnery? he wondered. Louis, though a boy of no great brain, had a good instinct for right and wrong, for normal and peculiar. And there was something quite wrong and peculiar in the way the Marc was following the cart. He seemed to be ducking behind the bushes, and moving rapidly between one bush and the next and so on. Obviously he did not want to be seen. He was spying on them. He must have been asked to follow them! This was just what Louis had been told to protect them against, as he understood it.

Louis thought hard about what he should do. He could go straight up to Marc and challenge him to a fight. No, better, skirt rapidly around him, warn the gardener and the girl, and then come back and challenge Marc. Immediately, without more thought, he began to carry out this plan. There was some woodland to the right and he made his way into this and moved quickly through the trees, coming out well beyond the gardener and Eloise and the vegetable cart. He hid himself behind a thick bush and, as the cart approached, stepped suddenly out into the road and held up his hand. There he made a miscalculation. Seeing a man armed with a sword barring his way, the gardener took for him a thief and sprang forward with his dagger in his hand.

'Out of the road!' yelled the gardener. He was a big, burly man, with a quick temper.

'No,' said Louis, 'I am here to protect you!' And he stepped back.

Marc meanwhile had hidden nearby and was watching this development with interest. Marc recognised Louis, but realised that he might be an enemy rather than a friend, since he knew that he was no spy for Drogo.

'What on earth is Louis doing, though?' muttered Marc to himself.

Then Louis said loudly again, 'I am not here to harm you, but to protect you!'

'Is that so!' replied the gardener, relaxing a little. 'And what would a young puppy like you do to protect us, then?'

'The Countess sent me to make sure that El... El...' he stumbled – 'that, that the young girl came to no harm.'

'And why should she come to harm then, eh?' asked the gardener gruffly.

'Well, I dunno,' said Louis. 'That was what she said, an' all!'

Marc retreated further into the bushes as he heard this conversation. If Louis or the gardener saw him, he would be in trouble, that was for sure. Marc leant back as far as he could among the branches, and was startled by a powerful buzzing around his head. He had placed his shoulder squarely against a wasp's nest. He was stung, once, twice, three times! No, that was enough. He sprang out of the bush, pursued by a swarm of angry wasps, and raced away down the path.

With a roar of anger the gardener turned, but Louis was ahead of him, off like a streak of lightning. He was the fastest boy in the village, and he began to make ground on Marc. The gardener stopped with his hands on his hips, after taking only a few steps. He began to chuckle, and remarked, 'He'll soon catch him.'

His chuckle was joined by the lovely lilting laughter of Eloise, whose eyes sparkled as she watched the chase. But the two soon disappeared around a bend in the road.

'Come, let's make our way,' said the gardener, and on they travelled towards the nunnery.

Back down the road towards the village, Marc was running, panting hard, with Louis closing fast, and Marc's stings were maddening to him. He had a sting on one of his big ears, another above his eye and on his neck, and still there were wasps around him. He would never outrun Louis, he realised, as he almost tripped over a loose stone. He would have to stand and fight, and as he said this to himself he abruptly turned and pulled out his dagger.

Louis almost cannoned into him, managing to swerve, but

receiving a nasty slash on his face as Marc lunged at him with the dagger as he went past. With a shout of fury, Louis drew his sword, and, swinging it wildly, dashed at Marc. Louis was no swordsman, and Marc no fighter. He turned and fled. Louis caught him a blow on the shoulder with the flat of his sword which almost knocked him down, and in its passage the sword removed a little part of Marc's right ear – but, unhappily for Marc, not the part which had the sting on it!

Marc managed to gather himself and pull himself upright before Louis could get his sword under control again. Putting his hand to his ear, Marc found it wet with blood. Fear and anger drove him wild and he threw himself upon Louis. Louis slashed blindly with his sword, almost losing his grip on it. Then, by a terrible chance, the blade plunged into Marc's breast. A look of disbelief crossed Marc's face, his eyes closed, the wasp stings faded and he collapsed and died, lying still in the dust at Louis' feet. Horrified, Louis stood for several seconds over the body of Marc, with his sword in his hand, as if turned to stone.

'Oh! God forgive me,' whimpered Louis. 'I did not mean to kill him.'

He put his hand to his face and felt blood coming from the slash that Marc had given him. It was just a shallow wound, but it had driven him mad with rage. Why had he attacked Marc so fiercely, and why had Marc been so stupid as to throw himself upon Louis, armed only with a dagger, and Louis with a sword? Louis stood gazing foolishly down upon Marc's body, as these thoughts went through his head.

At least, it can be seen that I killed him in self-defence, thought Louis. But then he had a vision of his trial and sentence… sentence to death, death by hanging… and he began to panic. No one must find Marc. He must hide the body. He put down his sword on the ground and began to drag Marc to one side of the path. Heaving with all his might, he pulled him among the bushes and into a small ditch beside the road, partly out of sight.

Then Louis began to feel faint and he sat on a fallen tree trunk, his head in his hands, blood seeping from his wound through his fingers. He realised that it would be obvious to the gardener and the girl that it was he, Louis, who had killed Marc. How could he prove that it was a mistake, that it was self-defence? There was no point in trying to conceal the crime. He could never deny it, he could not hide it! And he began to sob, tears trickling down his face, his fists clenched, pressed against his eyes.

That was why he did not notice three nuns come walking down the path from the nunnery, chatting gaily together. They fell silent when they saw him. He looked up at them before him, and they seemed to waver in the sunlight and then he shut his eyes. He was about to faint.

'This must be the boy that the gardener mentioned to us,' said one of the nuns.

'We were to see that he was not hurt, and send him on to the nunnery,' said another.

'Yes, but he is hurt,' said the third, pointing towards Louis' bloody hand on his face.

'*Poor boy,*' they said in chorus, advancing on him. Louis glanced wildly at them and then he fainted.

'Go back and fetch the gardener,' said the eldest of the three nuns.

'Yes, Sister Marianne,' said the youngest, and scuttled off holding up her habit. A short while after they could hear her voice shouting, 'Martin, Martin!' – calling the gardener to stop.

The remaining two nuns helped Louis to his feet. He stared about him, and then pointed towards the ditch where he had dragged the body of Marc. The nuns followed the direction of his hand, and then one gave a shriek and pulled at the sleeve of the other,

'Sister Frédérique!' she gasped. 'There's a man lying there. I think that he's dead.' Flies were buzzing around Marc's white face, which they could now see clearly.

'Oh, Sister Marianne! Oh, may the Lord forgive you, you have killed him!' she said, turning towards Louis.

Louis nodded hopelessly. 'I killed him. But by mistake. It was a mistake!' he cried. 'See, look here –' he pointed to his face – 'he slashed me with his dagger! When I threatened him with my sword,' (he adjusted the truth a little here), 'he fell upon me wildly. He would have killed me if he could. He almost threw himself upon my sword. I did not mean to push it in him. It's sharp, and it just went in,' he ended lamely.

'But what was the cause of the quarrel?' asked Sister Marianne. 'Why were you fighting?'

This was too much for Louis to explain. 'You had better ask the gardener,' he replied.

'Martin, you mean. What does he know about this?' asked Sister Frédérique.

At this moment they turned to look up the path towards the nunnery, and just turning the corner, only a couple of hundred paces away, was the gardener, with Eloise and Sister Natalie, the youngest of the three nuns.

'Martin, Martin!' shouted Sister Frédérique as they approached. 'This man has killed another man!'

At this Martin let go the bridle and ran towards Louis, Sister Frédérique and Sister Marianne. Eloise and Sister Natalie remained seated on the cart, staring at the bloodstained Louis, Eloise's hand clutching Natalie's arm, and Natalie with her hand clasped over Eloise's hand.

'You foolish boy! What have you done?' shouted Martin. 'Where is he?' he said. 'Ah! Over there…' He marched over to the corpse. 'Yes, he's dead alright!' said Martin grimly, and he sighed deeply.

He had been told by Marie to get the girl to the nunnery as quietly as possible and unnoticed, and hide her in his hut by the forest edge. Now the girl had been seen by these three nuns. He knew them well. Sister Frédérique was a gossip, and the other two not much better. The whole nunnery would know about Eloise within five minutes of their arrival. What should he do? And then there was the corpse. That had to be taken back to Romolue…

What was more, Louis looked as though he was about to faint again. He was certainly no hardened murderer.

'You're going to have to explain this. He was one of Father Drogo's men. You had better have a good story ready,' said Martin to him.

Louis nodded weakly, and sat down upon the log again, tears filling his eyes once more.

'He said that it was not his fault. He said that the dead man attacked him violently, and more or less impaled himself on his sword!' said Sister Frédérique.

'It's true,' said Louis feebly.

'Yes, but why were you quarrelling?' asked Sister Marianne again.

'It wasn't a quarrel,' replied Louis.

'What d'you mean? It looks like a pretty bad quarrel to me!' said Sister Marianne.

Here the gardener broke in. It was no good these nuns trying to get to the bottom of this. Louis would be sure to let out that he was protecting the young girl on the vegetable cart. Then they would want to know why, and then and then… there would be no end of it.

'Orders from the Château of Romolue, from the Countess herself.'

'What?' said Sister Marianne. 'The Countess…?'

'No further questions, good Sisters, please. Dangerous matters are involved here. Matters of the Church…' he knew how to quell these chatterboxes… 'matters of the Church which are far above us, good Sisters, far above us. Do not meddle with them. The Bishop, Father Drogo, these are all matters which are close to their hearts. Ask no more!'

Martin had no idea what he was talking about, though in fact he was closer to the truth than he realised. The three nuns, however, were silenced, and looked downcast at the mention of the Bishop and his ugly brother. There was no love for the Bishop or Father Drogo at the nunnery. The nunnery supported the House of Romolue. The Bishop, and they were sure his brother too, were for the House of Toulouse. If Toulouse were to triumph, then the nunnery would be stripped of its rich income, and the nuns moved elsewhere, while the Bishop took over all the surrounding lands and wealth.

Martin came to a decision. He could not leave the corpse beside the road. That would only cause more questions to be asked, if not by the nuns then by others, such as Drogo. He had no choice but to ask the nuns to accompany Eloise back to the nunnery. He and Louis would have to take the corpse back to Romolue.

'Sisters Marianne, Frédérique, Natalie. Listen carefully to me. This young woman here, this peasant girl, is precious to the heart of the Countess, and the Count. Do not question why. Her life is however threatened, not for any crime that she has committed, for she is entirely innocent of crime. Her life is threatened by, by…' then came inspiration… 'by a plot of Father Drogo.'

The nuns nodded eagerly. They had been sure of it.

'I must ask you to perform the task that the Countess gave to me,' continued Martin, 'for I must return with that corpse to Romolue. It cannot be left here. What was his name, Louis?' asked Martin, calling Louis over.

'I don't know,' mumbled Louis. 'I know that he's worked a short time in the château, a few months. I think he's got a brother there too.'

'Never mind, then; we'll find out soon enough,' said Martin.

Addressing the three nuns again, he said, 'What the Countess asked me to do was to hide the girl away securely. It was to be in my hut at the edge of the forest. But could you smuggle her into the nunnery, d'you think – without being seen? Is there anywhere you could hide her away undetected?'

The nuns looked at each other. Then Sister Frédérique said, 'Yes, I think that we could. Actually it would not be difficult. There's lots of ways in. Round the back, through the barn, yes?'

Sister Natalie turned and smiled at Eloise, who managed a tiny and uncertain grin in return. She had never liked the company of nuns. Dried up crows, she thought they were.

So it was arranged that the three nuns would smuggle Eloise into the nunnery, and hide her – somewhere – they did not say where. Eloise got off the cart, trying to act the part of a peasant girl, looking humbly at the ground, curtseying to the two older nuns.

The sun was now getting low and Martin and Louis hurriedly loaded the corpse of Marc onto the cart, as the women waited a little way off.

'And what about the vegetables?' said Sister Frédérique. 'They'll want to know at the nunnery why you haven't delivered them.'

'Tell them there was an accident on the road,' said Martin. 'Oh – on second thoughts, just tell them the truth. They'll find out soon enough anyway. Say I'll be back first thing tomorrow.'

He would not be back that evening. No one would travel at night, there were too many thieves and cut-throats about.

Eloise stood looking at the wagon. Instead of her sitting among the vegetables was the corpse of some poor youth. Not more than twenty-five years old, she thought.

Mind you, she said to herself, I'm not eating any of those carrots. They're packed right up against the dead chap! Ough!

Eloise had forgotten, as she stared at the cart with the body of Marc, to play the part of a peasant girl. She stood with her chin up and her eyes bright and she noticed that Natalie was staring at her strangely. Quickly, Eloise lowered her gaze to the ground again, did another little curtsey, and began to follow the three nuns as they turned to walk towards the nunnery.

It should have been a pleasant walk on a soft summer day approaching evening, the long rays of the sun playing through the bushes as the branches bent and swayed gently in the warm breeze. The air smelt sweet and butterflies danced about them. But Eloise was frightened, frightened at being separated from her home, from those that she loved, and from her very dearest love, Thomas! Her heart jolted as she thought of Thomas. Her eyes glistened with tears as her troubles gathered around her. When would she see him again? Perhaps never again! She did not know whom she could trust. These three nuns were just common women, of a kind that she had never talked to for more than a few moments in all her life. How long would it be before she betrayed her real self, the noble girl dressed as a peasant? And this *mud*! Now that it had dried, it did not smell quite so bad. But really! How long could she keep up her peasant girl act? How long before every person in the nunnery of Seiche-Capucins knew that Eloise de Narbonne was hiding there. How long before Father Drogo, or the Bishop, maybe, sent armed men to drag her back to the Château de Romolue and put her under lock and key, while they decided her fate? Or worse, took her off to Toulouse to face the Bishop, who would demand to know what she had been plotting with Thomas in the cupboard room… No! That was nonsense. These hateful men just wanted to use her as a pawn in their games of power. They were not frightened of her, but of each other.

They walked on, Eloise silently with her thoughts, Frédérique and Marianne talking of the murder that they had almost witnessed, discussing how much they would tell and what details they should give when they returned to the nunnery. They at least were enjoying the adventure. A murder on their doorstep for them to report, and a girl to hide, for secret reasons. Natalie, though, was quiet, walking close beside Eloise and seeming to understand that something serious was afoot. Eloise was grateful for her silence. Natalie was just a little older than Eloise, in fact. She was eighteen. Eloise cast a quick glance at her. She was a pretty girl, with fair hair, tucked away beneath the black drape of her ugly habit.

All of a sudden, Natalie put out her hand, and touching Eloise's hand, said, 'My dear poor girl, you have been through some terrible things today!'

Ha! thought Eloise. You should have seen me swimming the moat in the middle of the night, then… or cracking Louis over the head with that stick. How did I come to do that? she wondered.

'Tell me,' continued Natalie, as Eloise remained silent, her eyes on the ground, 'what is your name?'

Eloise was prepared for this. Swapping of names was bound to happen soon between two young women, even if one was a nun and the other a peasant's daughter, or supposed to be.

'Veronique,' answered Eloise, trying hard to sound shy.

'Veronique,' said Natalie, 'like the flower. That's pretty. Veronique…' And she gave Eloise's hand a little squeeze.

Eloise could see that Natalie wanted to make a friend of her. It was not, she thought, a good start to a friendship to lie about your name. Like Tommy, she could see that she was moving into a world of lies. But she smiled at Natalie and said, 'And you are Natalie. I heard the others calling you Natalie.'

'Yes,' said Natalie. Then keeping Eloise's hand in hers, she led her a little forward of Marianne and Frédérique and whispered to Eloise, 'We've got to hide you somewhere. I've been thinking. First we'll get you a nun's habit, and wash your face.'

Eloise grimaced and Natalie giggled. 'Don't like washing, is that it? Well, it doesn't look as if you do like washing, that's true.

But nuns can't go around with muddy faces, 'cos you're going to have to pretend to be a nun. Also, you'll never get a nice boy to look at you if you look like that.' Here Natalie paused a moment, and then added, 'Not that you aren't pretty enough, though. You're... well, you're beautiful!' said Natalie admiring Eloise's lovely pale and peachy cheeks, long dark eyelashes and sweet lips.

While Natalie gazed at her, Eloise was feeling amazed to hear Natalie talking about boys. Weren't nuns supposed to be the brides of Christ? What did Natalie know about boys?

Putting these thoughts to one side, Eloise mumbled 'Thank you' to the last compliment and wondered if she should return it. No, she decided. Do not offer any comments of your own. You're a silly, uneducated peasant girl, without manners, who could just as easily blow your nose on the ground as anything. She had seen peasant women do this. She would never have thought of it by herself!

They were only about a quarter of a mile from the nunnery now. Sister Frédérique said that she would go in and get a nun's habit from the washroom. They would just hope that no one would stop and ask her what she was doing, carrying it out of the nunnery. But in fact she was very soon safely back.

'Get behind the bushes,' said Natalie, and now Eloise was glad that Marie had insisted she remove her expensive underclothes and dress more or less properly like a peasant girl might dress. Natalie slipped the habit over Eloise's head and she emerged a nun.

If Thomas could see me now, would he still want to kiss me? thought Eloise. Probably not, she concluded, and she was right in fact. Kissing nuns was definitely taboo, even in the twenty-first century, even nuns as beautiful as Eloise.

'Come now, Veronique,' called Natalie, as Eloise hung back, 'we'll skirt around behind the nunnery. See you in there,' she called to the other two, who waved and walked towards the main door of the nunnery.

'Now if you see someone, don't run or anything. Nuns don't do that sort of thing. Just keep your head bowed down, and don't let them see your face. Just walk on.'

Eloise nodded. They picked their way through some trees and, following a rough path, came rapidly to a barn at the back of the nunnery.

'In through that door,' said Natalie pointing, 'Quick – some people are coming!'

They made a dash for the door. It was just a couple of farm workers, but they must have seen them enter the barn, perhaps just the edge of a habit as it was flicked in through the door. For one of them said to the other, 'Hey, did you see that, Jean?'

'Whaaa?' said Jean.

'Them nuns – busted in that barn. Shall we go in too and see if we can have a bit of fun, then?'

'Whaaa?' said Jean.

'C'mon,' said the other, and walked towards the barn door and pulled it open.

'We know you're in there, lovelies!' he bawled into the dark. But just then, a large porker came running at him, grunting.

'Oh, God!' he yelled, as he was bowled over and the large pig ran out of the barn door. 'Catch him, Jean!' he shouted. 'Damn it, we'll be in trouble if he gets away!' And off they went, chasing after the pig.

'Well,' said Natalie, closing the gate of the pigsty, 'that's got rid of them! A stick up the bum certainly gets a pig going, Veronique, don't you think?' And she giggled. Wisely, Eloise did not attempt to reply.

Out through the barn door at the other side, across a small cobbled courtyard, and they were in the nunnery itself. A faint sound of chanting could be heard in the distance.

'We're in luck,' said Natalie, 'most of the nuns are at prayers.' Eloise was wondering why Natalie was not meant to be there. Natalie read her thoughts.

'Not me, though. I'm only a novice, and no one expects me to take all this stuff very seriously!' She laughed her little infectious gurgling chuckle, and Eloise found she was really taking to this cheerful girl, who seemed only to be dressed as a nun. Underneath she was a proper woman, surely!

'Quick, this way,' said Natalie, and led Eloise down a dark and narrow corridor. I must look out for where I'm going, thought Eloise. I might need to find my way out quickly. But in a moment she was in Natalie's little cell.

149

'There's nowhere for me to hide here,' she whispered doubtfully to Natalie, looking about her.

It was as bare as bare could be! The only light came from a single tiny window in the roof, up high in the heavy stone wall of the nunnery, which was old even in 1599. There was a small roll of bedding on the floor, a crucifix on a simple wooden table, a rough wooden three-legged stool, and an earthenware pot with a few wild flowers in it. Eloise thought of her lovely room in the château, with the rich embroidered bedspread, the heavy velvet curtains, tapestries on the wall, showing hunting scenes, and a Turkish carpet on the floor. For the first time in her life she realised how lucky she was to be a noble girl and not some poor peasant. She had almost never seen how the poor live, and she had never thought about it. She turned to Natalie, put her hand on her arm, and smiled sadly at her.

When all this is over, she thought, I'm going to take Natalie up to my room, and she can come and be my lady's maid!

Again, Natalie looked strangely at Eloise. That look, when Eloise saw her room, it seemed like pity. But surely not... Her room was, well, not a palace. But it was surely more than a dirty little peasant girl was used to! She had seen how the peasants lived, half a dozen crammed into one room; mud and straw on the floor; bare feet. Come to think of it, Veronique had clogs on. How was that? And those slender delicate ankles!

'Veronique,' she said, 'take off your clogs. Let's wash your legs and things and get that mud off!'

'Oh!' replied Eloise, quite startled. 'Oh, very well!' She sat down on the stool and kicked her clogs free.

'My! You haven't been out much in the fields, then!' said Natalie, looking at her plump rounded feet, all smooth.

'No! I was, I mean, I am... a sort of favourite of the Countess really, you see,' replied Eloise, blushing and inventing furiously. 'I only do work in the château,' she mumbled.

Natalie eyed her doubtfully. Was there mud on the floor in the château, then? she thought to herself.

'Well, here's some water. Wash off that mud.' Natalie thrust a bucket of water, that had been standing in the corner, towards her. 'I'll be back in just a moment. I'm going to get you something to eat,' she added, and disappeared out of the door.

Natalie seems to have forgotten all about hiding me, thought Eloise. Suddenly Natalie put her head back around the door.

'Look, there's a couple of horseman turned up. Something about the boy who was killed, I think. They're sure to want to talk to us. You too!'

'Oh, save me, please!' pleaded Eloise. 'They're from Drogo, I'm sure. They'll kill me!' And she sprang up from the stool.

Just then they could hear men's voices in the passageway.

'Where is she, then?' one demanded.

'Down here, with Sister Natalie, perhaps.' It was Sister Frédérique.

'Quick, shut the door!' said Natalie.

'You can't just go in there. It's a nun's cell,' they heard Frédérique telling the men outside.

'I'm washing myself!' shouted Natalie through the door, swishing the water around. 'You'll have to wait while I put my clothes on.'

'Have you got her in there?' asked one of the men.

Natalie did not reply, but moved the table to the centre of the room and gestured to Eloise to put the stool on top.

'Out of the window,' she whispered to Eloise, 'quick!'

'Who's that you're whispering to!' demanded one of the men, and rattled the door.

'How dare you!' shouted Natalie. 'I'm praying!'

'While you wash?' The men laughed. 'Get a move on. Are you that dirty, then?'

Meanwhile, Eloise was up on the table onto the stool and pushing open the tiny window. Natalie grabbed her lower legs and pushed her up. Eloise got her shoulders through, and squeezed her way out onto the roof, just as the men lost patience and burst into the room. Natalie seized a leg of the stool and swung it at the first man as he came through the door. She hit him hard, square in the stomach.

'Damn you to hell!' he cried, clutching himself.

'Teach you to come rushing into my room!' yelled Natalie.

'What language is this?' demanded a voice from down the corridor.

It was the Abbess, a large lady, with tiny twinkling eyes, but a fierce temper when roused. And she was roused now. She bustled in to Natalie's room.

'Out of the building, you two,' she commanded, 'or I'll have you whipped!'

The two men had of course been sent by Drogo, when Marc did not return, to get hold of Eloise and bring her back from the nunnery. They had their orders. Brute force if necessary, Father Drogo had told them.

'Drag her out if you have to. She'll be delivered to the Bishop tomorrow, but we'll keep her under lock and key tonight.'

The question for the two men was, what did they fear more, Father Drogo's anger or a whipping at the nunnery? Anyway, the girl was not here. Natalie was alone in the room.

'Out, I said!' shouted the Abbess, 'Call the guards!'

Frédérique ran off to fetch them.

'Look, Ma'am,' said one of the men, 'we were told to come and fetch a girl here. We mustn't leave without her! Father Drogo will have us whipped too. Either way we're going to be whipped,' he added mournfully.

'Don't be a fool, man,' replied the Abbess. 'There's no girl here. Can't you see that?'

At that moment the Abbess's eye fell upon the clogs. Ah! she thought. Something's going on. I'll find out when we've got rid of these oafs.

'Come on, then,' said one man to the other, 'let's clear out of here. We're not going to find the girl like this!'

Turning to the Abbess, he added, 'I don't think Father Drogo will give up looking for her – the girl, I mean. I'm sure you've not seen the last of us.' And with that they strode off down the corridor, into the courtyard and rode away back to Romolue.

Eloise, meanwhile, was crouched on the roof. She saw them ride away in the twilight and breathed a sigh of relief. But did she dare come down? The Abbess was in Natalie's room still. She could hear their conversation.

'They were coming about the boy who was murdered, I thought,' said Natalie.

'What boy? Murdered? Where?'

Frédérique came running up, panting. 'The guards were having a nap, Ma'am. But they're coming now!'

'Tell them that the danger has passed. But I want them here in a few minutes. I think that we may well have another visit later on this night.'

'Now tell me,' the Abbess went on, 'what murdered boy are you talking about? No, wait a moment. Tell me after. First, what are those clogs doing here?'

Eloise's heart sank when she heard this. Her clogs! If she was found, the Abbess would recognise her straightaway. But then, what would it matter? Drogo seemed to know that she was here anyway. Better maybe to ask for the protection of the Abbess.

'Er... um... those clogs, you mean,' she heard Natalie saying.

'What other clogs?' replied the Abbess, beginning to lose patience. 'Whose clogs are they?' she repeated.

'Well, I... er... found...' Natalie began.

That settled it. Before Natalie could wade deeper into trouble, Eloise put her head through the window above the Abbess' head and said, 'Abbess!' At this the Abbess gave a cry of surprise, and her arms shot up as if to defend herself against some devilish vision.

'*Eloise!*' she shouted. 'What are—?'

'No – not Eloise,' interrupted Natalie. 'That's Veronique, good Mother.'

The Abbess could see it in a flash. Of course, Drogo was trying to kidnap Eloise. This did not surprise her so very much. He was a villain. Eloise had come to the nunnery secretly, in some sort of disguise, calling herself Veronique. Yes, of course. Best keep up the game.

'Oh! I got such a shock, I thought that it was someone else,' she said. 'Veronique, come down from the roof this instant. Natalie, you will go to the chapel and say one hundred Hail Marys for the lie that you were about to tell – to me, your mother Abbess!'

'Yes, Mother,' said Natalie, her cheeks reddening and her eyes on the ground. She did not like to be told off in front of this little peasant girl! But she went out of the room obediently.

The Abbess needed to talk alone to Eloise, and that was the

best way of getting rid of Natalie. The Abbess shut the door of Natalie's room as Eloise let herself down, jumping onto the table, with a crash.

'Careful! I should have helped you. I'm sorry,' said the Abbess.

'Oh! It's me who's sorry,' replied Eloise. 'I've brought troubles to the nunnery.' She explained how the Countess and Marie had sent her here. She did not mention Tommy, though.

'But why?' asked the Abbess. 'Why is Drogo suddenly after you now? After all these years...' she half muttered to herself.

'After all what years?' asked Eloise

'No, nothing, my dear,' said the Abbess.

Eloise had to confide in someone. She had always liked the Abbess, even if she did have a short temper.

'Well,' began Eloise, 'it's like this, you see.'

And she began to tell the whole story of what happened with Thomas. Except the bit with the scar, and of course about falling in love, and kissing and all that. She could hardly tell the Abbess that! But then she got into a problem. How could she explain arranging to meet Thomas at midnight? Well, she just said that Thomas had seemed so unlike himself, yes, that was it, quite unlike himself!

The Abbess tut-tutted a lot, just as Marie did when Tommy was telling her the same story, but just like Marie, you could tell from the twinkle in her eye – she could not suppress it – you could tell that she thought that Eloise was a brave girl. The thwack on the head which that guard got! They were at that bit now. Suddenly Eloise broke off and said, 'It was the same man, that guard I mean, who killed the other one today!'

'What?' said the Abbess. 'Natalie said something about a murder. Do you know anything about it?'

'Can I finish what happened in the château? It's all connected together, you see.'

The Abbess nodded and Eloise went on to tell how she had been smuggled out of the château by the gardener on his cart. Then Eloise paused. For something was still troubling her very much.

'You know when I said Thomas did not seem himself, Mother, well, I mean it really. He does not. Mother, I know this sounds really strange, but I don't think he is Thomas! No, he's not!'

'Eh?' said the Abbess.

And Eloise began to sob.

'He's not Thomas, he's not,' repeated Eloise, and tears began to stream down her cheeks.

'What nonsense!' said the Abbess, and reached over and took Eloise gently by the arm. 'What nonsense,' she repeated.

Nine: Hot Pursuit

ather Drogo had been carried unconscious to his room and laid on his bed. Marie and several of the servants gathered around, staring at the grey and mottled face of the good Father. There was a bandage wound around his head. This covered the gash on his forehead, where he had struck the altar as he had collapsed at the sight of the head of Christ dangling from the crucifix.

Confused thoughts passed through Drogo's mind. *The crucifix with which he had killed Eleonora. He had killed Eleonora!* It seemed to Drogo that this crime – his crime – it seemed that he had done it just a few moments ago, that he had thrown himself before the altar in the cathedral of Toulouse just a few moments before; that he had been shaken back to consciousness by his brother within the last few seconds.

Father Drogo lay stretched out on his bed and began to mumble words that no one could understand. Suddenly, he raised himself up a little, looked wildly about him, fell back once more and began to mumble again. Marie stood ready with a very potent medicine, a sleeping draught that should knock him out well and truly, she had told the Countess.

'The longer that we keep him unconscious, the longer that we will be safe, or at least Thomas and Eloise will be,' Marie had said, and the Countess had only smiled grimly in reply.

'Give me a hand to hold him up a bit,' Marie asked two of the footmen, seeing that Father Drogo seemed to be coming slowly round.

They bent down to the priest but Father Drogo opened his eyes as they approached and glared at them, baring his yellow teeth. They flinched and drew back.

'Good Father,' said Marie, 'please take this medicine that I have prepared for you. You collapsed before the altar and you have hurt your head, poor man!'

She motioned to the footmen to try again. This time they managed to get their arms around Drogo and lift him to a nearly sitting position. Marie quickly came with the flask and held it to Drogo's lips.

'*No!*' he shouted, but as he opened his mouth Marie managed to pour in a good deal. Drogo spluttered and coughed and Marie poured a bit more in.

'Hold him up, more!' she ordered the footmen, and as Drogo opened his mouth and tried to shout 'No!' once again, Marie managed to tip the rest of the draught down his throat.

'There,' she said, 'that'll make you feel ever so much better!'

And the footmen let him down gently onto the bed again. A few moments passed and already Drogo seemed to be settling. Quite soon his eyelids flickered closed. He was in a deep sleep.

Marie placed a guard outside Drogo's room, with strict orders that no one should enter. But when the two horsemen returned empty-handed from the nunnery of Seiche-Capucins, they came straight into the château and fearfully made their way to Drogo's door to report their news. Passing through Romolue, they also learnt that Marc, whom they knew was one of Drogo's men in the château, had been killed in a fight with Louis. So they came with this bad news also.

'We've got to see Father Drogo, my man, it's important,' one of them roughly addressed the guard.

'Strict orders, I'm afraid. You can't go in!'

'We must!' The speaker advanced threateningly towards the door.

'No,' said the guard, and barred the way with his pike.

The horsemen put their hands to their swords and the guard brought his heavy pike crashing down on the head of the nearest, who collapsed on the floor before him. The other fled out of the château, jumped on his horse, which was tethered nearby, and rode away. Within an hour he had reported to the Bishop that his brother was held prisoner in his room in the Château de Romolue, and that they had been attacked by men guarding the door.

Just moments after the fight between the guard and the two horsemen was over, Tommy turned into the corridor, and saw the guard bending over the unconscious horseman.

'Monsieur Thomas,' said the guard, 'I was attacked by these

two men.' He gestured towards the man on the floor and, pointing out of the window, said, 'There's the other fellow, making his escape. They tried to break into Drogo's room. They said that they wanted to talk urgently with him. They didn't make it, though! Shall we lock this one up in the guardroom?'

'Yeah!' said Tommy, 'and tie him up a bit too. He looks like a tough fellow! Take his sword off him.'

Other guards were arriving now. They had heard the noise of the fight. Among them hobbled Jacques. As he came up to Tommy, he slipped the mobile into Tommy's hand. 'Fully charged, Monsieur,' he whispered, and then turned rapidly away.

The guards picked up the man from the floor and dragged him along the corridor, the group quite blocking the passage. Somehow Jacques had managed to get the far side of them and Tommy could not follow him. Again he had escaped!

Tommy had been hunting everywhere for the Countess when he had come across the guard outside Drogo's door. He had the parchment, the confession of Drogo's crimes, stuffed down his tights, and he dearly wanted the Countess to read it. He'd asked the Countess to hide the crucifix in some secret place. So no doubt that was what she was doing. Ah! Perhaps the secret place was in that little room where they had had the conference before, the little padded soundproofed room? Tommy rushed up the stairs, two at a time, and bounded along the corridor, but then, to his surprise, when he reached the top floor of the château, he could see the Countess walking over the bridge, coming back from the geometrical garden, the fateful garden where all this strange story had started.

Tommy whipped around, rushed down the stairs, turned right into the salon, out of the French windows and met the Countess almost as she was coming in at the same place.

'Oh, Countess, Mother!' said Tommy, out of breath. 'Where is the crucifix?' Before the Countess could answer, he continued, 'I've got something that I need to show you. It's the secret. You were right. It's the secret of Drogo. The parchment.'

The Countess looked worriedly around, and put her finger to her lips. 'You found it? Good heavens! No one must hear this!' she whispered.

'No! of course not. I was just so… Well, anyway, tell me where have you put the crucifix?'

'You know the stone bench in the garden, the one with *Et in arcadia*?'

'Yes, yes,' said Tommy, impatiently. He knew it only too well. 'That's where I first arrived here.' Ignoring the odd look that he received from the Countess, he went on, 'Have you hidden it there? How could you do that, I mean…?'

'Well, yes,' replied the Countess, interrupting him, 'there's a secret compartment in that bench that only the Count and I know about. I'll show it to you.'

'Right,' said Tommy, 'but not just yet. It's more important you see the parchment. Let's go to the secret room and you can read it there.'

He took the Countess's arm and practically dragged her up the stairs. He could hardly contain himself from telling her that Drogo had killed Eleonora, but somehow they managed to get into the little padded room, doubly locked it, and sat down before he started to say anything.

'Look, before I show you this, it's going to be a horrible shock for you. So be prepared.' At that he pulled the parchment from out of his tights and handed it to the Countess.

'Written the 15th August, in the year 1585, at the command of my brother, Henri de Montfort, secretary to the Cardinal of Ferrara, Piero Vincenzo di Colonna, at the Palace of the Vatican, Rome, in my brother's apartments.

'Signed, Drogo de Montfort.'

The Countess read the text out loud at first, and then continued silently. Tommy watched her face intently. She is a beautiful woman too, he thought.

He could see flickers of emotion cross the Countess's face as she began to read. Apprehension of some horror to come, disgust and rising hatred showed themselves, and once even a slight grin as she read of Drogo's self-portrait: '… a misshapen scarecrow… long, thin and none-too-straight nose.' The Countess became more and more absorbed as she read of the deeper and deeper obsession which had gripped the priest, his obsession with her poor, beautiful sister.

Tommy turned away. He could feel the pain and anger that was filling the little room. The space seemed too small to contain it. He felt that they would be crushed by the power of the words which the Countess was reading. The Countess had come to the part where Drogo had sat with Eleonora on the couch in the library and had read that book together. The Countess looked up for a moment, her lips apart, thinking. She remembered the book. She remembered Eleonora's sweet lilting voice describing some of the strange pictures. The memory of the voice was so strong, that sweet voice, that tears came into her sister's eyes, tears of sorrow.

Soon there will be tears of rage, thought Tommy, looking up at her from where he sat on a low stool at the Countess's feet. The Countess read on in silence. Tommy watched her eyes moving over the words, sucking up their terrible meaning, as she read further.

'My God!' she suddenly cried. 'It was Drogo that destroyed the happiness of Eleonora, it was Drogo who forced Richard out of her life! The devil! It was Drogo who killed the messengers with the ransom. It's Drogo's fault that Eleonora and Richard, and Eloise, are not together now!'

She rose to her feet, grasping the manuscript in one hand as if she wanted to tear it in pieces. Tommy took her arm, but she shook him off furiously. She read on: 'This shows that I am a fair man!' she read aloud, raising her voice almost to a shout. 'The devil!' she repeated. 'He will suffer for this! He will suffer!'

Shaking with fury, she took a few paces around the room, looking from the manuscript to Tommy and back again. 'A fair man!' she said again.

Regaining some control, she sat down. Now comes the worst part, thought Tommy. The Countess sat stiff and erect in her chair, the muscles of her face taut with rising tension, and again the words of the parchment seemed about to burst the walls of the room apart. Suddenly she was there…

'I know I killed her with it,' she hissed. 'Killed her with it…' she repeated.

She rose again, and Tommy stood also and gripped the Countess's shoulders with both hands. He was not to be shaken off this time, but held her tightly, and after a moment of agony, she collapsed sobbing into his arms, shaking her head back and forth in sorrow at learning the true fate of her beloved sister.

'*Eleonora, Eleonora*,' she whispered. 'I was holding this wretched crucifix just now. I would have smashed it to pieces if I had known what it was. Oh! Thomas, how could you have given me that vile thing?' And she burst into tears once more, sobbing on Tommy's shoulder.

'We will destroy him,' Tommy said. 'We will destroy him utterly!' He held the Countess against him as her sobbing began slowly to subside.

'How could you give me it?' she repeated. 'How could you, knowing that Drogo had... had...' She couldn't bring herself to say the words.

'Countess, forgive me, please! But the crucifix will be part of our revenge. You were the person there to take it, to hide it until we can work out what we should do. With the parchment, with the crucifix, with everything. Look, you have read it, you know the worst. But did you read to the very end? Did you see the note added at the bottom?'

Tommy drew the parchment out of the Countess's hands and, pointing to very bottom of the page, read, 'The child grows so like her mother, that I may have to kill her too.'

The Countess snatched the parchment back from Tommy and stared horrified at this dreadful sentence. 'He's mad,' she whispered.

'Yes, he is,' said Tommy. 'In my time, he would be in a prison for insane criminals. But what this means is that Eloise is in real danger now, much more than we thought. It's not enough that she was sent to the nunnery of Seiche-Capucins. There's little safety there from an armed attack by the sort of people that Drogo can easily enough find. So first, I think, before we start to plan how to use this damning evidence against Drogo, let's make sure that he cannot reach Eloise. What should we do?' Tommy paused a moment, biting his lip, and then continued. 'I'm certainly going to go and see what's happening there, at the nunnery. Now that you've seen the parchment, I'm going to ride there straightaway. Eloise has to know the danger she is in.'

'Yes,' said the Countess, 'you're right. We've got to protect

Eloise from this vile devil! Thank God that he is lying unconscious in bed. Marie was right when she said that the longer he sleeps the longer you and Eloise will be safe! That sleeping draught should keep him in bed for many hours.'

'Fine,' said Tommy, 'but where shall we keep the manuscript? I forgot to tell you something important – how I came to find the manuscript.' Tommy began to tell the Countess about his frantic search, finding the key and eventually by chance that the manuscript was hidden inside the crucifix.

'The key I have replaced. So if Drogo goes back to the chapel to look to see if his secret has been discovered, he will be tricked into believing that it has not. However, he will certainly want the crucifix back. He's going to be asking where it is. I suppose you could say that it has been sent to be mended.'

'First, let's think about this parchment,' answered the Countess. 'I'll keep it where neither Drogo, nor anyone else, would dare to be found searching.' Here she dropped her voice to a whisper. 'With my jewels locked in the great metal-bound trunk in my bedroom. Now, if you want it – the parchment, I mean – and I cannot be found, the key for the trunk is in my boudoir, you know, the little room,' Tommy nodded. 'The little room off my bedroom where all my powders and creams and so on are. Beneath the pot.' (Ah! said Tommy to himself). 'In there, is a small loose flagstone in the middle of the floor. That's where the key is kept. Under that. Now, you are the only one in the château besides me who knows. Even the Count doesn't know where it's hidden.'

'What about the crucifix, though?'

'I'll think about that later. You had better be off as quick as you can to the nunnery. Take your sword. Be careful. You may not be my son, but...'

Tommy kissed her on the cheek. He left the room as the Countess rolled up the parchment and put it in the bosom of her dress. She looked both very sad and very determined. Yes, thought Tommy, Drogo will suffer, he will suffer miserably – I hope, he added.

Quickly leaving the château, Tommy ran to the stables, called his groom to saddle his horse, and within a few minutes he was off on Penelope. She was a thickset beast, thought Tommy, no racehorse in her. P'raps there were none in those days – these days – those days. Drawing on Thomas's store of memory, he certainly couldn't think of having seen anything like a real racehorse. He cantered along the path towards Romolue. Not too fast. He didn't want Penelope lame.

It was dark, but the moon had come up, throwing everything into very sharp shadow – like last night, thought Tommy. How long have I been here? I came on Saturday to Ellie-la-Forêt, not much more than a couple of days, and already I've... Penelope shook her head and snorted, and Tommy's thoughts were interrupted by a distant thundering sound. It was the hooves of many horses! He'd heard it before at point-to-point race meetings that he'd been at with his Dad. He'd won quite a bit one day. Concentrate! The sounds were getting louder! Tommy rode off the path and into the trees, dismounted and led Penelope deep into the shadows of the wood.

It was just in time, for thundering down the path towards the château came fifteen heavily armed riders, and at their head the Bishop himself! Each of the men wore a surcoat with the arms of de Montfort woven into them, red and white diamonds in the form of a shield. Among these fifteen fighting men, Tommy could see a rider more plainly dressed. This must be the man whom Tommy saw escaping and galloping away from the château a while ago, he realised. He must have gone straight to the Bishop and told him that Drogo was imprisoned in the château, in his room, with a guard at the door. That's what brought the Bishop on them like this. Well, there was little he could do about it.

One thing was clear. When the Bishop and his men heard from Drogo that Eloise had fled to the nunnery of Seiche-Capucins, they would be there in no time. With a bit of luck, Drogo would be too drugged to tell the Bishop much. But Tommy was sure that this simple piece of information would be passed from Drogo to his brother. He had to get to the nunnery to warn Eloise, the Abbess and everyone about the danger they were in. He began to get Penelope into a gallop. He would have to escape with Eloise. Where, in this foreign land? Why, yes, of course. He would make for where they least would expect to find him: back to the Château of Romolue. There they could hide Eloise away. Not behind his bed, perhaps. But with the help of the Countess and Marie, they'd find a place. Marie's room itself, maybe?

'Halt! Who's riding so fast, so late?' called a voice, for Tommy had just entered the boundaries of the village of Romolue. All the villages had guards posted, of course. There were many robbers, roaming in bands around the countryside. They had been known to attack a village and steal everything that they could lay their hands on, burning the peasants' huts to the ground. The guard had a horn, ready to raise to his lips. One blast on this and the village militia would instantly be out to defend their families and their homes. Tommy reined in his horse.

'My good man,' said Tommy, 'it is Thomas de Romolue whom you are speaking to!'

'Forgive me, sir,' replied the peasant guard, 'I did not recognise you in the moonlight. Please ride on, sir.'

Once out of the village, Tommy turned along the narrow road where Louis and Marc had fought to the death earlier that day. The moonlight made strange shadows of the bushes across the path. It was silent and lonely, with only the croak of a frog or the call of an owl, the creak of a branch to know that you were not alone on the Earth. The sound of Penelope's hooves on the hard ground was magnified by the silent world around. Tommy imagined that he could feel the cold rays of the moon beating down on him as if it were the midday sun. But instead of warming you, the rays of the moon made you feel colder. He shuddered slightly at the thought.

Now look, he said to himself, forget that! I'd better think a bit. How am I to get inside the nunnery so late at night? How can I find Eloise and get her out of the nunnery before the Bishop's men appear? I'm sure that they will soon be on top of me. How can I return to the Château of Romolue with Eloise, undetected? Thomas, the real Thomas, had only visited the nunnery briefly, once or twice, about two years ago being the last time, and so

Tommy had little knowledge of the place to draw on. He would have to play it as it came. Anyway, he was very excited about seeing Eloise again. He had not seen her since that morning. He imagined her beautiful face. Her lovely long dark eyelashes, her...

Crack! An arrow thwanged into a tree beside him, and a man emerged on horseback from the shadows. Fool that I am, thought Tommy, of course the nunnery has posted guards. There I was, dreaming of Eloise. Anyway, if they've put guards out, they must know that something is up! Good. They're already partly ready for the Bishop.

'Thank you, my man, for shooting wide,' said Tommy.

'Your name!' snapped the guard, ignoring Tommy's comment.

'Thomas de Romolue,' replied Tommy.

'Oh my God!' replied the guard, 'thank the Lord that I am a bad shot!' He drew nearer to Tommy. 'I'm sorry, sir.'

'You did not recognise me in the moonlight,' said Tommy. 'It's alright, you're not the first.'

'But may I ask why you are here?'

'Yes. I am pretty sure that the Bishop and fifteen heavily armed fighting men will be galloping up this path in the next half an hour or so. You must be prepared to receive them, however best you can. But I must get into the nunnery and rescue a young girl whom they are out to kidnap.'

'But there's nothing but nuns in there,' said the guard, wondering what the meaning of this was. The Bishop and fifteen armed men! 'Have you seen the Bishop and his men?'

'Yes,' replied Tommy, 'down beyond Romolue. They'll go to the château first and then, from there, on to here. I think that the best thing is that I wake up the Abbess. She'll know where Eloise is – or she can find out, surely!'

'Eloise de Narbonne, my Lord?' asked the guard.

'Yes, have you seen her here?'

'No, my Lord, but why should the Bishop want to kidnap her?'

Tommy was beginning to lose patience. 'Look, there's no time for talking. You have a fight on your hands very soon. Get your commander and get organised. First, follow me and let me into the nunnery to the Abbess.'

And with that, Tommy galloped off towards the nunnery, followed by the guard. At the main gate, there stood another guard.

'It's Thomas de Romolue, let us through!' shouted the first guard as they galloped up, and the gate swung open.

'The Abbess's rooms are over here,' said the guard, turning to the left. Tommy followed.

The guard jumped from his horse and banged loudly on the heavy oak door of the ancient building in front of him.

'Are they come, then?' They could the hear the Abbess calling from within, and the door opened an inch, held back by a chain.

'Not yet, Mother,' replied the guard, 'but Thomas de Romolue is here, with news.'

Thomas interrupted him. 'Good Mother Abbess, I am sorry to come like this. But I am sure that within a short time you will be visited by the Bishop at the head of fifteen heavily armed men.'

'Thomas! How is it you are here with this news? Could they find no other messenger from the Château de Romolue?'

'Good Mother, I come on a very special mission. First to warn you about the Bishop and his men. But also to tell you that they come to kidnap Eloise de Narbonne, who is hiding here. D'you know she's here?'

'Why, yes, I do,' said the Abbess. 'Come in, come in.'

'We have no time to spare,' replied Thomas. 'Where is she?'

'Asleep in the cell of Sister Natalie. You cannot wake her now!'

'Good Abbess, if I do not wake her, then the Bishop's men will wake her and carry her off!'

'It's true. Yes. Two men came earlier on today to try and take her away already. That's why we were expecting another attempt tonight. That's why guards are posted.'

'Take me to her, please,' said Tommy.

The Abbess came out of the door and as fast as her legs could carry her, panting as she went, led the way across the courtyard into the long low building where the young novice nuns lived. Passing along the narrow corridor, the Abbess counted the doors, 11, 12, 13, 14; yes, this was it. She rapped sharply on the door. A sleepy noise could be heard inside.

'Veronique, get your clothes on!' called the Abbess loudly through the door. 'As fast as you can.'

The Abbess knocked on the door again.

Scuffling noises could be heard, and a voice called, 'We're getting ready, Mother.' It was Natalie.

Tommy was getting very impatient. The Bishop and his men would be here at any moment.

'Eloise!' he called. 'It's me – Tommy!'

'Tommy!' called Eloise's voice through the door.

'The Bishop's men are coming to kidnap you. Come on out as fast as you can!'

The Abbess was rousing all the nuns in the nunnery.

'All into the abbey to pray,' she shouted.

And there was scuttling and shoving in all directions as nuns, half dressed, ran out of their dormitories and towards the abbey.

The door of Natalie's room burst open and Eloise came rushing out into Tommy's arms, dressed as a nun. The Abbess was too busy to notice this unseemly behaviour.

'Lead us to the barn, and we'll go out the back way, that way where we came in,' said Eloise to Natalie.

Natalie nodded. What was a peasant girl like Veronique doing falling into the arms of the heir to the house of Romolue? she wondered. Anyway, she led the way racing along the narrow passage, out of the door, across the cobbled yard and into the door of the barn.

Just then there was an uproar at the gates of nunnery, the sounds of angry voices roaring orders.

'Admit the passage of my men!' the Bishop was yelling.

This was followed by the sound of the main door slamming loudly, and bolts being forced across.

'You'll pay for this!' cried the Bishop. 'Round the back and enter that way, then,' he called, and they could hear the thunder of hooves around the nunnery, making for the barn – just where Tommy and Eloise had planned to leave!

'Post guards around the back!' shouted the commander of the guards of the nunnery, but already two of the Bishop's men were rattling at the barn door.

'Go, Natalie, go!' said Eloise urgently. 'I am not Veronique. I am Eloise de Narbonne. One day you will be my lady's maid. Go to the abbey and pray for me and Tommy. Go now!'

But Natalie, instead of running off, lifted her habit over her head, and thrusting it into Tommy's arms, said, 'Put this on. In the dark, you will look like a nun. I'll get my spare one from my cell.'

Tommy and Eloise ran into the darkest corner of the barn. Eloise pulled the habit over Tommy's head, and indeed he could pass for a nun, especially if he put the bonnet up – which Eloise did, and kissed him as she did it. There was a lot of last year's hay in the barn, lying in loose bundles. Tommy and Eloise burrowed into this and lay still. The two men at the barn door had been joined by others, and the door would surely give under the weight of so many of the Bishop's men. And suddenly it flew open, and they stumbled in, looking around in the darkness.

'All the nuns are praying in the abbey,' came the sound of the Bishop's voice.

'Ha! There's one who isn't – a pretty one too,' came the cry of one soldier. He was already out through the barn at the other side and was running towards the novices' rooms.

'You let me go! You devil!' came Natalie's voice.

'Leave her now!' came the Bishop's command. 'Find Eloise first. Whoever finds Eloise has the pick of the nuns, I promise you that!'

'Should we search the barn?' asked the soldier, returning from releasing Natalie.

'No, Jean,' said the Bishop. 'Eloise is most likely in the Abbess's rooms.'

Tommy and Eloise breathed a great sigh of relief. All the guards went out of the barn and there was silence for a moment.

'What should we do?' whispered Eloise.

'We ought to get out straightaway,' said Tommy, 'before they come back and really do search the barn.'

Just that moment, a guard came back inside. It was the same one who had just grabbed hold of Nathalie. He reckoned that it was worth a quick look in the barn, anyway. He began to prod around in the loose straw with his sword, moving slowly towards where Tommy and Eloise were hiding. Tommy and Eloise could hear him muttering to himself...

'I really fancy that blond one I got my hands on just now. If I can find this Eloise, p'raps...' Just then he stuck his sword deep into something soft, which gave an almighty squeal, grunt and snort, rose up and charged with all its might into the unfortunate man. He had spiked the porker, and it was in a rage. It jumped and stamped on him, and since it was the prize porker of the nunnery and weighed 300 pounds, the poor boy's ribs were crushed and bruised and he was lucky to escape alive. He backed against a wall, and the porker charged again, swerving neatly as he attempted to sidestep, and catching him a tremendous thump on his backside. This sent him sprawling and tripping out of the door into the cobbled courtyard, cursing and calling on God's mercy.

Tommy and Eloise saw their chance.

'Thank God for angry pigs,' said Eloise. 'That's the second time today that they've done us a favour!'

Tommy had no time to ask about the first time, for they were off running for the woods, two nuns, hand in hand, covered in bits of straw.

'No, stop!' whispered Tommy. 'We're nuns, remember!' He let go of Eloise's hand. 'While we're near the nunnery, we'll try and behave like nuns. No kissing me now!' And they giggled, despite the danger.

'Keep your face well hidden, and brush some of that straw off,' said Eloise, and they walked on in silence, looking at the ground and keeping in the shadow of the trees, away from the bright moonlight.

Ten: Cave of Demons

ho are these two lovelies, then?' said a rough voice. A heavily armed figure, wearing the red and white diamonds of de Montfort, walked from behind a tree, where he had been standing relieving himself.

'You heard the Bishop, your master,' said Eloise. 'You must not touch us!'

'I didn't hear anything like that. Cor, you're a beauty, and no mistaking it!' he said, catching a quick glimpse of Eloise's face in the moonlight.

Tommy drew his sword under the nun's habit. The man came closer, and putting his hand under Eloise's chin, he held her face up. That was the last action that he ever performed, for at that instant, Tommy plunged his sword into the man's heart. He dropped to the ground with barely a sound.

'Quick, this way,' said Tommy leading Eloise into the darkness of the trees.

He was shaking. He did not know that he could do such a thing as kill someone, in cold blood, like that. Eloise too was gasping with fright, whether at the danger which they had just been in or at the terrible deed which Tommy had done to protect her, she was not sure.

In the shadow of the trees, Tommy stood with his head bowed, looking at the ground, resting on his sword, his heart still beating as though it would burst from his body. He could not get quickly enough back into the twenty-first century, where he did not murder people to protect his girlfriend from being abused. Eloise stood beside him, feeling the weight of his thoughts bowing her down as well.

But they could only rest for a moment. Tommy put his sword back in its sheath beneath the nun's habit. It would not be long before the man's body was found, and the Bishop's soldiers would surely work out that Eloise had escaped. They must make the greatest distance that they could, and go in the most unlikely direction, where they would not be followed.

'This way,' said Tommy.

Some memory was aroused in him, some memory from Thomas. They moved as silently as they were able, but there was constant danger of detection. They cast flitting shadows as they moved from shade to moonlight to shade again. When guards emerged from the abbey, they would be spotted easily. They must get further away.

The ground began to descend. Ah! That was it. Once when I was very small, I came here, and the Bishop, yes, the Bishop, walked with me here in this little gully, thinking that a child would like the place. Probably he had been here as a child too. They were moving still lower. Now they were out of direct sight of the abbey.

But anyone standing on the roof of the abbey might still see us, thought Tommy.

'Keep down,' he whispered, 'we're far from safety yet.'

There was a sudden shout behind them. The body had been found. So soon!

'Quickly, this way!' said Tommy. They could hear the sound of several men crashing through the woods behind them. 'I remember, there's a cave here somewhere...'

They stumbled on. The voices seemed to be getting closer.

'*Fan out!*' Tommy could hear the Bishop's voice shouting in the distance.

They found a small path and a little stream. Following it, they moved deeper into the gully, the sides becoming steeper. They could easily be caught here, thought Tommy. Too late to find another path. Then just to one side of them opened the mouth of the cave that Tommy remembered. He also suddenly could remember that, if you crept along the cave far enough, there was another small hole in the roof where you could climb out! That was what was driving him in this direction. Otherwise, the cave was a deadly trap.

'In here,' whispered Tommy to Eloise.

'But...'

'There's another way out,' Tommy said to her, and she nodded vigorously, following him into the pitch dark mouth of the cave.

They waited just one or two seconds to let their eyes adjust. They could wait no longer, for the voices were very close now. The soldiers were gaining on them fast, with no need to move silently, and were slashing their way through the undergrowth, using their swords to clear a path. But Tommy and Eloise were not seen. Their black habits in the blackness of the cave were quite invisible. They moved as fast as they dared, feeling their way along the walls. A stream ran noisily along the bottom of the cave. This was lucky, because the slightest sound that they made was greatly magnified by the echo of the cave.

The cave went slightly upwards, becoming narrower. They could not see where the roof lay, but Tommy remembered that it was a large cave, high enough easily to stand in. But he simply could not remember how it was that he had been in this cave... The Countess may know. They could see nothing, not a tiniest spark of light entered their eyes. Tommy groped out his hand to Eloise. She grasped it firmly. In such blackness, you could lose all sense of where you were, and Tommy had begun to feel that he was floating off the ground. This contact brought him back to reality. He stopped for a moment, and Eloise put her head close to his. Just the feel of her breath on his cheek revived his courage. He rubbed his nose gently against her face, and felt her mouth against his cheek, planting a tiny kiss. A little pressure from her body said 'move on'.

They could hear the voices of the soldiers, the words obscured by the echoes. They could not make out what the shouts were saying. Would they attempt to follow them in here? The noise of their pursuers seemed at last to be fading. Perhaps they could escape now, if only they could make their way safely and find the way out. Let's hope that the Bishop does not know of the other exit to this cave, thought Tommy.

They moved more and more slowly now, for fear of falling into a chasm, or just a small hole. Even a twisted ankle at this stage would be a disaster. They kept well to the side of the cave, passing their hands over the clammy walls. All at once, they were startled by a few tiny shrieks and the flapping of wings. Bats! The bats might give them away. But fortunately the bats settled again. As they pushed farther and farther into the cave, they could feel that the space around them was getting narrower and lower. Water began to drip from the ceiling, turning into a slow trickle. They were becoming completely soaked, and the cave was cold. Both began to shiver. Tommy slipped on some loose stones and fell on his backside, dislodging pebbles, which rolled and splashed into the stream which still ran in the centre of the cave.

'Alright, Tommy?' whispered Eloise, the first words that they had dared to say since they had entered the cave.

'Yes,' said Tommy. 'I've torn my habit a bit. It caught on the wall as I fell over. Mind – there's a slippery muddy bit just here.'

The depth of blackness was becoming very oppressive. They could feel their eyes pulling and stretching to see just one little glimmer of light. But there was none. They took each other's hands again. Tommy's head had begun to swim. He leant very gently against Eloise, and they stood just feeling each other's presence, trying to overcome the darkness around them. Suddenly Tommy felt a new sense of strength. Was that just a tiny movement in the air, from in front of them? Could that come from the exit of the cave? The thought drove him on, and he squeezed Eloise's hand.

'Did you feel that breath of air?' he whispered to Eloise.

She did not answer at first, but then she said, 'The cave is getting quite a lot smaller.'

Tommy put his hand up and he could feel the roof coming sharply down. After a few more steps they had to crouch, to pass an overhanging rock, which Tommy felt with one arm outstretched in front of him. Several more rocks jutted from the ceiling, and they had to squeeze between them after a couple more paces.

'I hope that there is only one way,' said Tommy. 'If the cave branches, we could simply walk past a larger branch and go down a dead end.'

'Yes, I was thinking the same thing,' said Eloise. She stopped a moment, and felt on the ground for some larger rocks.

'I'm going to arrange these in a little pile here,' she said. 'So if we are forced to come back this way, we will know where we are. At least, we'll have some idea.'

'That's a good plan,' said Tommy. He picked up a large stone and feeling his way, placed it on Eloise's little cairn.

'If only we had a light!' said Eloise.

Then Tommy had an idea.

'Eloise, look, we've got a whole lot of straw. Lots of it is still warm and dry under our habits. Maybe, if we could risk it, I could make a spark by bashing my sword against a rock and light some straw, or even better, if there's flint here, we might get a spark that way!'

So they began to explore inside their clothes, pulling out what bits of straw they could find, holding them out of the way of the drips of water from the roof. Tommy felt around for two pieces of rock and he struck them hard together. A loud crack but no spark, not even a glimmer.

'Wait a mo!' said Tommy. 'I'll try to find some sharp stones. They might be flints.' And he scrabbled around in the pitch black.

'Here's something quite sharp,' he said, and he struck two stones together.

A spark! That little spark was so welcome; that little flash of light after total blackness was like a beacon of hope to them.

'How do we do this?' said Tommy. 'Bring the straw over here.' He took Eloise's hands in his and placed them against his chest.

'Mind your fingers,' he said and struck the stones together again.

Again a spark, but not enough to light the straw. Again and again Tommy struck the stones together, and each time a vivid spark lit up a small area of the cave. At last a red-hot fragment of rock fell onto the straw and it flared up, casting an eerie yellow light around them.

'Quick! More straw!'

Eloise threw more on as Tommy placed the burning bundle on the ground. He was just about to burn his fingers! In the brief time that they had before the straw burnt out, they could see that the passage that they had taken was indeed a dead end. Tommy gathered the burning straw in his habit and they moved quickly back along the way that they had come. Cinders of straw still glowed red and there was a smell of hot damp cloth. They could see nothing again, but even these little red glowing embers were a comfort.

They had to cross over the cave. There must be a passage turning to the left, which they had missed, clinging as they were to the wall on the other side. They waded through the little stream, holding hands in case one of them fell. The stream was freezing cold and swirled hard against their legs. The cave was much larger again here. Pressing against the wall of the cave they made their way further back. A few more bats rustled in alarm and several flew whizzing about their heads, defending the colony. Tommy and Eloise ignored them. They had to find the other tunnel. That was all that occupied their thoughts. They pressed with their hands, running their fingers over the cold, damp rock, for minutes on end, or so it seemed.

'Please, please,' muttered Tommy, and just for an instant Eloise placed her hand over his, and they stood for a few seconds without moving, trying to calm themselves. And then they began to edge along the damp rock again. Ah! Here at last the wall began to bend around.

'I think we've found it,' whispered Tommy, with a little gasp of relief.

But as he said this, they could hear in the far distance the echoes of voices again. The soldiers had returned! Eloise gripped Tommy's hand. Of course, they must have realised that we'd gone in the cave, thought Tommy. They've gone back for torches and lanterns to find us. They can see out footprints in the mud, too. They'll think we're trapped here.

'Let's go,' he whispered to Eloise.

Still gripping her hand, he pulled her gently around the corner into the larger passage. They crept on. The soldiers' voices were clearer now. They had lights and were moving rapidly along the cave towards them. All Tommy and Eloise could do was to move on as fast as they dared. If they dislodged a stone now, though, they would give away where they were.

The voices of the soldiers came still closer. They were nearly at the junction of the two passages, only a hundred yards or so behind Tommy and Eloise! The light from the soldiers' lanterns cast a faint glow even where the two fugitives were now crouched, fearful to move, in case they made a telltale noise. The soldiers reached the junction. Tommy and Eloise could hear that they had stopped and were discussing what they should do.

'I don't like it in these caves,' said one of them. 'There's people what say that demons live in these caves. It's no place for men to be!'

'Aye,' said another, 'that's true!'

'Why don't we just go back and say that they're not there and be done with it?' said a third, his voice sounding shaky with fear.

'Because the Bishop will tan our arses, that's why,' said the first soldier. 'Let's split up and get out of here as fast as possible. You go that way and we two will try this way!'

'I'm not going alone down there.'

'Nor me!'

There were only three soldiers, and they were going to stick together. That was a bit of luck, thought Tommy. But which way would they try?

'Look, there's footprints there,' said the first soldier, pointing, though Tommy could not see it, down the dead end that they had just come back from.

'Where?' said another, and, turning too fast, slipped and fell, letting go his lantern in the river. It sizzled out immediately.

'Careless oaf! Now we've only two left,' said the first soldier.

'You shut up!' said the fallen soldier, picking himself up off the ground.

This gave Tommy an idea. If they could put out the soldiers' lights, they would be pretty helpless. If only he had a bucket. Now it so happened that the nun's habits were held up around the waist with corsets made of whalebone. Perhaps he could use a bit of this to act as a scoop for enough water to throw over the soldiers' lanterns. They could ambush them.

'Let's follow those footprints, then,' said the third soldier.

'Yeah, let's go.'

The three soldiers disappeared up the dead-end passage.

'They'll soon be back,' said Tommy and explained hurriedly to Eloise what he'd thought of doing.

'Let's try it,' they agreed, and Tommy hoisted off the nun's habit. If only they had some light! He'd kept the flints in a pocket and they used them to rip the cloth off the whalebone, feeling their way as best they could. Then, suddenly Tommy realised what a twit he was. The mobile! They could use the light from the mobile. There wasn't much, but at least they could see what they were doing with the corsets! He pulled the mobile from the depths of his trouser pocket.

There was one thing, of course. Eloise had not seen the phone before. Eloise did not know anything about Tommy and the twenty-first century! Well, there was no time for explanations now, and he just switched it on. Eloise gasped and recoiled from the ghostly green light.

'Sorry, my darling,' whispered Tommy, 'but don't ask me to explain now, please! I'll tell you later.'

Eloise nodded, eyeing the mobile with fear, and shaking her head as if to cast out the strange vision of this little glowing object. They continued to work frantically at the corset, tearing and pulling with all their might. They managed to get the whalebone out. It would indeed act as a scoop. Two scoops in fact: one for each of them. Tommy pushed the habit back over his head. It flopped a good deal around the waist, but he could still wear it anyway.

'Let's find a good place for an ambush,' said Eloise, still eyeing the mobile.

They could just see a large puddle in front of them and they filled the whalebone scoops from there.

Holding the mobile up, Tommy led the way rapidly along the passage. After a few yards, there appeared a little corridor to the left, which they could easily squeeze into, and not be seen by anyone coming along the main passage.

'I'll tell you what,' said Tommy. 'Let's get some rocks. We'll let the soldiers pass and throw the rocks at them from behind. They're sure to turn and then we'll put their lights out with the water.'

'That sounds alright,' said Eloise, 'but we'll have to get past them to get out of the cave.'

'Yeah, that's true,' said Tommy. 'Let's bung the rocks at them just as they pass our hiding place.'

'Right. I'll take the closer, you take the further!' said Eloise.

Tommy and Eloise waited in silence. Water dripped on their heads and they shivered again with the cold. Tommy was wet underneath too, from when he'd had the habit off, fishing out the whalebone just before.

They'd laid the scoops full of water carefully on the ground beside them and armed themselves with a heavy rock each. It seemed an age before they heard the soldiers' voices again.

'Well, that was a waste of time,' they heard one say.

'We'd better try this passage, then,' said another.

'Oh, God protect us! Do we have to? Must we?' said the third.

So, holding their two remaining lanterns well forward in front of them, the soldiers began to make their way along the passage towards where Tommy and Eloise were hidden. Very gingerly, Tommy bent down and picked up his whalebone scoop, and Eloise did the same. They both stood tense and poised, a rock in one hand, the water in the other. The soldiers came closer.

'Don't you slip over,' said one. 'I don't want to be left in the dark in here!'

'Oh! By all the saints, nor do I!' said another.

'Ssssh, now,' said the third. 'We want to surprise them if we can!'

'Oh, come on – they'll see our lights anyway, you fathead!' was the reply.

Tommy and Eloise could indeed see the lights of the lanterns, coming very close. Tommy looked at Eloise and nodded. A soldier's foot appeared and then both soldiers carrying the lanterns were clearly in view.

'*Now*!' roared Tommy, and two heavy rocks caught the soldiers on the side of their heads, and water was poured over their lanterns before they had a moment to recover. There were squeals of fright and rage.

'*Demons*!' screamed a soldier, flailing around in the pitch dark, and connecting with something soft.

'Fool!' yelled a second, and Tommy could hear that he had drawn his sword!

Tommy and Eloise darted out of their hiding place and were about to escape when, by bad luck, one soldier, clutching wildly about in panic, caught hold of Tommy's habit.

'What this?' he shouted. 'I've got one of them!'

In desperation, Tommy pulled the mobile from his pocket. Switching it on, as he grappled with his other hand with the soldier, he shone the green light on his face from below and grimaced.

'*A demon!*' screamed the soldier, falling over backwards onto one of his companions, and letting go of Tommy's habit.

'That's them!' shouted the third soldier from behind. 'Don't let them get away!'

But the two in front were stumbling and slipping in the dark, clutching the cave wall, back towards the entrance as fast as they could go. The third, feeling himself alone in the dark, with demons or at least human enemies lurking somewhere in front of him, turned and groped his way back too, cursing his luck, slipping and falling in the icy stream, and cursing again.

Tommy and Eloise stood quietly for a moment holding hands while the three fighting men retreated out of the cave. But they could hear the men calling for help to their companions at the entrance. Tommy and Eloise had earned only a short time to get away.

When the Bishop saw three soaked and muddy frightened men come bounding out the mouth of the cave, he cursed them loudly as he heard their account of demons in the cave, a green-faced monster and many dreadful imps, who put out their lanterns and attacked them with cold fire.

'*Nonsense!*' he thundered. '*Demons?* You idiots – there are no demons!'

'What, no demons, sire?' said the commander of his little brigade – only fourteen of them now. 'You preached just last Sunday – and what a moving sermon it was, sire – that all who opposed the will of the true Church, would be thrown among the demons of hell, and...'

'Enough of that nonsense!' shouted the Bishop.

This was not the time for theological arguments. He wanted Eloise, dead or alive, captive in his palace.

'You, you, you and you,' he ordered, pointing with his drawn sword at four of his men, 'into the cave and capture whoever and whatever it is in there! I'm going to lead you myself. Where's a lantern?' he said, turning to one of the bedraggled men who had just emerged.

'We, we, er...' gulped the man, 'we dropped them in the cave!' and fell on his knees before his master.

The Bishop seemed about to strike the man with his sword, but a solider handed him a lighted lantern, saying, 'There's one left, sire.'

The Bishop marched determinedly into the cave, holding the lantern himself, followed with doubtful steps by the four whom he had ordered to come with him.

'It's all very well for His Lordship the Bishop to say there are no demons in there,' remarked one of the men who had been in the cave, 'but I saw this monster, it's got a black tail, and black hooded head, with a green face, green! A strange light...'

'Oh, shut yer face, for the Lord's sake!' said one of the soldiers. 'You're giving us the jitters.'

'But I saw it!'

'And so did I!' chimed in another of the unfortunate men.

Meanwhile, Tommy and Eloise had been making their way rapidly along the broad passage of the cave, using the weak light of the mobile to help them. Eloise was burning with curiosity about the strange object lighting their way, but she could not expect an answer to any questions now. They knew that the Bishop's party was after them, for they could hear the five men in the distance. They pressed on.

The cave was becoming narrower and lower again. Tommy held the mobile up to the ceiling. The roof of the cave fell rapidly over the next few metres, and they had to push between ledges of rock projecting from the walls, just as in the other passage.

'Let's hope this isn't a dead end too,' said Tommy.

'But you said that there was another way out!' whispered Eloise, urgently.

'Yes, but I hope that my memory... No, I'm sure of it!' said Tommy.

They could hear the echoing footfalls of the men behind them, but Tommy kept the green light of the mobile on. Their pursuers had only one route to follow anyway, and they were not trying to remain hidden any longer. A second surprise attack would not be possible. What they needed to do was to get out and away before the Bishop and his men could see the path that they would follow, once free of the cave.

But the cave was really narrowing now. Sharp shelves of rock, which they had to clamber along, blocked the path. At one point two projecting rocks allowed their passage only when they half slid along them on their stomachs.

Those fighting men behind are going to find this tough, thought Tommy. So long as we do not get completely caught.

Just then they turned a corner to find the path apparently blocked! Frantically, they searched for an opening. At last Tommy found a tiny crack, and beyond that a way through. A rock fall from the roof had blocked the cave, but pushing and scrabbling with their hands, they made the opening wider.

'Quick,' said Tommy, and lifted Eloise's habit over her head. 'We'll never get through with these things on.'

She did the same for him. They could hear the voices of the soldiers much more clearly now. The Bishop's voice rang out.

'They can't be far ahead. They're trapped. Like rats!' he laughed.

'Do you see that green light, sire?' one of the men said, and Tommy could hear that all of them had stopped in their tracks. Tommy switched off the mobile.

'Where?' demanded the Bishop.

'Oh, it's gone!'

The men started off again, and Tommy switched on the mobile once more,

'No, there it is!' shouted the same voice, and all the men stopped again.

Tommy and Eloise in their underclothes managed to press themselves through the little hole that they had made, and dragged the nun's habits after them. The cave was still very narrow, but seemed passable at least for the next few metres. The passage turned an abrupt corner and moved sharply upwards. They were scrambling now, climbing up a narrow slippery slope, with rock bulging out in smooth surfaces, where it was difficult to find a foothold. The roof was coming down to meet them, closer and closer.

They could hear the Bishop shouting at his men, 'You fools, that's no demons! They've got a green light with them, that's all.'

Still, he was thinking, what the devil is it, that light? He had never seen anything like it in his life. A strange cold green light. He felt the hairs on the back of his neck rise. Perhaps there was some truth in the absurd stories that the Church used to frighten the peasants?

He managed to drive his men further into the cave, but the narrower parts that they were entering now slowed them up even more than they had slowed Tommy and Eloise. For one thing, they were heavily armed, with swords and belts and buckles catching on the rock. The Bishop himself was no small man, taller than his brother Drogo and twice the width. It was getting clear that only the two smallest men could hope to get much further, and they would have to remove their weapons.

Tommy and Eloise ahead of them were lying flat on their stomachs, with rock just a few centimetres above their heads. They were clawing their way up the smooth rock by their fingernails. Water must have flowed down here once, taking the roughness off the rock. They could feel the weight of the rock above them, pressing down, crushing them. It was difficult to breathe, difficult not to panic. The cold rock pressed against them, crushing against their ribs, till they felt that they might crack. At one point Tommy had to turn his head on one side to press his face through, with a cheek pushed hard against the cold surface, his shoulders and hips almost wedged and a strong smell of earth and moss in his head. He could feel his trousers being torn off as he tried to lurch upwards and free himself at the narrowest part. Would they be jammed fast altogether? A dizziness filled his head. He gasped and pushed again. The rock tore at his ear. Push, push! At last, he was through, grazing his head and his legs, and exposing quite a lot of his bare bottom to Eloise, who followed directly behind him.

Eloise however had no time to notice Tommy and his bottom. Her problem was more that she might slip and slide back down the narrow crevice and fall into the arms of the Bishop's men below. Seeing Tommy was through the worst, she made a grab for his ankle to steady herself but caught the bottom of his trouser leg instead. She pulled his trousers still further off and he lunged down to hold them. Tugging herself up, slimmer and more supple than Tommy, but still with one hand hanging on to Tommy's trousers, she managed to squirm her hips through even the last tightest bit without losing any of her own clothes.

They lay breathing hard. 'Gosh, that was horrid,' whispered Tommy and Eloise nodded silently lying by his side.

Just a few metres higher and the ceiling rose a little and they could breathe more freely. Pulling at his trousers with one hand, Tommy held the mobile up with the other and looked ahead of them. The place smelled even more strongly of damp earth, and above their heads they could see tree roots growing down through the rock. They must be close to the surface. Perhaps they were going to need to dig themselves out with their bare hands, Tommy thought. There was certainly no going back.

Coming to the top of the slope, the rock curved smoothly over, and together they slid down a few metres and landed on soft gravel. Here they could almost stand, but the cave seemed to spread out in all directions. Which way should they take?

They walked a few paces forward, straining their eyes, peering into the gloomy darkness. Eloise stumbled on a tree root and fell, stretching out one hand to the ground as she did so. Tommy took hold of her arm, but she gently resisted his attempt to pull her upright, and crouching as she was, pointed her finger at the ground a short distance ahead. Tommy swung the light round to follow where she pointed and there, lying before them, to their astonishment, they saw a small wooden horse, a child's toy.

'What? How strange!' said Tommy. 'But it's...'

'It's your old wooden horse,' said Eloise slowly. 'It's your old wooden horse!' she repeated more excitedly. 'I remember it! I wanted one too. But it was only for boys.'

'Yes,' said Tommy thoughtfully, 'I remember it now; old Rabelais made it for me.'

He picked it up carefully, as if it might break since it had not been touched for so long. It had a strange feeling of something familiar, but not quite familiar, something familiar to another Tommy – one, he reminded himself, now stuck in the twenty-first century. They stopped for a moment, and as Tommy held it in his hand they both fingered it carefully, rubbing off some old dried weed that had stuck to the side. It was nicely made, looking like a real horse, with the mane carefully carved.

'It's rather beautiful, isn't it?' whispered Tommy half to himself. Eloise nodded and they walked on in the direction in which they had found the toy.

'How very strange,' repeated Tommy. A memory was hovering in his mind. A nightmare, in which he had been lost in total darkness in a hole in the ground. The memory of Marie's panic-stricken voice, calling his name, shouting, 'Thomas, Thomas!'

He had thought that this had been a dream. Perhaps it was real. It was surely Thomas, the real Thomas, who as a little boy had dropped his toy here in the cave. He remembered now that the horse had somehow disappeared from his childhood, and a small sense of loss came into his mind, a little pang, which set off the thought that... Of course! That must be how he knew that there was another entrance to the cave, and why he knew that they could get through to it! For Thomas, as a little boy, the cave would have not been so narrow.

I wonder how far I got down into the cave? thought Tommy, but he could not dredge any more out of his memory.

Anyway, the exit to the cave could surely not be far now. He switched off the mobile to see if there was a glimmer of light ahead. Not yet. The voices of the Bishop and his men had faded, but they could still hear a sudden loud shout of fear.

'No, sire, no! I can't go any further. I'll die down here, jammed in this rock. Mercy. Don't prick me with your sword, sire!' And again a shout of, 'Mercy!' and a cry of pain. Then came a muffled shout, 'Don't leave me here! Pull me out. I'm stuck. Help me!'

This was followed by a moan from the wretched man. He must be jammed on that last narrow bit on the slope where we came up, thought Tommy. Surely they won't leave him there? No! There was a scream of pain, no doubt as they pulled him free.

'My ribs are broken, sire!' cried a voice in agony.

'Is there no way through?' asked the Bishop, completely ignoring the suffering of his poor soldier. Then he added, 'You two, you stay here and make sure that they don't come back this way!'

'Oh, my Lord,' said a shaky voice, 'swear to me there are no demons here!'

And a second soldier added, 'The lantern will only last a short time, sire.'

'Then come out in the dark. And just repeat the Lord's Prayer if you see a demon,' snarled their master, as he left the two of them standing miserable and frightened in the cave.

Eleven: Escape into the Marsh

ommy and Eloise moved on, Tommy clutching his old wooden horse. Speed was important, for though they might soon be out of the cave, they had to get well away, somewhere the Bishop's men could not easily follow them. Through the marshes, thought Tommy. Dangerous, but maybe the best way. The ground was muddy and wet, and again the cave was narrowing. The roof of the cave was partly earth, though, and did not give that terrible sensation of crushing weight which they'd felt before. They had to crouch now and then, and push around tree roots and jutting rocks.

They turned a corner and suddenly a strange and strong smell hit them. There was a scuffling and a growl. Eloise gave a little shriek and Tommy drew his sword, shining the light of the mobile ahead of them. A badger sett! They had stumbled into a badger sett! Badgers, Tommy remembered, were powerful creatures, with jaws that could bite through your leg. It was lucky he had his sword, though it was difficult to use it in this confined space. He advanced slowly and a badger lunged at him. Tommy caught it on the nose. The badger let out a hissing shriek, turned tail and fled. Then they saw that there were baby badgers! It was a mother defending its cubs. Tommy and Eloise could not help pausing just a few moments to admire the little mewing creatures. Their eyes were open and their fur was forming.

Were the badger tunnels big enough for Tommy and Eloise to creep through? They moved on as quickly as they could, crouching, bent almost double. The tunnel was just broad and high enough, and after a few turns began to rise sharply. Tommy held his sword pointing forward. He didn't want a snapping badger in his face, while Eloise was wondering about a snapping badger at her heels. Abruptly, fresh air greeted them and they could see moonlight on the high branches of trees. Clutching projecting tree roots, they hauled themselves up. They were out!

Eloise threw herself sobbing into Tommy's arms. He felt like crying too; to feel the fresh air on his cheeks, to breathe deeply, this was such a great relief. He held Eloise in his arms only briefly. Her sobbing subsided.

'We must get back into the nuns' habits,' said Tommy, stroking Eloise's hair, which he saw now Marie had managed to hold up with several large metal pins. They struggled back into the habits and in their black clothes they were all but invisible in the shadows.

'What's the best way for us now?' asked Eloise.

'We've got to get back to the château. Do you think that we could make it across the marshes?'

Eloise shuddered in reply. The marshes were famous for their danger. People disappeared there. Criminals escaped from justice were said to live there, where no one would hunt them down.

'I don't think that the Bishop and his men would follow us there,' said Tommy.

'From one danger into another,' said Eloise.

'So long as we're together,' said Tommy, and Eloise kissed him on the cheek, as they held hands and looked around in wonder at the world again. Then they walked quickly off, enjoying the great sense of freedom with the enormous sky above their heads, and endless space to move. There was silence in the wood, apart from the occasional rustling of leaves, as small animals roamed around.

'I hope that badger has returned to her babies,' said Eloise. 'You didn't harm it much, did you, Tommy?'

'I just nicked its nose, I think,' said Tommy.

The thing of course that Eloise really wanted to talk about was the strange object that Tommy made the green light with. What was it? Part of Tommy's strangeness, certainly. Had Tommy learnt some magic from... from whom? Not Drogo, surely. And Drogo was his tutor, after all. She was turning these ideas around in her mind when Tommy turned to her and said, 'I know that you must be wondering what the green light was, Eloise.' Eloise nodded; it had not been difficult to read her thoughts.

'Let's just say for now that it is a secret which I will tell you soon. It takes too much explanation, and now is not the time for that! It's very important to our happiness together, and I want to have lots of quiet time with you to describe what this all means!'

Eloise nodded again, and they walked on in silence for a few steps, while she thought over what Tommy had just said.

'Well, it will have to wait, then, I agree. I'll trust you... I do trust you,' she said quietly, almost to herself, when the silence of the night was broken by the opening phrase of Mozart's 40th Symphony. *Pee, pee, peep, pee, pee, peep, pee, pee, peep, peep...*

'Blast it all!' said Tommy, fumbling to find the off switch. 'Harry, I'll kill you. It's the middle of the night!'

Eloise had stopped dead in her tracks, and placing her hand in Tommy's, she looked him in the eye.

'Is that another secret that will have to wait too?' she demanded, shaking a little at the alien sound that she had just heard; though she remembered it, not so loud, at the banquet on Sunday evening. She traced her finger over where Thomas's scar should have been and murmured, 'Is there some connection between this,' she said, pressing on his forehead, 'and these strange secrets. That noise from, from... another world, and that green devilish light?'

'Yes, there is,' said Tommy. 'Please, please, I'll tell you soon. Please trust me! I know you trust me! The secret is more strange than terrible, really, but we must have time together for it!'

'I trust you,' Eloise whispered in his ear, and they kissed gently in the moonlight and moved on, like beings in a dream.

The bright moonlight lit up the woods around them, throwing sharp shadows. There was no wind, and the branches heavy with leaves were outlined harshly against the sky, with only a faint rustle in the still night. They could see that they were on a gentle slope that would take them far down the hillside. The ground fell away into the marshy land below, stretching out before them. Once they could get down to the marshy ground, they were sure that the Bishop's men would not follow them. Anyway, the Bishop had no idea that they were out of the cave. Perhaps he was hoping to starve them out, waiting at the entrance. The stillness, the quiet was absolute. There was just the trudging of their feet on the leafy ground, the occasional scuttling of some little animal for shelter, and then silence again, of a quality that Tommy could never remember from his own time. More important, there was no sound of pursuit. The Bishop and his men had obviously lost the scent.

'I think that we have really given them the slip,' he said to Eloise. 'Outwitted the twits,' he added, grinning.

Eloise paused and nodded. Tommy had put away the mobile, and they were walking hand in hand, moving slowly to lower ground. In his other hand, Tommy still held the toy horse.

'Let me put this safe,' said Tommy and he stopped and, lifting up the nun's habit, stuffed the horse inside a kind of pocket in its lining.

'I don't think that it will fall out there. I don't want to lose it, again!' he added, 'and I need a free hand just in case I have to use my sword.'

'Oh no! I hope not,' whispered Eloise, 'not again.'

She pressed her face against his shoulder, as Tommy relived the sickening feeling of sinking his sword inside the Bishop's soldier. He had tried to put it out of his mind, but he had killed someone. Alright, it was self-defence, or at least, defence of Eloise. But he had killed someone. Who was he? he thought, the man he killed. Did he have a family? Were there a whole bunch of little children sobbing at home now, because of what he had done? He would try to find out, he vowed, when he got back to the château. Perhaps he could help the family, if there was one.

'Of course, the family must not know,' he muttered to himself.

'What was that?' said Eloise. 'What family?'

'Oh, nothing,' said Tommy. 'Well, I was worrying really about that man I...' It was really difficult to say 'killed'. 'That man I...'

'...killed,' said Eloise, 'protecting me.' She half-turned and pressed his hand in both of hers.

She seems less concerned than me, somehow, thought Tommy.

'Well, people get killed, you know,' said Eloise vaguely, sensing his unease. 'I mean, well, people get killed.'

Well, I suppose they do, or did, at least more often than I am used to. But not killed by me, not by me! thought Tommy.

They had been walking on, concentrating hard on their

thoughts, quite preoccupied with their conversation, both of them looking more at the ground than about them. Suddenly Tommy noticed that the floor of the wood had changed. It was grassy, a simple grassy slope, and suddenly rather steep. Looking around, he stopped. A faint yellow glow filled the sky to his right, and he could hear a distant murmuring. A great rush of joy came to him, as he felt Eloise tense and gasp at his side. They were back in the twenty-first century! Those yellow lights, they were the street lights of Toulouse. He was home!

'Eloise,' he said. Then he shouted her name, letting go of her hand, and spinning round with his arms in the air, 'Eloise, Eloise, we are home!' Then he thought a moment. 'Well, *I* am home.'

He looked at her. She stood stock-still, with a look of anguish on her face, paler even than the moonlight could make her. He quickly took her in his arms, for she seemed about to fall. Indeed her body sagged against him as he held her.

'Eloise,' he whispered, 'I have had no time to explain to you.'

'Where are we?' he could hear her murmur, 'please tell me where we are!'

'We are four hundred years in the future, in your future, four hundred years in the future – where I come from,' he blurted out.

This was not how he had wanted to break the story to Eloise, but there was no time for long explanations now.

At that, Eloise pushed him away from her, holding him at arm's length. Looking into his face, she shouted, 'You are mad! What am I doing with a madman here at night in these woods? Oh!' And she stamped her foot in frustration, and burst out sobbing. Tommy tried to hold her close, but she fought him off.

'Look around you!' he said, 'look around. You are where you were, I mean, in the same place, but four hundred years in the future.'

And as he said this he swept his arm over the countryside around them. But Eloise just shook her head and sobbed some more. In truth, the view around looked completely unlike the forest and marsh of 1599. Not far below them there was a road, along the border of the old marsh. And, where the marsh had been, was cultivated farmland, full of ripe crops.

'There,' said Tommy, seizing inspiration, 'there!' He pulled

Eloise towards him by her lower arm, 'that's Romolue church!'

In fact, in the far distance, you could just see the tower of Romolue church sticking up against the horizon. Unfortunately a small steeple had been added in the eighteenth century, but the Norman tower was still the same. Eloise looked up on hearing a familiar name, and peered anxiously where Tommy pointed.

'But... it's all changed,' she said, 'in just moments...'

Her voice trailed off. She sat down upon the slope, and placed her face in her hands. Tommy put his arm around her shoulder, as her body shook with sobs. She tried weakly to shake his arm away, but he ignored her.

'Trust me,' said Tommy and at that moment, headlights lit up the road and a car came past driving fast.

Eloise gave a yell of pure horror and looked up into Tommy's face. Then another car followed, and she clutched at Tommy, burying her face in his nun's habit. Squatting beside her, he put his hands around her head.

'I've got a lot to tell you,' he said quietly, 'a very great deal!'

Suddenly a feeling of great happiness came over him. He was back home, and Eloise was with him. She could come too! She did not crumble into bones and dust when they crossed four hundred years. She was alive, unchanged. They could always be together.

Then another thought crossed his mind. The clothes they wore, these had come with them – so they could bring things, not just themselves. His wooden horse? He felt in his pocket. It was gone! It had crumbled into dust, centuries old, and fallen to tiny pieces which he could feel in the lining of the habit. Well, so only some things could come with them. Otherwise they would be standing naked here beside the road! But these mysteries would have to wait. If they just got on the road and walked along it, they would be back at the château gates in, well, maybe half an hour or so.

'Come on,' said Tommy. 'You're safe, really.'

He pulled Eloise up by her arm. She looked wildly about her, and tried again to pull away.

'You're mad!' she said once more, as Tommy held firmly onto her.

'Look around, are you imagining all this?' he cried, sweeping his arm around once more.

'Then it's me who's mad!' she cried.

'Now look, Eloise, you've believed and trusted me so far. This is all part of the same thing. The strange green light the…' God! I'm doing this badly, thought Tommy to himself.

'That funny noise that you heard – *de de dum, de de dum, de de dum dum* – y'know, they're all part of the same thing. The green light thing, the mobile, is something that I brought from the twenty-first century, you see. That's why it looked so strange to you – and to the Count and the Countess!'

'They've seen it!' whispered Eloise. 'What did they think?'

'Well, the Count thought that it was a new toy made by Rabelais – at least that's what I told him – and the Countess nearly died of shock when it did its peeping in front of her. Mind you, Drogo practically had heart failure when it went off during the banquet right beside his ear. Ha, ha!' laughed Tommy.

He was so giddy to be home that he had forgotten for a moment that he should be trying to comfort Eloise in her shock.

But seeing Tommy apparently quite happy was the best tonic for Eloise. She began to quieten down and to think a little more clearly. It was true that there was something strange about this boy. He did not have the right reactions about things. He was so upset about people getting killed, for instance. No one cared if a peasant or a soldier was killed. But he did. He seemed to have no respect for the Church, or at least for priests and bishops, for Drogo and his brother. Also he was a different person from the Thomas that she knew, not to look at, apart from the scar, of course, but in almost every other way. He didn't seem to be Thomas… but he knew about the wooden horse; how could he know the wooden horse if…?

'Show me the wooden horse,' she managed to whisper to him.

'Oh gosh!' said Tommy. 'It's gone.'

'You dropped it!' said Eloise, 'out of your habit!'

'No!' said Tommy, 'it's gone. I mean, it's turned into little bits of rotten wood. It couldn't survive the change of time, the four hundred years, I mean.'

'What? Show me! What do you mean, it's in little bits? It was in your hand just a few moments ago! I saw it!'

Tommy pulled open the habit and said, 'Put you hand in there,' pointing at the pocket made by the lining, and Eloise did so.

Her fingers found just a lot of small fragments of wood, and she gave a little gasp. She pulled out a tiny fragment.

'You did this!' she shouted, raging at him again. 'You did this, just to fool me, to make me think...'

'No,' said Tommy quietly, and scooping out small pieces of his toy horse, crushed them in his hand, letting them fall to the ground as dust. 'I cannot make wood soft like this, so I can crush it to powder! Time did it. It lived and aged four hundred years. Luckily our clothes did not – otherwise we would be standing here with nothing on!'

'Oh, shut up!' said Eloise, blushing.

'Well, it's true,' said Tommy. 'Anyway, do you believe me now? Look at the modern world around you! Look at the road. You saw the cars!'

'You mean, those rushing black chariots, with bright lights, with – with – horses in them?' She ended with a question in her voice.

'No, I mean, yes, but no, no horses. Well, there's far too much to learn. Look, you really are four centuries in the future. But you're alive and well, you survived the change. You are with me. You are safe.'

And without warning he took her in his arms. This time she did not resist, but just buried her face in the nun's habit, and stayed trembling close to him for some seconds. He stroked her cheek, but she turned her head away.

'No!' she whispered. 'No! Who are you?'

'I'm Tommy. I-I-I'm not Thomas de Romolue, just plain Tommy. Tommy Sanderson, if you really want to know.'

'You're not Thomas de Romolue. You are not the boy that I am in love with. But you are! I'm in love with Thomas de Romolue, who is you. Where is he, then?' she asked, getting more and more confused.

'Well, actually, he's with my parents staying at the Château of Ellie-la-Forêt.'

'What château is that?' demanded Eloise.

'It's the modern name for the Château de Romolue. I think they changed the name to call it after you, actually, Eloise. Ellie's your pet name, isn't it?'

'You mean, Thomas de Romolue, the real one, kind of swapped with you?' She ignored his reply about the château.

'Yes. Not that we wanted to, I mean. It all happened because of, well, through a picture of the garden in the Château de Romolue, or Ellie-la-Forêt. It was Jasper... Oh, heavens, I'm not making this clear at all. But it's me you love, isn't it?' he added, suddenly worried about what would happen if Eloise met the real Thomas de Romolue again.

'Yes, but... what I mean is... well, I've been kind of tricked. No, not tricked, but fooled. I knew there was something strange about you. Thomas couldn't change so quickly, from morning to afternoon! Foolish shy boy in the morning, and loving, kissing boy in the afternoon.' She blushed at her own words. 'On Sunday, I mean,' she added quietly.

'Don't say anything more, Eloise, please. Just nothing for the moment, about that! Please! Look, I have other very important things to tell you, that happened all those years ago, in your time. Things that I have discovered when I was at the château, your château, I mean. Things about Drogo and, and... well, later. I think that we should just go to the Château of Ellie-la-Forêt, now. Just walk there. I'll look after you. Trust me, please trust me, like you have up to now! It's just half an hour or so down the road. Come with me, now!'

Saying this, he urged her gently down the slope, with his arm around her waist. Releasing her briefly, he jumped down onto the grassy verge beside the road, holding out his arms for her and she followed him. Both of them stepped onto the tarmac. Eloise stopped as she did so, and looked at the surface of the road, pressing down on it with her foot. She stooped down to touch the smooth surface. She glanced at Tommy, shook her head a little, and then they walked on. Eloise began to look around with great curiosity, especially at the houses and the lights, and she kept glancing at the strange yellow glow in the distance, but asked no more questions.

It seemed to her that Toulouse, if that was where Toulouse lay, it seemed that Toulouse was on fire. But obviously not! At least, Tommy hadn't said anything about it. The light didn't flicker, like a fire. But it did look like fire. As they walked on, she was totally taken up in these thoughts and Tommy was also submerged in worries that Eloise might cease to love him now that he was not Thomas de Romolue.

So lost in thought were they, that as they turned a corner, they suddenly found themselves face to face with headlights almost upon them. A car, driven fast, seemed to be aiming straight towards them. Eloise gave a sharp cry and froze and Tommy grabbed at her arm, yanking her sideways – but too late! They could see the face of the driver for an instant, as the world wavered, shimmered and, fading, began to darken.

The impact was long in coming, thought Tommy, but no impact came. The world refocused. They were standing in a calm peaceful wood, on a gentle slope making its way down to marshy ground below. The only light was that of the sharp bright rays of the moon.

Tommy and Eloise stood and looked at each other in astonishment. Eloise ran her hands down her habit, as if to make sure that she was real, real and alive. Tommy rubbed his brow with the back of his hand and then sank to the ground, drawing his knees up to his chin. He looked up at Eloise, patted the ground beside him and Eloise joined him. She put her hands on her knees and leant her head sideways towards Tommy, resting her cheek on her hands. She gazed at Tommy. Tommy turned his head and returned her gaze. So they remained for a long, long moment. Eloise opened her mouth a fraction, as if about to speak. But Tommy moved his head with a tiny motion to and fro, and no words were said. The silence closed around them, and the leaves rustled slightly, as the approach of dawn caused a faint breeze to stir.

Tommy finally broke the silence.

'I recognised that man driving the car,' he whispered.

Eloise raised her eyebrows, opening her eyes wide.

'Yes, I recognised that ugly face, with a long thin nose. It was Drogo!' he said, 'Drogo!' He raised his voice. 'Drogo trying to kill us!' he almost shouted.

'*Ssshhh,*' whispered Eloise.

Tommy stumbled to his feet, and grasping Eloise's arm, pulled her rather sharply up.

'It *was* Drogo,' he said again, dropping his voice, suddenly remembering the danger that they were in, and holding Eloise tightly around the shoulders to control his anger.

'How could it be Drogo?' asked Eloise. 'You told me that it was... well, your time, the twenty-first century.' The words sounded so strange to her. 'The twenty-first century,' she repeated, half to herself. 'I only got a glimpse of it – your time, I mean.'

'You believe me, then!' said Tommy. 'You really do. Oh, Eloise, I knew that you would trust me at last!' Then he pulled her against him, but she put out her hands.

'Not here,' she said. 'We're in danger here. The Bishop's men. Have you forgotten? Come, let's go. You can explain as we move on.'

Tommy nodded quickly and they began to walk rapidly down the slope, as they had been doing before they were spirited into Tommy's time. They continued some distance in silence. There was still not the slightest sound of pursuit, and they began both to feel safer on that score.

'What did you mean, it was Drogo, in the... car?' asked Eloise, at length.

'Well, look,' replied Tommy. 'It seems it's possible to sort of slip between our time and your time. I wish I knew how it was done! Either Drogo has a kind of double in my time, or he actually slips back and forth, like I think that Jacques does.'

'Jacques?' said Eloise, 'You mean the chief servant at the château? You can't mean him. I mean, he's, he's only a servant!'

'Ha!' said Tommy. 'But he's a clever person, your Jacques. He knows how to get back and forth. And he has some purpose in all this. He's somehow using us, I'm sure,' he went on, wrinkling his brow over the terrible puzzle of it all.

Eloise was very confused by Tommy's comments, and silently let her thoughts run. She knew now that Tommy had emerged from another time into the life of the Château de Romolue. How, she could not understand, and nor could Tommy. That was clear. Why had he come? Maybe there was no 'why'. Tommy seemed to think that Jacques was maybe important in it. Jacques! A servant! As far beneath her as the Almighty was above her. And so her thoughts trailed on. All she understood was that Tommy and she needed to sit peacefully and have a long talk together. Since they had jumped in the moat – she shuddered at the memory of the cold water closing over her head – since then, they had not had two moments alone without pursuit or something horrid about to happen to them.

At these mournful thoughts, tears began to form in her eyes. Besides, she was exhausted, and could not keep going much further. They were walking between shrubs now, with dense thickets of alder and clumps of reeds appearing. They had stumbled into the marshes without realising that they had done so. The ground made occasional sucking and groaning noises, and Eloise's foot sank in to her ankle, and she almost lost her balance, dragging herself forwards out of the boggy patch.

'Couldn't we stop and rest for a bit?' she whispered. 'I feel that I am going to drop into the mud, if we go much further.'

'Yeah,' sighed Tommy. 'We've been going all night, I know. Do you think that it would be safe to have a little sleep, before dawn breaks completely?'

A pale light was showing on the horizon. They had better get some sleep now. If they were asleep in the light, they might easily be spotted.

'Let's find a really dense bit of bush,' suggested Tommy. 'Over there!' He pointed to the right and took Eloise's soft hand in his, gently stroking his thumb over her palm.

Eloise smiled and began to follow in the direction that Tommy was going. Frogs hopped and splashed about them as they moved off into more marshy parts, and bubbles came up from the little pools of water that began to appear between the earthy tussocks of grass which formed the only secure ground for them to walk on.

'Here, what about here?' said Eloise, after they had gone about a hundred metres. Alders had sprouted at the spot for many years, and there was a tangled mass of branches and leaves, and a dark hollow inside. What an adventure this would normally be! But now it was a deadly game. They had to be so carefully concealed that even a soldier walking past a few metres away – or one of the bandits in the marsh – could not see them. Their habits caught on the branches. Tommy's already sagged to the ground, after he'd taken out the whalebone in the cave.

'Let's get these off again,' said Tommy. 'We can put them on once we're well hidden. The black will make us even more difficult to see.'

Both he and Eloise lifted their habits over their heads. With the habits stuffed under their arms, they pushed their way through the narrow spaces between the springy branches, until they could go no further. The ground was wet but there were so many branches that they simply spread their habits over them and lay down as best they could.

'I think that we're pretty well hidden in here,' muttered Tommy.

But Eloise was already asleep, breathing gently, her long eyelashes fluttering as if she were already deep in a dream.

That was the last that Tommy remembered, until they both awoke with a start. A great racket was coming from outside their hiding place.

Eee-yor…eee-yor! A donkey. A wild donkey! But no! It had a red ribbon tied to one ear. It must belong to one of the robber bands of the marsh. But Tommy and Eloise, still half asleep, did not notice the red ribbon.

The donkey stood and pissed noisily over the alders, fortunately missing Tommy and Eloise. Then it shambled off, shaking its mane and whipping its tail over its back to fend off the hundreds of flies that seemed to like its rear end…

'Blast you!' said Tommy, and Eloise chuckled, propping herself up on her elbows. 'Gosh, it's lucky in a way that that stupid donkey woke us,' Tommy went on. 'It's light. What time is it?'

Again came that puzzled look from Eloise. 'The sun says that it's half way through the morning,' she replied. 'We've had a few hours' sleep, anyway.'

'Yes, and not been caught by the Bishop's soldiers. More good luck than being careful on our part! Gosh, I'm hungry,' Tommy added.

'And thirsty,' said Eloise.

'I think that we can make it to the château without dying of hunger or thirst, though!'

At that moment they both realised how hot and sticky it was, and also that biting insects were not going hungry or thirsty.

'Quick,' whispered Tommy, 'let's get out of here!'

They struggled to their feet, half toppling over trying to balance on the wobbling mass of branches under them. Tommy prised the alder stems apart and Eloise squeezed through, and she held them up as he came after her. At the same time they were trying to see if there was anyone about – bandits or soldiers.

Or maybe Drogo hunting us with bow and arrow, thought Tommy. I wouldn't put it past him. Suddenly he had another thought. How could he have been in that car? He was meant to be deathly ill in bed in the château! Still more that I cannot understand. I saw his face alright. It was that priest of Romolue, or Drogo, or both the same thing. And he sighed to himself. Eloise gave him a quick questioning look, but they needed all their eyes and senses to stay upright.

'Let's go in the direction the donkey went,' suggested Tommy. 'If the ground can support him, it'll probably be okay for us.' Eloise nodded in agreement.

As they moved further and further into the marshlands, the sun began to burn down upon them on this hot July day. There was little enough shade, and their thirst and hunger grew. They spent a lot of time slapping at mosquitoes. Also it was becoming more and more difficult to make progress. They had to walk carefully. The ground would quake and sigh, and emit little belches of mud, leaving with a plop a little hole, looking like a fish's eye. They had sudden visions of falling into a quaking bog and sinking slowly in over their heads. They held hands tightly, and helped each other from one piece of firm ground to another.

Clumps of reeds became more frequent and larger expanses of water appeared around them. But, just a little further on, they could see that the alders grew in greater numbers, some of them quite high and dense, and an occasional oak tree too, stranded in the marsh. They decided to make for that direction, if only to keep off the hot sun on their black habits. The path they were following did become darker and shadier, with sunlight coming through in smaller and smaller patches, but the mosquitoes increased too. They stopped for a moment, slapping to right and left, and squinted into the shadows ahead. Reeds grew in a large clump before them, and pools of water lay half-hidden beneath the rotting boughs of trees fallen on the mossy ground. But it did seem firmer here.

'Let's go on this way, then,' said Tommy.

They both realised that they were lost. Surely if they just went as straight as they could, due south following the direction of the sun, then they had to come out on the other side of the marsh. Then they could cut round and come to the château from the back side. Would they have to cross the river? wondered Tommy. It wound about so much that they might have to cross it several times, for all he knew.

Tommy stopped, bent down and picked up an acorn from a lone oak. It felt good to hold the tiny, familiar object in his hand. With his other hand tightly enclosed in Eloise's, he rubbed the acorn between his finger and thumb, and squeezed Eloise's hand. Her answering squeeze caused a little rush of warmth in his chest and he glanced towards her, suddenly shy, and then gently, just like before, rubbed his thumb on the palm of her hand. They were standing still now, and a sweet smile passed over Eloise's face.

She does still love me, thought Tommy, even if she knows that I'm not Thomas de Romolue; and he leant towards her. As their lips touched, the ground suddenly lurched, and Tommy grabbed Eloise around the waist, dragging her towards him as she began to topple over backwards. Her arms flew around his neck and by brute force he managed to pull both of them upright.

'*Hrmmmm!*' rasped a deep rich voice, sounding very close by.

Tommy and Eloise, clutching one another, almost fell once more, but regaining their balance, looked wildly about them, marooned on their small piece of turf, which just held the two of them. There were reeds all around, the oak tree some way off, and little cover.

'Where did that come from?' whispered Eloise, as she regained her voice.

'Up ahead, somewhere,' muttered Tommy, 'I think!'

'I don't think it's one of the Bishop's men, surely,' said Eloise.

Who could it be, deep in the marsh? It must be one of those bandits, who lived in the marshes, those robbers and criminals that she had heard people in Romolue talking about. Might he not kill them? How could they defend themselves?

'*Hrmmmm!*' rasped the deep voice again, and then about ten metres in front of them a strange figure jumped off a bough of the oak tree, where he had been carefully hidden by the dense leaves, and landed legs apart squarely on the ground before them, right in their path. Tommy and Eloise tensed and held still more tightly to each other. They were unprotected, stranded on the little patch of turf, which wobbled if they moved. They dared not even turn to try and escape back the way that they had come.

'Ha, *hrmmm*,' growled the figure once more, still louder and asked, drawing out the words slowly and with great emphasis, as though it took much effort to speak, 'What are you?'

Tommy and Eloise were dressed as nuns. They must indeed have formed a strange sight in the marsh, clutching each other on their little tussock. Had this man, this strange creature before them, seen them about to kiss? Two nuns kissing! Tommy and Eloise had the same thought and they glanced at each other, with just a tiny wrinkle of amusement in their faces, even in their dangerous situation.

'What are you?' demanded the figure again.

Tommy was thinking fast. Best not to reveal their true identities. Better to be one of the fugitives in the marsh, to be one of them – the bandits, the robbers, that is. Perhaps they won't harm us if we are running from the powerful lords of Romolue and Toulouse, thought Tommy, forgetting for a moment that it was he who was one of the powerful lords, or would be one day, maybe.

'We are running from the Bishop's men,' answered Tommy.

'You are no nun!' shouted the creature before them, hearing Tommy's boyish, mannish voice, and suddenly the figure began to caper from one leg to the other, performing a strange dance, throwing his arms out to right and left.

Tommy and Eloise looked at him, wonderingly, regarding him carefully for the first time, as the sunlight flashed and sparkled over him as he moved. He certainly did not look dangerous. He had no weapons visible, and what a strange figure in fact he made. He was barefoot, but all the rest of him was covered with leaves and branches, which rustled as he moved, and flowers of the forest and marsh. In his thick, curly brown hair were briar flowers, and these trailed down and around his neck. His shirt was held together with the broad leaves of beech, and his trousers, such as they were, supported with a sapling wound through the holes in the band at the top, and with bracers around his shoulders of supple elder. Around his knees, he had wound ivy, with the stringy stems hanging down to his feet. These flew around as he danced and danced, springing more and more wildly about. Holding his arms out horizontally, and trailing weeds and briars from his sleeves, he began to stamp and sing. Tommy and Eloise could make out these strange words:

'I am Joncilond of the forest,
I am Joncilond of the wood
I am Joncilond of the marsh,
Be my friend, or you will rot
In the marsh, in the marsh,
Be my friend for your own good,
Ha! Ha! Hee! Hee!'

And as the last Hee! Hee! rang out through the trees, just as suddenly as he had started, he stopped, slamming his feet into the ground in time with the last words. He stood and faced them, legs squarely apart, staring fixedly at them.

Tommy and Eloise, and the creature – Joncilond, it seemed that he was called – stood and looked at each other for some moments in silence, a silence heightened by the raucous song which had just ended. As they stood, the stillness of the wilderness closed around them and Tommy and Eloise realised that they were both holding their breath, scarcely able to breathe for the spell which the marsh, the trees and this strange creature seemed to cast. The dark green light with little patches of sun and the heavy, acrid smell of fresh leaves made the air seem thick. They felt that their eyelids became heavy, and that they would like to lie down and sleep in this strange place, and then to wake, Tommy in his bedroom at home in England, Eloise in the

Château de Romolue. Eloise rested her head on Tommy's shoulder, and both of them took a deep breath of the warm and rich air. And so they stood quietly, until the whine of a mosquito right beside Tommy's cheek broke the stillness as he slapped at it, and almost at the same time a donkey brayed loudly nearby, and a faint 'Halloa' echoed through the woods.

'The Bishop's men,' whispered Tommy to Eloise, both of them suddenly alert again.

But the creature shook his head and smiled in a strangely gentle way. Tommy and Eloise could see now that he was quite a young man, no more than about twenty-five years old.

'Poor man!' whispered Eloise, but Tommy put his finger to his lips.

'Who are you?' demanded the figure again.

'We are running from the Bishop's men, and from the Bishop himself,' repeated Tommy.

'What are you? A male nun?' said the creature and hopped around on one leg – one, two, three, hop! 'A male nun!' he repeated, and laughed with a little shriek, turning a cartwheel on the grass, exposing most of his bare bottom to Eloise and Tommy. They looked at each other and giggled. Another 'Halloa', closer this time, turned their giggle into a look of fright.

'Help us, please,' said Tommy, at which the creature suddenly became serious again.

'If you enter the quaking marsh,' he said, 'the quaking, quaking, quaking marsh' – each 'quaking' being emphasised with a jump and a thump of his fists on the ground – 'if you enter the quaking marsh, you will drown in mud, before the sun sets,' the creature informed them. 'You will soon die,' he added, grinning foolishly.

'Please,' said Eloise.

'Ah!' said the creature. 'A female nun!' He went on, 'Tell me who you are, what you want. Tell me quick. My friends are coming. You heard them.' And, cupping his hands to his mouth, he shouted 'Halloa' over his shoulder. 'My friends are coming and they can be dangerous friends. Oh yes! Dangerous. They will send their arrows into you if you do not tell who you are and what you want.' And he danced a few steps and laughed and stamped some more, his leaves and stems rustling as he did so.

'I'm Tommy and this is Veronique,' said Tommy on an impulse. 'We are running from the Bishop's men to escape the vengeance of the evil priest, Drogo de Montfort.'

'Evil priest?' whispered Eloise questioningly, half under her breath.

Tommy nodded vigorously. If only she knew the truth... He would have to tell her soon, and that would be hard, very hard.

'We must hide from the Bishop and from Drogo,' added Tommy.

'Ah!' said the creature. 'If you are enemies of the Bishop, you may be friends of ours! But of this Drogo, I know nothing.'

Twelve: Bandits

nother 'Halloa', very close now, rang through the air and Tommy and Eloise could hear the sound of running feet. A moment later, three men wearing rough leather clothes broke out into the path behind the strange creature of the marsh.

'Whaooo! What's that, then?' cried one.

'Tender meat!' cried another, as the third man came forward, leering at them and pushing the creature to one side.

'Do not touch us!' cried Tommy, as he tried to draw his sword from under his nun's habit.

This was a rash act, for in his struggle to pull the sword out, he overbalanced, grabbed furiously at the air, and before Eloise could help him, toppled sideways into the swamp. The bandits, who were preparing to draw their bows, relaxed and broke into laughter as Tommy floundered about in the mud and Eloise tried to get a grip on his arm.

'You are in the hands of God, now,' called one of the men, and they started to laugh again.

The mud around Tommy began to gurgle and blow nasty-smelling bubbles as he gasped and thrashed about, sinking lower into the quaking marsh. The men just stood and grinned as Eloise became more and more frantic.

'Help us!' she raged at them, and at that, seeing that Tommy was in real peril of disappearing altogether into the swamp, the strange marsh creature sprang from his crouched position, and leaping nimbly from hummock to hummock, landed beside Eloise.

Holding her tightly about the waist, he leant far out over the bubbling mud, as Eloise braced herself as best she could. The hands of the marsh creature and Tommy's touched, separated again, and then as Tommy gave a lurch upwards, they managed to get a hold on each other. The creature leant over backwards against Eloise, and the three men in leather began to clap and cheer.

'Go it, Jonci, go it!' yelled one of them.

Using all his strength, the creature slowly dragged Tommy clear, and at last, with a great sickening, sucking noise he shot out of the swamp. Joncilond, Tommy and Eloise landed all three in a heap on the tiny grassy tussock, barely managing not to roll off into the swamp on the other side.

For a brief moment, Eloise lay underneath, the creature on top of her, and Tommy on top of both of them, his filthy habit draped down over her face. Gasping for breath, she inhaled a terrible smell of rotting swampy mud and the never-washed body of the creature. She screwed her face up, and with both hands pushed Joncilond and Tommy to one side, and pulling Tommy's stinking habit away, she sat up. The creature clasped both of them, to stop them falling in again. And then, without warning, he stood up, with Tommy under one arm and Eloise under the other, and sprang from one hummock to the next as if he had no burden at all, landing neatly on the soft, safe grass where the three bandits were standing. Gently he placed both Tommy and Eloise on their feet.

What a fine sight they were! Bedraggled, too frightened even to be able to thank Joncilond for saving Tommy from the swamp, stinking of swamp mud, they stood looking at the ground, not daring to meet the gaze of the three men.

'Very pretty,' said one man sarcastically. 'Oh! So pretty.' And then, looking more carefully at Eloise, a more serious look spread across his face. 'Very pretty indeed,' he said more quietly.

'I don't think much of your choice,' said another.

'What d'y mean, my choice?' said the first.

'Him!'

'Him? They're nuns!'

'Have it your own way, I'll go for the female one!'

'No one takes nothing,' said the third man. 'Not before we take 'em to the Emp. You know the law.'

'Yah, but…' began the first man.

'But nothing! They've got to go before the Emp!'

Tommy frowned. What was the Emp? Searching his memory, he found no clue. Eloise shook her head at his brief questioning look. She didn't know what the Emp was either. It sounded though that it must be a person.

'Come on, you two,' said the third man, 'and you can give me your sword too, if you don't mind,' he added, addressing Tommy. 'Are you armed as well?' he asked Eloise. 'Armed nuns... I dunno! And you can take that stinking thing off as well,' he said, turning back to Tommy.

He came forward, and reaching inside Tommy's habit, pulled out the sword. Tommy did not resist. What was the point, with the two bowmen there at point blank range. Then he started to help Tommy get out of the nun's habit.

'There, I told you it was a boy!'

'Damn me, you're right!'

'Good God, someone's pinched the whalebone out of it,' said the third bandit, as he pulled the habit over Tommy's head. 'I used to make 'em for the nunnery, Seiche-Capucins, you know, before they caught me pinchin' the... Well, never mind that! Come on. You've got to come with us.'

He gestured to Tommy and Eloise to follow him and they set off through the deep shadows of the alders and oaks. The path was well marked here, with the trees making a natural canopy, with a few little splashes of sunshine coming through to light up the ground. The maker of nuns' habits led the way through the greenish light, Tommy and Eloise and the two other bandits following behind. They made no attempt to be silent. They were the masters here. The creature of the marsh capered about them, humming and chattering nonsense.

'Gobble, gobble, bubble... Mud, mud, mud,' he sang, and then snatches of 'Jonci, Jonci, Jonci, that's my name... We're off to see the Emp,' and so on.

The three bandits ignored him. They were clearly used to his ways. The little procession was completed by the donkey, with the red ribbon around its ear.

Suddenly the bandit in the lead stopped dead in his tracks.

'Lord!' he announced. 'We're right fools. These two mustn't see where they're going,' he said addressing the two other men. 'Our routes across the marshes are our secret, you see,' he added, turning to Tommy and Eloise. 'They're the secret of our safety. No one not sworn into the band is allowed to walk the path to our town. That's the law. We're going to have to blindfold you!

Now, where have we got something to put around your eyes?'

'Your town?' said Tommy. 'Do you have a town in here? A secret town!'

'Yes, and we have laws and rules. Some of us may be robbers and murderers even. But we have laws. Women too, children, born in the marsh and never known another place. Real children of the quaking marsh. But no church, no priests. If we want to pray, we pray under the trees.'

'Aye, that's right,' said another of the men, 'and it's a holier place than the high altar of Toulouse cathedral, with that rat-faced, grasping Bishop on his knees before it!' He spat on the ground.

'Yah!' said the third bandit. 'And in charge of it all we have the Emp!'

'The Emp?' asked Tommy.

'Yah! The Emp!'

'It's short for "Emperor", y'see: The Emperor of the Quaking Marsh. That's his title,' said the nuns' habit maker. 'And his court of course. And the court jester. That's him. Joncilond!' he said, jerking his thumb in the direction of the creature, who had sat himself down and was picking daisies.

Hearing his name, Joncilond sprang up, and advancing towards Eloise, fell upon one knee, and with eyes to the ground, offered her his bunch of daisies. Everyone, even Tommy, laughed, and Eloise blushed, taking the daisies delicately in her hand.

Entering into the game, she said, 'Arise, sweet knight!' and raised her arm slowly upwards.

Joncilond rose gracefully to his feet, bowed, and then spoilt it all by doing an absurd caper and a little screaming laugh. This broke the spell.

'What about those blindfolds, then!' said the nuns' habit maker.

He drew out his dagger, and cut two strips off one of the cleaner parts of the filthy habit which Tommy had been wearing.

'Told you I was a tailor!' he said, laughing.

'Do we really have to be blindfold?' asked Eloise. 'We'll fall into the marsh if we can't see where we're going!'

'I'll hold your hand, lovey-dove,' said one the men and Tommy scowled.

'Don't get worked up about him,' said the tailor, 'it's all talk with him. Chases 'em but doesn't know what to do when he catches 'em… Hey! Stop that!' he yelled, and put out his arm, as the other man picked up a branch and made to whack him over the head. The third bandit just laughed.

'I'll tell you what. We won't blindfold you until we're nearly there. Do we all agree to that? We'd get into trouble if the Emp found out. You're only children, and I don't think that you're going to cause us much trouble!'

'Only children!' said Tommy, disgusted. 'Okay! Fine,' he added, having second thoughts about saying any more.

'If the Emp asks, you were blindfold all the way, okay?'

Everyone nodded. They ignored Joncilond, who actually had been listening rather carefully to what they had been saying, and he hopped on ahead, disappearing around the next corner. As he did so, the donkey also came trotting past them, following him.

'Is that his donkey, then?' asked Tommy.

'Well, sort of. It follows him around. Recognises a kind of kindred spirit, I think!' And they all laughed.

They walked on in silence for a bit. But the talkative tailor couldn't keep quiet for long.

'What's your names, then?' he asked.

'Tommy and—'

'Eloise,' broke in Eloise, and then put her hand over her mouth.

Tommy frowned slightly, but said nothing. He'd told Joncilond that she was called Veronique, but maybe he'd forget, or probably no one would take any notice of him anyway.

They walked just a few more paces, and then the tailor started off again, 'I'm Jacques, him there, the one who tried to hit me with the branch, him, he's—'

'François,' broke in the bandit.

'And I'm Alain,' said the third.

'How do you do!' said Tommy and Eloise.

'You're our captives, but we may as well be polite,' said Jacques the Tailor. 'My wife… well, I call her my wife, but we've not been married in a church of course, just under the trees… my wife, Henrietta, she'll get you cleaned up. Maybe you can join the band! It's not a bad life out here y'know. Not so much of "do this! do that", no counts and barons to boss you about! Hey, you two, you look a bit posh, and you sound a bit posh too. You're not counts and barons – countesses, I mean?' he said, looking at Eloise.

One thing with Jacques was that he talked so much that he didn't really wait for an answer to any questions that he put. So when Tommy and Eloise said nothing in reply, he didn't seem to notice and just continued on as the next thought came rambling into his mind.

'I s'pose you could stay with us! Henrietta would like to mother you a bit, I should think. Right motherly she is. Right motherly. Pity we never could have no littl'uns.'

'What, couldn't y–?' François broke in.

'Yer shurrup!' said Jacques.

'But it was you wot said that I didn't know what to do when I caught 'em.'

'Yah! That's right,' said Alain, 'yer did!'

'See what a coarse lot I have to live with!' Jacques said, addressing apparently a large oak tree. 'Never get any sense out of them. Unless they want their clothes mending. Then it's, "Oh, please" –' he used a wheedling tone – '"you're really good at buttonholes… Look, the collar's fallen off… A bit of leather around the cuff, please… *pleeease*!"… "Go and ask Joncilond to do it," I tells them. "He'll cuff you." Ha!'

'You get the best mutton chops, y'do, from Henri, and when you do buttonholes real nice, you got a whole leg of mutton.'

'Tough it was, tough as hell…'

'You ungrateful–!'

But they never found out what sort of ungrateful creature Jacques was, for just then came the sound of galloping hooves.

'Oh, Christ!' said Jacques. He snatched the blindfolds out of his pocket and began furiously to fumble with the strips of the nun's habit.

'Help me!' he grunted, gesturing to Alain and François.

As the riders came into view, they had managed to get the blindfolds on their captives, but Jacques was still tying Tommy's at the back.

The foremost horseman stopped in their path.

'Who's this, then?' he said, and bending down from the saddle, took Tommy roughly by the shoulder.

Too roughly, as it turned out, for his blindfold slipped off one eye and fell across his nose and mouth. Tommy looked so comical that Alan and François tittered, but were silenced by a black look from the horseman.

'Your name!' demanded the horseman sharply.

'Tommy,' mumbled Tommy through the blindfold, as Jacques rushed forward to pull it back up.

'D'you think that I didn't see you putting it on just now?' remarked the horseman, waving his hand at the blindfold.

'Yeah, it'll be a thousand buttonholes for you,' chuckled François, and Alain giggled and turned away.

Even Tommy could not repress a grin.

'You'll answer to the Emp,' said the horseman, and Jacques went pale, 'and you two as well,' he added, addressing Alain and François, who just looked at the ground, refusing to meet the horseman's eye.

'No!' said Tommy. 'It was me! I'd just pulled it off on a branch, y'see…' Jacques threw him a grateful look.

'And you, who are you? A nun, I see!' said the horseman, ignoring Tommy and turning to Eloise.

As Eloise did not reply, the horseman jerked his horse's head over and made as if to grab hold of her.

'That's Eloise!' said Tommy abruptly.

'Eloise?' said the horseman. 'That's odd. Joncilond said her name was Veronique. Hmmm. We'll have to get to the bottom of this. Eloise, eh! Called after Eloise de Narbonne, no doubt. We hate the nobles here. You'll have to change your name if you want to stay with us – if that's what you do want. You'll not be allowed to leave, anyway. Now you've found the way, with your eyes open—' he growled at Jacques —'into the quaking marsh. Anyway you'll have to appear before the Emp before anything else is decided about what to do with you. We don't get many visitors in the quaking marsh – not that live through their visit, that is,' he added, and gave a nasty chuckle.

'They've been no trouble!' Jacques broke in. 'Just a couple of children, really!'

'We'll see about that,' said the horseman, and beckoning to the second horseman behind him, continued, 'They'll come with us now. We'll deal with you lot when you get back to Town.' He looked round at Jacques, Alain and François.

'I'll take the little nun, and you,' he said, pointing at the second horseman, 'take him – you take this Tommy.'

At that, bending over, he took a firm hold of Eloise around the waist and bodily lifted her into the saddle in front of him. Tommy, seeing how things were, let himself be set before the other horseman, and without another word, they galloped off.

The path was narrow with overhanging branches. Tommy and Eloise, with their blindfolds, kept their heads down as best they could. The horses knew the path and moved swiftly and surely, but, as is the way of horses, with no regard for their riders. So they were bent half double, and after just a few minutes, and several narrow misses, they came to Town. They knew that they must have arrived, because the cries of children playing could be heard. Tommy felt the horseman's fingers fumbling with his blindfold and it slipped away to reveal an amazing scene before him. Eloise was also free of her blindfold, and they both gazed in astonishment at the great stockade, the high wooden walls, stretching away on each side of them, curving to form a strongly fortified town, with watchtowers, a single gate, wide open now, wide enough to let four horses pass. So many people! Men, women, children, all suddenly quiet, stopped still in their work, in their games, standing looking at them, motionless. They were all silent, some sullen, all curious, suspicious of these creatures from a world outside, a world forbidden to them by the harsh laws of the land, the laws of the nobles, of the bishops and their soldiers; a world which some of them had never visited and, of these, few expected ever to visit – save to end on a gallows, perhaps.

A quiet murmuring and whispering of voices arose as Tommy looked on, as the children, who, more inquisitive than the grown-ups, began to move slowly towards them. These were the true children of the quaking marsh, in their rough leather clothes, many not much younger than Tommy and Eloise, staring with dark eyes. Of the boys, some had bows in their hands, and all had knives in their belts; the girls, with their hair tied back, wore skirts of coarse woven cloth.

Brown, thought Tommy, brown faces, brown sunburnt bodies, brown clothes, dark brown eyes, brown!

There were no colours except for the bright red ribbon in the ear of Joncilond's donkey, which stood in the middle of the crowd.

That must be a rare and valuable thing, that ribbon, thought Tommy, which Joncilond has somehow got hold of!

'Let us pass!' shouted Tommy's horseman, and the crowd around the gate moved reluctantly to one side, as if unwilling to let strangers into Town.

'A nun!' whispered someone.

'God!' said another. 'You don't think that the Church has come to us, do you?'

'Nah,' said another, 'it's just a young girl, look, don't you see?'

'She's lovely, she's a peach,' said another.

'I hope that she stays,' murmured a young man, as Eloise's horse brushed past him.

And so they rode through the gate, under the gaze of the people of Town. Guards stood on the parapet along the wall, armed with bows, bristling with arrows, ready for an attack. The people did not follow them, but as Tommy glanced round, he could see them standing looking with piercing eyes after them, and a faint murmuring growing to a noisy hubbub as everyone began to talk about these new arrivals.

Thirteen: The Emp

he whole of Town was made of wood, with buildings of rough planks and wattle of young saplings bound together with mud. To Tommy, it looked strangely like a scene from a Hollywood Western, with wooden balconies on some of the larger houses and small dark openings for windows. Here and there along the broad main street, there were wooden pens, which stank of the pigs grunting and snuffling in them. The heat shimmered and the air and heat and smell seemed to thicken around them. An uneasy peace settled on Tommy, and Town was quiet and still as if all the buildings were empty, the only sounds the pigs and the sudden whinnying of a horse and braying of a donkey, some way off, and the now distant murmuring of the people at the gate.

The heat was burning, hotter even than in the marsh, and the street was without shade. Presently they stopped before a much greater building, again roughly constructed, with large logs piled up at each side to support the high wooden walls. Guards, half asleep, were posted at each side of the double entrance doors, which stood a little raised above the street, up a few steps.

'Off!' said Tommy's horseman, gruffly, turning his sweaty face with an unfriendly look towards Tommy.

Tommy half dismounted and half tumbled off the horse, whilst the other horseman lifted Eloise off as though she were a sack of carrots and set her on her feet on the dusty road. The horses pawed the ground and one snorted, blowing flies away from its muzzle. Then silence fell again and the oppressive heat closed around them as they stood in the sun.

What now? thought Tommy.

The two horsemen seemed themselves at a bit of a loss. The still heat of the air glowed more strongly and a little wind devil scurried around them, causing dust to rise and fall, blowing itself out at one corner of the Emp's house – or palace – for that is what it must be, thought Tommy. As the wind devil passed, the horse beside Tommy tugged its head up quite violently and shook its mane as Tommy's horseman placed his hand on its heavy neck.

'Sssh,' whispered the horseman, and silence fell once more and the heat soaked through their bodies.

Tommy glanced at Eloise. God, she must be boiled in that black habit! he thought to himself.

Eloise turned, seeming to feel Tommy looking at her. She shut her eyelids and held them closed for a few seconds, to show her weariness. Tommy made as if to move in her direction, but a heavy hand fell on his shoulder.

'Still,' hissed the horseman.

They stood for several minutes in this way, the horsemen fidgeting and looking left and right along the street, as if hoping that someone would come to issue commands for what they should do now. Just as Tommy was beginning to get quite giddy, unable to stand any longer in the sun and feeling that he was going to fall in another moment, the stillness of Town was suddenly shattered by a deep bass voice bellowing from inside the building before them,

'Get out of my palace! Get out and don't come again with that rubbish, that slop. Out! Out!'

Then they heard the sound of bare running feet, a crash, a little scream and one half of the double door was jerked open. A young woman, dressed in rags, flew out of it, stumbled on the steps, landed on her hands, looked up wildly at the horses, who shied away, and at Tommy, Eloise and the horsemen. The guards by the door, however, being half or more asleep, scarcely seemed to notice.

'Disgusting!' yelled the enraged voice from inside the building. 'Don't show your dirty little face back here!'

The young woman scrambled to her feet, lifted her ragged skirts up with one hand, and on her short brown legs sped down the road leaving a trail of footprints and dust behind her. She rounded the nearest corner and was gone.

'Very fussy about his food,' said Tommy's horseman to no one in particular; the other horseman just grunted in reply.

Like one of the pigs in the pen that they had just passed, thought Tommy.

'That must be the third, or maybe the fourth this month,' continued the horseman. 'No, let's see. First there was Janine, and that raspberry pudding that tasted like marsh water, according to the Emp; I didn't think it was really so bad myself. What about you, Phillipe?'

'Grunt!'

'Then there was Emilie,' the other man went on. 'She lasted two weeks, maybe a record, until that business about an arrowhead in the pheasant and that brown sauce, with rabbit droppings in it – or so the Emp said – I could have sworn that they were just cranberries, past their best, mind you; and then there was… who was it then?'

'Grunt!'

'Oh! Yeah, she only lasted one day, can't remember her name. Veronique? No! Raisins in the bread. Why not? Anyway now Mathilde has gone too. He'll be looking for another. Who's to be the lucky girl? Can your daughter cook?' he added, again turning to Phillipe, the other horseman.

'My daughter? Hrummph, grunt!' was all the reply.

'What about you? Can nuns cook decently?' said Tommy's horseman, addressing Eloise.

Eloise looked at him in surprise and then looked away quickly.

'Sulky little thing, eh!' said the horseman, and chucked her under the chin.

Eloise took a step backwards and Tommy made to move towards her, but the power of the sun and the heat and the drowsiness of the street made him pause.

The other horseman was evidently getting impatient.

'No point in going in when a mood's on him like this,' he muttered, half to himself.

However, just then both doors of the palace were flung open and the two guards, wilting in the heat, managed to come out of their stupor and jump to attention, one so hurriedly that his pike fell with a great clatter onto the planks in front of him.

'Fool!' shouted a tall, very fat and bristly man, his face a mask of anger, with a black beard, two beady eyes and a large mouth with a full range of teeth – brown, as Tommy noted. The little eyes sparkled with anger.

'Fool!' he yelled again. 'Radishes, radishes, radishes, every day, radishes!'

He stamped his foot in rage so that the timbers of the veranda rattled. In one hand, the Emp, for it was he, brandished a baguette; in the other, three large red radishes with their tops intact. These he shook furiously as he stamped his foot again, throwing them far out into the road. Tommy's horse jerked sideways, almost pulling the horseman holding him off his feet, and began to munch this unexpected gift.

'Ha!' yelled the Emp. 'Only fit for horses!' And then, as if he had only just noticed them, the Emp turned towards the little group sweltering in the road in front of him and roughly demanded, 'This is them, is it?'

'*Yes, my Lord*,' said the horsemen in chorus, and bowed.

Eloise did a little curtsey and Tommy sort of inclined his head in what he hoped was a respectful way.

'Hee, hee, indeed it is!' called a familiar voice from behind the Emp, and out capered Joncilond, a garland of radishes around his head and a couple sticking rather rudely out of his trousers, too.

At the sight of him, the Emp burst out laughing, a great guffawing bellowing that started in the stomach, worked up the throat and issued forth like an explosion.

'Away, you scamp!' he said as his laughter subsided. 'We have important matters of state to discuss! Can you cook?' he asked, turning towards Eloise.

'I-I never…' stammered Eloise.

'You never?' shouted the Emp. 'You…?'

'I can cook!' interrupted Tommy suddenly.

'What?' exclaimed the Emp. 'A boy who cooks? I'm to have a boy to cook for me?' He paused a moment, thinking over the women whom he had recently employed. 'Well, why not? You're hired!'

Eloise looked at Tommy in astonishment. Actually he was rather astonished himself. He'd had cooking lessons at school last year – 'Domestic Science', they called it – or home something or other. 'Home Economics' – yes, that was it. He'd spent most of the time flicking pastry dough at Harry and trying to smuggle enough flour out to make a really big flour bomb. All he had learnt was how to make toad-in-the-hole. Well, okay, toad-in-the-hole it would have to be. It had no radishes in it, anyway, so far as he could remember.

'Come in, you two,' ordered the Emp, interrupting Tommy's increasingly desperate thoughts about his cooking skills, and beckoning to Tommy and Eloise. 'And you, too,' he said to the horseman, the grunter, who had carried Eloise. Turning, the Emp called over his shoulder, 'Dismissed, the rest of you!'

Joncilond however still capered about them, rudely waving the radishes and shouting out, 'Jonci, Jonci, Jonci!' and making faces.

They made their way into a large and dark hall. At one end there was a roughly carved chair, set upon a pile of logs, pinioned together. Below this chair, which Tommy guessed must be the Emp's throne, was a long table with benches on each side and a few stools along the walls. There was a strong smell of oak resin mixed with a smell of pitch, which was used to block the holes between the logs which made up the walls. A dark and smelly place, but cool at least. They stood as the Emp made his way to his throne.

'Sit,' he commanded them, as he took his royal place.

At that moment, he realised that he still held in his right hand the baguette, upright, like some royal emblem of power. For a moment he looked at it, as if unable to make out what it was and then, trying to preserve his dignity, he threw it to one side and pretended to ignore how it slid noisily across the floor.

But Joncilond pounced on it and began to worry it, like a hungry puppy.

'Stop that!' shouted the Emp, and obediently, but on all fours, Joncilond took the baguette in his jaws and made his way, rolling his bottom in the air, into a corner, where he continued to mumble it unnoticed.

The radishes, however, had fallen out of Joncilond's trousers at the feet of the Emp as he had pounced on the loaf. These radishes did nothing to add dignity to the scene, but fortunately the Emp did not notice them. Tommy however found his eyes continually straying to the little pile of bright red in the gloom of the hall.

'Tommy and Veronique,' boomed the Emp, bringing them back to serious business, 'what brings you here, where all others fear to come? You're lucky to be alive, do you hear?'

'Good sir,' began Tommy, 'we were pursued by…'

But up jumped Joncilond from his corner and interrupted.

'She's not Veronique,' he sang out, 'she's Eloise!'

'What…?' Tommy began. He thought that Joncilond thought that… Oh, heck!

'She's not Veronique,' said Joncilond again.

'She's—' Tommy started once more.

'Silence!' roared the Emp, and silence fell as he glowered around at his two captives and the horseman, Phillipe.

'What's your name?' he said, turning to Eloise.

Eloise looked at the ground and muttered, 'Eloise.'

'Look up and speak up!' said the Emp sternly, and Eloise raised her head and looked him full in the face.

Casting back the bonnet of her habit, she said loudly and clearly, 'Eloise de Narbonne, my good man, and I know who you are too!'

God! thought Tommy. The fat's really in the fire now! What's come over her?

'And he – your cook,' continued Eloise, emphasising 'cook' with irony and gesturing towards Tommy, 'he's—'

'No!' interrupted Tommy, loudly, 'I'm, I'm… your cook!' he ended lamely.

'He's Thomas de Romolue,' went on Eloise unperturbed. 'And if you think…'

'Stop, enough!' yelled the Emp, and put his hand up for silence. 'I'm the leader of Town and my word here is law. We care nothing for Counts and Countesses, nothing, do you hear?'

But in truth, the Emp was troubled as he thought over what he had heard.

Were these two really what this girl, Eloise, had made out… what that beautiful angry young girl had stated? What was more, she had recognised him – or so she said. Here was a great danger, but also a great opportunity. He might lead his people back to freedom and a place in the wide world, or he might bring down upon them the full force of Romolue, and maybe Toulouse as well, for all he knew…

Town is strong and difficult and dangerous to find, he continued to himself. But if trained fighters were to come in large numbers, Town would be overrun and all of us destroyed. If word got out that I have kidnapped Eloise de Narbonne and Thomas de Romolue, I and my followers would be dead men, no doubt of that!

Whilst these thoughts passed through his mind, he eyed the pair of youngsters – little more than children – before him. Seven years had passed since he had escaped the gallows in a daring raid by his friends, with him now to a man: his court, he called them. Seven years since an arrow flew past his face into the gallows post and in the alarm and confusion, his four faithful friends rushed in on horseback, into the main square in Toulouse, in front of the cathedral, grabbed him -- to the cheers of the crowd – and rode so fast out of the town that no one could catch him or even close the gates in time. Seven years since they picked their way through the marsh, led by Joncilond, who had lived there all his life. Seven years to build Town, seven days to destroy it, if he chose wrongly now.

'I'm told that you were found, stranded in the marsh,' he began, in a less aggressive manner, 'by Jacques the Tailor, and François and Alain. How did you come to be there? If you really are Eloise de Narbonne and Thomas de Romolue, how were you in the marsh, where no one comes, alone and unprotected?'

'Why should we tell you?' demanded Eloise. 'What do we owe you? We've been manhandled, treated like worthless peasants. And you, a common thief, yell at us!'

'Silence!' shouted the Emp. 'You were not invited here,' he growled. 'Your presence here, if you're what you say you are, is a great danger to us! If word were to get out that we held Eloise de Narbonne and Thomas de Romolue captive in the marsh, how long would it be before the count and his soldiers were burning Town around our ears? A day? Two days? No more!'

'Treat us with respect!' replied Eloise. 'Why should I bargain with a robber, a sheep stealer, a…' And she stamped her foot, her eyes blazing.

Tommy looked at her in wonder. Where was his sweet and loving girl? There was too much of the twenty-first century in Tommy to understand the great gulf that opened between Eloise and the Emp, which made her rage that she should stand in his presence, that he should demand anything of her. It was for her to command and for him to obey, and so it would remain for centuries to come.

After this outburst from Eloise, there was silence in the hall as the Emp looked from Eloise to Tommy and back again. Then the Emp sighed.

'Take them away, but treat them well. Do not let them escape. Who knows what they might tell if they made their way out of the marsh!'

Phillipe took the arm of each of them but Eloise shook him off disdainfully. He just shrugged and escorted them out.

'One last thing!' called the Emp as they left. 'Tommy, or whoever you are, can you really cook?'

The three of them stopped and turned. Tommy could not help grinning.

'I'll do you toad-in-the-hole if you like!' he said.

'Toad!' spluttered the Emp. 'Toad!'

And Phillipe began to laugh, a long snorting grunt of a laugh.

'No! no!' said Tommy. 'It's just a name. Get me some sausages, flour, eggs, milk, butter, a hot oven, and salt, of course. You'll not regret it!' Well, they might, actually, he said to himself.

Without giving the Emp time to reply, Tommy strode out of the door, followed by Phillipe with Eloise. Joncilond had disappeared. The Emp was left brooding on his throne, thinking of the difficulty he was in, but also thinking how disgusting it would be to spike a toad with a fork, and watch it wriggling – ugh! He'd have to find another cook! Tommy would not do.

Tommy and Eloise passed through the double doors of the Emp's palace and came out into the brilliant white light and scorching heat of the street. As they stood blinking in the sun, they noticed a low murmuring, which could be heard at first in the distance but then getting louder, as they stood to listen.

The horseman, Phillipe, paused a moment, raised his eyebrows in puzzlement at the noise and then led them at a rapid walk towards the main gate along the road from which they had come. The noise grew louder and they could make out voices. It was the noise of a large crowd, an ugly sounding crowd, which suddenly burst upon them, children running in front, with Joncilond in the lead. The crowd swelled out into the main road from a narrow alley to one side, and in a moment they were surrounded by most of the inhabitants of Town chanting, 'Narbonne, Romolue! Narbonne, Romolue! Down with them, down with them! Narbonne, Romolue! Down with them, down with them…!'

Phillipe put out his arm and shouted, 'Away with you! Orders from the Emp. No harm is to come to them!'

But no one took the slightest notice. And most of them could not hear what Phillipe was shouting anyway. Several men came running forward carrying chairs made of rough logs, and others with rope. Pulling Tommy onto one chair and Eloise onto the other, they wrapped rope around them until they were both so firmly bound that they could barely move their hands or feet. Then, taking each a chair leg, eight men raised their captives high above the heads of the crowd, and along they marched through the main road of Town, keeping up their chant of, 'Narbonne, Romolue! Down with them, out with them! Narbonne, Romolue! Down with them, down with them!' They passed the Emp's palace, until they came to a small square with a broad oak tree and a patch of dusty brown grass around it.

Phillipe meanwhile had rushed back into the Emp's palace. But the Emp was not to be found. He knew that he could not control this crowd alone and was at a loss how to act. He was in fact escaping from his palace through a small back door, out of sight of the crowd.

No harm must come to those two! he exclaimed to himself. Where were his court? Out hunting! The fools! The five of them could perhaps control the crowd and persuade them to give up Thomas and Eloise. But by the time that he found them, perhaps it would be too late!

The crowd entered and filled the little square. Tommy and Eloise, bound to their chairs, were placed in the oak tree, two metres from the ground, the chairs jammed between the lower branches. The men who had carried them there roughly pulled the leaves and smaller branches away, so that Tommy and Eloise could be seen by everyone.

'Now,' shouted one of the ring leaders, cupping his hands to his mouth, 'now we will try, and condemn to death, these nobles – just as they try and condemn us to death where they rule, so unjustly!'

God! Joncilond must have betrayed us! thought Tommy, as a great roar of approval greeted the words just shouted.

'Yes! My Jean!' cried a woman's voice from the crowd.

'And my Martin!' cried another woman.

'Bertrand, Maurice, Jean, Jacques, Roger…' The chorus of names rang through the square.

'Yes, all murdered by the nobles and the Bishop – yes, that Bishop,' continued the same man, and as he said 'Bishop' the second time, he spat on the ground. 'He's the worst, and his lying treacherous brother, what's he called? What's his name?' demanded the man.

Tommy saw his chance. '*Drogo,*' he shouted with all his might.

'Yes, Drogo,' yelled the man. 'A friend of yours, I suppose,' he said, turning to Tommy.

'*No!*' cried Tommy, 'He's a murderous villain, worse even than you suppose. He killed… he killed…' No! Tommy thought. I can't say it in front of Eloise like this.

He looked at Eloise. Tears were running down her cheeks. But whether they were tears of rage or tears of terror, he was not sure. So long as she did not blast off with another speech of noble outrage… He looked at her, as if to say, 'I'll handle this!' and she nodded just perceptibly and closed her eyes. But tears continued to roll down her cheeks, and Tommy felt his anger rising against these brutes around him.

'Hear us!' shouted Tommy. 'Before you condemn us… First, we are far too young to have had anything to do with Jean, Jacques, Maurice, Martin and all the other…'

'Silence!' yelled another of the ringleaders. 'We'd like to have the hounds. But we've only got the puppies. We'll make do with the puppies!' he shouted, raising his voice to a roar which mingled with another great yell of approval from the crowd. People pushed closer to the oak tree.

'String 'em up!' screamed one woman's voice.

'Revenge for my children!' cried another, and shook her bony fist at Tommy and Eloise.

'Roast them – burn them like witches!' shouted a third, and the crowd pressed closer still.

'It was the Bishop's men who were out to kill *us*,' yelled Tommy, desperately. 'That's why we're here!'

A murmur ran through the crowd at this.

'Don't believe you!' yelled a woman.

'Revenge for my Maurice!' cried another… 'And my Jean,'… And my Jacques!'

This is getting bad, thought Tommy, bad, bad, bad!

It was just this moment that Harry chose to phone him. *Peep, peep, peeeeep, peep, peep, peeeep… peep, peep, peeeeep… peep.* Mozart's 40th rang through the boughs of the oak and out around the square. For an instant, the crowd was struck quite dumb, and there was dead silence except for the phone ringing. Tommy, bound as he was, could not turn it off, though he struggled violently trying to free a hand.

'*Witches!*' screamed a voice, and one of the ringleaders echoed this.

'*Ungodly witchery!*' he shouted, backing away from Tommy, who was still struggling to release a hand. The phone started up again: *Peep, peep, peeeeep, peep, peep, peeeep… peep, peep, peeeeep… peep.*

'Witchcraft!' yelled another voice.

'She's a witch!' cried a woman in rags, thrusting a finger up at Eloise. Tommy recognised Mathilde, the lady of the radishes. She did not seem such a figure of foolishness now; more of a devil, as she stretched her thin bare arm up at them. The crowd became silent again, listening to the telephone ringing. Harry, getting bored, the ringing ceased. Then the crowd began to rage.

'Burn them for witchcraft! Burn them, burn them, burn them both!' they cried, and surged forward. The eight ringleaders grasped hold of the chairs again and Tommy and Eloise were carried once more, this time back towards the gate of Town.

Tommy's head was swimming and he found himself shouting, 'We hate the Bishop and Drogo as much, no! more than you do!' again and again.

But no one listened; no one could hear. Eloise he could not see. She must be behind him. To his horror he saw that a group of men had come with burning torches.

'*Stop*! *Stop*!' he yelled, as loud as he could; but on they rushed, to a horrible death by fire.

Just then Tommy heard the sound of horses' hooves. Five men swept into view, riding hard. It was the Emp and his court! They rode regardless of the safety of the townspeople at full tilt into the crowd, swords held high, two grabbing hold of Tommy's chair and two of Eloise's, as the ringleaders leapt to one side and ran for their lives. People scattered for safety, and those holding torches rushed to douse them in a great vat of water close to the gate. One man in his rush stumbled over a fallen townsman and the torch leapt from his hand, falling on a pile of hay stacked against the wall of Town. Flames burst up and raced along the wall, as guards sprang from their posts on the parapet to avoid being burnt to death.

At this unexpected turn, the Emp and his four followers reined in their horses and began to bellow commands for water to be brought from every corner of Town. This was the very disaster that all in Town feared most. The dry wood of Town burnt like so much tinder. The crowd forgot their murderous purpose and began to run like crazed ants to save their town and their own houses and children from the fire. The flames began to roar as air was sucked into the spreading blaze, and smoke rose in a great cloud, visible in Romolue, Toulouse and all the hamlets round about. The atmosphere became a choking fog and then, as this dispersed in places, the heat became unbearable and everyone retreated from the burning walls of Town, pressing back against the surrounding houses, some of which were starting to burn through airborne cinders falling on them. Tommy realised that their escape from burning might only have been a brief escape. He and Eloise might yet be burnt to death, in the company of half the inhabitants of Town.

With two slashes of his sword, the Emp freed Tommy and Eloise. Then, ignoring them, he turned back to fight the fire, which raged more and more strongly. Tommy and Eloise were left free to go wherever they could find safety. Taking each other's hands, they fled along the main road, unnoticed by all.

'Perhaps there's a gate at the other side,' shouted Tommy to Eloise, through the smoke and confusion.

Eloise nodded, and they both began to run as fast as they could. Glancing back a moment, Tommy could see flames leaping high around the main gate and on both sides, far along the walls.

'Create a firebreak,' Tommy could hear the Emp yelling. 'Pull down a section of the wall!'

Tommy and Eloise ran on, but then Tommy moved his hand to Eloise's arm and they slowed, and stopping, Eloise fell sobbing into Tommy's arms. He held her and she gasped with fear and relief at their close escape from death at the hands of the people of Town. As he stroked Eloise's head, Tommy could hear the Emp calling in the distance.

'Axes, axes!' And the word was passed on. 'Axes!' everyone shouted to each other.

Tommy glanced around. Leaning against a nearby wall, by chance, were two axes, roughly made but they looked effective.

'Eloise,' he said, 'let's help them. We need these people as our allies. They'll track us down and kill us in the marsh if we try to leave alone. If we help them save their town, then maybe they'll help us on our way to the château!'

'Yes!' replied Eloise, nodding briefly. 'Yes, let's do that!'

They took the axes and began to run down a little side street, making for a section of the wall far beyond the fire. As they ran, others joined them, some with axes, others just with lumps of rock in their hands. They reached the wall and all began to hack at the great oak uprights which held it from falling. Splinters flew and the great oak trunks began to sag. Glancing to one side, Tommy could see the fire advancing.

'Now, push!' shouted Tommy, and fifty shoulders were launched against the wall, as others continued to hack at the cross-spars which bound one section to the next.

The fire was leaping towards them, like a hungry animal, a dragon belching sparks with gusts of burning wind. All their work would be in vain in a matter of minutes if this section did not topple.

'*Push!*' yelled fifty voices together, and with a great cracking and groaning and rasping, twenty metres of the wall fell outwards.

'Drag it away, drag it away!' yelled Tommy, and all were now wrapping ropes around the fallen and scattered logs.

Sweat pouring from them, blinding their eyes with salt, they dragged the wood clear of the advancing fire, just as the heat was becoming impossible to withstand.

It was this that saved Town from destruction, with the same manoeuvre on the other side of the gate, where the Emp was in command. The fire was halted, and as it died, it could be approached with buckets. But many houses were destroyed, and many pulled down, to stop the spread of the fire, before all was under control.

Fourteen: Drogo's Shame

he fire and the struggle against it had lasted just one hour. But as they wandered through the smouldering wreckage, the citizens of Town felt a great weariness, a sadness and a regret for their foolish condemnation of Eloise and Thomas. The madness of the crowd had vanished, replaced with remorse. For now they saw these that two young people, noble or not, whose horrible murder they had screamed for, just an hour earlier, now they saw that these two had helped to save their town. Robbers, cut-throats, pickpockets to a man, they were ashamed. Some turned to Tommy and Eloise in the street and thanked them, some came and silently shook their hands. Tommy and Eloise said little, but only smiled and made their way back to the Emp's palace, to seek his help.

As they arrived, they could see that the veranda was partly burnt, set alight by the intense heat of a nearby fire. Otherwise the palace was still standing much as before. Without ceremony, they pushed open the double doors, unguarded now, and made their way into the great hall. As they entered, from behind a pillar sprang the form of Joncilond, carrying an axe in one hand and with a wooden bucket strapped to the back of his head. He bowed to the ground before them, and falling to his knees, tried to kiss Eloise's feet.

She moved smartly out of the way to avoid his tongue, which he stuck out as far it would go, wiggling it up and down. They giggled at this crazy display, and supposed that it was Joncilond's way of saying 'Sorry' for leading the crowd upon them. His tongue still wriggling around, Joncilond stood up, as the sound of horses announced the arrival of the Emp and his court.

The double doors were pushed roughly open and in strode the Emp and his four followers. Joncilond sprang out of sight behind a pillar. Tommy supposed that he was strongly out of favour for his part in the events of the day.

'Ha! You two are here, are you? A lot of trouble you have caused!' announced the Emp, arching his thick black eyebrows at Tommy and Eloise. 'You should have stayed in your château! That's the place for the nobles. In their castles – and me in mine!' he added, waving his hand expansively around the dark hall. 'Ah! damn it all! You were useful at the fire, though. Perhaps you are not all the same rotten, grasping, arrogant and bloodthirsty monsters like that Bishop and his disgusting brother. Eh? Speak up!'

'I will speak up!' said Tommy. 'Now hear us out! First, we thank you for saving us from your townspeople. But you want to know how we come to be here. Well, we were pursued by the Bishop and his soldiers. They were trying to kidnap Eloise, who was hiding in the nunnery of Seiche-Capucins! We fled into the marsh. From one hell into another, it would seem! Is this enough? Well, we hate, we loathe Drogo more than you can imagine!' Again he saw that glance of surprise from Eloise. 'Oh! Eloise, you do not know,' said Tommy, turning to her. 'You do not know!'

'What... what don't I know?' asked Eloise. 'More mystery, Thomas?'

'Yes, but please let it wait. Be patient. Listen all of you,' he continued, 'I must plead, we must plead with you. Get us out of the marsh and back to the Château de Romolue. Drogo and the Bishop are plotting our ruin and that of the Count and Countess, of the whole House of Romolue. If you help us, we will do everything that we can to grant pardons to you, so that you can rejoin the world – live here if you wish, but not as outlaws, to be hunted down one day, as you know, at the whim of the Lord of Toulouse, or Bishop Henri, or Drogo. In fact, I can promise to rid you forever of Drogo, and disgrace his brother too!'

This speech was greeted by murmurs from the Emp and his four followers, who, looking at each other, tried to find in their faces some wisdom where none had been found before. For these men were leaders of a kind, but their only policy was survival. They had come close to death so often that they saw the future in terms only of weeks, and thanked the Lord for every day that passed. This young lad, Thomas de Romolue, was offering them a future which stretched years, perhaps decades, ahead. This was difficult to grasp, and what was more, could they bargain for their lives, and the lives of all their townspeople, with the nobility? Would the nobility not require service in return? Would they not have to run, here, there and everywhere, at every command of some noble lord, losing the freedom of the quaking marsh? Could they truly, as Thomas de Romolue promised, continue to live in the marsh, but as a free people, able to visit their families, to trade, to take part in the outside world, to have stalls in the market, to marry in church, if that was what they cared to do?

'There's the problem,' said the Emp, 'the Church.' The Church would never give up its authority over them, never agree that they were free from the priests and bishops or the heavy payments which the Church demanded of everyone – even the nobility had to pay up, large sums too, if the rumours were true of golden cups, covered with jewels, and suchlike. 'The Church, the oppressive Church,' he muttered to himself.

These musings were broken by the clear, sweet voice of Eloise.

'I too will help you, all that I can. If you would agree to rejoin our world, we could forget the crimes that some of you have committed...'

'These must be long forgotten,' Tommy broke in, 'you—'

'Not all!' interrupted Eloise, her voice hardening. Oh no, thought Tommy. 'Not all!' repeated Eloise. 'Do you have the man here who stole the saddle and jewelled bridle off my pony, and broke its legs, leaving it to die in a ditch?'

'Eloise!' pleaded Tommy. '*Please*!'

'On the road between Romolue and Seiche-Capucins!' continued Eloise.

One of the court put his hand to his mouth, and looking pensive, said quietly, 'That was your pony, my Lady?'

'Was it you?' said Eloise loudly, turning sharply towards the speaker.

'No! No!' he replied hastily. 'But I think that I know...' And his voice trailed off.

Eloise opened her mouth to speak again, but Tommy got in more quickly.

'We must not quarrel now about these things! We will help you, we promise. You will no longer be outlaws. But help us return to the Château de Romolue!'

Holding up his hand for silence, the Emp began to speak.

'These things require deliberation – thinking about! We need to consider these... these...' he paused for a lack of words. 'But,' he resumed, 'you helped us with the fire, even after the people were about to burn you to death. You have earned something for that. For now, we need to go around Town and start to rebuild the wall, send out parties to cut down and shape staves, organise the townspeople. There is a lot of work to do. We'll leave you here for a time. There are no guards – but you will not attempt to escape. You know that if you do, you will meet your death in the marsh, if not in the quaking mud, then at the hands of one of our people, seeking revenge...' He paused a moment. 'We will eat together this evening, at sunset.' With these words he turned to leave, striding out of the hall.

However, as he got to the door, followed by his court, he stopped abruptly, put his hand to his forehead, and, turning, exclaimed, 'My God! We will have no dinner. I've sacked my cook!'

'What, not again!' exclaimed one of the court.

'Yeah!' replied the Emp. 'Every meal had radishes, she was crazy about radishes. I never want to see another radish, curse them to hell!'

Just then, as if by magic, a ray of late afternoon sunshine pierced the gloom of the hall, through a crack in the wall, and fell directly upon the little bunch of radishes that had tumbled from Joncilond's trousers earlier in the day and still lay on the floor before the throne. They shone brightly in the sunlight, while everyone held their breath and gazed at the bunch of radishes in wonder, as if the Emp had indeed summoned them up from hell. The dark figures, suddenly still and silhouetted against the walls, the smell of resin, the shaft of light and the little bunch of offending radishes, glistening scarlet in the dark hall: time ceased for a moment, but the moment soon passed.

'Joncilond!' yelled the Emp, breaking the spell. But no Joncilond appeared.

'He must have scuttled off,' murmured Tommy to Eloise.

'Joncilond!' shouted the Emp again, stamping his foot in rage. The Emp gave a long-drawn-out sigh, motioned one of his followers to pick up the radishes, and marched out of the hall, with as much dignity as he could still muster.

For the first time since midnight on Sunday night, Tommy and Eloise were left together, alone and in no danger.

'If Drogo could see us now!' breathed Tommy, as he held Eloise's head against his shoulder.

She turned her face towards him and placed her cheek against his, and he pressed her gently in his arms.

'Drogo,' she whispered. 'What is it about Drogo?' She straightened up and looked into Tommy's eyes. 'Tell me now. You know something, don't you?'

'Yes,' replied Tommy. He had been dreading this, but Eloise had to know what the parchment said, what Drogo's confession revealed.

'Well, Eloise,' he began, and then faltered. How should he begin? 'Well, it's like this...' He could not find the words. 'Well...' he started off again, and paused.

'Yes...?'

'After you went off disguised as a peasant girl...' He trailed off again. 'Look, Eloise, this is going to be really nasty, what I'm going to tell you. So be brave! Just be ready for something really horrible!'

'Alright, alright, please just tell me,' said Eloise, letting go of Tommy's hand and sitting down on the bench along the table in front of the Emp's throne.

'Come,' she said placing her hand on the space beside her, 'come and sit here! I am ready now, really.'

Tommy did as he was asked, and began his story.

'When you left, with the gardener guy, whatever his name was—'

'Martin,' chimed in Eloise.

'When you left with Martin... No, before you left, that was it, yes, the Countess...' Eloise looked at Tommy in surprise. 'My mother, I mean,' said Tommy and then hesitated, 'well not really my... er my mother... but anyway,' he continued hastily, 'she had seen Drogo coming out of the chapel clutching a manuscript in his hand. She had watched him stop outside the chapel door, and then return inside. Then there were scraping noises in the chapel, and... Oh, never mind all that! Anyway, Drogo came out without the manuscript, which obviously was hidden somewhere in the chapel. I had a feeling, a strong feeling, that Drogo had some dark secret to hide, and when I heard about it, I was sure that this manuscript had something to do with it! I was right,' he said, and added, 'horribly right!'

Eloise nodded and placed her hand on Tommy's arm.

'Go on,' she said.

'After you had gone, Drogo lost his temper with me and sent me to the chapel to say the Lord's Prayer five hundred times. Now the Countess – mother – had told me about Drogo and the manuscript. She's on our side, very much so; I haven't told you. Well, anyway, when I got to the chapel, I started to hunt for the manuscript, of course. There's not much in the chapel. But the big trunk in there had clearly been moved. So I took the crucifix off the altar and... Oh, gosh!' exclaimed Tommy, as he saw the look of horror on Eloise's face. 'Yes, I know that I shouldn't have. But the trunk was very heavy. Anyway, I sort of prised it along the floor with the crucifix. And I broke it!'

Eloise gasped. 'No! You really will have to do penance now! That was my special crucifix. I often went to pray before it, for my mother...' And, dropping her voice very low, she whispered, 'and my father too, wherever he is.'

'Oh, gosh! Did you?' muttered Tommy. 'Anyway, underneath the trunk was a block of wood and I found a key. But it didn't fit the lock of the trunk. In fact, there wasn't a lock. I got pretty frantic, especially when I found that Christ's head was almost broken off the crucifix. But eventually I found that the crucifix had a hollow bit in the base, which the key fitted. Inside the crucifix, I found the manuscript, rolled up, obviously the one that Drogo had been seen clutching. I pulled it out. Drogo's confession...' Tommy broke off for a moment.

'Yes, his confession to what?' demanded Eloise.

'Oh! Wait a second. I'm going to tell you,' said Tommy.

Putting his hand on her shoulder, he drew her closer to him.

Pressing him gently away, she said, 'Tell me the rest. Please, I can't bear to wait any longer! Do you have the parchment with you?'

'No, no, it's hidden. What it said was this: when Drogo was younger, before your mother was married, he came for the first time to Ellie-la-Forêt, I mean, the Château de Romolue. He met your mother, Eleonora.'

'Yes, Eleonora, how did you...? Well, of course...' Eloise fell silent.

'Drogo met your mother and fell hopelessly and passionately in love with her! She was so beautiful. Drogo was consumed by his love. It drove him mad! Then came Richard, your father.'

'My father? Richard! I never knew his name! Richard what? What was his name? Please, please tell me!' begged Eloise.

'You never knew your father's name?' exclaimed Tommy. 'Why not? Why was that a secret? Well, anyway his name was Richard de La Courtablaise.'

'La Courtablaise... CB,' whispered Eloise. 'CB... That's why...' She held out her hand. On the fourth finger there was a small gold ring with *CB* engraved on it.

'La Courtablaise,' murmured Tommy.

'Yes, yes, now go on, go on,' urged Eloise.

'Your mother married Richard not long after meeting him. She was quickly... er... going to have a baby, and when she was near to giving birth to you, Richard set off to collect his old nurse as a midwife. But he was captured by pirates and ransomed.'

A look of shock passed over Eloise's face.

'But that was not Drogo's fault, was it?' she asked.

'No! No, wait,' said Tommy. 'Drogo learnt how the ransom was to be paid. The ransom had to be delivered somewhere, the bay of Labeyrie at midnight, I think it was,' Eloise nodded. 'And the money was got ready, and two messengers went off with it. But that evil Drogo arranged through his servant, Roland, that these two messengers, carrying the ransom, would be murdered on the road. And that was what happened. The murderers made off with the ransom, and Richard was never freed by the pirates. No one knows what became of him! As you know, your father has never been seen since.'

'Oh!' cried Eloise. 'The evil man! I can see why you call Drogo evil. He loved my mother and he made sure that my father could not return, out of jealousy. Yes, Drogo is evil, you are right. And my poor mother. Did she die of grief? Is that how she died?'

'Oh, Eloise, it's worse, much worse!'

Eloise looked up at him wonderingly, her eyes glistening with tears.

'How could it be worse?' she asked.

'After you were born, Drogo became more and more consumed by his passion for your mother. He worked himself up to a mad, furious, jealous rage. One day your mother had arranged to go to the cathedral of Toulouse to pray for Richard. As she walked down the aisle, alone in the cathedral, but holding you in her arms, Drogo, hidden behind a pillar, stepped out, and killed her, with... Oh, Eloise!'

Eloise had gone very white. Tommy caught her in his arms.

'Eloise, Eloise!' he cried.

Eloise opened her eyes. 'Killed her,' she murmured. 'No, no!' she shouted, sitting suddenly upright. 'It's not true! He didn't. He couldn't have done that! How did he do it?' she demanded, turning on Tommy, her eyes blazing.

'With the crucifix,' said Tommy, 'that very crucifix in the chapel in the Château de Romolue!'

'No, no!' sobbed Eloise, her head in her hands. 'With the crucifix, that crucifix!' And then she grasped Tommy's shoulders with both hands, holding him tightly with all her strength. Anger transformed her.

'He will pay for this! He will pay dearly!' she raged. 'I will tear him into pieces if I can find him,' she said between her clenched teeth.

She made to get up, but Tommy held her down.

'Eloise, my dear Eloise! Now you see why I hate him. He destroyed your family – first your father, and then your mother. I hate him.'

Holding her firmly by the shoulders, he waited for her to calm herself a little. They looked long at each other and she allowed herself to be comforted a little as Tommy kissed her cheek gently.

'There is more,' he added. 'First, his brother knows this

confession. It was Henri who found Eleonora in the cathedral the next morning, and Drogo fallen against the altar, fainted from… I don't know what, but unconscious anyway. In fact the Bishop made Drogo write down the confession, to keep for blackmail, I suppose. Also, at the end of the manuscript, added later, but in Drogo's hand, was written: "The daughter grows so beautiful, I may have to kill her too." No! "The child grows so like her mother that I may have to kill her too." That's what he wrote! Your life is in danger, Eloise. The man is a criminal lunatic. In my time he would be in a prison for madmen.'

'Your time!' muttered Eloise. 'Your time…' she shook her head.

'Let me go on with what happened next,' said Tommy, and Eloise nodded weakly. 'I tried to fix Christ's head back on his shoulders, and got it to sort of stay on.' Eloise winced slightly at this. 'At any rate, I thought, Drogo probably wouldn't notice that I had been moving things in the chapel. As it was, I took the parchment and hid it in my clothes, but I met Drogo on the stairs, coming up to the chapel – to check on me, I suppose. We went back up to the chapel together. As we opened the door, a gust of wind took it, it slammed and the jar caused Christ's head to spring from his shoulders, where it dangled, jerking about from the crucifix!'

'*God*!' breathed Eloise.

'Drogo was mesmerised with fear. He saw the dangling head as an accusation against him, I think! He blacked out, striking his head hard against the stone altar.'

'Good!' cried Eloise, clenching her fists.

'Yes, his punishment has started,' said Tommy. 'The last I saw of him, he was unconscious in bed in his room, with a great gash on his forehead. I gave the Countess the crucifix to hide. Oh! I forgot to say. Drogo had earlier sent a horseman off to the Bishop to tell him of you and me, and our midnight meeting and all that. When two of the Bishop's horsemen came to the château, they could not get in to talk to Drogo – he was lying in bed with his bleeding hand – and there was a fight outside his door. One horseman escaped. Then the Bishop came to the château with his armed men – I saw them come past as I was on my way to you. Drogo must have been awake enough to say that you had fled to

Seiche-Capucins. That's why they arrived looking for you there so quickly. We were lucky to escape!'

'We wouldn't have if it weren't for you being so brave and clever,' said Eloise and kissed him.

Tommy looked into her pale face. She had just learned that her mother had been murdered by the priest whom she had known all her life, as the guardian of the souls of Romolue. She also knew that he had betrayed her father. He took her head in his hands and kissed her sweet mouth. She sighed, and placing her arms around his neck, held him close.

'Hrmmm!' The loud noise came from behind a wooden pillar in the darkest corner of the hall. 'Hrmmm!' sounded again. They jumped and pulled apart, looking wildly around.

'Joncilond!' shouted Tommy. 'The idiot! He's been hiding in here all the time. Did he hear what I was telling you, d'you think?' he added in a lower voice to Eloise.

'I don't know. I bet that he heard something.'

And as if to show that this was true, Joncilond leapt out from behind his pillar, and prancing from one foot to the other, gambolled about them, chanting, 'Drogo, Drogo, Drogo! Evil, evil, evil!' Then he ran off out of the hall and into the main street.

'Well, blast it all! It's important that this does not get around – especially not back to Drogo. But not much gets out of the marsh. I've got a plan to expose Drogo! That can wait. I must tell you the rest.'

'What! Is there more?'

'Yes. Listen. The Countess hid the crucifix in the stone bench in the garden – you know, the one with *Et in Arcadia ego* written on it...'

'Yes, yes,' said Eloise, eagerly. 'How, I mean, is there...? Anyway, and...?'

'Also, in her secret room,' continued Tommy.

Eloise raised her eyebrows at this.

'Yes,' Tommy explained, 'she's got a little secret soundproof room up at the top of the château. Anyway, in there, I showed her the manuscript. In fact I gave it to her to read. You can imagine. The poor Countess. She had loved your mother, her sister. And they could never understand why Richard did not return. They never knew the story of the ransom. Drogo covered his tracks. The Count still knows nothing. So it is only us three: you, me and the Countess who know the story.'

'And Joncilond,' said Eloise.

'And Joncilond,' agreed Tommy, 'but we'll just have to forget about that and hope there's no harm done!'

They sat there, holding hands and looking at each other, trying to think each other's thoughts, trying to guess each other's feelings. The stillness of the late afternoon filled the hall as Tommy studied Eloise's face. Her colour had returned a little. The beautiful colour of her cheeks, her lips, her soft, firm hands, he tried hard to imprint these on his memory, for he knew that, in the twenty-first century, maybe he would never see these again.

How could all this be resolved, and how could he escape with Eloise to his own time? He lifted her hand to his lips and kissed her index finger. He was rewarded with the curving of her mouth into a beautiful smile, but a sombre smile, as she remembered her mother's terrible fate.

Who was this boy, Thomas, or Tommy, who seemed half Thomas, but not quite Thomas? Much more exciting, she thought to herself and blushed slightly. What was that strange land of which she had caught a tiny glimpse, with burning lights, and dangerous… 'cars', was that what Tommy called them?

'What were those things,' Eloise broke the silence, '*cars*?'

Tommy did not reply immediately, but just looked at the wooden bench, at the grain of the wood.

'Mmm?' said Eloise, lifting his head with the tips of her fingers under his chin.

He looked her full in the face. So much beauty. He could never meet another girl with so much beauty. All his life would be second best after this. He must not lose her! If only they could find out from Jasper how to cross back and forth, perhaps they could live in both centuries at once? But what about that other Thomas? Perhaps he was in love with Eloise too.

'Cars?' said Tommy.

And then, sitting upright and alert again, it came to him very strongly that he had told Eloise nothing of who he was, and he had not tried to explain the mystery of the scar, or of the mobile, or of anything. But at least she had seen his century – briefly only – but she had seen it.

'Cars,' repeated Eloise. 'What are cars?'

'Oh, Eloise,' he began, 'there is so much to tell! Where can I begin? Let me tell you my story, of how I came to be here in the first place.'

So Tommy told of the holiday swap, and arriving in Ellie-la-Forêt, of the painting of the beautiful lady, who must have been Eleonora or maybe Eloise, Tommy explained. He told her of the etching and how he had found himself on the stone bench. Eloise listened, astonished, as little glimpses of this strange world crept in and out of the tale. Cars, telephones, so many people, what did they do, whom did they obey, nobles, the Church? As Tommy drew towards an end, they noticed that the sun was beginning to set. The Emp and his court would be returning soon.

'There's time for a quick telephone call, I think,' said Tommy.

Eloise looked nervously at the mobile as it lit up, the eerie green light showing clearly in the dark hall. The little alien peeping noises unsettled her, and then the squeaky voice of Tommy's mother.

'Ah! Tommy, at last. I did not dare to phone you.'

'You were quite right,' said Tommy. 'Harry nearly got us burnt as witches! Could you tell him he mustn't ring me, never, not at all! You've got his number, I think!'

'Yes, yes, darling. But how are you?'

'We're alive anyway... with the Bishop of Toulouse after us with fourteen armed men!'

'Oh! Gosh! Really! Who are "we"?'

'It's me and Eloise, Eloise de Narbonne. That's her picture, as a grown-up, in the salon, I think. She's fifteen here. Oh! Mummy, she's so beautiful!'

'Heavens alive, Tommy, we want you back. Never mind romance just now! By the way, they came on Monday morning to take that picture you're talking about away to be cleaned. Anyway, I've tried to catch Jasper, but he's very wary. He knows of course that I know all about his jumping between us and you. I'll corner him soon, and I'll get him to tell me what's what, if I have to hold a knife to his blooming neck! He said to mind that priest that we met.'

'Yeah! Right there. Eloise and me found ourselves back in the twenty-first century for about five minutes last night. God knows how – but you see, it can be done. Anyway, we were on the road and this wretched car comes straight at us, driven by that priest. Drogo's his name here, and he's the most evil man you ever heard of! He murdered Eloise's mother, he murdered Eloise's mother,' repeated Tommy, raising his voice, and Eloise drew in her breath sharply. 'Anyway,' went on Tommy, 'we landed straight back into 1599, just before he hit us. Not because of anything we did, of course; but it saved our lives. Perhaps it was Jasper watching over us. I don't know. Eloise was absolutely petrified.' Tommy paused for a moment.

'Tommy, Tommy, you've got to get back,' whispered his mother.

'But what about Thomas, the real Thomas de Romolue?' he added and then wished he hadn't, glancing at Eloise.

'He's adjusting okay, in fact,' replied his mother. 'Dad and he get on really well, discussing history. He's a mine of information about what you used to eat... Oh, gosh! Obviously he wants to be back home! He misses the Count and Countess and Madeleine. He hasn't talked about Eloise.' *Good*, thought Tommy... or, maybe, not so good?

'Look, just at the moment, we're in an outlaw town in the middle of a marsh, not far from Ellie-la-Forêt. I'm definitely going to be here until next Sunday. Could you come completely clean with Jasper? Don't threaten him or anything. Tell him there's going to be a big showdown on Sunday! He's a friend, in a way. He's certainly saved me from Drogo at least once, quite apart from the thing with the car. Tell him where we are – in the quaking marsh – but we've made friends here, and I think that we can get back to the Château de Romolue – that's Ellie-la-Forêt – tomorrow evening... Wednesday evening. The batteries are going to get low soon. Oh, Mum, I miss you and Dad!'

'We miss you. But you'll be back soon. For God's sake be careful. They're a bloodthirsty lot where you are.'

'You don't have to tell me! I killed... I killed...' Suddenly it stuck in his throat. He couldn't get it out. 'I... killed.' His voice dropped to a whisper.

'Tommy, no!'

'I did, Mum. I did! Oh! Look, it's a horrid story, awful, awful. It must wait.' He paused a moment, forcing himself to speak normally. 'Eloise is sitting here goggling at me as I'm talking to you. Would you like to say hello to her? She's saved the situation once or twice, I can tell you! Here, Eloise.'

'Is that you, Eloise?'

Eloise held the phone as if it would bite her. 'Yes,' she whispered.

'Louder,' said Tommy.

'Yes, it's Eloise. You're Tommy's mother?'

'Yes. And we want him back. Will you come too?'

Gosh, thought Tommy, just what I wanted to ask.

'I want to be in both places,' said Eloise. 'I want to be with Tommy – Thomas, I mean – he is so brave, so noble, but I also want to be here, or at any rate, I want to be Eloise de Narbonne in my own time. Both!'

'Ah! We shall see. Something will work out.'

'First I will have revenge, terrible revenge, on this evil priest, Drogo!' said Eloise, her voice rising.

'Yes,' said Mum, sounding slightly shaken. 'Yes, I can see that you would feel that way. But be careful. Please be careful. I must go now. Keep the battery for emergencies. I'll talk to Jasper. Goodbye.'

'Goodbye, Mum!' shouted Tommy.

'Jasper?' said Eloise, turning to Tommy, as he reached over to shut the phone off.

'Jacques – I told you, you remember?'

'Ah! Yes, of course.'

Eloise still held the mobile. She began to run her finger over it, then held it to her nose and sniffed at it.

'Strange, smooth stuff,' she said, 'with no smell at all really. Perhaps a tiny bitter smell, maybe.' Then she handed it back to Tommy, who hid it away in his clothes.

'What story should we have for the… um… mobile going off in front of all the townspeople? The Emp is bound to want to know about that,' asked Eloise.

'Oh! Let's just say that it's one of Rabelais' toys!' suggested Tommy.

Before they could discuss it further, the Emp and his court entered. Behind them came a procession of men and women carrying trays of food, hot and cold, and earthenware jugs of drink. All these things were placed on the long table where Tommy and Eloise were sitting, and the Emp and his four courtiers sat down around them, without any ceremony.

The Emp drew his dagger from his belt, and lifting the lid of the nearest tray, speared a small chicken and sank his brown teeth into the breast, motioning to the others to do the same.

'Don't you say Grace?' asked Eloise in a shocked voice, and everyone laughed.

'Sometimes I say it afterwards, if the food was any good,' chuckled the Emp. 'Remember, we're outlaws. We don't have to even pretend to believe all that stuff!'

Tommy pressed Eloise's hand, as if to say, 'Bear with these uncouth men. We need their help.'

Eloise gave a very slight nod.

'Well, not so bad so far!' announced the Emp, as the juice from his second chicken ran down into his beard. 'It's Phillipe's daughter – you know, Phillipe who brought you to me earlier on horseback – it's his daughter that cooks here now. You're sacked, by the way, Monsieur Thomas. I didn't fancy your idea of grilled toad. What's under this one? Let's see,' he said, lifting the lid from a second tray.

'Nettles. Hmmm. We'll see. Let's hope that she picked the young sweet ones, or she'll have a bunch of them where she daren't show her father!' At this the court chuckled and Eloise frowned.

'There's ladies present, y'know,' remarked a courtier.

'Oh! Pardon me,' said the Emp.

'Nettles,' said Tommy, 'I've never eaten nettles.'

'Ah! Not dainty enough for the nobles, that's for sure,' said the Emp.

'No, I mean, at home in Eng—' Tommy blurted out, without thinking, but just stopping in time, as Eloise kicked him under the table.

'In where? Eng... what?' asked the Emp.

'No, nothing,' said Tommy. 'They're good though, the nettles.'

The meal progressed, each dish carefully inspected and judged by the Emp: fair, middling, good stuff, rubbish and so on. To mark the end of the meal, the Emp gave an enormous belch, which lasted several seconds.

'That's Grace after meals,' he announced loudly, and everyone laughed, except for Eloise, who still seemed shocked by the lack of respect these outlaws showed for Christian customs.

And then, to Tommy's amazement and disgust, the Emp put his hand in his mouth and pulled out his teeth. So that's why his teeth were brown, they were brown false teeth, made of wood! Taking a small splinter, the Emp began carefully to clean them, flicking the bits on the floor. No one paid much attention to this, and even Eloise only raised an eyebrow slightly. Wooden false teeth? Whatever next? thought Tommy.

Finishing his teeth-cleaning operation, the Emp turned to Tommy and Eloise. 'Now,' he said, 'you two have got a bit of explaining to do. First of all, what was that thing that went off making weird noises in front of the townspeople, before they decided that they would make a nice grill of you?'

'Oh, that,' said Tommy, wincing at the last phrase. 'Yes, well, that, it's something that old Rabelais made, in Romolue. You remember old Rabelais? It's a kind of toy. If you press the buttons on it, it makes squeaky noises.'

'Yeah, but what possessed you to set it off in front of everyone then? I mean, it was hardly the time for showing off your toys!'

'Well, it was a bit daft, I agree. I thought that it might sort of divert them a bit. I mean, get them interested in something other than hanging us from the nearest tree. I had to do something. Things were getting very hot, as you know.'

'Look,' replied the Emp, 'these people are very upset about losing their sons, brothers and sisters on the gallows, for no good reason at all, most often. Just the brutality of the Church or the greed of the nobles. You can't expect them to get carried away by some silly toy that Rabelais made!' He looked around at his followers, who all nodded wisely in agreement.

'Anyway, I'd like to see it,' continued the Emp. 'Can you give me a look at it?'

Tommy had been expecting this. Best just to show it directly, like he did for the Count. So, to Eloise's surprise, he fished inside his clothes without hesitation, finding the mobile and pressing the off button several times to be sure, slowly pulled it out to show the Emp.

'Here. Careful, though. It's delicate. Don't drop it.'

'What're these button things for, then?' asked the Emp, as he ran his fat and greasy fingers over the surface of the mobile. 'And, heavens, it's made of strange stuff. Not wood, is it? Not metal either? What did Rabelais say it was?'

'I think it's wood,' replied Tommy.

'You can't see no grain,' said one of the courtiers, peering over the Emp's shoulder.

'That ain't wood,' said another.

'Perhaps it is a kind of metal then,' said Tommy, getting a bit worried as the mobile went from hand to hand. What if one of them turned the light on?

'Hey, give it me back,' he cried, 'you're making it all greasy!' He took it back, and put it away out of sight inside his clothes.

'Well, okay,' said the Emp, dismissing the mobile from his mind. 'Now, you want to get back to the château, don't you? Well, we've talked about it and there's a couple of things. First, ways into and out of the marsh are secret. You're going to be blindfolded – properly this time!' Here the Emp thumped the table with his fist. 'Second, we just want to be left in peace. We don't want no special privileges. But, we want to come to market. To come and go as we want. But no one comes to us. Y'understand? None of this "Yes sir, no sir," for us anymore. It's mostly the Church what'll object, you'll be sure. See what you can do for us! '

Tommy and Eloise both nodded and smiled at each other.

'They are going to help us, you see,' whispered Tommy.

'I knew that you would,' said Eloise, as she turned to the Emp's courtiers and gave them one of her wonderful smiles.

Fifteen: The Bishop at Romolue

hrough the grey and misty light of dawn, the Bishop and his followers, fourteen men only now, rode wearily towards the Château de Romolue. Some were so tired they were held awake only by the sudden motion of their horses, which now and then tossed their heads, snorting in the cool air of the approaching day. Only the Bishop, tight-lipped and angry, seemed alert, at the head of the troop, peering this way and that, as if in the hope of catching a glimpse of Thomas and Eloise. The Bishop was an evil-tempered man even in good times, and these were not good times. He was always quick to take offence, never more so than now, and slow to forgive any lack of respect, real or imagined. He had a hatred of failure whatever his purpose.

To be fooled by two children! He scowled as he thought of it. To be made a fool by two children, outwitted, led into a trap – that cave… and his brother imprisoned in the Château de Romolue, or so his man had said. We'll see… And so his thoughts ran on.

'Keep in line,' he ordered, and his men tugged roughly at their reins. 'There might be bandits about! Not to mention demons coming out of the ground, you dumb idiots!'

Several of his followers shuddered at the memory of the strange green light and the monstrous face, which they had seen as they had attempted to pursue Thomas and Eloise in the cave.

'I'm never going near any bloomin' caves again,' whispered one man aloud, half to himself and half to his friend in front.

'Silence!' shouted the Bishop, who overheard him. 'If I order you to descend into hell, you'll do it. D'you hear?'

'Yes, my Lord,' mumbled his followers.

'I don't like caves, though,' muttered the same man again.

For it was the poor fellow who had got jammed in the rocks and broken a couple of ribs when he was roughly pulled out. He winced in pain and cursed loudly as his horse put a hoof in a pothole in the path and stumbled.

245

'Silence, I said!' shouted the Bishop.

'Sorry m'Lord,' said the poor fellow, 'but what with m'horse and m'ribs…'

'God's blood, it'll be sentry duty for you for a week, if you don't shut your trap,' retorted the Bishop, turning to glower at his soldiers.

And so the little group made their painful way, through the lightening landscape, arriving as a pale red sun began to rise, at the great door of the Château de Romolue.

'Open in the name of the Church!' shouted the Bishop, and as there was no immediate reply, he ordered one of his men to dismount and beat on the door.

'Patience, m'Lord, patience is a virtue!' a small voice inside the château called to them, accompanied by the sound of chains being moved and the grating of a large key.

The door swung open to reveal the bent form of Jacques, smiling welcome as best he could to these rough and dangerous men.

'Patience you said? I'll have you hanged, man!' said the Bishop addressing Jacques. Then, turning towards his followers, he ordered, 'You and you,' jabbing his finger at them, 'stay at the door here. The rest, stable the horses and get in the kitchen. Be ready to come on the instant, if you are called!'

Swinging himself down from his horse in a swift movement, the Bishop entered the château, plumped himself into the nearest chair, and pointing at Jacques, said, 'Boots!'

'Boots, m'Lord?' said Jacques, puzzled.

'Yes, boots! Take my boots off!'

'Well, of course, m'Lord, I'll fetch…'

He hurried off as fast as he could, as the Bishop opened his mouth to order him once more to take off his boots. Jacques was not going to stoop to removing the Bishop's boots. That was work for the most humble servants, not for the steward of the household.

'Boots, indeed!' he muttered, as he cuffed awake a young footman who was snoozing by Drogo's door. 'Meant to be guarding it, aren't you?'

'Guarding…?' said the footman, half asleep.

'Go and get the Bishop's boots off!' ordered Jacques, waving his hand along the corridor in the direction of the main door, 'and shut that door after you!'

The footman, coming rapidly awake, stumbled off with his hand over his mouth suppressing a yawn.

The door of Drogo's room was left unmanned. As Jacques paused a moment, from inside he heard a muffled noise as Drogo cried out in his sleep. Alarmed at the sound, Jacques quickly put his head around the door to see Drogo sprawled beneath heavy blankets, his head just showing from under the bedclothes. As Jacques watched, Drogo turned, and kicked with his legs, as if spurring his horse, and kicking again, woke with a start, jarring his hand and moaning at the wave of pain that travelled through his arm and up into his injured head. Jacques closed the door noiselessly and departed to warn the Count and Countess of the arrival of their noble guest, the Bishop.

Drogo meanwhile lay still for a moment, letting the pain recede, breathing in shallow breaths through his thin lips. His grey face matched the pale light of the room, the windows hidden by cloth draped around them to keep the light from the sickroom. He stirred again, with great care, and slowly raised himself on one elbow, letting the bedclothes fall to one side. His watery eyes opened and closed, blinking like those of a large lizard, and the rough skin of his wrists looked like the scales of a reptile. He peered around the room, as if to be sure that he was alone. Now wide awake, a sneer came to his lips and he began to mutter to himself.

'I will have them soon in the palm of my hand. Eloise...' He shuddered a moment as he said her name, and then fell back upon the bed and whispered, 'Eleonora, Eleonora! Why, oh why, are you not here to comfort me?'

And he lay still for a moment as he relived his crime, as he had done each of these days for fifteen years, bringing once more the heavy crucifix crashing down upon her head, down, down, as she fell and died upon the flagstones, the baby tumbling from her arms, lying whimpering in the cold nave of the cathedral of Toulouse.

'Why are you not here to comfort me?' he repeated more

loudly. Then, crying out, 'No!' he pulled himself from the bed, putting his feet on the cold floor. Dragging himself up by placing his good hand on the chair beside his bed, he rose to his feet. He stood, breathing hard, his thin body covered only in a long linen robe, finding his balance and looking around, his eyes darting this way and that. His glance finally fell on the heavy door of his room. He placed one foot forward, and then with great care, for every step caused his head to burn and pulse with agony, he made towards the door.

'I must free myself from this prison,' he hissed, his eyes on the door. 'How dare they lock me up here. I, Drogo de Montfort, brother of Henri, the Bishop of Toulouse!' A look of anguish passed over his face as he mentioned his brother's name, but he continued, 'Of a great and ancient family, among the first in France...' Driving himself on, he reached the door, raising his voice almost to a shout, as at the last syllable, 'France', he grabbed at the door handle to support himself from falling.

But to his surprise the door was not locked, and as he put his weight on the handle, it turned and the door began to open outwards, dragging him along with it, as he held on with all his strength. With a cry, he tripped, his hand slithered down the door, and he fell across the threshold of his room, half stretched out on the floor of the corridor. The wound he had received from the chapel altar, loosely bound as it was, reopened, and blood spilled on the ground, trickling between the fingers of his hands which he held pressed against his forehead.

The corridor was deserted, the doors at each end shut. No one saw this latest accident. Then a noise from behind the closed door leading to the entrance hall of the château startled him, and he tried to raise himself. Surely that was the voice of his brother, cursing a servant? His brother was here, to protect him, to take him away from this place where every shadow, every shaft of sunlight reminded him of his pain, his torture, his Eleonora, born again as Eloise, taken from him again. Thomas, ah! He would have his revenge.

These thoughts put life back in him and he struggled to his knees, crawling a little way forward, his lank hair falling over his bloody face. At just that moment, the door of the corridor flew open, and there, revealed on a chair in the hall, was his brother Henri, with two footmen struggling to remove his boots, tugging and swearing, and a third at the open door, gazing down at Drogo. The curses died on Henri's lips as he followed the footman's gaze, and the Bishop sprang to his feet, kicking all and sundry out of the way, and stood, his face purple, his mouth still open to yell some insult; but he stopped in mid-breath as he stared upon the form of Drogo, on his hands and knees, gazing up at him, just a few yards away, blood in rivulets running slowly down his face from the gash on his forehead. The Bishop's hesitation lasted only a moment.

'My brother!' he shouted, running forwards, arms outstretched, and coming down on one knee on the ground beside Drogo. 'What have they done to you?'

'Revenge!' cried Drogo, raising a weakly clenched fist. 'Revenge!' Then he collapsed in a faint, as Henri managed to hold his head from striking the floor.

At this moment, footsteps could be heard on the grand staircase, and the voice of the Count could be made out.

'Bishop Henri is here, you say? It must be an important mission that brings him here at this hour. And with ten or more soldiers? What does this mean? But where is he, on the chair, waiting in the hall, you said?'

'Yes, Count,' said Jacques, 'indeed he was, but...'

Coming to the bottom of the staircase, they glanced down the corridor and at once saw Henri kneeling beside his brother, holding Drogo's head in his hands. The Count came rushing forward.

'What is this?' he shouted, working himself immediately into a rage. 'Who did this?' he shouted again, turning to Jacques.

'But, Monsieur le Comte, you know that...'

'Yes, who did this?' repeated Henri, grinding his teeth with rage. 'But we know! We know who did this! It was your Thomas, whom I pursued through the night. Pursued but failed, yes failed, to capture!' His voice rose to a shout. 'And Eloise was with him! That we extracted from the fat Abbess.'

The Countess came hurrying down the staircase as these last words were said, and hearing this remark of the Bishop, realised that serious danger was upon them.

'Ah! Drogo, and my good Bishop!' she exclaimed, as she hurried up to them. 'Let us discuss all that has happened later. The first thing is to get Father Drogo back into his bed and settled. Whatever came over him to leave it? Was there no one sitting with him?'

She looked hard at Drogo, thinking as she did so. Is this the man who murdered my sister? This pathetic, thin rag of a man? I will see that he suffers as much pain and horror as I can arrange!

'Don't just stand there gawping, fetch a sleeping draft from Marie,' she ordered a footman, who was peering over her shoulder trying to get a glimpse of Drogo.

The man ran off.

At that, the Bishop took his brother in his arms and, kicking the door fully open, strode over to the bed.

'Gently!' whimpered Drogo, as his brother laid him not very tenderly on the hard mattress.

'I hope that you are not too injured to talk sense to us,' muttered the Bishop in his ear.

'No! I'll have revenge, I'll—'

'Ssshh… not now,' interrupted the Bishop, as the Countess came up to the bed with the Count hovering behind her.

At that moment, Marie herself came bustling into the room.

'My good Bishop,' she began. 'Your Grace,' she added, and did a little curtsey.

The Bishop turned and glowered at her.

'Don't you give him anything that knocks him out as you did before!' he said. 'We need to talk together, my brother and me.'

'Ah! My Lord, that was only to relieve the pain and help his wounds to heal. But he has been walking about and the wound has reopened. I need to put a bandage on it again. Bring warm water,' she ordered a footman.

'Should we not all leave whilst Marie attends to your brother?' suggested the Countess, moving towards the door.

The others, including the Bishop, followed her out, as the footman arrived with water.

'Stay!' Marie ordered the footman.

Together they washed the blood from Drogo's face and bound up the wound again.

'Hold up his head,' said Marie and as the footman did so, Marie pinched Drogo's nose between finger and thumb.

In the half stupor in which he lay, his mouth fell open and Marie, drawing a small bottle from a hidden pocket, emptied the entire contents down his throat. Drogo coughed and spluttered feebly for a moment, and then with a deep sigh, sank back among the bedclothes. Marie smiled grimly to herself.

Leaving Drogo's bedroom, Marie could hear voices raised nearby.

'The Abbess knows Eloise when she sees her.'

It was the Bishop, his voice loud with irritation.

'Yes, that's true, Henri,' the Count could be heard replying, as Marie stopped to listen.

Well she might listen, for it had been her doing, the escape of Eloise to the Abbaye de Seiche-Capucins. Obviously, Eloise had not been able to keep up the deception in front of the Abbess.

'But Jacques told us that Eloise had departed after the feast on Sunday night with, with… er…' said the Countess.

'She cannot have done!' interrupted the Bishop, thumping his fist on the dining-room table, for it was in the dining room, the scene of the feast on Sunday night, in which they stood.

'Perhaps we should hear again from Jacques,' suggested the Count. 'Send for Jacques,' he said, marching to the door and calling down the corridor towards the kitchen.

Jacques appeared immediately. He had been in the kitchen, making sure that the Bishop's men were so well supplied with wine that they were all now fast asleep on the floor and the benches.

'Jacques,' said the Count, adopting a kindly manner, as the Bishop scowled beside him, 'tell us once more what Eloise said to you, after the feast on Sunday evening.'

'Well, sir, as you know, there was a great deal of coming and going, a great deal…' answered Jacques, spinning out his words as he formed a plan in his mind.

'Yes,' said the Bishop, with an impatient movement.

'Well, as far as I remember, Mademoiselle Eloise shouted over the heads of several people that she was going… er… somewhere, and that she did not want to disturb you' – he turned towards the

Count and Countess – 'because you were so busy with all the guests. She had changed into a simple dress for travelling, I remember, yes.'

'Somewhere?' exploded the Bishop. 'Somewhere! Can't you remember where she said?'

'There was a great deal of noise,' replied Jacques, 'but now you mention it, she may have said something about an abbaye... She was always talking about, well, she, er...'

The Countess was grinning faintly. 'An abbaye?' she said.

'Well, that's probably it then,' said the Count. 'She probably went off to the Abbaye de Seiche-Capucins, that night. That's what the Abbess said, wasn't it?' he added, addressing the Bishop.

The Bishop clenched his fists in fury. It was true that all the Abbess had said was that Eloise had been in the abbey, and that she was now gone. But Drogo had told him that she had been smuggled out of the Château de Romolue, that Thomas de Romolue had run off with her – not that this made any sense, but Drogo had been drugged.

At this point, in the short silence that followed, a small shaft of light seemed to penetrate into the brain of the Count.

'What was that you said before?' he demanded of the Bishop, 'that you pursued Thomas, my son, through the night, and he had Eloise with him? With fifteen soldiers?'

'Well, Drogo told me...' began the Bishop, on the defensive, as he saw the colour coming into the Count's cheeks. 'Er, Drogo told me...'

'Drogo be damned!' shouted the Count, and the Countess began to look alarmed, damned though she wanted him – and the sooner the better.

'My Lords!' she broke in, as the Count and the Bishop tried to stare each other down, but they ignored her.

'Why was this man pursuing my son with fifteen armed men through the night?' demanded the Count, thrusting his hands on his hips.

'Look!' shouted the Bishop. 'My brother has been badly injured, because of your stupid little son and his stupid little cousin. And they aren't just stupid, they're also dangerous, meddling in things, in important matters of state! You know well what I mean.'

'I'm sure that I don't,' retorted the Count, 'and if you think that you can go trying to murder my children because they get in the way of your plans, by God, I'll break your head!' And he advanced threateningly towards the Bishop.

Henri de Montfort backed away, and feeling less than safe, called loudly, opening the door to the passage leading to the kitchen, 'Men! Come to my aid!'

The Countess ran forward between the two of them.

'Count,' she said, 'the Bishop felt himself wronged. And quite false information was given him… in the heat of the moment,' she added trying to calm them.

'Men! Here!' shouted the Bishop again, and at that, one sleepy soldier tottered into view, supporting himself on the door frame.

'They're all drunk, sir. Good wine, sir, and we didn't get no sleep chasing after them two nuns last night!'

'Forget your men,' said the Countess, and she slammed the door in the face of the soldier as he started backwards at her approach. The Bishop stamped his foot in rage as the Count stood aghast. 'No one will harm you here,' she added, casting a powerful look at the Count.

'"Them two nuns!"' shouted the Count. 'He said *nuns*!'

At this he grabbed the Bishop by his coat and threw him bodily into one of the heavy chairs, half turned from the table. De Montfort steadied himself, and eyed the Count carefully.

'You will pay for this,' he muttered.

'And you had better explain your actions, my good Bishop!' said the Count loudly and with fury still in his voice.

'I'm not required to explain anything to you,' replied the Bishop quietly. He rose from his chair, regaining his composure and trying to be dignified, turned to the Countess.

'I thank you for your hospitality,' he said, and walked out of the dining room, along the corridor and entered Drogo's bedroom.

He paused for a moment at the door, so that his eyes could adjust to the weak light inside. Then, walking rapidly over to the bed, he pulled back the corner of the blanket, seeing immediately that Drogo was deeply asleep.

'Damn them!' he muttered. 'They've drugged him again.'

He pulled a small bottle of smelling salts from a pocket. Shoving these under the nose of his brother, he roughly shook his shoulder. Drogo moaned, and came half awake.

'Careful, good brother,' Drogo murmured, seeing Henri standing over him.

'You must come with me,' said Henri. 'You cannot stay in this château a moment longer. In your drugged state, something may be revealed... you know what I mean!'

Drogo nodded weakly. It was this fear that had led him to the chapel, to check on Thomas. What had happened there? With a shudder he remembered Christ's head wobbling on its shoulders, and he stared wildly at his brother, fear settling on his face.

'What?' said Henri urgently, suspecting something. 'Does anyone know anything?'

'The Almighty knows! The Almighty,' said Drogo in a trembling voice.

'Don't give me that rubbish,' retorted the Bishop, relieved. 'I mean, someone in the château!'

'Listen to me!' whispered Drogo. 'Listen! The crucifix, the one which...' he could not say the words, but the Bishop nodded, to say he knew very well which one... 'the crucifix,' said Drogo in hushed tones.

'Get on with it! The crucifix...?'

'The crucifix is damaged!'

'So what! You've still got the key for it, haven't you? No one's got inside it, have they? Your parchment is safe?' For the Bishop knew all his brother's secrets. 'Anyway, where's it damaged?'

'The head, Christ's head. Oh! It's a judgement!' said Drogo and his head fell back upon his pillow.

'Christ's head *what*? Man alive!' demanded the Bishop.

'Christ's head sprang from its shoulders as I entered the chapel,' whispered Drogo. 'It's a judgement!' he repeated.

'Christ's head?' began the Bishop, and paused for a moment, wondering if his brother had finally gone quite off his rocker. 'It must just have come unsoldered. That's all! For heaven's sake, you're not starting to believe all that poppycock we tell the people in sermons, are you?' But then, remembering the green light in the cave, he felt a little queasy.

As Drogo made no reply and seemed to be drifting off again, his brother shook him once more,

'Get up and get ready. We must be off!'

'Where are we going?' muttered Drogo.

'To Toulouse, to my palace. I'll keep you safely there until Mass on Sunday. I have decided to announce the betrothal of Thomas de Romolue to Clarice in the cathedral that day.' As he said this, he realised that he had quite forgotten that this matter needed urgent discussion with the Count and Countess.

Give them a day or so to forget the quarrel – the Count would calm down soon enough. He was always flaring up, at the least thing, although the Bishop realised that hunting Thomas through the woods with armed men was perhaps a bit more of an issue than pigs running wild through the village streets, or whatever it was that usually got the Count so hot under the collar. Anyway, it was only for Thomas's own safety. Yes, of course, that was what he should have said... He was protecting Thomas, trying to capture him to save him from the dangers of the forest at night! And like a little fool, he ran off. Henri thought of returning to the Count and Countess with this tale. But it was certainly better put off till tomorrow.

As these thoughts were passing through the Bishop's mind, Drogo was muttering incoherent words, of which the Bishop could only make out 'crucifix'.

'What, what's that?' demanded Henri.

'I'll come with you, of course. Get out of this cursed château. But I must take the crucifix!' replied Drogo.

'No, don't take *it*!' said the Bishop. 'Just take the manuscript from it. Check that all's in order.'

'Yes, yes, yes,' muttered Drogo. 'All in order. Check the crucifix!' He raised himself on one elbow, the sense of purpose giving him sudden strength. 'Help me from my bed, Henri. We'll go up to the chapel. If you come with me, I can make it. Support me,' he said, stretching out an arm.

So, using the Bishop as a crutch, he levered himself out of bed and allowed himself to be half dragged and carried from his room, and slowly, step by painful step, his head throbbing with pain, he went up the grand staircase, coming finally to the door of the chapel.

As Drogo and his brother arrived there, they were overtaken by a startled maid, who running up the stairs, almost tripped over with surprise at the sight of them. She curtsied, mumbled something about m'Lords, and ran off in the direction of Marie's room. Henri and Drogo entered the chapel. Immediately, to their horror, they saw that the crucifix was gone, the gap on the altar staring at them with all the force as if they had seen the devil himself perched there.

'Mon Dieu!' cried Drogo, and pushed past Henri towards the chest. 'Help me move this! No, shut the door first – put the catch down. Quick, before someone comes.'

'What are you doing?' asked Henri, and Drogo explained about the key. Nervously Drogo fumbled with the block in the floor.

'Ah! The key's there. Thank God!' he exclaimed. 'My secret's safe. Or... no, what do you think? That sly little boy might have read it all, put it back and put the key back. No! Thomas is merely a little fool,' he added, shaking his head to put away the image of Thomas sitting in the chapel, reading his confession.

'Yes, but what about the crucifix? That can't be allowed to fly about the place with your manuscript inside it!' said Henri urgently. 'Obviously it's gone because it was damaged in some way, the head, you said. We'll have to find out...'

He stopped abruptly as they heard footsteps on the staircase. The Countess rattled the door of the chapel, finding it locked, and the Bishop sprang forward to remove the catch, leaving Drogo, very pale, leaning against the altar.

'Ah, Madame,' said Henri, 'we need your assistance.'

The Countess eyed them with surprise, seeing Drogo on his feet after the medicine that Marie had given him.

But of course! Drogo would want to know that his precious murderous confession was safe. They'd been looking for the key – hence the locked chapel door. Well, the crucifix was safe indeed, and she gave a tight little smile as Jacques hurried into the chapel behind her.

'Father Drogo,' she said, 'you should be in bed. You need rest and sleep.' *And we need you out of the way*, she added to herself.

'No!' said Henri. 'He's coming back to Toulouse with me.

Back to his family, to recover from the terrible wounds he has received here, in the Château de Romolue! This will not be forgotten!' he added, and threw a threatening look at the Countess.

'You must understand that it was Drogo who fainted and hit his head on the altar,' replied the Countess coolly. 'We did not injure him. It was perhaps the sight of the damaged crucifix that brought it on – though why that had such a powerful effect, I cannot imagine,' she added slowly and loudly. 'You know that he is a delicate man, with terrible headaches and blackouts, for many years, ever since my poor sister died...' she continued, with a break in her voice, looking at Drogo and at the vacant space on the altar.

'And his hand, how did that happen?' demanded the Bishop, making to ignore the last remark.

'That was the poor girl who drowned,' replied the Countess.

'Yes, we found her dress in the river,' put in Jacques.

'She stamped on Drogo's hand, when he...'

'Poor girl, you say! Drowning was too good for her,' interrupted the Bishop.

What was this absurd story? Drogo had reported that it was Thomas who had stamped on his hand, driving shards of glass into it. What girl had drowned? He would get to the bottom of this at some later time. First the crucifix...

'The crucifix,' Drogo blurted out, getting there before his brother. 'Where is it?' His crabbed fingers gripped the altar to steady himself. Henri came to his side to support him. 'The crucifix,' repeated Drogo.

'It was damaged somehow, as you know,' Jacques explained, standing behind the Countess. Making his way forward, he placed his hand on the altar where the crucifix should have stood. 'I can't think how it could have happened. Surely no one would have touched it. And even if they did, how did the head come loose? It's a mystery.'

'Yes, but where is it?' demanded the Bishop, repeating Drogo's question.

'Oh! I sent it down the village, to... er... ummm... to Rabelais, for repair. Rabelais is a clever chap, you know. He'll do a good job. It will look like new, when he's soldered the head back on. Of course, it'll get a bit hot. Need shining up afterwards. I was looking at it, actually. Kind of compartment underneath. Funny thing, but you need a key to open it. Nothing in there of any value, is there? I mean, it's going to get a bit hot, and if it starts smoking when Rabelais starts to heat it up… Well, we'd better avoid that, really. But Rabelais will probably have a key, or make one, to fish out anything that might be inside before he starts, I expect…'

'Oh, God!' muttered Drogo, clutching still more feverishly at the altar.

'Who did you send it down to the village with?' asked the Bishop abruptly.

'Oh – one of the kitchen people, Marc, actually. Haven't seen him around much since,' replied Jacques.

This was little surprise to Jacques or the Countess, for as they both knew very well, Marc was dead, killed on the road to the Abbaye by that trusty fool of a boy soldier, Louis. What is Jacques' game? wondered the Countess.

'I think that I want the crucifix mended by one of my expert jewellers in Toulouse. It's too valuable to let loose on this Rabelais fellow,' said the Bishop hastily. 'We'll call in at the village and collect it off him before he does any damage to it! There is no time to lose. Come,' he said, turning to Drogo. And indeed there was no time if they were to stop Rabelais finding the parchment – if he had not already done so. If he had, he would die, mused the Bishop and he fingered thoughtfully the little vial of poison he kept around his neck.

Although haste was of the greatest importance, it took the Bishop some time to assemble his drunken, sleepy soldiers, threaten them with hell and damnation, frighten them into obedience and get them on the road, groaning in their saddles. Each step that the horses took jarred their heads. Jacques had soaked them well in strong wine, which they had gulped down gratefully to drown the memory of the night, of the cave, of the fruitless pursuit of the nuns – or some creatures dressed as nuns. De Montfort led an extra horse, on which Drogo was held, in a special saddle made for wounded men, but in great discomfort.

Their pace was slow, despite the impatience of the Bishop.

The sun was high and the morning hot and well advanced as they entered the village of Romolue. One of the soldiers was a native of Romolue, and like all the villagers, knew where Rabelais lived, among the crude huts, wattle and timber houses, and small, stinking winding alleys. Villagers gazed at them in surprise as the company made their way through the streets. It was rare, almost unknown, for the Bishop – for all knew him – to enter the village. And so many fighting men, though they looked as though they had not much fight left in them, as several village lads joked, seeing them sagging in their saddles and wincing at each lurch of their horses.

At length they came to Rabelais' house. Timbers stood at all angles, holding up the walls, and in some places the roof and the thatch reached almost to the ground, with a space cut out to make way for the tiny front door. The Bishop would have had to stoop if he had wished to enter. But he had no intention of dismounting into the puddles of filth that marked the path in front of Rabelais' house.

'You there,' he said, pointing at the soldier directly behind him, 'get this man out!'

The soldier gingerly dismounted and, stepping on the cobbles, and avoiding the puddles and rotting refuse, he made his way to the door.

'Get a move on, man!' shouted the Bishop. 'Knock the door down if you have to!'

But before this was found necessary, the door flew open, and a large but stooped old man stood peering up at the soldier advancing on the door, and the mounted men behind him. Bright black eyes gleamed from beneath the old man's enormous bushy eyebrows and the mass of grey hair, sprouting in all directions, which framed his face. Suddenly, he spied the Bishop.

'My Lord!' he said, and tried a little bow, and made his way out of the door in his high wooden clogs. 'My Lord!' he repeated, and waited respectfully for a reply.

'You are Rabelais…' said the Bishop; it was half a question, half a statement.

'Yes, my Lord.'

'Good! Then hand over the crucifix which Marc delivered to you yesterday.'

'The crucifix, my Lord?'

'Don't fool around!' snapped the Bishop, and Rabelais raised his remarkable eyebrows at him. 'Yesterday, a young lad, Marc, came with a crucifix from the Château de Romolue. We're in a hurry. Give it me and let us be off!'

'Yes, come quickly now!' broke in Drogo, angrily, and Rabelais looked up at him, startled by this sudden new voice, which he knew well from the church.

'But, my good Lords, Father Drogo, I do not have this crucifix. I know nothing of it. If I did, you would have it on the instant. I know no one called Marc. I know nothing of it,' he repeated, his voice dropping to a whisper, his hand raking through his grey hair.

He was frightened. What false accusation would be made against him? Would he be accused of stealing the crucifix? What crucifix was this, anyway? Not the one in the church of Romolue. He had seen that one just this very morning.

'This cannot be true!' said the Bishop angrily, hearing this reply, and turning to Drogo with a shrug of his shoulders. Had Jacques deliberately lied to him?

'Search the house!' shouted the Bishop. 'You and you!' he commanded, 'and you there by the door!'

The three men pushed past Rabelais, who had barely time to move aside to let them enter. It was dark inside Rabelais' single little room. There was a rough bed and a workbench, with many tools and wooden toys of all sorts lying about on it, some to be mended, some partly carved.

'Ah!' said one man. 'I'd like this for my young 'un.' He picked up a toy horse with a bushy tail made of horsehair.

'Hands off that,' said Rabelais gruffly. 'That's for Madeleine de Romolue.'

It took only a brief inspection to show that no large crucifix was concealed in Rabelais' hut. Where could a poor peasant hide such a thing? The three soldiers came out again, blinking in the sharp sunlight.

'Nothing, my Lord!' said one.

'Nothing?' exclaimed the Bishop and Drogo together.

At this moment, de Montfort was distracted by a glimpse out of the corner of his eye of the tall figure of a man standing some twenty or thirty metres away, looking fixedly at them. The man was dressed as a sailor, with a red scarf around his neck, a leather jacket, and baggy canvas breeches.

'Who is that man?' he asked, pointing towards the figure, and everyone turned suddenly.

Almost as they did so, the man disappeared around the corner of the hut by which he had been standing.

'Fetch him here!' commanded the Bishop, and two horsemen pulled hard on their reins and swinging around spurred their horses in the direction in which the stranger had stood, splashing through the puddles, and halting abruptly to peer down the several little alleyways along which the sailor might have run. One horseman went to the right, the other to the left. The villagers, slipping over the few cobblestones, pressed themselves against the walls, or fled down gaps between the huts, to avoid the horses' hooves, as the two men riding fast churned the narrow paths into a welter of mud.

But they found no trace of the stranger as they rode this way and that through the village. They were soon covered in mud themselves and, smelling of rotting vegetables thrown up by their horses' hooves, they gave up their search and returned to the Bishop and his party.

'He's nowhere to be found, my Lord.'

'What was that?' said the Bishop. 'Ah – that stranger!'

He seemed distracted, and the two horsemen, who had expected a round of loud curses, guard duty and cleaning the latrines, moved away before their master turned on them.

'No matter,' added the Bishop, though something about the stranger had troubled him; and, exchanging a look with Drogo, he wrinkled his brow, as did his brother.

'Now, look here,' said the Bishop, turning again to address Rabelais, who stood before him in the doorway, 'you were saying that a young lad was brought into the church yesterday?'

'Yes, my Lord. He was dead, my Lord, or badly wounded, or both; or, I mean…'

'Don't be a fool!' said the Bishop sharply. 'Did you know him?'

'No, my Lord, I mean, I don't know, I didn't get close enough really to see him. But someone said that he had been working up in the château,' he added in a doubtful tone.

'Ah! Who was that, now?'

'Well, my Lord, it was my...' Rabelais broke off, regretting the remark and unwilling to drag a friend into this.

Any dealings with the Bishop and Drogo were always avoided. The village people kept well out of their way. Not like the Count, thought Rabelais! He was often in Rabelais' little hut, admiring his carving.

'Out with it! We're in a hurry. *Who*?' demanded the Bishop, breaking into Rabelais' thoughts.

I've no choice, Rabelais realised, and so he replied, 'I'll fetch him, my Lord'

'You! Go with him,' ordered the Bishop, shoving a finger in the direction of the nearest horseman. 'Make sure he doesn't run off. There's something smells wrong here,' he added, turning to Drogo, who nodded miserably, letting his eyes close and his head fall upon his chest.

'It most certainly do. Poooh!' said one of the horsemen, and several of them chuckled, silenced by an acid look from the Bishop.

In a moment, Rabelais returned.

'He's out in the fields, my Lord. But,' said Rabelais hastily, seeing the Bishop apparently about to ride him down in a fury, 'but his wife said that the body in the church... He's dead, you see... The body was a young lad, sir, called Marc, sir, who worked in the château. Run through with a sword, he was. Young Louis done it! Brought him in with the gardener chappy, what's his name, from the abbey. Yeah, Martin, that's him. They brought him in, yesterday. Louis was right cut up, sir. Never meant to hurt him. Tears bubblin' down his cheeks, sir. A good lad. Can't understand it, really!' Here Rabelais broke off.

'Marc,' exclaimed Drogo in surprise. 'One of my... er... servants in the château. Lent to me, that is, of course. Marc is dead,' he muttered. '*Damnation!*' he burst out suddenly, with so much life in his voice that he startled his horse, which reared, causing Drogo to give a yelp of pain.

The Bishop quietened the animal, stooping from his horse to hold the bridle.

'One of your men, eh?' said the Bishop. 'Killed by, who's this, Louis?' he said, turning to Rabelais.

'Yes, my Lord. Just a young lad, sir. A good lad, like I said! It was all a mistake, on the road to the abbey...' Here his voice trailed off, for the Bishop had turned his horse away and was giving orders to his men.

'We go to the church. I want to see the body of this Marc. Perhaps he has the crucifix with him. Perhaps it was stolen from him by this young thug, Louis.'

'Oh, no, sir! Louis would never steal a Church possession, my Lord. Never!' exclaimed Rabelais.

But the Bishop, with Drogo and his escort, had already ridden away from his door. Breathing a sigh of relief, Rabelais crept back indoors. Putting on his cape, against the sun, he came unseen from his house and, leaving the village, made his way across the fields as fast as he was able towards the Château de Romolue. Louis must be warned that the Bishop and Drogo knew of his hand in killing Marc, or Louis' life would be not be worth more than... *that*! And he snapped his fingers.

Meanwhile, the Bishop's party arrived at the church.

'The body will be in the villagers' mortuary,' said Drogo, indicating a little wattle hut, standing some way from the church, under a clump of plane trees, their mottled trunks and dense leaves shading the hut from the sun.

Rapidly dismounting, the Bishop pushed open the door without ceremony. On a rough plank on the floor lay the body of a young man, his face covered with a cloth. Drogo, helped by one of the soldiers, had followed the Bishop into the hut. De Montfort leant down and pulled the cloth away from the face.

'That's Marc,' said Drogo, turning away in disgust at the swollen features and the strange look of surprise on the young man's face.

'Damn me!' said the Bishop. 'Part of one of his ears is missing. Good swordsmen they have at the Château, I see!'

Then he laughed, a sound so out of place that the soldier supporting Drogo drew back, and Drogo stumbled, cursing him for his carelessness.

The Bishop replaced the cloth and, emerging from the hut with Drogo, said to the soldier who was helping him, 'You! Search the body and the hut for the crucifix! I give you special sanction to do this,' he added, seeing the man's reluctance; for plundering the bodies of the dead was a crime for which the punishment was hanging.

Despite the Bishop's words, the man barely moved.

'Get in and do it!' commanded de Montfort roughly, 'or do you wish to join him in there on his little wooden plank?'

Accompanied by a few sniggers from the others, the soldier entered the hut, and as the Bishop looked on, rummaged through the clothes and oddments lying with the body of Marc. Just a glance was in fact enough to see that the large and heavy crucifix was not there. The Bishop cursed himself for the waste of time. Of course Rabelais would have mentioned if Marc had been in possession of anything so large and obvious – the whole village would have known. That damned Louis must have taken it… The Bishop swung round.

'Georges!' he shouted to his most trusted horseman, the leader of his band. 'Georges – ride as fast as you can to the château and root out that Louis, the man who killed Marc. Find him, and bring him to me, as a prisoner. If you can force anything out of him about the crucifix, then it's a gold coin for you.'

A gold coin! Half a year's pay! The other horsemen stirred. They would all of them willingly have ridden after Louis for that money.

'The rest of you, back with me to Toulouse!'

Georges turned his horse smartly and galloped off in the direction of the Château de Romolue.

Sixteen: Leaving Town

ight had fallen upon Town. In the Emp's palace, the dishes had been cleared away, the Emp's false teeth replaced in his mouth and the Emp and his court departed. One of the Emp's men brought rough bedding into the hall of the palace. This was laid out for Tommy and Eloise in a dark corner. The hall was lit only by a single flickering and smoky candle, making a wobbly light, with strange shadows playing on the walls.

'Best pig's fat candle,' said the servant who brought it in, 'not that you two will be wanting no candles!' he added, leering at them.

Tommy looked at Eloise, dark patches playing over her face, and for an instant her nose was caught in the glow, making a pattern like a little pyramid on the floor, and then her cheek caught the yellow candlelight. Her eyes flashed briefly in the flame and she pursed her lips, as if, as she probably was, holding back some sharp comment to the servant.

Instead she muttered, 'Thank you,' and Tommy echoed her words with, 'Thank you, and do not wake us too early!'

At this the servant chuckled, and Eloise gave an angry toss of her head.

'God, I wish there was somewhere we could wash a bit!' said Tommy, as the man left.

He was no great one for washing, but since their dip in the river, if you called that a wash, they had been in sweltering heat, fallen in the mud, nearly smothered in it, in fact... he remembered how Joncilond had pulled him out, and saved his life by dragging him out of the bog.

'I'm sure I smell horrible,' he added.

'Me, too,' said Eloise, and smiled. 'But if we both smell just as horrible as each other, perhaps it won't matter.' And she pressed her head against his shoulder.

Tommy stroked her hair. This was their second night together! The first was being chased by the Bishop's men, and ended in a nasty prickly bush in the swamp. Now, for the second, they were more or less prisoners in a very smelly hall – a palace, at least by name…

Ha! thought Tommy. Even our little house in England is a palace beside this!

He looked around at the wavering shadows and felt a sudden burst of longing to be back home, far away from Romolue, away from the violence and hatred and passions of 1599, back to the… violence, hatred and passions of the twenty-first century.

But the violence of his time did not invade your life, as it did here. At least, only through the television set, as another fanatical bomber blew ten people apart in the streets of Jerusalem or Baghdad. These thoughts made him wonder what Eloise was going to make of his world. Anyway, he'd decided that whatever happened she would come back with him. They'd work something out, he thought, as he stroked her hair more firmly. Also, he noticed that instead of being sleek and smooth, Eloise's hair was wiry, full of dust and had a certain smell. Well, she needed a bath too, that was certain! Unaware of Tommy's thoughts, Eloise gave a little murmur of content at the pressure of his hand on her head and snuggled a bit closer still to him.

'There's no way of washing, so let's just lie down and go to sleep,' she whispered in his ear. 'You can hold me and we can sleep like that,' she added, and found herself blushing to hear herself say such a thing.

She had only known Tommy four days! And here she was, ready to sleep in his arms! She did not even know who he was. That strange world of his, so fascinating, so dangerous…!

Pushing these thoughts from her mind, she turned suddenly and, putting her hand behind his head, kissed him hard on the mouth, pulling away so quickly that Tommy had no time to react. She stood at arm's length from him, her hands on his shoulders and in the dancing candlelight, nodded her head vigorously, as if to say, 'Well, that is how it is!'

In the silence that followed, Tommy, taking Eloise's hands in his, and still a little dazed from her kiss, sat down on the edge of the bedding. He looked up at her. She nodded her head again, more gently this time, and smiled so sweetly that Tommy felt an ache inside him.

'Do you think we can get these boots off?' he asked, breaking the silence. 'I don't want to be kicking you all night...'

He started to struggle with a muddy leather boot, which had been on his foot since he set off to the Abbaye de Seiche-Capucins to save Eloise from the Bishop and his men.

Eloise knelt down.

'Well, this is the first time I've taken off a man's boots!' she said, and giggled, as they both relaxed.

'Poof! I bet that doesn't smell very nice,' said Tommy, as Eloise managed to get one boot off and turned to the other – keeping her face well away from his feet, Tommy noticed. Stinky socks, thought Tommy, remembering his friend, Harry; stinky socks.

'Thanks, though!' he added as Eloise removed the other boot.

They snuggled down together, Eloise laying her head on Tommy's arm and her face close against his chest. She was asleep almost immediately, but Tommy lay with his eyes open, watching the flickering candle and the dancing shadows.

Should he put it out? Candles were probably quite a luxury. He ought not to let it burn down. Very carefully, so as not to wake Eloise, he raised himself on one arm, and stretching forwards, pursed his lips, to blow out the candle. But the flame just leapt about and the shadows danced even more madly as he blew. So he leant much further forward, removing his arm from under Eloise's head, which he laid back on the bed as gently as if it were a bird's egg, feeling her breath on his hand as he did so. He put his face right up against the candle and drew in a long breath. But just as he was about to really blow the candle out, the door of the hall creaked open. Tommy sat up suddenly and Eloise woke with a start.

'What – what is it?' she said loudly, and Tommy put his hand on her arm.

'Someone's coming in,' he whispered. 'I'd thought they had put a guard outside; at least, I hoped they had. Some of those people probably still want their revenge on us!'

Eloise clutched Tommy's arm. 'Oh, God! Will it all end here?' she murmured; for they had no weapons.

Tommy's sword had been taken and not returned. They had just their bare hands. The door creaked again. Was there more than one of them? Eloise squeezed Tommy's arm more tightly still.

'Is there a back way out?' she whispered.

Tommy shook his head.

'Dunno,' he muttered.

They could be seen in the candlelight, but they could not see the intruders. Would someone spring forward with a sword or dagger and kill them both?

'Come, into the dark corner over there,' whispered Tommy, pulling Eloise after him. 'Perhaps we can see who it is.'

They scuttled out of the light and, holding hands tightly, peering through the darkness they began to make out the form of a large man, with a mass of untidy hair. Suddenly, the smell of the intruder hit them across the room.

'*Tchk, tchk, tchk!*' it said, '*tchk, tchk, tchk!*'

'*Joncilond!*' shouted Tommy, angry with the fool, but greatly relieved that it was not a peasant from the town, come to take his private revenge on the nobles.

'Joncilond, you idiot! Creeping in here… We thought that you, you… well, in the middle of the night. Eloise was asleep. You woke her up. Bad Joncilond!'

'*Tchk, tchk, tchk!*' said Joncilond, '*tchk, tchk, tchk!*'

'Oh, shut up!' said Tommy. 'And let us go back to sleep!'

'I guard,' announced Joncilond loudly, and taking off his headdress of leaves and twigs, laid it on the floor. Using it as a pillow, he then lay down and went, it seemed, instantly to sleep.

Tommy and Eloise made their way back to their bed, breathing freely once more, though the smell of the most unwashed man in France did not freshen the air.

'I'm glad he's here, really,' whispered Eloise.

'What, don't you trust me?' said Tommy.

'What d'you mean?' replied Eloise, sounding surprised.

Tommy could see that she really did not understand that he was being a bit naughty. Of course, things must be different in

1599. Boys and girls, well, I dunno, he thought, I mean, she kisses me... Tommy had kissed girls before of course, but this was, well, somehow... not really the same.

'Things are different,' he murmured to himself, 'different,' and he felt Eloise relax and begin to drift back off to sleep.

Tommy whispered in her ear, 'No, I mean, well, of course it's good he's here, apart from the smell and...' The silence of the room was ripped apart by a tremendous hogging snore and a grunt... 'And the snoring,' added Tommy, with a giggle.

Eloise opened her eyes, gave Tommy a little smile, made a little kiss with her mouth and fell asleep once more.

Damn the candle! thought Tommy and, shutting his eyes, was also asleep in a few moments.

They slept long and deep. Tommy had some vague memory of the occasional thunderous snore and scuffling noise in the night, of Joncilond standing looking down at them in the early dawn, of the loud chorus of birds as the sun came up. And, as the bright sunlight finally came flooding between the gaps in the logs of the palace walls and woke him, he felt ready for everything that the Bishop and Drogo could throw at them, ready for a fight if need be, ready to get home, ready to see his Mum and Dad again – with Eloise, of course; with Eloise.

He turned towards her and as Eloise moved in her sleep, sunlight fell upon her face, her eyelids flickered, and she woke too. Her first glance fell upon Tommy and a smile came to her lips. Tommy looked with wonder on her beautiful face, and felt still more determined to overcome the dangers that lay in front of them. The first thing was to get back to the château, get Eloise well hidden. Perhaps in the Countess's little soundproof room?

'Come,' he said, 'we've got to get going! We'll be back in the château in a few hours. They're going to guide us out.'

Eloise nodded and stood up, smoothing down her dress. Just at this moment, the door of the hall flew open and the Emp strode in.

'Had a good sleep then? Not been playing with your toys, I hope, Monsieur Thomas, eh?' And he grinned at them, a toothless grin.

Where are the wooden teeth? thought Tommy, but felt that he should not ask.

'No teeth, huh!' exclaimed the Emp. 'Is that what you're gawping at?' Tommy blushed slightly. He had not meant to stare. 'Well, they're going to need repairing. Broke them badly on a bit of grit in a bun this morning. I'll have that miller's arse tanned for that! Great bit of grinding stone in the flour. Damn it! Anyway, that's another reason for sending someone out to Romolue. Only Rabelais can do a decent job mending them. Someone can take 'em along to him. Rabelais made them, and he's mended them before.'

'When can we get going, please?' said Tommy.

'Heavens, you haven't had your breakfast yet. Georgine!' he yelled. 'That's Phillipe's daughter, y'know, her that did the cooking last night. Not bad. Georgine!' he yelled again. 'Where is the little minx? Off with Alain, I expect. Oh! Excuse me,' he said glancing at Eloise.

At that, Georgine came flustering in.

'Yes m'Lord, sir, Milord and Lady,' she said curtseying in all directions.

She was a sweet-faced, round little girl, with auburn hair done up in a bun for working. She was all of a sweat with running.

'Breakfast!' ordered the Emp.

'But – but… You've already had yours, sir!' said Georgine.

'Damn me for a fool!' shouted the Emp, and Georgine stepped back, blinking in panic, as the Emp went on. 'What about these two, eh? Anyway, I had mine hours ago. Bring a whole lot of rolls and butter and ham and… whatever you can find. They've got a tough journey in front of them.'

Georgine scuttled off.

'Eggs!' shouted the Emp after her. 'D'you think she heard? You'd like some eggs, wouldn't you? How d'you like 'em cooked?'

He didn't bother waiting for a reply, for as far as he was concerned, everyone liked everything, and wanted everything that there was to eat. It was just a matter of making sure that you got hold of it, that was all.

'What time is…?' started Tommy, and then stopped himself.

'How long will it take to get from here to the Château de Romolue, please?'

'Ah, let's see now,' replied the Emp. 'Look, do you think that it's safe for you to arrive in broad daylight?'

'Well, we might arrive in the light, and lie a bit low for a time, and spy out what's happening... who is coming and going, and so on,' replied Tommy; Eloise nodded.

'Yeah,' said the Emp. 'Not a bad idea. I expect that Drogo and the Bishop will be on the watch for you, mind. The Bishop will be furious about your escaping him. He's a vicious bast... erm... fellow,' said the Emp, correcting himself. 'But they might not be expecting you back in the château. Have you thought about how you might warn 'em and get back in?'

Tommy and Eloise exchanged looks. They really hadn't thought about it at all. If only they could get a message through to someone – Marie or Jacques, thought Tommy. Jacques! Yeah. He could ring his Mum, tell her to tell Jacques – Jasper, that is – to expect them back... Then he could ring back to his Mum to make sure that Jacques had got the message. Yeah, right.

These thoughts were interrupted by breakfast. Georgine came struggling in, carrying a heavy wooden board laden with small loaves, ham, cheese, butter, fruit and a steaming jug of something like tea, with a kind of vanilla smell, Tommy thought.

'Great!' said the Emp. 'Tuck in!'

And he took a bun, dug his thumb into the side of it, shoved a thick slice of ham in and a wodge of butter with his dagger, and took a large bite.

'Damn me, m'teeth!' Tommy and Eloise heard him mumble, as crumbs flew out of his mouth. 'Get m'teeth!' he spluttered, and gestured at Georgine, who stood gaping at him.

'I think he wants his teeth,' said Eloise to Georgine. 'D'you know where they are?'

The Emp worked his jaws up and down heroically, managing finally to swallow the large mouthful he'd taken.

'Blast, I'd forgot m'teeth,' he said, shaking his head. 'And what about them eggs?' he demanded of Georgine.

The poor girl went pale. Teeth, eggs, it was all too much for her.

'Don't worry about the eggs, Georgine,' said Eloise kindly. (I would have liked an egg, thought Tommy. Ah well!)

'Ah! Miss, Your Ladyship, I mean. Teeth! What teeth?'

'Gimme a jar of that tea, will y'. I'm half choking with them crumbs!' announced the Emp, ignoring Georgine. 'And help yourself quick, before I eat the lot!' he added to Tommy and Eloise.

So Tommy made a ham and cheese bun: 'A sandwich,' he announced.

'What's that?' asked Eloise, who was more daintily holding a small piece of bun in one hand and cheese in the other. 'A sand...wich?'

'Yeah,' replied Tommy, 'invented by the Earl of Sandwich, a hunting-crazy nobleman of...'

'So only noblemen eat them, then?' broke in Eloise.

'Hardly,' chuckled Tommy. 'You just wait and see. The first railway station buffet will be enough... oops!' he said, catching Eloise's eye and noticing the look of blank astonishment on the Emp's face.

'Railway...?' muttered the Emp. 'Another thing that Rabelais invented, I suppose. Thomas de Romolue, you're a strange lad. Almost like you don't belong here. You say some funny things.'

At this, Eloise and Tommy tried to concentrate on biting into their buns.

As they were finishing breakfast, in came Jacques the Tailor and behind him, capering about as usual, Joncilond.

'Right,' said the Emp. 'You're off now, then. Joncilond knows all the paths. He may look a bit mad, be a bit mad, in fact. But he's alright. He saved you from the bog didn't he?' added the Emp, seeing the doubtful look on Tommy's face. 'And he's the best with the paths, he is. Yeah. Anyway, it will be just Jacques, here, Jacques the Tailor, and Joncilond.'

Eloise put on a dark cloak that Jacques had brought with him. She was no longer disguised as a nun. After all, the Bishop and his men would be on the lookout for nuns. In a few minutes they there were off.

'We'll be going out the back gate,' said Jacques, and Tommy nodded, lost in his own plans.

'Can you make a cuckoo noise?' asked Tommy, turning to Joncilond as they walked side by side down the main street of Town.

Joncilond nodded his head up and down, stretched out his neck and gave a perfect 'Cooo–kooooo' imitation. So much so that there was an answer almost immediately from the nearby wood. 'Lots more,' said Joncilond, and started off on a whole range of chuckling, burbling, whistling and trilling noises.

'Yes, thanks… beautiful, great, that's enough, please… lovely, yes,' said Tommy as Joncilond cooed like a pigeon and frightened the birds with the cry of the screech owl.

As Joncilond ended his performance, they turned abruptly into the front door of a low, long house. Eloise gave Tommy a little look of surprise and he just shrugged. They followed Jacques and Joncilond into the darkness, stumbling on some rough stones as they entered. Joncilond's arm shot out to steady Eloise, and they all stopped for a moment to accustom their eyes. Before them was a large and deep hole, with some tiny steps cut in the side. They clambered down about three metres then crossed over a muddy floor and climbed up on another little staircase on the opposite side. Before them they could see the outline of a heavy door, chained closed with a metal stake through a massive iron hoop. Joncilond pulled this free as though it were a toothpick, jerked the door inwards and they found themselves outside the wall of Town.

'They'll come and close the door for us from the inside, in a bit,' explained Jacques, as they began to walk rapidly off along a well-marked path.

After a few minutes they were deep in the wood and the ground was breaking up into wet patches, signs that they were entering the quaking marsh.

'I'm afraid that we'll have to blindfold you soon. I've already been put to sewing a thousand buttons after last time,' said Jacques the Tailor.

'Yeah, sure, we understand,' said Tommy, and Eloise smiled.

They were now out of sight of Town, with Joncilond leading the way, with an occasional skip and hop. Tall trees surrounded them, leaves thickly sweeping the ground with a haze of sunshine and the buzzing of insects, the smell of warm grass and a waft of wild mint, which made Tommy think of Sunday roast lamb. Tommy stopped a moment and whispered something in Eloise's ear, and she gave a tiny nod of agreement.

Trotting a bit to catch up Jacques, Tommy asked, 'Can we just go and, ummm, go to the toilet, a moment, please, me and Eloise?'

'Sure,' said Jacques. 'Joncilond!' he called. 'Pipi... pipi!'

Joncilond nodded and went leaping and crashing off into the bushes crying, '*Pi-pi, pi-pi, pi-pi!*' as he went.

It must be infectious thought Tommy, as he pushed his way between the low branches. He wanted to make sure that he was quite out of sight, not because he was specially shy, but because what he really wanted to do, as well as 'pipi', was to ring his mum and arrange the message for Jacques. The cuckoo call, three times, was to be the signal.

His mum answered the phone immediately.

'Oh, Tommy!' said the squeaky voice, and Tommy explained his plan.

'In a couple of hours or maybe more, I'll ring back to see if you've been able to catch Jasper. Remember, three cuckoo calls will be the signal, repeated three times. Okay! Tell him, we'll come in through the window that we escaped out of on Sunday night, through the pantry, up the servants' stairs and... and up to Marie's room. Have you got all that? He'll know what to do!'

'Tommy, be careful!' said Mum.

'I will, I will... no time now to talk,' replied Tommy, 'I'm meant to have just gone for a wee. I'll ring soon. Find Jasper.' Then Tommy turned off the phone.

Tommy came out onto the path to find Eloise standing there looking a bit rumpled. Suppose she's not used to pipi in the wild, thought Tommy. Joncilond was stretched along a low bough, with his legs crossed, a long blade of grass in his mouth, his arms behind his head. Jacques stood leaning with his elbow on the bough on which Joncilond was lying.

'What took you so long then?' he asked. 'Couldn't find it among all them clothes?' He chuckled, and Eloise's angry glance went unnoticed. Tommy suppressed a smile.

'Joncilond thinks that you should be blindfolded now,'

Jacques went on. 'We're going off the main path, he says, so we'd better do it.' He pulled two long pieces of cloth from a pocket.

It was rather horrible walking along blindfold, stumbling all the time, holding hands with Joncilond in front, then Tommy, then Eloise. It was nice holding hands with her, anyway, and then Eloise holding hands with Jacques.

'Never thought that I'd be walking the forest here holding hands with Eloise de Narbonne,' he chuckled and Eloise pulled a little face under her blindfold. 'Tell me grandchildren. I walked in this 'ere wood, holding hands with, who do you think? That great lady! Beautiful she was…'

'Stop it now,' said Eloise.

'Oops! Sorry, Your Highness!'

That started Joncilond off. 'Highness, highness, lowness, lowness, highness!' he bawled, prancing along, addressing the trees.

'Aren't we meant to be being quiet?' asked Tommy. 'If the Bishop and his men are about, they'll hear us from miles away.'

'Oh! According to Joncilond, they've all gone back to Toulouse. He was out scouting yesterday. Saw 'em going that way. Carrying Drogo along too, they were.'

'Drogo, Drogo, evil, evil, evil!' chanted Joncilond.

'Yeah, Joncilond,' said Jacques, 'but he's no worse than his brother, maybe not as bad!'

That's what you think, thought Tommy and he felt Eloise squeeze his hand.

'Evil, evil…' Suddenly Joncilond went quiet, putting his finger to his lips.

'Okay, from now on, we'll keep quiet,' said Jacques, almost in a whisper. 'We're not that far from a path which you can follow between the château and the village of Romolue, joining the main route for Toulouse.'

They walked on in silence for a long while, an hour or more, branches whipping around them, sinking in the mud, gurgles of gas following them, and the smell of bad eggs, hydrogen sulphide, Tommy remembered from school, but it seemed a bit unimportant now. Suddenly they stopped and felt themselves pulled to the ground.

'There's someone on the road!' whispered Jacques, 'not a word!'

As they waited in silence they could hear the sound of approaching feet scurrying along, scuffing the dusty ground, and the heavy breathing of someone not much used to exercise, or not in his first youth.

As the traveller passed, Tommy could hear him muttering, 'Thank the Lord that I got there quick! Louis's safely hidden. The Bishop would have had him killed, poor boy! Had him killed!' the man repeated to himself.

I know that voice, thought Tommy. Why, it's Rabelais, of course.

'Rabelais!' Tommy heard Jacques mutter beside him, 'What's he doing here? Never leaves Romolue except...' Then Jacques paused, making a decision. 'Stay here,' he whispered to Tommy and Eloise, and he got up and strode out onto the path.

'Rabelais!' he called.

Rabelais almost leapt off the path in fright. Stopping dead in his tracks, he turned slowly, shading his eyes against the sun, half expecting one of the Bishop's men.

'Jacques!' he exclaimed. 'What a relief! What brings you here? I've been to the château,' he panted, 'to warn them. Lay low there a bit! I'm just back from warning 'em.'

'Warn 'em what?'

'It's er...' Maybe he shouldn't tell, thought Rabelais.

'A secret, eh!' broke in Jacques. 'Well, I'm on a secret mission too.'

Good! thought Tommy, he's not going to say we're here!

'But, anyway,' added Jacques, 'take these.' He handed a small bundle to Rabelais. 'They're the Emp's false teeth. Need mending! You'll see.'

Then, as Rabelais turned, Tommy secretly pulled his blindfold up a bit and saw him full face.

God! he thought. He looks like... with that mop of grey hair, bright eyes, like... Einstein. Yeah, really like him! Kindly, wise, maybe he could really make the mobile phone, after all!'

Before Tommy could look more closely, Rabelais was off again at a rapid trot. But then, after a moment, he stopped and called over his shoulder.

'It's Louis! Killed Marc, he did! But I warned 'em at the château, just in time. Georges, the Bishop's man, he got there just when I did. Nasty bit o' work. Wanted to grab 'old of Louis. But Jacques calmed him down.' He paused a moment and added, 'Funny business about a crucifix! But Louis killed Marc all right, he did!' and then Rabelais was off once more and gone around a corner.

'Marc – who's Marc?' exclaimed Jacques, and turned off the path back to Tommy and Eloise. Eloise was struggling with Tommy's blindfold as Jacques reappeared.

'Marc,' Jacques was muttering, 'and who's Louis? I wonder if it has anything to do with you two,' he said, addressing Tommy and Eloise, and, absentmindedly lending a hand in adjusting Tommy's blindfold.

Joncilond was nowhere to be seen. Jacques knew that they should just stay where they were and wait for him, so he sat down on the grass beside Tommy and Eloise.

'Wonder if what's got something to do with us two?' asked Tommy, replying to Jacques' question.

'Rabelais, yeah, it was Rabelais on the road, y'know,' said Jacques.

'I heard you calling him!' said Eloise.

'Of course. Silly me,' said Jacques. 'Anyway, Rabelais was in a right state. Something about warning 'em at the château about... something. I couldn't follow it. Some Georges or other wanted to arrest some Louis, because he killed Marc, whoever he is! Does that make any sense to you?'

Tommy shook his head slowly. Louis must be, well, *might* be, the one he and Eloise cracked on the head. But Eloise bent forward to him and whispered in his ear, 'I know something about this. Should I say?'

Tommy raised his eyebrows slightly and, pursing his lips, gave a little shrug. 'Might it help?' he murmured in reply.

'Don't know,' whispered Eloise.

Jacques was lying back, ignoring them, looking at the sky through the trees, thinking of the nice fruit pudding which his wife Henrietta had made last night. A few blackberries would have made it even better, but they would come a bit later in the year. There were more fruit puddings to look forward to. Ah, life was not so bad! A bumblebee buzzed gently by his ear and a long grass tickled his chin.

'Jacques!' said Eloise quietly. 'Jacques! I know what it's about.'

'Y'do, m'Lady! Well, what happened, then – Louis and Marc, I mean?' said Jacques, sitting up, his legs stretched out, his arms extended behind him. 'Let's hear, then!'

'Well, I was on a cart with this gardener man, being taken to the Abbaye de Seiche-Capucins... I was escaping from Drogo, you see, disguised as a peasant girl, like now, really. And this young man Marc was following us, and Louis, it seems, was following him. Well...' And Eloise went on to describe how Louis had, it seemed, killed Marc on the road, the nuns finding Louis in a state of shock, near the body of Marc, and how the gardener (she was careful not to give his name, Tommy noticed), how the gardener and Louis had left her to go on with three nuns to the Abbey, so that the gardener and Louis could take the body back to Romolue.

'Marc must have been working for Drogo and the Bishop,' said Tommy. 'P'raps they've been in Romolue, found out that Marc's dead, and gone to arrest Louis at the château.' His guess wasn't far off the truth, in fact. 'But,' he added, 'Joncilond said that the Bishop and Drogo and his men had returned to Toulouse.'

'Perhaps Joncilond's wrong!' said Eloise.

'Joncilond's not wrong, he's right, right, right!' whispered a voice suddenly in her ear, and she jumped with surprise. They had been so taken up with the story of Marc and Louis that they had not heard Joncilond approach, for he could be as silent as a deer.

'It's clear ahead,' said Joncilond quietly, and holding up his hands, wiggled all ten fingers.

'That means, "come along quick now, while the going's good!"' said Jacques.

'What means "come along quick"?' demanded Tommy.

'Joncilond wiggling his fingers, like he just did. Oh, of course, silly me! You couldn't see him, could you, with your blindfolds on!'

Eloise gave a little snort of annoyance and Tommy asked, 'Can't we take these blindfolds off, please? I mean, you said that we had got to a well-known path.'

Jacques looked at Joncilond, who nodded, once slowly, three times fast.

'That means, oh… er, yes, you can now, you can take them off. We're not that far from the château. In fact we're out of the marsh really. Here, let me help.'

'Gosh,' said Tommy, 'that's better! Phew!' And Eloise blinked in the sunshine and smiled at him.

Joncilond led the way up to higher ground, the route rising more and more steeply. The undergrowth got thicker and they made noisy progress. Suddenly there was a loud grunting and scuffling. They had stumbled over a wild boar. Tommy didn't see the creature except for a streak of coarse black hair, but the sound of a large animal crashing through the wood seemed to have started just beneath his feet. Briefly he remembered stories of people gored to death.

'We've spoilt his siesta,' whispered Tommy to Eloise as they recovered from their fright, and she grinned.

But Joncilond raised his hand, commanding them to be still, and waving his arm down, made them crouch among the long grass as the sound of the wild boar died away in the distance. Edging his way to just beside Eloise and pressing his lips against Eloise's ear, Tommy whispered, 'Time for pipi!' Then held his hand up beside his ear, meaning the mobile phone. Eloise nodded and they waited.

Joncilond stood in perfect stillness, just occasionally turning his head this way and that, listening to see if there were scouts on their way placed in the woods by the Bishop or Drogo, for the wild boar might well have given them away. But complete quiet reigned, against the hum of insects and the occasional feeble twitter of a bird. It was siesta time in the forest, just as Tommy had joked, and all of nature was drowsy.

If we wait here any longer, I'm going to drop off, thought Tommy. But Joncilond remained like a statue for another minute or more, until certain that no one was on their track. Then he waved them on, with a great sweep of his hand, and stretching out his arms, wiggled all his fingers. *Come along quick*, thought Tommy and mouthed *Pipi* to Eloise, who nodded again. Tommy tapped Jacques on the shoulder.

'Pipi,' he whispered.

'No! Where?' said Jacques. 'I'd love a nice juicy one.'

'Eh?' said Tommy, puzzled. 'Pipi,' he repeated, a bit louder, and Joncilond turned, putting his finger to his lips.

'Oh! I thought you said pear tree,' replied Jacques. 'Yeah, pipi, sure, of course.' He took a few quick steps to catch up Joncilond.

'They need pipi,' he whispered, jerking his thumb towards Tommy and Eloise, and Joncilond stopped, putting his hands on his hips, as if to say, 'Pipi again?'

He looked back at Tommy and Eloise, waggled his head around at all angles and wriggled his bottom, making Tommy and Eloise giggle as they went off into the bushes. A very quick call told Tommy that his Mum had been lucky and had caught Jasper almost immediately after Tommy's call. Yes, he'd be ready for them. Three times three cuckoo calls. Great, said Tommy to himself, and grinned. We're as good as back in the château already.

As he rejoined the group, he exchanged a quick look with Eloise, who inclined her head just a tiny fraction to show that she understood that all was well.

It was not long till they came to the crest of the high ground. Joncilond led them very cautiously to the edge of a row of trees, motioning to them to crouch down. Below they could see the Château de Romolue in the bend of the river, the black slate roof glinting in the sunshine, and the geometrical garden where Tommy thought that he could just make out the stone bench where all his adventures had started. All around were fields of vegetables, empty of people at this, the hottest time of day.

How can we get down to the right-hand side of the château without being seen? wondered Tommy. Maybe we shouldn't hang around, but go in quickly. As soon as the peasants come back out in the fields, I'll be seen and recognised, and Eloise too.

Then he said to Jacques, aloud, 'We've got to go to the right, keeping the cover of the trees, all the way down to the château. How far will you and Joncilond risk coming with us? I need

Joncilond quite close to the château, for a signal he has to make, by the way.'

'Well, I dunno,' answered Jacques, hesitantly. 'I don't want to get caught. For me, it would be...' And he drew his thumbnail sharply across his throat and stuck out his tongue.

'What about Joncilond?'

Joncilond gave a brief nod, and pulled back from the ridge, with a sweep of his arm urging them away from where they could so easily be picked out. Tommy pointed to the right, but Joncilond was already off in this direction, and they all followed him as rapidly as they could.

They made their way at an angle down the hillside towards the river, keeping well inside the cover of trees and bushes. Looking down at the river between the trees, Tommy saw the wide stone bridge over to the château, and remembered that there was a small boat tethered beneath it. The bridge lay in the direction that Joncilond was leading them. Tommy had the idea that he and Eloise could get across the river in the boat, pulling themselves along on the underside of the bridge, and remain unseen. Then they could creep along the side of the river, hidden from the château by the high bank and the rushes and some small willow trees that were growing there. Then up onto the roof of the pantry, in through the little window, where they escaped on Sunday night, and they were home and dry!

'Joncilond,' Tommy whispered as loudly as he dared.

Joncilond stopped and stared back at him, looking almost as if he wondered who Tommy was! Then he grinned, gave a little skip, and sat suddenly down upon the grass, patting a patch beside him, inviting Tommy to come and join him. Eloise and Jacques gathered around as Tommy outlined his plan.

'When you see us getting close to the château,' said Tommy, 'you've got to do the cuckoo sound three times, then again, and then once again! No, no, not now!' he added, as Joncilond put his thumbs to his lips.

Tommy sprang up and put his hand over Joncilond's mouth. Joncilond made a sound as though a cuckoo had been strangled in mid-cuckoo.

'*Cuck... ooooo*,' replied a real cuckoo, while Jacques looked around surprised, and Eloise gave a little grin, almost as if it had been she who replied and not a cuckoo.

'Listen, Joncilond,' said Tommy. 'It's a signal, the three times three cuckoo sounds. Okay?' Joncilond nodded, three times three. 'When they hear it inside the château, they'll be ready for us. You've got it?' Joncilond nodded again, three times three. 'But only when we're really near to the château. Okay?'

Seventeen: Muddy Waters

hey were almost at the bridge now. There was a last little bit with no cover. They decided that they just had to risk it and, crouching, they all four ran down the slope and scuttled under the bridge. Huddled together in the dark shadow of the arch, Tommy pointed at the tiny boat lying in the mud beside them. Without delay, Eloise and Tommy stepped carefully in, as Joncilond pushed the boat slithering over the mud into the strong current of the river.

'Sit down,' Tommy whispered to Eloise, as he stood half bent over, grabbing at the rough stones on the underside of the bridge.

It was difficult to keep the boat from breaking free and floating off in full view of the château, even though Joncilond still gripped the boat at one end.

'I'll keep hold at this end,' whispered Eloise, half standing, 'or it'll swing round!'

Tommy nodded, and as Joncilond let go, Tommy and Eloise hand over hand manoeuvred the boat across the river, holding on to the bottom of the bridge mostly by the plants that were growing there and roots that were poking through the stones. At any moment they could be swept away, and Tommy could feel his heart thumping as he struggled, using all his weight, to heave the boat sideways. With a final tug they were over, and Tommy leapt from the boat, holding his end with one hand, as Eloise came forward. Both were covered in mud up to their knees by the time they managed to drag the boat out onto the bank on the other side of the river.

Resting a moment in the cool air beneath the bridge, Tommy took Eloise's hand and squeezed it, giving a grin of encouragement for the next and still more dangerous part.

Cupping his hands round his mouth, Tommy whispered, 'Thank you,' as loudly as he dared across the river, the words echoing under the bridge, and he and Eloise set off along the bank. The river turned sharply here, and was screened from the road by a line of trees.

'Why don't Joncilond and Jacques make a break for it?' he whispered to Eloise, who just shrugged in reply. 'They shouldn't just sit there!' he added.

But then to their dismay, they realised why. They could hear the sound of horses on the road – several horses.

'We're there now,' said the Bishop, and Tommy and Eloise ducked fearfully down onto the muddy bank behind a thick alder bush as they heard this familiar and hated voice. 'Good brother, the château's just around this corner.'

Peering through the branches, Tommy and Eloise could see Bishop Henri de Montfort and Drogo, and an escort of two horsemen, making their way along the road, just a short distance from the bridge.

'Quick,' whispered Tommy urgently, 'they'll spot us when they cross the bridge unless we get further around the bend here.'

They stumbled off as fast as they could, hoping that none of the Bishop's party would look too closely in their direction.

Gosh! What about Jacques and Joncilond? thought Tommy, as they increased their distance. What about the signal! Blast our luck! Why did they have to come now? They were pretty close by this time to the château. Surely, the Bishop and Drogo must be crossing the bridge by now…

'*Cuckoo, cuckoo, cuckoo*…' And again, and once again, the call rang out through the hot afternoon air.

'Oh, you genius, Joncilond! Thank you!' muttered Tommy, and he exchanged a smile with Eloise.

'Good God! That was close, that cuckoo!' exclaimed the Bishop, halting his horse at the start of the bridge. He motioned the others to pass.

'Aye, m'Lord, I could have sworn it came from right under the bridge, m'Lord,' said one of the soldiers.

'D'you think so, really?' said the Bishop. 'I can't remember seeing a cuckoo – not for years, not close up, anyway.' He edged his horse over to the parapet of the bridge. 'I wonder if I can get a glimpse of it!' he muttered to himself.

'What's stopping you, Henri?' asked Drogo, impatient to get to the château and get his hands on the crucifix once more, wherever it might be. 'Come on!'

'I just want to see if I can see…' replied the Bishop, craning his head over the side and bending down as far as he could from his horse.

His long robe fell over the edge of the bridge as he did so, and before he could finish the sentence, a strong hand rose up, grabbed the robe and pulled it so hard that the Bishop tumbled sideways off his horse. Clutching at the air, he balanced for a moment on the parapet, and then fell with a great splash of mud and water onto the river bank below, letting out a roar of anger as he did so.

Drogo and the horsemen, now a little way ahead, turned at the sound of the Bishop's cry. They watched in frozen amazement as a second hand appeared, launching the body of Joncilond over the parapet and into the saddle of the Bishop's horse. Before anyone could react, Joncilond had turned the horse's head and spurred it away. At the same moment, Jacques fled from the cover of the bridge. Joncilond, bending down, scooped him up with one arm and they were off at full tilt up the slope and into the forest.

'After them, you fools!' screamed Drogo, as the guards held their horses, rooted to the spot. 'After them!'

At this second command, the guards reacted, and turning and kicking hard into their horses, rode as best they could up the hillside after Joncilond and Jacques. Drogo, shading his eyes with his hand, caught a brief glimpse of the chase as the riders disappeared among the trees.

Only then did a groan from under the bridge cause Drogo to wonder if his brother had been injured. He approached the edge of the bridge fearfully. Would another hand reach up and pull him over the side to join Henri? Holding his robes tightly around him, Drogo leant out and peered over the parapet. His brother lay stretched on his back, eyes tight shut, his fists clenched in fury and in pain.

'Henri,' whispered Drogo.

At the sound of his name, de Montfort's eyes suddenly blinked open and meeting Drogo's gaze, he snarled, 'Help me up from this mud and filth! Where are my men? Get them down here! That mad horse! It will be straight to the knackers when I get back to Toulouse. The finest horse in south-west France, I was told. Ha! What a price I paid for it. The finest horse!' he repeated, his voice rising. 'The finest at throwing people, I should say! Don't just sit on your horse and stare at me, for God's sake, man!' he raged. 'Where are those two soldiers, eh! Bring my horse down!'

At that, he began to struggle to sit up, putting out an arm which sank into the mud up to his elbow, causing him only to fall back again.

'Help me, damn you!' cried the Bishop, raising his voice to a shout, as Drogo continued to gape at him.

'Try to roll over,' said Drogo. He had never seen his brother so helpless before, and he was rather enjoying it. 'Try to roll over,' he repeated. 'The ground's a bit firmer...'

'Where're my men? Stop fooling with me!' yelled Henri.

'Oh,' said Drogo, 'they've galloped off in pursuit. I ordered them to. Didn't you hear me?'

'I was out cold. Of course I didn't hear you!' replied Henri.

He tried as he spoke to follow Drogo's advice to roll over, grabbing at some grass as he did so. This just tore in his hand, and he cursed Drogo again. 'You damned imp! In pursuit, you said! In pursuit of what?'

'Look! Listen to me, Henri,' said Drogo, 'someone reached up from underneath the bridge and pulled you off your horse. When... when you were looking for the... er... cuckoo!'

Henri had managed to get on his hands and knees by this time, and he looked up at Drogo with a puzzled scowl upon his face

'What damned cuckoo?' he asked, and then shouted, 'Cuckoo!' thumping the ground with his fist and losing his temper once more.

And, at this moment, a cuckoo in the nearby trees chose to give his call. Henri's head spun round in the direction of the sound. He would have strangled the bird if he could have got his hands on it, but instead he staggered to his feet, leaning heavily against the lower parts of the bridge. Drogo was unable to suppress a chuckle as the cuckoo called once more and Henri shot him a glance of hatred.

'You think it's funny, do you? Seeing me lying in the mud.'

'No, no, Henri,' replied Drogo hastily.

'Then lead me down my horse!'

'Henri, you don't understand. Your horse is gone. Whoever it was that pulled you over the parapet, he stole your horse too!'

'What? It didn't throw me, then?' retorted the Bishop who had been too dazed to follow what Drogo had just told him.

'No, no, Henri,' replied Drogo. 'As I said, you were pulled over the side, by someone hiding under the bridge!'

'Hiding under the bridge? What in the name of the Virgin were they doing there?'

'The… whoever it was,' continued Drogo, 'pulled himself up and leapt on your horse and rode away!'

'What! He stole my horse? The finest in this part of France! I paid a fortune for him! And you let him do it! You just stood and watched as he rode off on my horse! Damn me for having such a brother! No, damn *you*…!' spluttered the Bishop, working himself up into another rage.

'Henri, it happened so quickly. You've no idea! Your two horsemen rode off after him of course. They should have a good chance of catching him. For as the thief made his getaway, his accomplice ran from under the bridge and he managed to grab him, and they both rode off together. Quite a burden for a horse!'

'Not that horse!' replied Henri. 'We'll have to mount an expedition to recover it, and hang that thief from the nearest tree. Steal my horse – within sight of the Château de Romolue? And now, I suppose, I will have to walk to the château!' Henri exclaimed.

Again, Drogo had great difficulty in suppressing a grin, and Henri could certainly see the corners of his mouth twitch up and down as Drogo imagined the Bishop of Toulouse arriving on foot at the great door. Such a sight would be remembered for many a year at the château… And for a moment Drogo pictured the Bishop, holding the bridle of Drogo's horse, with its special saddle to hold the injured man; the Bishop, walking beside Drogo's horse; the Bishop, his face streaked with grey stinking mud and half his body smeared with it… Drogo's eye gleamed with amusement at the thought.

Drogo's wish was not, however, to be satisfied. For as the Bishop stumbled back onto the bridge, standing rubbing his head and grimacing in pain, supporting himself on the parapet, one of his guards came galloping down the slope towards them.

Pulling hard on the reins, he called, 'We lost him, sire. He seemed to know the way through the woods like the back of his hand, darting this way and that. It was impossible to follow him. And Jean, he's lamed his horse. He's leading it back. Put its leg in a bog, sire. Jean tumbled off. Lucky he only landed in the stinging nettles, sire. Could have really hurt himself.'

'He could really have hurt himself, could he?' muttered the Bishop. 'Bring that horse here,' he suddenly yelled to the guard. 'Off it! Hop it! I'll ride to the château on this old beast rather than walk!'

'Should I wait for Jean, sire?' asked the guard, dismounting.

'No, you will not. You come with us,' answered the Bishop.

All the while Tommy and Eloise had been creeping along the river bank towards the château. They were well hidden from view and saw nothing of the drama on the bridge. They had been moving on as fast as possible after Joncilond gave the cuckoo calls, and as they approached the kitchen wing of the château, they could faintly hear the church bell of Romolue strike four o'clock.

'Let's get in,' whispered Tommy. 'The peasants will be out in the fields in a few moments. The siesta's over.'

How were they to get onto the roof? Tommy wondered; but then they both saw that Jacques had solved the problem for them. Leaning along the wall of the kitchen was a ladder. Quickly, they struggled up the bank, grabbed the ladder, shinned up it, pushed it away from the wall, to cover their tracks, found the skylight, still broken from Sunday, and dropped through into the pantry below – praying that no one was about. They landed as quietly as they could, standing for a moment listening for footsteps or voices. But all they could hear was their own heavy breathing, and, it seemed, a gentle snoring. Holding hands, they smiled at one another.

'To Marie's room, then,' whispered Tommy, and they cautiously made their way into the kitchen.

One of the cooks lay sprawled on a bench, alongside the kitchen table. Dregs of wine from lunch and a hot afternoon, and he was far away... It was his snores that they had heard before.

But as they crept past, he turned sharply in his sleep, and muttered, 'Larks in butter: first remove the beak...' Then he almost fell on the floor.

Tommy grabbed his shoulder and eased him back onto the bench, whilst Eloise steadied his legs.

'Phew!' whispered Tommy, as they started to climb the servants' stairs. 'If he'd fallen, I'm sure that he'd have woken up.'

They moved as noiselessly as they could and they had just reached the first floor when a door opened in the corridor around the corner and a quick footfall could be heard coming towards them, tapping along the flagstones.

'Quick, in here!' squeaked Eloise, pulling Tommy sideways through a small door.

They found themselves in an enormous linen cupboard. Tommy had never seen it before.

'Oh, God! They might come in here, if it's a servant!' whispered Eloise. 'We'll have to hide.'

And indeed the footsteps were approaching. They had no time to lose and dived in among a heap of pillows. Eloise grabbed a large pile of sheets and attempted to pull them over the two of them. Now, the pillows were stuffed with goose feathers and in their rush to hide among them, lots of little feathers had been stirred up. Some of these found there way right into Tommy's nose...

'I think that I'm going to sneeze,' he muttered desperately. 'I am!' Eloise grabbed his nose as Tommy went red in the face and made a loud snorting noise.

'God! That's done it,' he said and then from outside the door Tommy could hear someone whistling a little tune... 'Für Elise'!

'Oh gosh, it's Jacques!' he said quite loudly, struggling to get up from among the pillows.

'How d'you know?' whispered Eloise urgently. 'How d'you know that it's Jacques?'

'That tune, Eloise. It's not from now – I mean, it's the tune the mobile phone plays. It's Beethoven!'

'Who?' exclaimed Eloise. 'You said it was Jacques!'

'No, the tune. Never mind!' said Tommy, dusting off the feathers. 'Let's get out of here.'

'Are you sure it's safe?' whispered Eloise.

But by way of answer, Tommy just opened the cupboard door, feathers settling around them, with Eloise peering out nervously behind him. There stood Jacques, his finger to his lips. Then he beckoned with his forefinger, and pointed up the stairs. Tommy nodded. In no time they were at Marie's door, with Jacques following behind them. Tommy made as if he was going to knock, but Jacques came running forward, waving his forefinger.

'No, no,' he whispered. 'Just go straight in!'

Tommy gently pushed the door open, and as they entered, a white halo of hair turned in the chair facing half away from them, and the brilliant and twinkling blue eyes of Marie fell upon them. Jacques closed the door behind them and they could hear the *tap, tap, tap* as he departed down the corridor.

'Why, you are a muddy mess!' said Marie, as if they had just come back from a Sunday afternoon ramble in the woods. 'Quite a muddy mess! Here, change into these trousers, Master Thomas, and you, Milady, go in there.' Marie gestured with a little wave of her hand. 'You'll find a change of clothes in there. Be quick,' she added.

Eloise and Tommy needed no second telling to be quick, because they knew that the Bishop and Drogo were approaching the château. In just a few moments, they stood before Marie, still smelling a little of mud, perhaps, but less like football players on a wet Saturday afternoon, than before. It was none too soon, for they could hear a heavy blow at the château door.

'The Bishop,' whispered Tommy, and Marie nodded.

'Into the padded room with you,' said Marie, 'quick!'

'But…' protested Tommy, for he knew it was locked.

'The Countess will be there to open it,' said Marie, reading Tommy's thoughts. 'Go, quick – but silently!' she said, and they tiptoed as fast as they could out of the door of Marie's room, and, meeting the Countess, with her finger to her lips, made their way in silence into the little padded room.

'The Bishop,' began Tommy at once, 'the Bishop is—'

'Yes, and Drogo too,' interrupted Eloise, 'the man who – the man who – killed my mother,' she blurted out, her mouth tight with passion.

'Ah! You know!' said the Countess, turning pale and putting her hand to her head, and taking Eloise's hand with the other. 'You know!'

'Countess... mother,' began Tommy, 'we met Drogo and the Bishop, I mean, we saw them, they didn't see us, when we were getting into the château. They were coming over the bridge. The crucifix is safe, isn't it? Still in the stone bench? And Drogo's parchment?'

The Countess nodded.

'Look, I've got to find out what Drogo and the Bishop are planning. They're bound to ransack the place if we give them half a chance. I'll just go out on the landing – I'll keep well hidden, don't worry!' said Tommy, seeing the alarm on Eloise's face.

Tommy crept through the door onto the corridor. From there he could hear all that passed below.

The main door to the château was open, and he heard the Count exclaim, 'My good Bishop! Good heavens! What has happened to you? Jacques, fetch two footmen. Lead His Grace to Drogo's apartments. Clean clothes, warm water. This instant!' Turning back to de Montfort, he added, 'You look as though you fell off your horse.'

The Bishop clenched his fists in rage and snarled, 'Someone, something, pulled me from my horse. And by God, he's going to pay dearly for it. I'll hang him over your bridge.'

'Pulled you from your horse? But, your men, sire, your men...' replied the Count.

'No, it was the cuckoo call,' broke in Drogo.

'The *cuck...oooo!*' yelled the Bishop. 'If you mention cuckoos again, I'll have my archers exterminate the little brutes from every tree around Toulouse.' He thumped a dresser with his fist, grimacing in pain as he did so.

'Cuckoos?' said the Count, with a puzzled look on his face. 'What have cuckoos—?'

'Enough!' bellowed the Bishop. 'I was on the bridge and I was

291

hauled over the side, my horse stolen, the finest horse in southwest France, worth a fortune. My horse stolen from under me! On *your* land, my good Count.'

On the landing above, Tommy grinned gleefully, *Joncilond*! he exclaimed to himself, clenching his fists in delight.

'And now,' Tommy heard the Bishop continue, a little more calmly, but with acid in his voice, 'and now we will retake my horse and the lives of any who resist. I will personally put the rope around the neck of the man who did it, and swing him over your bridge!'

You'll have to catch him first, thought Tommy.

'And this is what we're going to do,' the Bishop went on. 'My man here will ride fast back to Toulouse and return with fifty of my horsemen. You, my good Count, will certainly assist me in this! We will advance together into the forest, into the marsh; we will sweep through, driving all like frightened deer before us. Twenty-five of my men will accompany me. Twenty-five archers will remain at the outskirts of the wood. We will drive them into the arrows of the bowmen. They will be crushed between muskets at their back and arrows at their front, squeezed like an apple with the juice running out, until the pips squeak!' As he spoke, de Montfort took an apple from a bowl beside him, and in his great fist, he squeezed until juice began to run on the floor and squashed apple pulp pushed out between his fingers.

'But, my good Bishop, your horse! How are you going to get your horse?' asked the Count, looking from the apple to the Bishop and back again.

'I will personally see to my horse,' replied the Bishop, 'and to the man who stole it!' His voice rose dangerously.

What a violent piece of work he is, thought the Count, images of ropes and bridges swimming into his mind.

Turning to his horseman, the Bishop ordered him away to Toulouse adding, 'Bring muskets, remember! That'll terrify them. And also six pistols for my belt!'

Tommy had heard enough. Silently he re-entered the padded room, closing all the doors behind him as he came. Eloise and the Countess were waiting anxiously.

'Well,' said the Countess, letting out her breath, as though she had been holding it all the time that Tommy had been out of the room. Eloise's gaze seem to bore into him as she too breathed a sigh of relief at seeing Tommy safe from detection.

'Well!' repeated the Countess, 'what did you hear?'

'The Bishop is planning to attack the people of the quaking marsh!' said Tommy. Suddenly he was in a terrible hurry.

'The people of the...' began the Countess.

'Yes,' interrupted Tommy talking rapidly, 'there's a whole town out there. They're good people!' At this, Eloise raised her eyebrows and seemed about to speak, but Tommy put up his hand. 'Well, if they're not always good, they have reason, hunted down by the nobles, the Church... But, look, some of them have helped us, the leaders there, they helped us escape. I mean, in fact they brought us back here. We've got to warn them about the Bishop. There isn't much time. I've got to go in, find Joncilond.'

'Who?' said the Countess.

'Joncilond,' said Eloise, 'he's a kind of forest spirit, but he's a man... I mean.' She paused, seeing the puzzled look on the Countess's face. 'Well, sort of a man, anyway' – she smiled – 'Wait till you meet him!'

'Yeah... Joncilond,' said Tommy, 'he's the only person who can guide me to the Emp.'

'The Emp!' muttered the Countess. 'There are stories of criminals living in the marsh. The Emp! The Emperor of the Marsh...'

'You've heard of him, then?' said Tommy excitedly. 'He's our friend. I've got to warn him,' he added, standing up, and starting to pace about the room.

'Sit down a moment,' said the Countess. 'I can't think with you pacing about!' Then there was a long moment of silence, as the Countess wrinkled her brow, and Tommy and Eloise looked hard into her face.

'The main thing,' began the Countess, 'is to destroy Drogo! Now—'

'Yes,' interrupted Tommy, 'I've thought about that...'

'Wait a second!' snapped the Countess. 'What's the point of warning these people, these escaped robbers and murderers – yes, some of them are,' she added as she saw Tommy about to protest, 'some are murderers, and witches, maybe! If the Bishop kills them, so much the better! What use are they to us? They may have helped you once, it's true, but...'

'No!' said Tommy, and Eloise shook her head, adding quietly, 'No! we've promised. We can't just let them be murdered by the Bishop and his men. The Emp, and some of the others, Jacques the Tailor, Joncilond...'

'We can't,' said Tommy, 'and anyway, they can be useful to us. We need as many friends as possible. They'll help us to destroy Drogo.'

'What can they do?' demanded the Countess. 'They can't resist the Bishop's men, you admit that.'

'Yes, but look, I've got a plan. On Sunday, when we are all at the cathedral...' And Tommy began to outline how Drogo could be overcome.

The Countess and Eloise listened with close attention, nodding, Eloise clapping her hands at one moment, the Countess grinning, a tight-lipped smile curving around her mouth.

'Yes,' she said as Tommy drew to a finish. 'Yes, that might do rather nicely. Rather nicely,' she repeated quietly to herself. 'Yes, I can see that the people of the marsh might be useful, mmm. Very well, so you want to try and warn them? There's not much time!'

'I know,' said Tommy, standing up again.

'I think that it's best if you wait until dark – when all the peasants have gone in from the fields,' said the Countess.

'Yeah,' replied Tommy, 'I can let myself down from the window of my room, slip into the moat, swim across the river and be in the woods and out of sight in a few minutes.'

Eloise shuddered, 'Do we have to go through the moat again?' she asked.

'You, you're not going with him!' said the Countess firmly.

'The only thing is,' went on Tommy unperturbed, 'is how am I going to find my way at all in the dark? I've got to make for the road, and cross that, where we met old Rabelais... Oh gosh, that was something else,' said Tommy, turning to Eloise.

'I'm not coming with you?' asked Eloise, ignoring his last comment, her voice rising.

'Sssh,' whispered the Countess. 'No, you're not!'

Eloise knew better than to argue. But she would see. She wasn't going to let Thomas go off alone. He needed her. Joncilond would do anything for her, and maybe he wouldn't help them at all if Thomas were alone. And the Emp and his friends, they'd only behaved themselves halfway decently because she was there. No, she had to be at Thomas's side. For the moment however, she kept these thoughts to herself.

'Rabelais, Rabelais,' muttered Tommy. 'What was it? Ah, yes,' he said, turning to the Countess. 'Rabelais was hurrying back to Romolue. We met him on the road. He'd been here to warn you that Louis, you know, that thick-headed guard who Eloise and me, we bashed over the head... well, Louis killed Marc.'

'Louis!' exclaimed the Countess, 'Well, heavens – and who's that... Marc?'

'One of the servants in the château, and...' began Tommy.

'Oh! Just one of the servants. Still, there'll be a trial. Hang him, probably,' she added, dismissing the business from her mind.

'Yes, but the trouble is that Marc was also one of Drogo's men, here. Spying and working for Drogo in the château.'

'It happened on the road to the Abbey, when I was on that cart,' broke in Eloise. 'Marc was following us, I think, and Louis was following him – probably Jacques sent him – and well, they met, because Marc came running out the bushes where he was hiding, and Louis chased him and killed him. Accidentally. He was very sorry about it. But—'

'Rabelais' message got through, though?' interrupted Tommy.

'I don't know,' said the Countess, 'Jacques will, though. I'll send a servant to find him.'

At that moment, there was a noise outside of someone quietly clearing their throat, followed by a gentle tapping at the door. All three of them jumped.

'Who's that?' whispered the Countess sharply.

'It's Jacques, my Lady!' whispered a voice through the door.

The Countess moved rapidly to the door, unlocked it and let Jacques in.

'That's lucky, we wanted to talk to you. Have you seen Rabelais?' she asked.

'Yes,' said Jacques. 'But, let me see now. We haven't got much time, y'know, Countess. The Bishop…'

'Yes, yes,' said Tommy, 'I heard all that. I was listening on the landing when the Bishop was telling the Count how he was planning to wipe out the people of the marsh. Tell us first about Rabelais!'

'Right! Yes, Monsieur Thomas. Anyway, the people of the marsh don't matter much in all this, do they?' replied Jacques. 'But you remember when the Bishop and Father Drogo came looking for the crucifix? Well, I told them that Marc had taken it down to the village to Rabelais, to be mended. Drogo seemed very fixated about that crucifix, and the Bishop said that it was far too valuable to go to the village, and that they were going to go and get it. That wasn't exactly true, my Lady, about Marc taking it down to Rabelais. Not exactly true at all. Please forgive me for telling untruths to these noble churchmen.' He smiled.

'No, I know it wasn't true,' said the Countess, 'but it was a good idea!'

Tommy and Eloise nodded.

'Well,' continued Jacques, 'Rabelais arrived just as one of the Bishop's horsemen rode up outside the château. Georges, he's called. Watch out for him. He's a bad one. He didn't even dismount, just shouted, "I'm sent to arrest Louis for killing Marc. Bring him out and search him for a crucifix we reckon he's stolen!"

'Several of our guards came running when they heard this,' continued Jacques, 'and a bit of an argument started. Louis is maybe a bit dumb, but he's good-natured, and no one believed the story – especially the bit about stealing. I could hear what was going on, and so what I did was to find Louis and warn him to hide. He's in your bedroom, sir,' explained Jacques, turning to Tommy, 'hiding in your bed, sir; I mean, sorry,' he added, as Tommy's eyebrows shot up, 'not in it, under it, you know, the sliding bit!'

'Yes, I know,' whispered Eloise and blushed.

'Anyway, I went out to Georges, and quietened things down a bit. We sort of pretended to search where Louis might be, but, as you can imagine, we didn't actually find him! "Obviously gone to earth, Georges," I said. "If he's gone and killed Marc, and pinched the crucifix from him, Louis has probably made off. P'raps into the marsh, taking the crucifix with him... Melt it down maybe. It's very big to hide."

"'But the Bishop offered me a gold coin if I find anything out about the crucifix!" said Georges. "I'll reward you if you can help me!" he said.

"'Well," I replied, "you can tell the good Bishop that the information about the crucifix is that it's probably gone walkies into the forest with Louis. I expect you'll get the reward that you deserve for that!" Fancy, he thought that he could bribe me! Anyway, all Georges did was to give me an ugly look, and then he spurred his horse off, without any reply.'

'Good, good,' said Tommy.

'Certainly, certainly; but now we've got troubles. The first thing that Father Drogo asked me was, just a few minutes ago, "Where's that crucifix? You gave it to Marc," he said. "Marc's dead. We've seen his body in Romolue. Louis killed him. Where's Louis?" – and so on! "My gracious Lord," I answered, "this is terrible news! We've searched the château, that was when Georges came earlier, sir. There's no sign of Louis, good Father."

'Then I told him the rest of what I told Georges. It seems his brother the Bishop hadn't said anything about the crucifix probably being in the forest with Louis, because he broke out in a terrible rage, and then threw himself in despair face down on the bed – we were in his room – waving with one hand for me to leave... which I did, quickly enough!' Jacques paused for a moment to catch his breath and then went on.

'There's something more to that crucifix than meets the eye, Countess. What's so special about it that it sends Drogo off into fits? Because, when the Bishop's men appear – which will be in a few hours at the most – fifty of them, they're going to be combing the château for it like cats comb their fur for fleas, if you will pardon the expression, Monsieur Thomas and Mademoiselle Eloise! Excuse my asking, but where is this crucifix? Because if they do find it, it'll be the chop for me, I think!'

'I reckon that we should tell him,' said Tommy.

The Countess pursed her lips.

'He's a very faithful servant, Mother,' said Eloise.

'It's in the stone bench,' whispered the Countess suddenly.

'But the parchment's not in it any more!' The words came tumbling out of Tommy's mouth. 'Ooh – you don't know about it, do you? Look, Drogo, he – oh gosh, this is something awful! Look, Father Drogo, he – he – murdered Eloise's mother, Eleonora. He killed her himself. With this crucifix, in the cathedral. It's all written down in a confession, a parchment, which I found inside the crucifix. We've taken the parchment out and we've hidden it somewhere else, very safe. But, if they did find the crucifix, and Drogo finds that there's no parchment in it, then it's going to ruin all our plans for his destruction. He mustn't be warned that we have it, or that we know about the parchment in any way at all. Anyway, that's why he's so crazy about the crucifix going missing. He knows it's only a matter of time before someone looks underneath, finds the keyhole and wants to know what's inside. So you're right, they're going to search the place like mad.'

Jacques was looking at Tommy, staring and dazed by all that he had heard. 'Say that again!' he managed to stutter out. 'Say that again!' His hand was on his brow and he was shaking his head. 'What are you saying!' he muttered, half to himself. 'Then it's true... the old stories... I was right, the old...' he whispered, and then he broke off, looking around at the faces before him and seeming to recollect where he was.

Tommy gave him a puzzled look.

'Drogo killed Eleonora and wrote about it,' Jacques added, addressing them directly, 'even down to how he did it! With the crucifix, of all things! The crucifix! He must be mad, quite mad! Why would he do such a thing? And why write it all down?'

'Blackmailed by his brother, I think. You have to read the manuscript. But not now, we've got too much to do,' added Tommy.

'Humph!' said Jacques. 'I knew that Drogo was a man capable of evil, and his power-hungry brother – oh, forgive me for talking of these churchmen in this way!'

'Nothing that you say of them can half match how evil they are!' cried Eloise, and stamped her foot.

'Ssshh!' warned the Countess.

'Are you absolutely sure that the compartment in the stone bench is unknown to Drogo?' Tommy asked the Countess anxiously.

'Yes, yes. Only the Count and I know about it.'

'And what about the Count, Madame? Does he know anything of this? I mean, he might show them the stone bench, I mean the place in the stone bench where you could hide things,' asked Jacques.

'Well, I must admit that I haven't told the Count anything,' the Countess replied. 'You know that he would fly into a rage, and nothing could stop him confronting Drogo and the Bishop with the parchment, and publicly accusing them. There would be open war again. I had to keep them apart just the other evening, when the Bishop made the mistake of describing how he and his men had been hunting Thomas and Eloise through the forest.'

'Heavens! Was he?' exclaimed Jacques, shaking his head.

'Anyway,' went on the Countess, 'it's clear that we have to catch Drogo off his guard. It's a dagger that we want, not a sledgehammer. And Monsieur Thomas has had a good idea.'

Jacques gave Tommy an enquiring look, but only replied, 'Right, my Lady. I'll stay near the Count, and if he shows any sign of talking about the stone bench, I'll divert him. But now, I must be back to attend on His Lordship, the Bishop!' And with that he turned and rapidly left the room.

'And now,' said the Countess, 'we've got to hide you two!'

Eighteen: Warning to the Emp

Fifty heavily armed men with bows and muskets were moving fast down the road towards the Château de Romolue, the banner of de Montfort flying high over their heads. They were riding hard, and the thunder of the horses' hooves was matched by a darkening sky. Evening was coming early as great thunderclouds massed. The heavy air darkened further and large raindrops began to fall.

Georges, at the head of the column glanced anxiously upwards. The pennant that he was carrying was a perfect target for a lightning strike. He'd had that happen once, in one of these violent summer storms. He could still remember the extraordinary shivering of his arm and the feeling as though his body was suddenly pulled taut by a great engine of torture. He had woken, groaning, with his teeth clenched together, lying face down on the ground. He shook his head to chase the memory from his mind. And as a precaution he handed the pennant to his second in command, who took it none too readily. Perhaps he too knows what can happen, thought Georges, and he gave the man an unpleasant grin.

A powerful gust of cold wind and the rain began suddenly to roar down upon them, with hail in it, clattering off their tough leather jerkins and making the horses toss their heads and shy away. It was tempting to shelter under the trees for a moment. A brilliant flash and an enormous clap of thunder and a strange acrid smell in the air put an end to that idea. Better to be soaked in the open than mashed by a tree falling on you! The path turned to mud, and the horses began to slip, with each man jerking hard at the reins, this way and that.

'Break ranks,' cried Georges, 'and make the best of it!'

On they rode. The pennant no longer streamed boldly out above them but sagged and dripped. A second flash, and Georges felt his hair stand on end. The clap of thunder came just a split second later.

God, we're right in the middle of it! he thought. This is one of the bad ones. And, as if to confirm his thoughts, a tree seemed to explode nearby, coming crashing down just fifty metres in front of them.

'Hold that pennant up!' commanded Georges, as he turned to see the tip of it pointing more at the ground than the sky.

'It's damn heavy – waterlogged!' yelled his second in command. 'You take the bloomin' thing! There's no one to see it anyway.'

His words were lost in the pouring rain, the last comment cut short by another flash and a clap of thunder. The explosion was so close that the poor man's horse bucked and bolted sideways off the path. The pennant jammed crossways between two trees, catching the horseman around the waist. The reins were pulled from him and he grabbed at the pennant pole as his horse, still more panicked by being restrained, pulled with all its strength to be free of its rider. With a great rip, the saddle came off and for a moment the horseman and saddle, stirrups and all, were left suspended between the trees, as the horse crashed its way into the surrounding wood. Then, in slow motion, the solider slithered and collapsed into a mass of wet leaves and muddy, soggy grass, the breath taken completely out of him.

'Oh! Damn me!' said Georges. 'You there,' he gestured at one of the men close by, 'go and see to him. Catch his horse. And you –' gesturing at another – 'take the pennant!'

'But it's snapped in two!'

'Well, hold it up as best you can.'

'I don't want splinters,' muttered the man.

So it was that forty-eight sodden, dejected men arrived at the door of the Château de Romolue, with a muddy pennant almost trailing along the ground, their clothes steaming in the humid sun, which now flickered between the dark clouds.

The Bishop gave the troop one cold look, then beckoned Georges and informed him that they would meet in an hour to discuss their planned attack for the morning. An hour later saw the men crammed into the kitchen, with a couple of barrels of wine, one already nearly empty, on the table.

'We're down one horse, my Lord,' Georges told the Bishop,

and then described the accident in the thunderstorm.

The two guards had just arrived, the injured man on the horse, and the other leading him.

'Get that pennant mended!' ordered de Montfort. 'Now, men,' he said in a commanding voice.

There was immediate silence. Even the beakers of wine were placed on the table. Outside you could hear that another great downpour had started.

'Tomorrow,' continued the Bishop, 'we...' But his words were drowned in a thunderclap.

'What's he say?' whispered one of the men.

He was stone deaf and had never heard a sound since a musket had exploded by his ear when he was a young lad. Mind you, the man that fired the musket died of his wounds; so he was lucky, but deaf.

'What's he say?' he whispered again.

He couldn't even hear the thunder, but he was good at lip-reading. Unfortunately he was also rather short-sighted, and he was sitting too far away from the Bishop.

'What's he say?' he repeated.

'Dunno,' said his companion.

'But...'

'Yeah, but the thunder...'

'Oh! Right!'

'Tomorrow,' the Bishop began again, 'we are going into the forest and we'll—'

A second clap of thunder obliterated his words. This time some of the men exchanged grins. The deaf one just looked puzzled, and took a long slurp of wine.

The Bishop decided to go on regardless. What the men heard was something like this:

'We'll divide... some people... with muskets... drive them... sheep... Shoot on sight... just robbers and murderers, condemned men,' and so on.

He did not mention his horse. He hadn't worked out how to explain how it had been stolen from under him without making a fool of himself. Not that anyone would have heard him. None of them was much the wiser about what they were expected to do, except that they had some idea that they would be shooting defenceless men, women and children in the marsh. That sounded okay – simple enough, and not too dangerous.

As the Bishop drew to a close, Drogo entered the kitchen, a flash of lightning showing his pale, thin face and sharp nose in the shadow by the door.

'May I say a word?' he asked, addressing his brother.

The thunder was dying away and the thin voice of Drogo could be heard.

'One of these thieves, the ones that you'll be hunting down tomorrow, has stolen a valuable crucifix from the château – from the chapel!'

There was a sharp intake of breath. This was a crime that everyone could understand, a very serious crime. You'd be hanged for that, on the spot.

'What's he say?' said the deaf one. 'What's he say?'

'He said… oh, I'll tell you after!'

'This crucifix will certainly be hidden somewhere, where they live, these robbers, in a hut or a cave, or whatever miserable place they have. I want you to search where you can. Search hard. This crucifix is of very great value to me, to the château, to the Count and Countess of Romolue, and to the Bishop, of course. Search, and the man who finds it, he will be rich for life. Five gold coins. *Five…*' But the rest was drowned in a clamour of voices from the soldiers.

'What's that?' said the deaf one. 'What's he say? I'm really missing somethin' now!'

'Later, later,' said his pal.

'Five gold coins,' repeated several of the men, 'five gold coins!'

'For a crucifix!'

'Must be some bleedin' crucifix!'

'Jewels in it, maybe.'

'Hey, Father Drogo,' called out one of the bolder men. 'Has it got jewels in it, like? Encrusted with diamonds, emeralds and such?'

'No, my good man,' replied Drogo. 'The value of the crucifix is… is… its sentimental value. An ancient heirloom. Priceless!'

'Ah!' A sigh went up from the soldiers, many of whom were still muttering, 'Five gold coins, eh!'

Amid all the noise of the men, and sound of the rain, no one in the kitchen heard the faint splash of Tommy entering the moat, and a few moments later, a second splash as Eloise followed.

'I've put a pillow in the bed – if they don't look too hard, they'll think it's me!' whispered Eloise to Tommy, and grinned.

'Maybe!' answered Tommy. 'Mind the swans! At least we won't be seen tonight.'

A great sheet of rain swirled around them and a gust of wind blew a warm mist across the moat.

'We're in the river soon, aren't we?' asked Eloise, and just then her foot slipped on the muddy stones and Tommy grabbed her arm as the swift current took her.

'Hold on to me!' said Tommy, as he struck out strongly for the other bank.

The rain poured so hard upon them that they could barely see across the river. The water slapped on their backs and stung their faces, as they screwed up their eyes against the wind and raindrops, scrabbling and pushing with their legs.

At last they were able to drag themselves up the bank. They were already as muddy as they had been when they had returned to the château just hours before. Moving away from the bank, they slithered across the fields, looking back at the château, with the friendly candlelight beckoning from the windows. It was strange to Tommy, how much it seemed like home. He had only been here for a few days, and for Eloise, it really was home. Just for a brief moment, he put an arm around her and cuddled her.

'Come on!' she whispered – though there was no need for whispering; you could have shouted out loud, and no one would have heard in the roar of the wind and rain. 'Come on! There's no time for that.'

She smiled at him and unwrapped his arm from around her and ran on. He followed, and soon they were at the border of the forest.

'What... what are we going to... how... I mean, which way...?' began Eloise.

'Gosh, you know, I'm not really sure. I was sort of half hoping that Joncilond might be scouting around. But in this weather!'

They stopped and looked about.

'There's the bridge,' said Eloise pointing down to the left. 'Why don't we try and retrace the way that we came yesterday? D'you think that we could?'

'Well, it's something to try,' said Tommy and they began to cut across up the hill so as to meet the route which had led them down to the bridge earlier that day.

The wood sheltered them from the wind but it howled among the upper branches and from time to time a bucket of water seemed to hit them full in the face. They waded through a muddy torrent at one point, as the rain ran off the hillside.

'This is not going to make it too easy for the Bishop and his soldiers, anyway,' said Tommy. 'The marsh will be overflowing.'

'Yes, I was thinking that!' said Eloise. 'I wouldn't want to be one of those soldiers,' she added.

'Nor me,' said Tommy.

It was getting more and more dark. Trees loomed up before them unseen except in the last few paces, like silent guards, waiting to pounce on them. Eloise drew close to Tommy. It was difficult not to trip over the rough ground, and she took hold of his sleeve.

'I'm glad there's two of us!' she whispered.

'Me too!' agreed Tommy. 'Y'know, I was wondering if I did a cuckoo call…'

'What! There're no cuckoos at night,' said Eloise.

'Exactly. I mean, if Joncilond were about, he'd know it was us. Three times three cuckoo calls! Then he'd know.'

He tried it: three times three cuckoo calls.

'I suppose it won't carry far, though.'

'Not more than fifty or a hundred paces, I should think,' said Eloise, 'or maybe even less.'

'Oh, well! Here goes again.'

Three times three, again and again, every few hundred paces. Three times three, but there was no answering call, no Joncilond. After a time they came to the top of the rise. The lights of the château were a faint glimmer between the trees, a distant patch of light that went in and out of their sight, as branches swept to and fro in front of them.

'I think we should turn down about that sort of direction,' said Tommy, raising his voice against the rushing wind and waving his hand to the left.

'Yes, but perhaps not quite so sharply down as that. I think we came up at a bit of an angle, perhaps. Let's go, then.'

They began to walk down the steep slope, which became a more gentle slope, after a little while. 'Just as it should,' said Tommy.

'Yes, it was gentle at first and then got steeper,' replied Eloise.

They had to talk to keep from being frightened by the swaying black shapes, imagined creatures, strange sounds, grunts and creaking noises of a forest at night in a rainstorm, with a high wind blowing overhead. There was the sound of running water everywhere. Each little gulley became a stream in this weather. The wet leaves were slippery, and several times both Tommy and Eloise landed on their backsides, sliding down a muddy bank, grasping at the tough ferns to stop their fall, their clammy clothes sticking to their skin, as they pulled themselves upright.

'Should we try the cuckoos again?' asked Eloise.

'Y'know, I think that we stand a much better chance of finding Joncilond, if he's out at all, on the other side of the road. Oh, well! Why not...?'

And again the unlikely sound of a cuckoo could be heard faintly through the rain and wind.

The forest began to break up ahead of them. They could see the moon showing occasionally between the billowing clouds, which were racing wildly across the sky. Moonlight shone for a moment on a path.

'Ah! The road – there it is!' said Tommy.

'Down!' whispered Eloise, and Tommy sat on some thistles.

'Ow! And what is it anyway?' he asked.

'Sssh! There's someone on the road!' whispered Eloise beside him.

Tommy crouched down further.

'Ow!' he muttered again and shifted himself sideways.

He peered out into the blackness. A flicker of moonlight showed, just for an instant, a man walking towards them, walking with a firm and rapid step, and, as he approached, they could hear that he was singing quite loudly to himself. It was a strange song, of which they could only make out a few notes here and there, a strange song, in a language which seemed somehow familiar to Tommy: English, it was English – with a funny accent! As the stranger passed, they could see that he was dressed as a sailor, a tall, strong figure. His face was weather-beaten, and his dark eyes shone for an instant as a flash of moonlight passed across his face. High cheekbones, a large and clear forehead, a strong nose, a handsome face... more like the face of an aristocrat than a sailor.

'*Twenty men...*' Tommy heard him singing.

'*Twenty men on a dead man's chest!*' sang the sailor, as he passed them.

'*Yo, ho, ho! And a bottle of rum,*' muttered Tommy.

'Eh?' whispered Eloise.

'A bottle of rum,' said Tommy and grinned at Eloise, whose face became a question mark.

'It's an old sea song,' explained Tommy, 'an English one.'

They both looked at the back of the sailor as he disappeared into the gloomy shadows of the trees.

'Yes, but why should this man, this sailor, be marching along the road to the Château de Romolue in the middle of the night?' asked Eloise. 'Singing in English?' she added.

This sailor, or whatever he was, had made her feel uncomfortable, but in a way that was strangely attractive. She had felt an urge to run out into the middle of the road and take his hands in hers. She felt unsettled and asked again, almost to herself, 'Who could this be?'

'Well, a sailor...' began Tommy.

'But he didn't *look* like a sailor,' said Eloise, 'just his clothes.'

'And the song,' said Tommy. 'Only a sailor would sing that song! Come on, let's get across the road before we're spotted by someone. Perhaps he wasn't alone!'

Taking Eloise's hand firmly in his, they clambered through the ditch along the side of the road and ran across into the cover of the woods. Now they were truly in the quaking marsh. The ground seemed unstable under their feet, just as soon as they had moved a few paces.

'We daren't go much further,' said Eloise and Tommy nodded.

His one dip in a bog was quite enough to convince him of that. They both stopped.

'If only we could find Joncilond, or Jacques the Tailor, or anyone!' said Tommy.

'Why don't you try the…?' And as Eloise was about to say 'Cuckoo' they heard, '*Cuckoo, cuckoo, cuckoo!*'

'It's Joncilond!' cried Tommy. 'It's Joncilond!'

He danced up and down with glee and suddenly his leg sank up to his knee in the bog and he was left lurching at an angle, but still grinning.

'Ssssh!' said Eloise.

'*Tchk, tchk, tchk,*' said Joncilond, springing down beside Eloise from the branch of a large old oak beside them. Eloise got such a fright that she jumped backwards, tripped over a tree root and fell on her bottom.

'*Tchk, tchk, tchk,*' he repeated, as he gallantly stretched out his hand and drew her up as if she were light as a feather.

'Now help me out!' said Tommy. 'Please.'

'I heard you, I heard you, I saw you, I smelt you!' sang Joncilond, doing a little caper.

'You smelt us!' said Eloise, as Tommy struggled to get loose.

'Help me out!' he repeated.

'Yes,' said Joncilond, ignoring him, 'you smell of roses, roses, roses, Mademoiselle Eloise, roses. But he smells of puppy-dogs' tails, pooh, pooh, pooh, puppy-dogs' tails. Ugh!'

'Never mind what I smell of!'

'I mind,' said Eloise, laughing, but then she could not help remembering that Joncilond was the most smelly person that she had ever met.

'Just help me out, please, kind Joncilond!' said Tommy, and a sucking, gasping gulp came from the mud as Tommy sank still further in.

A sharp blast of wind caused Eloise to shiver, and Joncilond slipped off his filthy cloak which was flapping about him and placed it over her shoulders.

'Thank you!' and she shuddered again, but this time at the smell which rose from the cloak around her. He smelt us, she thought, but if it had not been for the wind, we could have smelt him, I reckon!

Whilst Eloise was trying to shift the cloak away from her nose, Joncilond took Tommy's arm and bodily lifted him out of the mud, practically dislocating his shoulder in the process.

'Thank you, thank you,' mumbled Tommy, furiously rubbing and stretching his arm, to make sure that it still functioned. 'Now, Joncilond!'

'Yessir, yessir, yessir!' gabbled Joncilond, looking from Tommy to Eloise and back again. 'Yessir!'

'Now, Joncilond. This is really important!'

'Yessir!' said Joncilond again, springing into the air, landing on one foot and turning round and round on one leg.

He would be a terrific ballet dancer, Tommy could not help thinking.

'Joncilond!' began Eloise in her sweet voice. 'Please!'

Joncilond stopped in mid-turn, and, still on one leg, bowed down and kissed Eloise's muddy shoe. His other foot projected high up into the air. Silhouetted against the moon, Tommy could see that he was missing the third toe, which was just a little stump.

'Your toe!' began Tommy. 'No! Listen, Joncilond. There's no time. Lead us to the Emp, please.'

'But, Master Thomas de Romolue,' replied Joncilond, suddenly reasonable and standing normally, 'we just led you from the Emp. Dangerous too!' he added. 'And now you want to be back with the Emp!'

'Oh, good Joncilond,' said Eloise, 'you saved us. And we have not said thank you. But thanks, thanks! It will not be forgotten when I have the power to reward,' she added, rather grandly, and Joncilond bowed once more, but with both feet on the ground.

'Yes, gosh, thanks, Joncilond. I did not mean to seem ungrateful. You were great. And Jacques, too. The horse, the Bishop's… yeah… that was fantastic.' Eloise cast him a puzzled glance. 'But you see,' said Tommy, 'something's happened, or going to happen. The Bishop and fifty men are going to attack the people of the quaking marsh, tomorrow. *Tomorrow*! The Emp must be warned. Please take us to him!'

'The Bishop, the Bishop!' shouted Joncilond. 'And Drogo... Drogo,' he added in a whisper, drawing out the name.

Eloise clenched her fists as she heard the name of the hated priest.

Joncilond had heard them talking in the Emp's palace. Joncilond knew. He knew! thought Tommy.

'You've told no one, Joncilond?' Tommy whispered anxiously, as if they could be overheard here in the forest.

'Told no one,' echoed Joncilond, and nodded slowly.

'You must tell no one,' whispered Eloise, and the three of them stood for a moment listening to the wind gusting through the trees and the swish of the rain, slapping against the branches.

'Come,' said Joncilond, breaking the trance, 'Come, to the Emp, to the Emp!' And he set off at a rapid pace.

Tommy and Eloise hurried to follow, so as not to lose him in the dark. They stumbled on, it seemed for hours. At last they hit the main path.

'We are close, now,' said Tommy quietly to Eloise.

Joncilond turned, his finger to his lips. Then he gave three short calls, the sound of a dove, and stood still. They waited. The wind had dropped, just whispering now among the higher branches, which cast hard shadows on the ground from the brightly shining moon, with the clouds dispersed. They waited and again Joncilond called the dove calls. Then very faintly in the far distance they could hear a response. Three dove calls – or was it an echo? No, for Joncilond nodded, turned, grinned, did a little hop, and they were off again.

Soon, turning a corner in the road, they could see the wooden walls of Town caught in the moonlight. It looked the picture of a quiet, safe little village. Tommy wondered whether the next night it would be a smoking ruin. He would do all he could to stop it, and he gripped Eloise's hand. She turned to him and nodded, as if reading his thoughts.

Again Joncilond made the three dove calls, answered this time immediately and quite loudly nearby. Drawing close to Town, they saw a door open, and a figure appear, beckoning them to hurry in. They moved into a trot. They were going in the back way – the way they had left Town, just the day before – no! that morning! In no time they were in the dark streets of Town and before the Emp's palace.

Dinner of course was being served, or at least, they were on the dessert, when Tommy and Eloise entered, ushered in noisily by Joncilond.

'Well!' said the Emp, without looking round, annoyed at the interruption to his meal. Then, turning, he started out of his chair in surprise. 'You two! Gods alive! You'll bring ruin on us all!' he spluttered, his mouth full of stewed pears and cream and pastry.

'That looks quite nice,' said Tommy cheekily, knowing well that the best way to get the Emp's attention was through his stomach.

'Yeah, well,' said the Emp, 'it's Phillipe's daughter, what's-'er-name, er... Yeah, she's pretty good at sweets anyway. No radishes, either, yeah, these pear... Hey! You didn't come here to discuss the food, you little... er, Monsieur Thomas!' he ended a bit lamely, remembering that he was addressing the heir to the House of Romolue.

Eloise frowned beside Tommy.

'Yes, well,' started Thomas.

'It's *not* well!' shouted the Emp. 'You'll be the ruin of us!' he repeated.

'Wait, wait,' said Tommy. 'You're right, we're not here to talk about the cooking! We've come to warn you about...'

'The Bishop, the Bishop, the Bishop!' sang out Joncilond suddenly, prancing from one foot to the other. 'And Drogo, Drogo,' he added quietly, drawing out the name as he had before, and wriggling and shuddering his arms and legs about as he did so. 'Drogo!' he shouted abruptly.

'Quiet!' yelled the Emp, stamping his foot, causing the plates to rattle on the table beside him. His companions looked up at him.

'Let's hear it, then! Warn us, he said,' growled one of the Emp's men, jerking his thumb in Tommy's direction.

'Well,' said Tommy, 'the Bishop is collecting fifty men, in fact they're in the Château de Romolue now already, and he's going to attack you tomorrow.'

'Oh, God! It must be that bloomin' horse. I knew it! Joncilond, you wretched ape!'

At that, Joncilond sprang up, and, scratching himself under his arms, went whooping around the room.

'Shut up!' yelled the Emp again, and Joncilond crouched down into a huddle on the floor, almost at the Emp's feet, peering up at him anxiously. 'Yes, you, you...' he said, poking a finger at Joncilond, and then thought better of suggesting anything more to Joncilond. 'You – you – you, stealing the Bishop's horse...'

'What! He stole the Bishop's horse. Fantastic!' whispered Eloise to Tommy, and then frowning, added, 'You didn't tell me!'

'Sorry,' muttered Tommy, 'in all the rush...' and the Emp continued.

'You've really stirred things up. How many men? Fifty. Armed to the teeth, I expect. Tell us what you know.'

Tommy had heard the Bishop, of course, talking to the Count and had also pumped Jacques for information, and he told the Emp all he had learnt.

'So it's going to be twenty-five with muskets, and then bowmen outside to shoot us down as we run out of the cover of the woods! Hmmm.'

And there was a silence, broken by the murmur of voices from the Emp's companions. Mostly all that Tommy could hear was 'Blast! Damn! Damn it all! The Lord protect us!' They're not much use, thought Tommy. The Emp's our man.

Joncilond uncoiled and rose slowly to his feet and stood before the Emp, who looked at him sternly.

'Joncilond,' he began, 'could you...'

'Yes, my Lord and Master, yes, I could,' replied Joncilond. 'I could lead them all, the Bishop, anyway, he'll be after me specially, I could lead him so that he disappears into the bog, never to be seen again. Oh! Yes, I could! I would! I should!' he sang out, getting excited again.

'You took the words out of my mouth,' said the Emp, grinning.

'I'll ride his horse, Master, Lord Emp, sir. That will drive him really mad. He-he!' he added. 'He-he, tee-hee, he-he!'

Tommy looked up sharply. Could they really trust the tactics of the battle to Joncilond? Well, the Emp knows him best, he thought. Perhaps it's safe, if anything is.

'Well,' said the Emp slowly, 'come and sit down. Since you're here, you might as well try some pear tart... both of you, Mademoiselle, Monsieur Thomas,' he added, beckoning the two of them to the table as he returned to his own place.

As they sat, both of them munching a large slice of tart, with custardy cream, the Emp began to talk about the coming battle.

'What we can do is this,' he began.

Joncilond crouched on the ground beside him, begging for scraps like a large and smelly dog.

'What we can do is this,' he repeated, handing a large chunk down to Joncilond; and he began to outline a plan to outwit the Bishop and his troops, with Tommy and Eloise and the Emp's companions all nodding, giving the thumbs up and so on as the Emp developed his ideas.

'We've got to be off, back to the château,' said Tommy as the Emp drew to a close.

'Yes, if they miss us there, I mean, if the Bishop finds out that we're gone, then...' began Eloise.

'Yeah!' said the Emp. 'Take 'em back, Joncilond. No tricks! Meanwhile, I'll wake the townspeople. They've got to be warned of the plan. We'll meet maybe tomorrow. If not, come to the road where you met Joncilond today. Three times three cuckoo calls at dusk will bring someone to lead you to us.'

'Yeah!' said Tommy. 'That's important. Because I've got a plan for you, too. Something important. For Sunday. But let it wait. Let's see off the Bishop first!'

'Sunday, you say! That's just a couple of days. But, okay, okay, let's let it wait.'

With that, Tommy and Eloise and Joncilond made their way rapidly out of Town, through the back door, out into the forest, picking their way through the quaking marsh, and across the silent moonlit road. There, Joncilond waved them goodbye, and with a single dove call was gone, fading into the darkness of the trees like a deer of the forest.

Tommy and Eloise, alone now, and hand in hand, crept from tree to tree, keeping as best they could out of the stark moonlight, in case they should be spotted from the château. Suddenly they stopped. For leaning against a tree just a short way in front of them, with his back to them, was the sailor they had seen on the road before. But he had not seen them, and they crept behind the trunk of the large oak under which they were standing. After a short time, Tommy peeked out. The man remained there, motionless, gazing at the château.

Surely, he's not just admiring the architecture, thought Tommy. But the man continued to stand and gaze, without moving. Tommy felt Eloise tug at his hand.

Very quietly, cupping her hand over her mouth, she whispered in Tommy's ear, 'Thomas, there's something about that man...'

There was pain in her voice, and Tommy brushed her cheek with his lips. She shook her head.

'No, no, I mean...' And she took his hand and kissed it, muddy as it was. 'There's something strange about that man,' she said again.

'Well, he's just a sailor!' muttered Tommy.

'No! He's...' But just then the man began to turn, and Tommy pulled back behind the tree.

'What if he comes this way?' whispered Eloise, her voice urgent with fright.

Indeed the man began to walk in their direction, apparently not caring if he were seen from the château. He strode past them, looking straight ahead, as they huddled behind the broad trunk of the oak, a look upon his face of anger, hatred, fury and revenge, a grim and frightening look.

I wonder what that is, what that look means! thought Tommy as he passed. Eloise was shaking beside him, with fear and a strange passionate need to rush out and... what, fall into the man's arms? Tommy put his own arm around her and she felt more calm as the man walked rapidly away, towards the road to Romolue.

Tommy felt almost jealous at the strong effect which this

sailor stranger seemed to have upon Eloise; yes, he did feel jealous.

How odd, he thought, and shaking his head, whispered, 'Come on, let's go.'

Keeping within the sharp-edged moon shadows of the trees and of the château, they arrived unseen by any guards, and, shortly after, soaking wet, Tommy and Eloise pulled themselves through Tommy's bedroom window, left open this time by arrangement with Jacques and the Countess. As Tommy turned to shut the window, he heard voices from below.

'What's that, you say?' spoken quite loudly.

And, 'Ssssh, you deaf twit!'

'I'm sorry,' said the voice more softly, 'but…'

'Ssssh!'

Good God, thought Tommy, I thought that it was Joncilond out there. 'Eloise,' he said aloud turning into the room, 'did you hear that?'

'What's that?' said Eloise who was making her way quietly towards the door. 'Hear what?'

'That voice outside. One of the guards. It sounded exactly like Joncilond!'

'Huh! Well, I hope not!' said Eloise, and they both put it out of their minds.

Nineteen: Up to his Neck

ommy awoke early the next morning to the sound of noisy activity in the château. Impatient shouting, orders given, and then counter-orders given again, could be heard clearly from his room. The soldiers were preparing for their attack on the people of the quaking marsh. At least the Emp was well warned, thought Tommy. He pulled on his complicated clothes as fast as he could. No time for the pleasant wandering fingers of that girl, what was her name again? He paused for a moment; he could only think of Eloise. Well, so much the better.

He had something important to do, but he had to keep well out of sight of the Bishop and Drogo – or indeed any of the Bishop's men. He crept out into the corridor outside his room. A quick glance out of the window showed him that the Bishop and Drogo were outside, with all the men before them, at some distance from the main door of the château. The Bishop was speaking. It must be a repeat performance of last night, Tommy thought, but this time without the interruption of the thunder, for the day was bright and sunny.

Tommy could just catch some of de Montfort's words.

'No mercy... Drive them into the bowmen!' yelled the Bishop, brandishing a horsewhip.

Onward, Christian Soldiers, thought Tommy, and smiled to himself.

This was the moment. He tiptoed as fast he could down the main staircase, keeping a close lookout, but it seemed that everyone – including the household staff – were outside listening to the Bishop. Muskets were stacked in the kitchen. Real museum pieces, thought Tommy, as dangerous for the man firing as for the man fired upon – or women and children, in this case, Tommy added grimly to himself. Well, he would see about that. Now, where had Jacques said...?

'Monsieur Thomas, it's all ready!' said Jacques behind him.

Tommy jumped, but turning, grinned at Jacques.

'Right – quick!' he said, and together they manhandled a large sack of flour and another of charcoal out of the little room where Tommy and Eloise had so fatefully met the last Sunday night. There was no time to lose. The Bishop might finish at any moment.

'Ah!' whispered Tommy. 'Drogo has taken over now!'

He had glimpsed the scarecrow figure waving his arms about in front of the soldiers, holding in one hand a crucifix – perhaps just in case they would not recognise one otherwise! thought Tommy.

'Come with that shovel,' said Jacques, and together they began to mix flour and charcoal into the barrel of gunpowder standing beside the muskets. Each man would have his share from this barrel just before they left for the attack.

'We'll have to take some out, so that they don't see there's too much,' said Tommy.

Jacques nodded and pointed to another empty barrel beside him.

'Into there first, then,' said Tommy, and they shovelled a good half of the gunpowder away.

Jacques grabbed hold of the barrel and grasping it around the middle, made off as fast as he could upstairs.

'To the clothes room,' he whispered to Tommy.

Tommy meanwhile was furiously shovelling flour and charcoal into the remaining gunpowder, digging it in with the shovel and mixing it well.

'A bit too pale,' he muttered, putting in some more charcoal.

Jacques came tumbling down the stairs.

'They're coming back!' he whispered urgently. 'I saw them from the landing. Quick, get this stuff out of here! That'll do!' he added, glancing into the gunpowder barrel. 'It'll have to. They won't suspect, anyway!'

They grabbed the two sacks of flour and charcoal and rushed them back to the little room, where they had come from. Tommy skidded out through the kitchen and leapt up the back stairs, just as the Bishop entered.

The Bishop, however, was much too preoccupied with listening to Drogo to notice Tommy.

'We must get that crucifix back, brother. We must! Think what...' Drogo was saying.

'Yes, you don't have to spell it out! How could you be such a fool?'

'How was I to know?' protested Drogo in reply.

But soldiers were now entering and the Bishop, putting his finger to his lips, stationed himself at one end of the kitchen. His mind was now fixed upon the coming attack – or slaughter, as he hoped – and important matters, such as the filling of the powder pouches for each man with a musket.

Within a few minutes two groups of soldiers set out from the château, twenty-five armed with heavy muskets, their brimming powder pouches strapped to their waists, twenty-five with bows, some of them crossbows which fired lethal bolts, that would instantly kill even a boar as it charged you down.

Crossing the bridge, the soldiers divided, the bowmen moving down the road towards Romolue, and the men with muskets, the Bishop among them, entering the woods. The Bishop alone was on horseback. He had six pistols thrust into his saddle.

'Each one a dead man,' he had explained to the soldiers, who eyed them enviously.

They would much rather a pistol than their heavy and dangerous muskets. But pistols were only for short range – muskets should panic people from far off.

Tommy watched them go, hidden beside a window on the top floor of the château. Marie stood beside him.

Placing her hand on his shoulder, she said, 'You've changed a lot, young man, and I like what I see! The old Thomas was, I thought, maybe a bit of a faint heart. But I was wrong!'

Tommy winced inwardly as heard this. He would have to do something about the 'old Thomas' when the time came. The time... for what?

This is not the moment for thinking about Eloise and my future with Eloise, he told himself sharply. This is the time for action!

'I'm going to follow them in,' he announced out loud to Marie.

'Oh no, my boy! A little more of the old Thomas, please.' She smiled. 'What good could you do?'

'Well,' he said, and he told her about the gunpowder.

'Ha! Good!' she laughed. 'Yes, yes! Good, very good. Their silly little machines will only go "pop"! Won't frighten more than a sparrow!'

She clapped her hands together at the thought, rather as Eloise liked to do. Maybe that's where Eloise got it from, thought Tommy.

'This time, though, Eloise stays at home,' added Tommy. 'Where is she now?'

'She's in her room,' replied Marie, and then in a voice of surprise she added, 'By Heaven, no she's not! She's standing by that tree down there. Heavens,' repeated Marie, peering through the window, 'she's beckoning to you! She's dressed as... Stop her, will you! Someone's bound to see her. Drogo, perhaps.'

Drogo had gone to the chapel, to pray for success of the attack, or so he said. More likely to hunt for traces of the crucifix, thought Tommy.

Following Marie's gaze, Tommy could see Eloise frantically waving her hand to him from down below.

'She's dressed as a boy!' exclaimed Marie. 'Disgraceful!' she whispered to herself.

Tommy gave Marie's arm a gentle squeeze – he thought Eloise looked rather nice in trousers – and he set off rapidly down the main staircase.

'Eloise! You might be seen! Drogo...' said Tommy, getting his breath back.

'Oh! Drogo won't be going anywhere very quickly,' replied Eloise, squatting down behind a tree. 'I just happened to pass the chapel and, well, he'd left the key in the lock, on the outside. So I turned it.' She giggled, and Tommy grinned and clenched his fist.

'Quick, let's get out of here!' he said, and quite forgetting that Eloise wasn't meant to be coming with him, he grabbed her hand and they ran off after the Bishop's men, dipping from bush to bush, trying to keep out of sight.

Marie saw them go from the window, but she just sighed and muttered to herself, 'God protect them,' and turned away, suddenly startled by a thumping, coming – it seemed – from the direction of the chapel.

Tommy and Eloise followed the route of the night before. They could hear the Bishop's men, struggling through the undergrowth with their heavy muskets. Impatient as they were to get on, Tommy and Eloise had to wait silently, hidden in the bushes, whilst two of the soldiers stopped to relieve themselves together against a tree.

'Shouldn't 'ave drunk that second mug of wine at breakfast,' they heard one of the men announce.

Occasionally they caught a glimpse of the Bishop himself, on horseback, riding from side to side, trying to keep his men in some sort of order. He was obviously not interested in a surprise attack; they were making enough noise to warn the people of the marsh miles away. In the distance, Tommy heard the faint sounds of a cuckoo call, three times three. He turned and grinned at Eloise.

'I wonder what sort of reception they are preparing for the Bishop and his men,' he whispered in her ear, and she gave her little nod, by way of reply.

Soon after, from another hiding place, they could see de Montfort cantering down the hill towards the road. The Bishop assembled his men by the side of the woods. Tommy and Eloise crept closer. Again they heard the cuckoo calls.

Ha! If only they knew! thought Tommy. Their every movement is being watched. Meanwhile, the Bishop was giving his men a last minute pep talk.

'They've got a town in there. Wood. Set fire to it – use a little gunpowder – and shoot at them as they run out. Don't care if you don't hit 'em. Drive them like sheep into the arms of our archers. They'll hit them, all right! Oh, by the way, mind the bog when you get into the woods, it can be a bit slippery in places!'

The Bishop then gave a powerful wave of his arm, and they turned and started into the quaking marsh.

'This is going to be interesting,' whispered Tommy, and Eloise grinned.

Almost at once they could hear exclamations from the soldiers.

'Christ, the ground's moving!'

'Get over here! Hell and damnation, give me a pull out, will you!'

The Bishop's horse leapt instinctively from tussock to tussock and he just turned and shouted, 'Look where you're putting your clumsy feet, you oafs! I told you that it was a bit marshy in here.'

'M'Lord!' Georges called out. 'M'Lord, it's more than a bit marshy. Half the men are stuck. The other half are trying to pull them out. Who's got some rope? I'm stuck myself, m'Lord!'

The advance of the Bishop and his party was slow, very slow indeed. Tommy and Eloise waited cautiously at the border of the woods, watching several of the men sink up to their backsides.

'I've lost me musket!' yelled one of the soldiers. 'It's disappeared, m'Lord, in the bog!'

'That's a month's pay for you,' said Georges.

'I'd give two months' to get out of here,' said another.

'How far can we sink in, d'you think?' said a third.

'All the way!' shouted Georges and gave an unpleasant laugh.

'Oh! God preserve us!' said one soldier and began to struggle, grabbing at some loose sticks, lying on the surface of the bog, and sinking still further down.

'It's like bloomin' blancmange. We're all going to suffocate in bloomin' blancmange...'

'Never did like the stuff, meself,' said another soldier, standing on a firm piece of ground nearby.

'Oh, shut up, and get us out of here!' gasped one of the soldiers, who was already up to his waist.

'They'll get themselves out!' shouted the Bishop. 'Let's get on. And watch your big feet!'

Most of the troop then made their way off, leaving several men still struggling in the mud.

'P'raps if you take your trousers off,' said one.

'What's that he said,' asked the deaf one. Yes, for he was one of the trapped men.

'Yeah! That's an idea.'

'What?' said the deaf one.

'They've gone and deserted us! The mean...'

But before he could finish the sentence, men dropped from the trees around them. Tommy and Eloise watched breathlessly. Men from Town! Would they just kill the soldiers? No!

'Chuck us your muskets!'

'Get out o' y'trousers, and stand on 'em, to give a bit of push!'

Pulling the men out, one at a time, they bound them tightly with rope, and led them away each held by a noose around his neck, and wearing only their sixteenth century underpants (funny baggy things, thought Tommy). There were five prisoners in all, among them of course the deaf one. The men from Town made off into the woods, taking a direction quite different from that of the Bishop and his party.

'What do we do now?' whispered Eloise.

'I dunno,' said Tommy, 'but I do want to see what happens when they try and fire their muskets!'

Suddenly they heard three cuckoo calls, close by. And again, and once more.

'Joncilond,' breathed Tommy, 'but where is he?'

'Let's just wait for him,' whispered Eloise, sure that she would smell him before they would see him.

But in a moment he appeared before them, melting out of the leaves and branches, silently and with his finger to his lips. His expression was very serious. He just beckoned to them, and they followed as he led them rapidly in the direction the men from Town had taken. In the distance they heard the whinny of a horse. Tommy tensed. Was it the Bishop? Joncilond turned and shook his head, reading Tommy's thoughts, and pointed his hand towards himself.

'It's your horse,' whispered Tommy, 'or the Bishop's horse!'

Joncilond grinned and nodded, three times three.

Coming to a small clearing, they found the Bishop's magnificent animal, tethered to a tree.

Releasing it, Joncilond leapt onto its back, and patting its rump, said, 'Get up on here. It can carry the three of us for a bit, three, three, three!' And he whinnied like the horse.

Oh! My gosh! thought Tommy, and soon they were galloping off in a direction to intercept the Bishop.

'You get down here,' whispered Joncilond to Tommy and Eloise.

Tommy and Eloise slipped off, and making their way a little forward, crouching low, they could see between the leaves the Bishop picking his way carefully through the swamp. Georges was close behind, with the others strung out in a long line. Kicking the horse back into a gallop, Joncilond set off to cross right in front of the troop.

'What's he doing? Gosh, doesn't he see...?'

Georges caught sight of Joncilond before the Bishop did, and kneeling down, frantically began to fumble with his musket, shovelling powder down the muzzle and ramming it in, checking the flint, trying to hold Joncilond in his line of sight.

Pop! it went. *Fzzzzz*, *splut*! and the bullet rolled out of the end of the muzzle.

'Damn me!' he yelled, and Tommy, forgetting himself, laughed out loud.

Georges looked wildly around, with a look on his face as if he believed he were hearing devils. Then he shook his head and began to shovel more powder in, calling over his shoulder to the men behind. 'Contact, men. We've got 'em!'

Ha! thought Tommy.

The Bishop had spotted Joncilond, and pulling his horse around sharply, pushed his spurs so far into his horse's side that he drew blood. An arrow whizzed past his horse's head. With a great roar of rage, he drew one of his pistols and fired wildly in Joncilond's direction. It was a lucky shot, for it hit Joncilond's horse on its massive backside.

'My horse, damn me!' yelled the Bishop.

Pop! went another musket behind them... *F-zzzzz*, and *pop* again, with a good deal of cursing from the soldiers.

'This gunpowder...' Georges began, but his words were lost on the Bishop, for as he fired off a second pistol, the horse, on which the Bishop sat, found it had suddenly had enough.

It bucked and bolted. Joncilond too was having trouble with his horse, which reared in panic as it felt the sting in its backside, stumbled, and snorted, shaking its great head. Wisely, Joncilond slipped from its back, and, leaving it to calm itself, ran like the wind after the Bishop, leaping the quaking bogs as he went.

Not so de Montfort. His horse, mad with fear, careered along without thought of the ground beneath it. The Bishop clung on, clasping his arms around the horse's neck. Suddenly the horse lurched to a halt, stumbling to its knees at the edge of a massive muddy swamp, sensing the danger. The Bishop was flung head over heels, performing a graceful curve in the air, ending in a massive splat of mud and water.

'Men, men, to me!' he yelled, half dazed but clutching at the mud to try and stop himself sinking.

But before any help could come, Joncilond was there, and at the other side of the pool, the man who had narrowly missed the Bishop's horse with his arrow, just before. Joncilond had a lasso of rope in his hand, and flinging this at the Bishop, it looped around the Bishop's waist. Joncilond pulled it taut. Again he flung a rope attached to the lasso, and this time it was caught by his companion opposite. The Bishop gave a cry of surprise, as suddenly he was hauled half out of the mud, dangling from the lasso which slipped up to his armpits and held him tight. One end was made fast around a tree, and the other Joncilond just wound once around a tree trunk, holding the end in his hand.

'Men!' yelled the Bishop, but the word 'help' disappeared in a gulp of mud, as Joncilond let his captive smartly down into the bog.

As they pulled him up, dripping with stinking mud, spluttering and spitting, Joncilond whispered to him as loudly as one can whisper, 'Not one word, or we dip you in again!'

The Bishop turned his head sharply from right to left looking at his captors, and began to struggle on the rope.

'Keep still,' hissed Joncilond, and released the rope a little.

The Bishop froze as he sank in up to his waist.

'My men will find us soon. You'll hang for this!'

'It is more you, sire, that is hanging, just now,' said the Emp, emerging from the bushes behind Joncilond. 'By a thread, I should say. By a thread,' he added threateningly. Then he continued in a more friendly tone, 'The hospitality of the marsh, my Lord! If we had not saved you from the bog, you would have gone, by now, sire, disappeared sire, as so many others before you! Are you not grateful? Also, your men are a little occupied at the moment. Some of them you may meet later. Some, you may not! But just now, they are enjoying the pleasant air of the forest in the company of some of the men of Town, sire. Hospitality, sire, hospitality! It seems as though you are not good at gunpowder in Toulouse, my Lord,' he added.

'What, what?' spluttered the Bishop, trying unsuccessfully to get his hand to his mouth to wipe the mud away.

'The mud tastes bad, sire?' enquired the Emp. 'Why, you should have tasted some of the cooking... but no matter. We are not here to discuss cooking!'

'Cooking?' shouted the Bishop. The word reminded him of cuckoo, which enraged him still more. 'Cooking!' he yelled again.

'Silence!' commanded the Emp.

'Silence!' yelled the Bishop, but the end of the word was lost in the mud as he disappeared altogether into the bog.

'That's enough!' said the Emp to Joncilond, as apparently Joncilond had forgotten to pull the Bishop out and the mud began to settle over his head. 'We don't want to suffocate him, just yet,' he added as the Bishop emerged into hearing.

By this time Tommy and Eloise were close by. They were careful still to keep out of sight of the Bishop, but they could hear every word and could see de Montfort dangling on the rope, covered in mud. Tommy turned to Eloise, with his hand over his mouth. Eloise gave a little frown. This was too much for her, too much of turning her values on their head. The Bishop of Toulouse having a mudbath at hands of outlaws? The very Church being made to look weak and stupid!

'No!' she muttered, and turned her head away.

Then, remembering that this was Drogo's brother, an accomplice who had concealed Drogo's crime, she looked back. Turning to Tommy, she gave him a tight-lipped grin.

'I think we have a bible,' said the Emp.

'What, what?' gabbled the Bishop.

He was beginning to feel very frightened. Were these outlaws going to murder him? In a sudden moment of clarity, he knew that he had come to murder them. But, what did they want with a bible? The answer came immediately.

'We want you to swear to leave us in peace, my good Lord

Bishop,' announced the Emp. 'Where's that bloomin' bible?' he shouted suddenly.

'Oooh! It's on my horse,' said Joncilond. 'I'll go and fetch it. Sorry!'

Letting go of the rope without thinking, he ran off.

'*Aaargh-gluff!*' went the Bishop, as the Emp grabbed the rope, yanking it back around the tree.

The Emp and the Bishop eyed each other, like two sharks circling the same prey, as they waited for Joncilond to return. Joncilond came cantering back, the horse recovered. The Bishop's bullet had only winged it.

'We want you to swear on this bible,' began the Emp, 'swear to—'

'Swear?' yelled the Bishop. 'Promise you outlaws, villains, murderers, cut-throats… that's my horse! … *rrruurrrlll, glub!*'

'Swear!' shouted the Emp, as Joncilond hoisted the Bishop out again. 'Swear, that you will leave us in peace, that you will allow us to come to market, in Romolue, that—'

'Nev… *rrrlllup, fllllpp!*' said the Bishop, spitting mud in all directions.

And so the interview between the Bishop and the Emp continued, interrupted at last by the arrival of five very sorrowful figures, with ropes around their necks, led in by men from Town. The Bishop was still refusing to agree, even after his tenth visit to the mud, and comments from others like, 'Just leave him in there this time'… 'He'd show us no mercy'… 'Break his legs for him,' and so on.

'You foolish idiots!' cried the Bishop, as he hazily saw his captive soldiers approach, through a film of mud over his eyes.

His men just gaped.

'You'd better swear, my Lord,' said one of them, hearing the Emp again make the same demand.

'Yeah, you'd best…' said another.

'Hold your tongue!' ordered the Bishop.

'But, my Lord, we'll never get out of here alive if…'

'Hold your tongue, I said!'

'They can't, sire, their hands is tied!' said one of the men from Town, and everyone laughed – except the Bishop, that is, and the deaf one, who whispered, 'What was that then, eh? What am I missing now?'

While the Bishop remained hanging there, thinking how to escape with just a tiny piece of dignity, the deaf soldier muttered, 'Well, I might as well make meself a bit more comfortable.'

He moved towards the tree which Joncilond was using to hold the Bishop, pulling his captor with him.

Unfortunately for the poor deaf man, the rope around his neck was just too short, so as he plumped himself on the ground against the tree, he practically strangled himself, and with a gasp, half fell against the tree trunk. Joncilond grabbed his shoulder with his free hand, and the man holding the rope around his neck released it. The deaf soldier collapsed to the ground, his face right up against Joncilond's left foot.

'*Pooooh!*' he shouted, regaining his breath. 'My God, man, do you ever wash?'

And all the people of Town began to laugh again.

'No he don't, actually!' said the Emp.

'Yeah, but hey, look,' shouted the deaf man. 'He's missing his third toe!'

'Less to smell,' said the Emp.

'His third toe!' shouted the deaf soldier.

Most people knew that Joncilond had lost his middle toe, somewhere, sometime. He had always been a toe short. So what?

'Martin!' yelled the deaf man at Joncilond. 'Martin, Martin, Martin!'

Joncilond's face twitched slightly. Suddenly, all eyes were upon them. Even the Bishop turned his head.

'Martin,' whispered Joncilond, and then shook his head. 'Joncilond,' he said, pointing at himself.

Meanwhile the Bishop was praying that Joncilond wouldn't let go of the rope. He'd suddenly had enough; he'd swear anything they wanted him to... on the Bible.

'I'll swear!' he shouted.

But everyone, including the Emp, was more interested in Joncilond and the deaf soldier. The Bishop was ignored. He looked wildly around, to see everyone's attention fixed elsewhere.

'I'll swear!' he shouted again, but no one paid him the slightest notice.

'Martin,' said the deaf man again.

Joncilond shook his head slowly. 'Joncilond,' he whispered, and a tear came into his eye.

No one had ever seen Joncilond cry before. Everyone pressed closer.

'Oh, Martin!' said the deaf man. 'I'm Henri, your brother!'

And this time Joncilond did let go of the rope, and clasped the deaf soldier in his arms.

'No, no! *Glurpplplpl*!' screamed the Bishop.

'Henri, Henri,' muttered Joncilond.

'He's stone deaf!' shouted out one of the captured soldiers.

'The Bishop!' yelled the Emp suddenly, as everyone noticed that he had disappeared into the bog.

'Quick, catch hold of that rope!'

Joncilond lunged for it and missed as it slithered rapidly into the bog, fell in the bog himself, grabbed the rope, and pulled himself up on several outstretched arms.

'I'll swear,' gulped the Bishop, swallowing another mouthful of mud. 'I'll swear. Give me the bible!'

In the meantime, Joncilond had tied the rope tightly around the tree trunk, so that the Bishop remained safely suspended. Joncilond now was clasping his brother Henri in his arms, both of them covered in mud.

'Okay! You'll swear, will you?' said the Emp, turning away from Joncilond and Henri; and whilst the Bishop swore, on his knees, on all things holy, that he would never, never, etc., etc., Joncilond – or Martin – and Henri began to talk.

'Yeah! You disappeared as a small boy. Six or seven you were,' said Henri, as Joncilond released his arms from the ropes which bound him. 'You disappeared one day into the forest, taken by gypsies, you were, we thought, or bitten by a snake, or... I dunno. We never found no trace of you!'

'I... I...' began Joncilond.

'Please look at me when you speak,' said Henri. 'I lost my hearing when I was... however old I was. Gun went off. But I can read your lips.'

'I… I,' began Joncilond again.

'Yeah! You lost that toe when you were really little. Playing with an old rusty sword. Swinging it about. I remember. God! How you screamed! So did mother. That old priest came running, and old Mother Madge – d'you remember her? Mother Madge! Could cure anything. Anything. Except what she caught herself, of course. Killed her quick, it did. Mother Madge. And do you…?'

'I… I,' began Joncilond again.

'And what have you been doin' here in the forest then, all these years?' demanded Henri.

'I've been… cuckoo, cuckoo, cuckoo!' Joncilond called out.

At this the Bishop looked up sharply, and Henri looked startled.

'He's a bit queer in the 'ead, sometimes,' said one of the men from Town,

'Always!' called out another.

'But you get used to it, like,' said a third.

'He can be a bit daft, capering about and so on. But he's a good chap. Terribly strong! Amazing. Lifts things that three of us can't hardly budge!' added another.

'He knows the forest paths like no one else,' chipped in the Emp, as he finished tying up the Bishop, for transport back to the Château de Romolue. 'That's nicely done, then, shouldn't come apart before it reaches home, eh!' he laughed. Then he added for the Bishop's benefit, 'And no funny business, mind. We're sending Joncilond with you. We're not always so kind and understanding, like.'

The Bishop just glowered in reply.

'These men of yours, do you want them back – or should they best stay with us?' asked the Emp. 'How about you, Henri?'

'Yeah, well. Now that I've just found me brother… he was just tellin' me how he stole the Bishop's horse! Hee-hee, that's something! Think I'll stay with you lot, if you don't mind. Bein' deaf and all, that is!'

The Emp just nodded. 'And the rest of you?'

The remaining prisoners all just looked at the ground.

'Families at home, eh? I suppose that the Bishop might do something nasty to them, what? You wouldn't though, would you?' said the Emp, turning back to the Bishop. 'Not a nice kind-hearted man like you, that got my little sister burnt as a witch! Only eighteen, she was...' The Emp's voice rose dangerously. 'Oh, no! Not a nice Bishop, Your Holiness. Take him away, before I do something that I might regret later!' said the Emp, and he turned on his heel and strode off towards Town.

'Quick,' whispered Tommy to Eloise, 'we've got to catch him – the Emp, I mean – and we mustn't let the Bishop, or any of his men, see us!'

Eloise just nodded in reply. They skirted around the group of prisoners and men from Town, keeping well out of sight behind bushes, and avoiding the worst of the bog. Joncilond seemed quite to have forgotten them. Anyway, he had to lead the Bishop and the other captives back to the Château de Romolue. Tommy and Eloise managed in fact to catch up with the Emp quite quickly. He was standing surrounded by a group of people from Town, just a little way off.

'Why did you let him go?'

'Should have just trussed him up and thrown him in the bog!' said another.

They were seething with hatred for the Bishop. All of them had lost close relatives – mothers, brothers, fathers and daughters – at the hands of the nobles and of the Church.

'I was tempted, I was tempted, I can tell you, to do just that,' replied the Emp. 'But if we'd done it, we'd have been dead meat, all of us, double quick! It wouldn't be fifty men, it would be five hundred. It's going to be quite tough as it is. These churchmen are not going to like it that the Bishop of Toulouse has been dipped in the bog, you know, much as he deserved it. They might be thinking that it's their turn next.'

'Yeah, it is an' all,' said one man.

'If we want to survive, we'd best keep a low profile for a bit,' reasoned the Emp. 'Hey! Look, what about those bowmen, waiting for us to come running out, eh? Twenty-five bowmen, remember?'

'D'you think that they'd dare come into the quaking marsh? Their orders were to stay put and wait for us, weren't they? So Thomas de Romolue told us!'

'Yeah, I reckon that they'll just go home, when nothing

happens. Not come looking for trouble, I should reckon, yeah!' said another, and everyone nodded hopefully.

'We've posted a good few lookouts, haven't we?' demanded the Emp of one his close followers who had just joined them.

'Yeah! I think that they're taken care of!' he replied.

It was at this point that Tommy and Eloise came panting up.

'Here's trouble!' said the Emp loudly.

'Gosh! That was great,' said Tommy. 'The Bishop, I mean!'

'Oh! You saw it all, then?'

'Yes, we met Joncilond, earlier on, and we went along with him, till just before he rode out in front of the Bishop. We were careful the Bishop didn't see us – or any of his men, either!'

Eloise said nothing, but gave a tight little smile. The Emp looked at her and nodded.

'You see what I mean? She doesn't approve – Eloise de Narbonne, there. She don't approve. You see what the nobles will think of what we did with the Bishop!' said the Emp. Then he added, eyeing Eloise, 'Ladies wear trousers, do they, then, eh? Funny lot, these nobles.'

Eloise frowned, but Tommy interrupted the proceedings by saying, 'Look, we need your help!'

'What – again?' said the Emp. 'I'm hungry. I can't think when I'm hungry. Why don't we all get back and find out what Phillipe's little daughter has cooked up for us!'

'Radish soup,' said someone.

'That's not bloomin' funny!' said the Emp angrily, and everyone laughed.

Twenty: Squirrel Stew

o Tommy and Eloise found themselves once more in the dark hall of the palace of the Emp, with the strong smell of resin – and other things, thought Tommy, not so nice, bad drains… Oh, well!

'It's like this,' he started, as soon they had all sat down, 'it's…'

The Emp rapped the table with a large wooden serving spoon.

'No discussin' o' nothin' till we've eaten,' he announced loudly, 'and that includes Monsieur Thomas de Romolue,' he added with a slight bow in Tommy's direction. 'Food's too important to waste on words, as me good ole Dad used to say!'

'It weren't your dad, he was…' began one of the company.

'Well, it were someone's dad,' interrupted the Emp.

Tommy had the feeling that the Emp did not want his Dad discussed in public. Anyway, all discussion fell rapidly to a close as Phillipe's daughter came in staggering under the weight of a great wooden dish, covered with a heavy steaming cloth. The evening sunlight, coming through gaps in the walls, caught the vapour as it rose, causing eerie shadows to play about the hall. It looked strange, but it smelt good.

'There y'are, sir,' announced Phillipe's daughter grandly, as she stretched forwards over the table, grunting with the exertion, and letting the dish down heavily in front of the Emp – just about bursting out of her rough sack-like dress as she did so. It had rather a lot of holes in it in need of darning, and one or two of the Emp's followers sniggered as they gazed at her; and some were fairly gaping.

Tommy turned towards Eloise, who grinned slightly and blushed, putting her hand to her mouth. Phillipe, who was standing guard by the end of the table, shuffled his feet noisily and made a funny coughing noise in his throat, trying without success to catch his daughter's eye. The Emp however paid not the slightest attention to anything but the food.

'What's this then?' he asked loudly, grasping the large wooden spoon again.

'Well, sir! Your favourite, my Lord, sir!' replied Phillipe's daughter, standing to attention beside him.

'Radish...' began one of the Emp's men, but the Emp ignored the titters around the table and ceremoniously pulled back the cloth covering the dish, pushing his face into the steaming mess beneath.

A few drops of gravy attached themselves to his beard, and glistened in the rays of sunlight as he did so. Then his mouth broke into a broad grin, and he lifted his head to let the aroma fill his nostrils.

'Perfect, perfect, after a successful battle!' The grin seemed glued to his face.

'Yeah, we did them,' broke out several voices.

'Did 'em proper!'

Then everyone started to talk at once. The tension had broken.

'That Bishop...'

'Wish we had his nasty brother!'

'Yeah! I was going to say...' Tommy tried to break in, but no one paid him any attention, as shouts and laughter filled the hall.

The Emp began to serve the food.

'Pass your plates around,' he commanded, banging the spoon on the table once more, with bits of stew spraying in all directions.

'There's just one problem,' Tommy heard the Emp mutter to himself. 'Me teeth!'

At that, Tommy fished in his pocket and shoved a pair of wooden teeth across the table to the Emp.

'Spare pair. Found them in my room,' explained Tommy; in the toilet, actually, but he didn't add that.

The Emp smiled gratefully and shoved them straight in his mouth, waggling his jaw around.

'They fit great!' announced the Emp.

Meanwhile the conversation was getting pretty lively around them.

'Did you see when he disappeared in the mud!'

'Gloop, gloop…'

'*Goooopffff*!' said another.

'*Gluuuuuuurp*!' said the townsman opposite Tommy, belching loudly to imitate the quaking mud. He suddenly put his hand over his mouth, looking embarrassed, and bowed towards Eloise.

'Did you see Joncilond? Hey, pass it round!'

'Yeah! His brother, think of that!'

'Deaf as a post!'

'Deafer, I reckon!'

'When Joncilond let go that rope…'

Here, everyone around the table laughed, and even Eloise could not help a grin. The conversation tumbled back and forth, as all began to tuck in.

Not bad, thought Tommy, not bad at all! And he shot a glance at Eloise, who was gobbling away as happily as the rest of them.

'What is it then?' asked Tommy, turning towards the Emp during a brief lull in the conversation.

'Eh! What's that?' said the Emp, spoon in mid air between plate and mouth, savouring the smell of the stew. 'Ah! Yes, well, this…' said the Emp, waving the spoon towards the now empty dish… 'this is… the finest food of the forest, the finest food that ever ran up and down a tree. This, my dear Monsieur Thomas, is… squirrel.'

'*Squirrrel*!' sputtered Thomas, his mouth full. 'Sorry,' he muttered, and his host nodded impressively.

'Squirrel,' repeated the Emp.

'Oh, gosh, squirrel… I mean,' started Tommy.

'Yes! Never had it before, then?' asked the belcher opposite, looking puzzled, while Eloise sent Tommy a furious glance.

'Yes, well, yes, of course…' mumbled Tommy, feeling all eyes on him. 'But not for some time,' he added lamely.

'Hey!' shouted the Emp to Phillipe's daughter as she reappeared with a second bowlful. 'Give this 'ere Thomas de Romolue some more squirrel stew. He hasn't had it for a long time – or at all, eh? There's something funny about you, Monsieur,' he added turning to Tommy, and shook his bushy head.

Tommy found a great wodge dollopped onto his plate, and

Phillipe's daughter chipped in, 'It's good, isn't it? And you can use the tail to clean up after. Right soft, it is. Like all those bits nobility wears inside their underwear,' she added, and giggled.

'What d'you know about underwear, then?' asked one of the Townsmen, recalling the sight of her straining over the table with the bowl of squirrel stew. 'What d'you know about underwear?' he repeated, as everyone started to laugh, except Phillipe, who suddenly dropped his sword on the ground with a clang.

'Oops! Sorry, Milord Emp, sir,' he muttered.

'There's someone you can ask about nobility's under...' said another, pointing his finger at Eloise.

'About what?' interrupted the Emp, who had been concentrating on scowling at Phillipe.

'About...'

'That's enough... er... stew,' said Tommy loudly. 'I'm full, thanks. Very good stew, really was! Thanks!' he went on, trying to change the subject, for he could feel Eloise seething beside him; the underwear had been too much for her.

She mustn't blow up now – they needed these people's help.

Eloise let out her breath and gave her little nod, and Tommy relaxed. For a few moments all one could hear in the hall was the slurping of many spoons in many mouths and the cracking of small bones. Tommy thought that perhaps the time had come to try and get the Emp's attention. But no!

'Honey cake,' announced the Emp, as he stuffed a large hunk of bread into his mouth, dripping with the last of the sauce from his plate.

'Hon-ey cake!' he shouted, his mouth full, crumbs flying, and drawing out the words, so that the sound echoed around the hall.

Phillipe's daughter came scuttling in, her sackcloth dress flapping about her.

'Sire, with all the battle and things, sire,' she started off, 'Joncilond, sire, what normally gets the honey, sire, on account of his...'

'I know why Joncilond gets the honey!' bellowed the Emp. 'Are you trying to tell me that there's no honey cake, girl?' he demanded more quietly, but with a trace of menace in his voice. 'No honey cake?' he repeated.

'Well, sire, sir, Joncilond, sir, Milord,' began Phillipe's daughter again, still more flustered.

'Blast and blast Joncilond!' shouted the Emp. 'My God!' he added, in a much quieter voice and with a note of sorrow, looking down at the table top in front of him. 'No honey cake…' And in his clenched fist he banged the end of his spoon on the wood. 'My God!' he repeated, and silence reigned in the hall.

'Urmmmm…' Tommy cleared his throat, trying to choose his moment.

The Emp, lost in his thoughts, dark thoughts of a life without honey cake, at least in the immediate future, turned his head slowly in Tommy's direction.

'Well?' he said mournfully.

'I've got something important to ask you,' began Tommy.

'Involves danger, I suppose,' said the Emp, and sighed, the gloom in his voice still echoing the memory of the absent honey cake.

The whole company remained very quiet.

'Well, a bit dangerous, perhaps, a bit, I suppose, but not so much, I mean, for brave…' Tommy trailed off. He wasn't very good at trying to flatter people.

'I mean…' he started again.

'You mean, mad, crazy people like us, who'd risk our lives…' broke in the Emp.

'For Thomas and me, please,' said Eloise suddenly.

But negotiations were abruptly interrupted by a loud commotion at the door.

'Let me in!' they could hear someone bawling.

'They're still eating. You've got to wait here!' shouted a guard.

'I've got to speak to the Emp!'

'That's Jacques!' said the belcher and at that moment Jacques, the Tailor, came bursting in.

'The archers!' he cried. 'The archers!'

The Emp leapt to his feet and the bowl of stew went flying. Jacques paused, getting his balance, one hand on the table, breathing hard.

'The archers?' demanded the Emp.

'The archers, sire!' He waived his hand in the air. 'The archers. They've gone, sire!' A sigh of relief passed around the hall.

'They've gone!' shouted the Emp, slamming his fist down on the table. 'Of course they've gone! Is that why you come haring in here, like the Bishop was on your tail, you... you... you *chump*!'

Jacques started back, and as if the word had struck him across the face, put his hand to his cheek.

'Well, sire,' began Jacques, falling over the words, 'we scouted them out like you said we should, sire. Found them at the edge of the wood, sire, down from the Abbey – y'know, where I used to make the nuns' habits.' The Emp nodded impatiently, 'They didn't see us, sire.'

'Good,' said the Emp.

'At least,' went on Jacques, 'they didn't see us, until I accidentally, like, fell out of this tree I was in, the bendy one, sire.' As the Emp gave him a bleak look, he went on, 'The, er... bendy... what's they called? Oh, well! But they took a shot at me. Missed of course...'

'Pity,' said a voice somewhere in the hall.

'Who'd do your buttons then, eh?' demanded Jacques, hands on hips. 'I'd like to see you...'

'Get on with it!' commanded the Emp, drumming his fingers on the table.

'Oh! Yes, well, anyway, I ran off, sire, and one of them shouted after me, "We'll be back," and then I saw them make off up the hill towards the Abbey, sire. They didn't dare follow us into the marsh!'

'No! Their orders were to shoot us all down as we fled from the Bishop and his men, and their guns. Pity they didn't try to follow you in. We'd have had some of them too, I reckon.'

His followers chuckled at the memory of the woebegone mud-covered prisoners they'd taken that day.

'Right then,' said the Emp. 'That's seen them off, too! Good, fine! You can go now, Jacques!'

'Just a sec,' broke in Tommy. 'Jacques, I want to say – and Eloise too – thanks for getting us back to...'

'Ooh!' broke in Jacques. 'Are *you* here?' He'd had eyes only for the Emp and hadn't noticed anyone else in the gloom. 'I thought...'

'Well, we're back! We wanted to say thank you for risking your life for us, to get us back to the château!'

'So, what are you doin' back here then, you dafties?' demanded Jacques. 'Er, I mean, Milord, Your Ladyship!'

'That's enough,' said the Emp. 'Jacques, dismissed!'

Jacques gave Tommy a puzzled frown and turned and left.

'Okay, where were we, then?' asked the Emp.

'Well,' started Tommy once more.

'We need your help, you see,' said Eloise in her sweet voice, with her lovely smile.

Tommy began to explain his scheme.

'At the cathedral on Sunday morning, at mass...'

Everyone around the table leant forward to catch each word.

The Emp and the others nodded now and then, grunted and grinned as the plan began to unfold.

'Yeah, sounds interesting!'

'You'll help us, then?'

'Anything to keep that Bishop off us, and his brother.'

'That monster!' said Eloise, between gritted teeth, but subsided as Tommy placed his hand on hers.

'But, y'know, a little diversion – like – at the right moment, that would be a good idea, y'know something...' added the Emp pensively, nodding his shaggy head.

'That's certainly an idea,' said Tommy. 'Something to throw them, make 'em really freak out! What d'you think?' he added, looking round the table.

'I know,' said Eloise. '*That gunpowder!*' she and Tommy exclaimed in unison, and Tommy held up his little finger and hooked it around Eloise's.

She looked quite startled at this and eyebrows shot up around the table. Tommy was embarrassed for a moment, and as he released Eloise's finger he mumbled, 'It's what we do, like, anyway,' and felt himself going a bit pink. 'Never mind! The gunpowder,' said Tommy, and everyone's ears pricked up again.

'Gunpowder!' said several of the men.

'Ain't got nought o' that,' said the belcher opposite.

'No, we haven't,' said the Emp, and taking his false teeth out of his mouth, began absent-mindedly to clean them with his fingernails.

'Right, but *we* have!' said Tommy, trying to keep his eyes off the teeth. 'You know how the guns didn't work at all – the Bishop's men, I mean?'

They all nodded.

'Well,' continued Tommy. 'Jacques and I, we spiked the gunpowder. Took half of it out and put flour and charcoal in instead! That's why they went "pop" and the bullets just rolled out of the end of the barrel!'

Everybody started to laugh and the Emp clapped Tommy on the back.

'I must admit,' said the Emp, 'I did wonder that the Bishop... Well, anyway, well done, lad!'

'Yes, but the rest of the gunpowder, I know where it is. There's quite a lot of it. Enough to create a diversion, like you suggested.'

'How much?' asked one of the men. 'I used to work on the cannons, y'see.'

'Yeah! He's the gunpowder man round here,' said another.

'Well,' replied Tommy, 'there's a full barrel, about this big.' He curved his arms around an imaginary barrel.

'Phew! That'll go up proper, if we pack it in nice,' said the gunpowder man.

'What'll we blow up, then?' asked the belcher.

'How about the Bishop's carriage, when he's at the service?'

'Or when he's in it!'

Here, several people laughed and banged their fists on the table.

'Mmm... well, we'll see,' said the Emp as the hall quietened down again. 'Got to get the timing right. But more important for now is that the gunpowder's in the Château de Romolue, I suppose' – Tommy nodded – 'and it's us what'll have to take it to Toulouse. We'll go late on Saturday night, maybe, or maybe, yes, well, we'll... Anyway, we've got places we can hide out.' He winked at Tommy. 'But you'll have to get the gunpowder to us. You can't go carting a barrel of gunpowder about, Monsieur Thomas.'

'No, that's true. Look, it'll soon be dark. We've got to get back to the château soon. The Countess... Anyway, I reckon that the Bishop and his men will be heading back for Toulouse by now.'

'With the mud washed off, d'you think?' said one of the Townsmen, amid laughter.

'Okay,' said the Emp. 'We'll go along with you – on Sunday I mean. Okay, everyone?' he added, sitting back in his chair, and surveying the faces of his followers.

There was a murmur in the room, which seemed to mean 'Yes,' and, shoving the false teeth in his pocket, the Emp got to his feet, followed by the whole company. Tommy and Eloise each clasped one of the Emp's arms.

'You'll not regret it,' said Tommy.

'You will be free men, women and children,' said Eloise, and the Emp smiled.

'Phillipe, you lead them back to the château now,' he said. 'Take your horse and something to hold that barrel of gunpowder. We'll think of something to blow up, don't you worry,' he added, turning to Tommy and Eloise.

'They seem completely to have forgotten about blindfolds,' whispered Eloise to Tommy a little while later, as they trudged back through the woods, with Phillipe leading the way, holding his horse's bridle.

Tommy just grunted assent and ran his hand down Eloise's arm. The gurgling swamp seemed almost familiar to them now, as they picked their way carefully from tuft to tuft. Tommy was preoccupied with a plan of how to get the gunpowder out of the château into Phillipe's hands without detection.

'Over the kitchen...' he muttered to himself.

'Not that way!' hissed Phillipe at them as loudly as he dared, and Tommy skidded and slipped thigh-deep into the stinking mud.

Phillipe's horse shied and stumbled, but he managed to grab Tommy's arm, and with Eloise's help, they dragged him free of the sucking clutches of the bog.

'Poooh!' said Eloise, wrinkling her nose at Tommy.

'Soon be at the road,' said Phillipe a little while later.

Darkness was falling fast as they came to the path.

'Here's the plan,' said Tommy, when the three of them were standing in the shadow of the trees, and he began to outline his scheme for the gunpowder.

'Okay,' said Phillipe, 'at the bridge, then. Good luck!'

Tommy and Eloise began to make their way into the darkness of the trees opposite, down the slope towards the château.

'Let's risk the bridge, shall we?' whispered Tommy, and Eloise nodded.

The rising moon, waning now, still cast a long deep shadow of the parapet across the bridge. They crept through the blackness, crouched low, listening for the smallest sound, but only the cry of a screech owl and the distant beating of heavy wings broke the stillness of the night.

'Down the bank,' whispered Tommy urgently, and he half pulled Eloise after him. 'I thought I saw a movement in the woods!'

Just then a large deer broke cover at the edge of the trees, and putting up its nose, sniffed the air, paused a moment, turned tail and rapidly disappeared again into the wood.

Tommy and Eloise both breathed a sigh of relief. They began to crouch and crawl their way, as they had the day before, along the cover of the river bank, keeping in the harsh moon shadows and listening intently, hearing only the rustling of the reeds and branches and leaves of the small willow trees in the brief gusts of wind. The river rippled and the moonlight fluttered from the surface and all seemed peaceful. Tommy took Eloise's hand briefly and planted a swift kiss on her mouth.

But suddenly they froze. Voices! Voices, loud and clear, but several hundred metres away, Tommy thought. Blast it! There are guards out. No wonder, I suppose, after the attack today in the quaking marsh. Tommy made a sign with his arm: *Keep down but let's go carefully on.* Eloise nodded. The voices receded and disappeared.

'They must have gone around the other side of the château,' whispered Tommy. 'We'll have to risk it. I hope that ladder's still there!'

It was. They scuttled up it and quickly across the roof, through the broken skylight, tiptoeing up the servants' stairs and straight into the airing cupboard.

Good God! There was one of the footmen, kissing that pretty little maid, whose fingers... Flore...! Tommy motioned Eloise back out of sight.

'What's going on here?' he hissed.

The girl gave a squeal and fled, and the footman performed a sort of weak bow, looked in amazement at Tommy half covered in mud, and rushed off down the stairs, making a good deal of noise.

Bother him! thought Tommy. But no one stirred in the house.

'Come and help me find the stuff,' he whispered to Eloise, ignoring her questioning look.

They began to search.

'Where could he have put it!' exclaimed Tommy, half aloud.

'Probably well hidden,' whispered Eloise and Tommy nodded.

At last, there was the barrel, behind a large pile of sheets. Shoving these to one side, Tommy took hold of it by the rim and Eloise took the other side, and they dragged the barrel up and out of its hiding place. Blast, it was heavy! This was going to be fun and games, getting this back to Phillipe... As noiselessly as they could, they were down the staircase, Tommy passing the gunpowder up to Eloise and out of the skylight.

'You hold the steps at the bottom, Eloise!' he whispered, and clasping the barrel so that it was almost in front of his face, Tommy began to wobble and squirm his way down the ladder. Halfway and the silence of the night was shattered by *Pee, pee, peep, pee, pee, peep, pee, pee, peep, peep*.

'Damn and blast it, Harry, you ape! I must have knocked the thing on with holding the barrel.'

Tommy, perched on the ladder, was madly struggling to brace the barrel between himself and the ladder with one arm, whilst fumbling hopelessly with the other hand for the off button on the mobile. Just then, voices could be heard around the corner of the château.

'What's that! For God's sake, what's that noise?'

Then came the sound of running feet. The guards!

'Here, catch!' said Tommy and chucked the phone down to Eloise. 'Get down under the bank and hide. I'll deal with the guards!'

God knows how, he thought. Eloise caught the phone and scampered off slithering down the bank, with the thing still ringing, Mozart's 40th blaring out over the river. Tommy just made it to the bottom of the ladder, and put the barrel down behind him, as the guards came running.

'Right, you there, stop or you're a dead man!' called one of them, practically colliding with Tommy.

'And who do you think you are, addressing Thomas de Romolue in that way, my good fellow?' Bluff it out, thought Tommy, bluff it out!

'Why, excuse me, sir, but, but... the ladder... that noise, sir.' But the guard was interrupted by Harry's voice.

'Tommy, Tommy, we won the championship, the whole, bloomin'...' rang out from the river bank behind the guards' backs. Eloise had been frantically trying to turn it off, but had pressed connect – she'd never handled it before.

The startled guards both turned suddenly at the squeaky voice, expecting to see a ghost behind them. Just then the moon passed behind a heavy cloud and total darkness descended.

'Tommy, can you hear me?' squeaked the phone again, very loud this time. Find the off button, Tommy prayed, not the louder button! 'Say something,' Harry went on, 'we won...' *Click*!

'Thank heavens, she's found it,' breathed Tommy.

A sharp gust of wind passed across the river, and the willows creaked. A green face, lit from beneath, showed over the river bank. The guards gasped in horror.

'The monster of the cave!' yelled one, his foot slipping on the muddy bank, and over he went, into the river. 'I can't swim!' he screamed, but he only stood in a metre of water.

The other guard stared transfixed. The guard in the river looked foolishly around him.

'I can't move,' he whimpered. 'I'm stuck!'

Noises and voices could be heard from within the château. It was now or never. Tommy turned and, grabbing the gunpowder barrel, squirmed around and ran crouching off towards the bridge, hugging the gunpowder to him, followed by Eloise.

'Quick, quick. If they see us, too bad! Surely that guard standing up to his waist in water will, if the moon comes out! He's bound to spot us!'

The moon began to form a wavering light. The cloud was thinning.

'Help me out!' yelped the guard in the river. 'The devil in the cave… it's here, help me! I'm stuck!'

'I'll get some others,' said the guard from the bank in a shaky voice, coming to life and running off.

'Don't leave me here. Aaaah! There it is again!'

For Eloise had stopped for a moment, as the moonlight faded again, and turned her green face towards the river. The guard swayed and splashed down with one arm, trying to crawl away, shielding his face with his other arm.

'That should keep 'em occupied for a bit,' said Tommy, giggling as they made their way as fast as they could, using the green light of the mobile to guide them over the roots and stones and mud along the bank.

But they were far from safe yet. Several guards were now assembled outside the main door of the château. One was holding a lantern. They were bound to come to the bridge. Tommy and Eloise could hear the babbling of one of the guards whom they had met.

'A green devil face!'

'Like the one in the cave!' said another guard in fearful tones. 'Where's Jean?'

'He's standing in the river, half dead with fright.'

'Don't blame him. I'll fight any man, but weird devils, no!'

'You'll meet a few in hell.'

'You too!'

'Let's take the light and go and see what's going on, then.'

The group, sticking together, made their way around the side of the château, arriving just as Jean, their fellow guard, was dragging himself, half dead and soaking wet, up the bank. The night was warm, but his teeth were chattering.

'I'm not… going… to… never…' he was snivelling. 'Over

there!' He suddenly pointed down the river towards the bridge. 'The green devil!' he announced and he lay slumped on the ground, holding his head in his hands. 'It's all true, it's all true, what them priests say in church, it's all true, we'll all go to hell!' And he shook his head.

'Well, I suppose we ought to go and have a look,' said one of the guards, 'at the bridge, I mean!'

'Yeah! That's a good idea,' said another.

But no one moved.

'The Bishop's going to skin us for this. What are we going to tell him?'

'I think I heard the green-faced devil's name,' said Jean, pulling himself up from the ground on the arm of another guard. '"Tommy," it said, "Tommy, Tommy," it squeaked! Oh, God!'

'Look, we had better do something. Who's coming with me, or do I have to tell the Bishop that I was the only one who wasn't such a bloomin' sissy?'

'Ha! You didn't see it!' said Jean.

Tommy and Eloise could hear every word of this conversation, as they crept as fast as they were able towards the bridge.

Keep it up, thought Tommy. Keep it up!

'I'll scout around the back to make sure that nothing's gone that way,' said one guard, and marched off quickly.

'Look, I forgot to say,' said another guard. 'I met Thomas de Romolue. Here, right here. Come to think of it, he didn't seem very frightened by the devil. Perhaps he's in league with devils!'

'More likely meeting some girl, here in the middle of the night! What's he got to do with it?'

'No, but he didn't seem to be frightened,' said the guard, and shook his head. 'Tommy, Tommy,' he muttered to himself.

'Anyway, I'm off to the bridge. Who's coming? Just you and me? Right!'

'Blast it!' said Tommy. 'They're on their way now.'

'Look, there's Phillipe,' whispered Eloise, and they could make out the dark shape of a horse in the shadow of the bridge, and Phillipe, standing in the shadow. He waved briefly to them. They could hear footfalls crunching on the gravel of the path to the bridge from the château – the two guards. Phillipe ducked under the bridge, but he couldn't persuade his horse to follow, tug and kick as he might.

'What are we to do?' whispered Eloise.

Tommy shook his head.

Then suddenly he whispered, 'You stay here. I'll decoy 'em out. Pretend I saw the devil. Make out it's, it's… someone from Town, come to raid the château, decoy 'em into the woods! Can you manage the gunpowder by yourself? Wait for me under the bridge after you've given it to Phillipe.'

Noiselessly, Tommy climbed up over the bank, and as if he had been waiting there for the approaching guards, called out, 'Hey, you, men!'

'Who's that?'

'Thomas de Romolue! About time you came. There's some robbers about, I think. Probably those convicts from the quaking marsh, again. I saw what looked like a green lantern flashing about before!'

'Ah – the devil!'

'What did you say?' asked Tommy.

'Oh! Pardon me, sir, one of our men thought it was a devil, sir. Silly superstitious fellow!'

'Devil or no devil, I think that you should try and stalk it. It disappeared into the woods up that way,' said Tommy, pointing in a direction up the hill to the left.

'Do you think we stand a chance, sir? I mean, at night and all,' said the other guard.

'Well, a quick look can do no harm. Let's go!'

Tommy led the way rapidly up the hill. The guards looked nervously around. Phillipe's horse shuffled about in the shadow of the bridge.

'Whatssat?' exclaimed the more timid of the guards.

Tommy shrugged. 'What sort of soldier are you, my man?' he exclaimed. 'Armed to the teeth, and you're frightened of a toad hopping out of the river, or a water rat, or whatever it was.'

'No, it weren't, sir, it's a bloomin' horse! Look, sir, under the bridge!'

'God, you're right!' said Tommy, cursing his luck. 'That

means the man we're looking for can't be far away. I'll go and stand guard over the horse. You go and have a quick scout around the woods. Quick now!'

Tommy dismissed them with a wave of his hand. He watched them disappear among the trees and then walked rapidly back to the bridge.

'Quick,' he whispered as loudly as he dared, and Eloise appeared at the other end of the bridge, lugging the gunpowder. Tommy ran to help her. 'Phillipe,' he whispered urgently, 'are you ready? The guards will be back in a moment! Get on that horse!'

'Right you are! Hand it me, the gunpowder... Quick, quick, there they are, coming back out the wood!'

'Eloise, under the bridge!' said Tommy. 'Phillipe, pretend to hit me, look as if we're fighting.'

Tommy pulled out his sword and clashed it against Phillipe's, which was already drawn.

'Ride now! They've got bows. Get going! The moon's coming out again! Now!'

An arrow whistled over their heads. Other guards were running down from the château. Tommy fell to the ground and crawled on knees and elbows for the cover of the bridge. Phillipe spurred his horse hard and set off up the slope, as a second arrow and then a third flew past him. The fourth arrow struck his left arm, ripping the leather protector, but then he was out of sight among the trees. The pursuit was over.

Under the bridge, Tommy was whispering urgently to Eloise.

'Wait here. I'll get rid of them, and then we'll both go back into the château – by the front door, this time! We'll make up some fib if you're spotted near the bridge!'

Tommy crawled out from under the bridge, groaning and rubbing his shoulder, as guards came running up from both directions.

'The villain was hiding under the bridge all the time. When I went back to the horse, he attacked me and rode off!'

'I think an arrow winged him, sir.'

'Oh, really? Good shooting. No, I'm okay,' said Tommy, as a guard came to take him under the arm. 'I think that you had best go and scout around all the grounds of the château. Where there's one robber, there's probably more! I'll go back inside in a few minutes. A bit of air will do me good for now.'

Tommy watched as the guards dispersed, thinking how easy it seemed to be to dupe these people. They'd believe anything he told them, just because he was a nobleman.

'I reckon he's got a girl out there,' whispered one guard to another, when they were out of Tommy's hearing.

'Yeah, that's why he wants us out of the way!'

'You watch, he'll be running after her in a minute!'

They glanced over their shoulders to see Tommy turn on his heel and walk back towards the bridge. As they watched, they saw him duck into the shadows. They glanced at one another and smiled knowingly.

'See what I mean!'

Twenty-one: Players in the Château

aggage!' came the voice of Marie loudly from her room, the door slightly ajar. 'Baggage – he called me an old baggage!'

'Yes, yes! Oh, Marie, you know…' began the Countess.

'Baggage!' repeated Marie, and Tommy could hear her stamping her foot as he walked along the corridor to visit her.

'Well, I've seen better dressed suitcases, it's true,' he giggled to himself and then he yawned. He'd slept very late. It was already nearly midday. He wondered how Eloise was. Safely in her room, he hoped. He tapped gently on Marie's door.

'Come in!' called Marie, still sounding irritated.

'That Drogo,' she said, as he entered, waggling her old head to and fro, her wispy white hair shaking with indignation, and forgetting to greet Tommy. 'That Father Drogo, he called me an old baggage! What do you think of that, young man?' she demanded of Tommy.

Standing behind her, the Countess was trying to stifle her laughter behind a frilly handkerchief held to her mouth. Tommy attempted to collect himself.

'The man's a criminal, a monster!' he said sharply, forgetting that Marie knew nothing of Drogo's crimes.

'Oh, Monsieur Thomas!' gasped Marie, clasping her hands together.

The Countess frowned and pursed her lips.

'Well, look,' started Tommy, 'what has he done to you? I mean, why did he call you a… er…?'

'Baggage!' exclaimed Marie, and the Countess gurgled into her handkerchief. 'He was locked in the chapel! What are you grinning at?' asked Marie, as Tommy remembered how Eloise had said that she had turned the key on him, and a smile spread across his face.

He made no reply and Marie continued, 'I heard this

thumping, y'know, soon after you left me and you went down after Eloise. That naughty young lady! Countess, I haven't told you…'

'Yes, but let's hear about Drogo, er, Father Drogo, first, please, Marie,' interrupted Tommy.

'Well, he was locked in the chapel, you see,' continued Marie. 'I don't know how he'd done it, because the key was on the outside, in the lock, I mean.'

'Someone must have turned the key on him,' said the Countess.

'Yes, I suppose so, yes, of course,' replied Marie, 'but why should they…?'

'Probably a trick to keep him out of the way while the Bishop and his men went off into the marsh,' suggested Tommy.

'Yes, but…' Marie shook her head. 'Anyway, I opened up of course. He was shaking the door handle so hard I could hardly get the key to turn. Father Drogo came out, angry as a dog that's lost its bone. He turned and snarled at me, "What do you think you're doing, you old baggage?" – and strode off, without so much as a thank you! What do you make of that, then?'

'He's a brute,' answered Tommy.

'He is that!' said Marie and plumped herself in her armchair, frowning.

Then, shaking her head as if to put Drogo out of her mind, she sat up and said, 'Ah well, today's another day!'

Then she peered out of the window to see just how the day was. Her window commanded a long view over the moat, over the tops of nearby trees, stretching right across the fields, as far as the eye could see. Tommy and the Countess followed her gaze.

'What's that?' Marie asked, squinting and pointing. 'No, there, more to the right. It looks like a sort of… wagon… and some people.'

'Probably just some peasants at work,' said the Countess.

'No, I don't think so,' said Tommy.

With his keener eyesight, he could make out a horse pulling a wagon, and a good many people, mostly walking alongside.

'Hey!' he shouted. 'It's the circus! Great!'

'Circus?' exclaimed the Countess. 'What are you talking

about? Oh! Maybe you mean players, come to do a show. Do we have time to think about watching plays?' she added, turning to Tommy.

'Well, anyway, it's fun!' said Tommy, feeling rather glum that that they did not have time for a circus, really.

'You mean those newfangled things from Italy – rude jokes and capering about? Never mind them,' said Marie. 'It'll be some time before they get here, anyway,' she added glancing out of the window again. 'Tell me what happened with the gunpowder.'

Tommy gulped. He thought for a moment that Marie meant the gunpowder he'd smuggled out the night before, which was pretty much at the front of his mind, when he thought of the narrow escapes that he'd had. How could she know about it? But, no, of course, the gunpowder that he and Jacques had spiked: that was what she meant.

'Yes, well,' replied Tommy, recovering quickly, 'yeah! That really worked. Just like you said, their guns just went *pop*, and then pathetic little bullets sort of rolled out of the end of the barrels. You should have seen their faces!'

'What, you were there?' exclaimed Marie.

'I was hiding,' Tommy said guiltily.

'What's all this about?' asked the Countess.

'Well, me and Jacques…' Tommy began, and he described to the Countess what they had done.

He did not mention, though, where the extra gunpowder had gone, and fortunately the Countess did not think to ask.

'Good! Good!' the Countess kept on saying. 'That explains why the Bishop got caught, and several of his men, of course! We had a terrible time untying the rope,' she continued with a grin. 'He was dumped on the bridge. I think that it is really time to let the Count in on all this, y'know,' she added, an edge coming into her voice.

'All what?' asked Marie, and seeing the looks that Tommy and the Countess exchanged, she added, 'Alright, I can wait. When you're my age, a couple of days doesn't make any difference.' She squinted out of the window again. 'My, my, they've come on proper quick,' she remarked.

Tommy went to the window. 'They'll be here soon,' he said.

'Just right in time for lunch,' said the Countess. 'Good timing!'

In fact they could hear the sound of laughter and shouting and the tinkling of many bells, and a kind of hooting noise, as the travelling players approached. One of the players seemed to be almost entirely covered in leaves and was jumping about, jerking and twitching.

'Look at him!' exclaimed Tommy, thinking that something about the figure was familiar.

'Oh! That'll be the harlequin,' said the Countess. 'They always act rather barmy! You know that.'

Tommy looked closer. 'Good God – that's Joncilond!' he cried.

'Who?' said Marie sharply. But Tommy was already gone, out of the door, muttering, 'Brill, brill, brilliant!' and punching his fist into the air.

The noise in the kitchen was tremendous. They were all there, the Emp, his followers, Phillipe, Jacques the Tailor, Alain, François and more than a dozen other townsmen. And capering around, in and out, everywhere at once, Joncilond. Each of them wore some sort of costume, and a mask. But everyone was stuffing their faces, lifting up their masks, swigging the wine and shovelling in the bread, cheese, pickled walnuts, raw onions, hard-boiled eggs, skinny chickens, venison and oatmeal patties and savoury cabbage spread out before them. The Emp looked fatter than ever, with a cushion stuffed down his enormous trousers. His mask was a great half moon, with his beard tucked into the lower bit and the top projecting right out of his forehead.

'Well, well, well, Mr Pulchipulchi!' cackled Joncilond, and stuffed his elbow in the Emp's paunch.

The Emp almost choked on a chicken leg.

'You oaf!' bawled the Emp.

'I'm a harlotquin, a hurletquin, a hurlyharlybarlyquin!' sang out Joncilond, doing pirouettes, and everyone grabbed for their mugs of wine as Joncilond's arms flew across the table, succeeding only in catching a large lump of butter on the back of his hand.

'Oooh – butter! I love it!' he exclaimed.

'You pig!' said one of the townspeople, unwisely, as Joncilond wiped his hand on a piece of bread and took an enormous bite.

'Oink!' said Joncilond. 'Oink, oink, oink, I'm a harleypig!' And he cannoned into him.

'Ooof, you twit!' roared the unfortunate fellow, and rebounded into his neighbour, and wine went shooting over the table.

'Look what you made me do!'

'No! It was Jonci – er – the harlequin!'

'Silence!' roared the Emp. 'Eat like civilised people, please!'

'Yes, I should think so too!' said a rather high-pitched voice, and with a flick of his long hair over his shoulder, and a jerk of his nose in the air, and a suitable little sniff, an elegant figure, Gerome, dressed as Colombina for the show that they were to perform, entered the kitchen.

'Oooh, look! Where have you been, then? I thought you'd got lost looking at your own reflection in the moat!' shouted Jacques.

'None of your tongue!' retorted Colombina, daintily taking his place beside the Emp, who looked sideways at him.

'Getting into the role, are you?' said the Emp

'Doesn't need to! It comes natural to 'im,' butted in Jacques, who liked to use Gerome to model his latest creations of the forest.

'I don't understand nothin',' said the Emp, looking down at his plate, 'but these are dead good venison patties.' He licked his fingers happily.

'Hey, you lot, remember, we're *in disguise*,' said the Emp dropping his voice suddenly to a hoarse whisper, addressing a group of his men who were discussing the defeat of the Bishop loudly at the other end of the table, drinking down large gulps of wine as they did so.

'Whoever thought a nun's habit could make such a fetchin' dress,' said François, grinning at Gerome-Columbina.

'And revealing... Look at that neckline!' sniggered another.

Colombina blushed beneath his mask.

'Dipped the Bishop in the mud, right up to his holy nose. Ha!'

'And over it. Right over his anointed head,' yelled the group at the other end of the table.

'I'll drink to that!' shouted another, taking a mighty swig of wine, and slopping some down his front.

'I said shut up down there!' bawled the Emp.

'Why? What 'ave we done... Oh, yeah! Sorry. Disguise, yes, disguise, yes of course, sir!'

'We're not to bawl out about defeating the Bishop!'

'What y'say?' said his companion. It was Henri, Joncilond's deaf brother.

'Not to bawl about defeating the Bishop!' yelled his friend into his face. 'Oops!' he said and put his hand over his mouth, looking down the table at the Emp, who just put his hands to his head in despair.

'Gor, these onions are strong! Gimme some more wine!' said the Emp, slamming down his empty mug.

'This chicken must ha' needed a crutch to get about, it's legs are so thin.'

'Looks a bit like that Drogo.'

'Bloomin' scarecrow!'

'Bung us an egg. Not that hard! God, you nearly brained me!'

Raucous laughter, shouts, grunts and twitterings, the last from Joncilond, continued to fill the kitchen, until even these men began to feel that they had eaten enough.

Pathetic little chicken bones lay strewn over the table, the odd crust of bread, the butter with finger marks in it, wine swilled this way and that, seeping into the wrinkled old oak surface. Eggshell mixed with scraps of venison patty, and, lying full length on the table among the debris was Joncilond, trying to balance a pickled walnut on his nose.

'Gerroff!' said the Emp sleepily. 'Gerroff that table, Joncilond, before you ruin your harlequin outfit.'

The sound of snores was his only reply. After the long trek with the wagon – they had had to bring it in pieces from Town and assemble it at the borders of the quaking marsh, all the time remaining on the lookout for any of the Bishop's men – they were flat out. And what with the wine and the warm afternoon air wafting gently through the kitchen, sleep gradually overtook them all. The still air of the kitchen was interrupted only by the occasional grunt and snort, shifting of bottoms, and turning of heads laid on the table. Only Joncilond seemed still awake, going cross-eyed, wriggling his nose, trying to keep the pickled walnut from rolling off it.

Meanwhile, the noble lords and ladies of the Château de Romolue were having a very different, and rather less enjoyable kind of lunch. There were just the three of them, the Count, the Countess and Tommy. Eloise had not yet appeared.

'Are not the roast larks a little tough, dear?' muttered the Count, as he chewed long and hard at part of a leathery wing sticking out of his mouth.

'Wine, m'Lord?' A footman stepped forward.

'*Wrrrh!*' mouthed the Count.

'Excuse me, my Lord, but was that…?'

'*Wrrrrrrrhh!*' repeated the Count more emphatically, waving the footman away with his arm.

The Countess was looking speculatively at a ghastly little lark on her plate and was mulling over how to start to tell her husband about Drogo. She had not yet noticed the drama with the footman.

The Count, he really had to know, she said to herself, he had to know about Drogo, about Eleonora: she forced the name to the forefront of her mind. He had to know… now! It was only Sunday, Sunday that… How to start, without her husband flying off the handle?

'The Bishop, my dear,' she began and then stopped as, looking up, she saw her husband fighting with a bone caught in his mouth, with an alarmed footman hovering behind him.

'*Wrrrhhhrrrr!*' repeated the Count, louder this time, pointing frantically towards his mouth with the index finger of his right hand and pulling at the lark's wing with the other hand. '*Wwwrrrrrhhhhh* – itth sththtuck!' he managed to gasp out, choking at the effort.

Tommy stared fascinated at the Count.

'Gosh! What a lark,' he muttered.

The Countess, rising to her feet said sharply, 'What was that, Thomas?'

'Nothing, nothing,' he mumbled going slightly pink.

'Let me…' began the countess, ignoring Tommy and taking the end of the bone from her husband's hand.

The Count, with a look of anguish, let his arms fall to his sides as his wife pulled the bone back and forth, peering into his mouth, and wiggling and wiggling harder and harder.

At that moment the door opened and Eloise entered the dining room. She looked so beautiful that Tommy quite forgot the antics of his adopted parents and just gazed at her. She gave him a little smile but then stopped in her tracks and gasped as she saw the Countess bending over the Count and apparently trying to saw off his nose – or so it looked from where she stood.

'Mother!' she cried.

The Countess looked up. 'Ah! Eloise, perhaps you could try. He's got a lark bone caught!'

But just then there was a sickening, cracking noise. The Count, losing patience, had decided to test which was stronger, his teeth or the lark bone, and grasping the bone in his hand, he had bent it sharply sideways. It was a dead heat. Both the lark bone and the tooth broke, a large fragment of tooth flying out of his mouth and landing plop in the middle of the apple purée, which, it seemed, was intended to accompany the larks on their final flight down the human gullet.

The footman, grabbing a spoon from the sideboard, ran quickly over to the table, as everyone craned their necks to watch the piece of tooth sink slowly and disappear into the apple purée.

'Just like the Bishop in the mud,' whispered Tommy to Eloise, their giggles stifled by an angry look from the Countess.

'Bishop?' demanded the Count, shifting his gaze from his disappearing tooth, becoming suddenly aware again of his surroundings, as the footman fished about in the purée with the spoon, trying to find the bit of tooth.

'Take it away!' yelled the Count, and the footman jumped, gave a little bow and ran out of the room, carrying the dish of purée with him.

'Bishop?' repeated the Count. 'What's this got to do with the Bishop?' he demanded, waggling his index finger towards his mouth. 'The Bishop!' He spat out the word, shaking his head.

Then he put up his hand as he saw his wife on the point of speaking, and started to explore the inside of his mouth with his tongue, to see how big a gap his tooth had left. Frowning to himself – the gap felt enormous – he muttered, 'The Bishop,' again, and raising his finger in the air, as he saw his wife once more about to interrupt, he started off again.

'And what's worse, I meant to say to you, before that stupid, failed attempt yesterday to kill off the people in the marsh – and he didn't get his horse back either, puh! – yes, the Bishop, he started on at me in the salon, cornered me in there, he started on about getting Thomas, Thomas here,' brandishing his knife in the air, 'Thomas betrothed to... who d'you think, eh? – who d'you think?' he repeated, raising his eyebrows and looking his wife square in the eye.

'I...' began his wife.

'Clarice,' whispered Tommy.

'Clarice,' bellowed the Count, seeming not to have heard Tommy. 'Robert's daughter!'

'Clarice!' exclaimed the Countess.

Well, she wasn't surprised, but they were certainly trying to push the pace. It was now or never to tell the Count about Drogo. So before her husband could recover his breath she began.

'My dear husband, I think that it is time that we told you some things that we have discovered about the Bishop and, er, about Father Drogo,' began the Countess, speaking quietly but firmly.

'Drogo?' exclaimed the Count. 'What has he to do with all this? It was the Bishop's horse that was stolen. Nothing to do with Drogo! Father Drogo hasn't got a horse, or only an old...'

'No, it's nothing to do with the horse, you're quite right. It has to do with Eleonora,' she added quietly and deliberately.

The Count looked up sharply. He knew that his wife had loved Eleonora dearly, and that she still missed her, all these years later. Sometimes that book would appear, Eleonora's favourite book, which she had sat and read with Richard – and, unknown to all except Drogo, with Drogo too. Sometimes in the autumn they would have woodcock pie with asparagus, Eleonora's favourite dish; sometimes he would surprise the Countess gazing at a little portrait that would disappear the instant she noticed that he had seen her. He had not heard his wife mention her sister's name in ten years, he mused.

'Eleonora?' he whispered.

'Yes, Eleonora,' replied the Countess in a firm tone.

'Thomas,' began the Count, 'Thomas, I think… and Eloise…'

'No!' said the Countess. 'This concerns Thomas too and Eloise. You forget, Thomas has come of age now,' she added.

Tommy remained wisely silent, but reached out and, hidden by the tablecloth, took Eloise's hand and held it firmly in his.

'Eleonora!' whispered the Count again.

'Yes. We – Thomas and me, and Eloise – we have found out how Eleonora died!'

The Count drew in his breath as he heard these words. Eleonora's death had always remained so mysterious. She had left that day for Toulouse, to pray for Richard in the cathedral, he seemed to remember, but she had never returned. He had never gazed upon her beautiful face again. For the Count had not been immune to Eleonora. She had only to smile at you and you fell in love, whether you were thirteen years old or eighty. But there had always been safety in numbers. Everyone was in love with her! He sighed at the memory, the sound loud in the quiet of the dining room, where the only noise, as the Countess, Tommy and Eloise sat very still, was the faint trace of shouts and laughter from the kitchen, where Joncilond still capered about.

The Count recalled the time of Eleonora's death. Her funeral was without special ceremony, quickly done, the coffin closed, bolted down as if she had died of some terrible disfiguring disease. They had returned to the Bishop's palace afterwards, he remembered. Father Drogo had seemed half crazed. You would have thought that he had been in love with her himself! Dreadful idea! The Count believed in an ordered world in which things fitted nicely together. That ugly scarecrow of a priest could not love such a beauty as Eleonora.

'Do you remember, after the funeral, Father Drogo seemed almost mad!' said the Count suddenly.

'And we know why!' exclaimed Tommy, and Eloise's eyes became dark and began to fill with tears.

'Eh? What d'you mean – you know why!' asked the Count.

Tommy opened his mouth to speak, but the Countess held up her hand for silence.

'You are right,' said the Countess, 'he did seem mad. And we do know why, indeed, we do!'

'Don't be so mysterious, all of you!' exclaimed the Count. 'If you know something, out with it!'

'My dear husband,' began the Countess, 'a terrible crime has been committed. Eleonora did not die a natural death! She was murdered, murdered in the cathedral!'

'My God!' shouted the Count, and rising from his chair began to pace about the room. 'Who did it? I'll kill them with my bare hands. Who did it?' he demanded.

'Calm, please, please try to keep calm. The criminal will come to justice, and you will be there to see it done. We all will be there! But that'll only work out if you do not rush into action. Revenge, we will have revenge, but we've got to be careful. You'll see why. Promise to hear us through. What we have to tell is secret, must remain secret. Promise!'

'Murdered!' repeated the Count. 'Murdered... Are you sure?'

'Oh yes!' Tommy blurted out.

'What do you know? I mean, how... what could... Thomas, or Eloise, tell me, please!' stammered the Count.

'First you must understand about not rushing out the door of this room shouting for your horse and your men! Promise me, promise!'

'Yes, promise, for my sake, for my mother's sake!' said Eloise, in a voice choking with tears.

Tommy gripped her hand tightly.

'*Mon Dieu*! you look just like Eleonora, Eloise! Just like her. How could anyone refuse you anything?' said the Count, forgetting himself.

The Countess pursed her lips. 'You promise, then?' she said.

'For God's sake, tell me. Who did it?'

'Drogo!' exclaimed Tommy, slamming his fist on the dining table.

'Impossible!' shouted the Count. 'Who told you that absurd story? Who could believe such a thing. Drogo!' his voice rose still further.

'Quieter, quieter, please! The servants, everyone, the actors in the kitchen, everyone will hear. You must promise to keep this secret!' said the Countess. 'Do you imagine that we made this up, that we heard it whispered about? No! We have proof – proof, I tell you! It's written down. He wrote it all down. Thomas discovered it. Wait, I think the best thing is that I go and fetch it… No! We'd better all go up to my room, the quiet room. There's too much danger here… spies, yes, there are spies in the household. One of them died on the road to the Abbaye, killed – Oh! that's another story.'

'Spies!' bawled out the Count. 'In my château? I'll have them hanged! Whose spies? Drogo's, I suppose,' he added sarcastically.

'You wait and you will see!' replied the Countess.

A few minutes later, they were all seated in the small padded room, all doors locked, the Countess clutching the roll of parchment which was Drogo's admission of guilt, Drogo's confession.

Eloise stared at the parchment, for she had never seen it before.

'That's the confession!' she blurted out.

'Confession?' exclaimed the Count.

'You remember when Thomas had to go and say the Lord's Prayer five hundred times,' the Countess began, and the Count nodded, as Tommy and Eloise sat on the edges of their chairs watching his every reaction. 'Well, a bit before, I happened to see Drogo coming out of the chapel – clutching this!' And she held the manuscript in front of her husband.

'What's written in that?' demanded the Count.

'Wait! I saw Drogo clutching this parchment. Then he went back into the chapel and came out a couple of minutes later without it. I told Thomas what I'd seen…'

'Yes,' said Tommy, 'and when I went into the chapel I started to hunt for this parchment, as you might imagine!'

'Well…' began the Count.

'I already was suspicious about Drogo,' Tommy went on. 'Well, anyway, I found it, inside the crucifix.'

'What? The parchment? Inside the crucifix – rolled up?'

'Yes, pushed in the bottom, and locked in. There was a key,

under a bit of wood in the chapel floor.'

'Astonishing,' muttered the Count. 'And I suppose that this piece of paper has some sort of story…'

'Yeah,' answered Tommy. 'Some sort of story, you could say. Let me read it to you, Father. Eloise knows what's in it, but she hasn't heard it read out. It's right that she hears it, too!' And he cast Eloise a glance of love and pity.

Unrolling the parchment, Tommy began to read.

'Written the 15th August, in the year 1585, at the command of my brother, Henri de Montfort, secretary to the Cardinal of Ferrara, Piero Vincenzo di Colonna, at the Palace of the Vatican, Rome, in my brother's apartments.

'Signed: Drogo de Montfort.'

'Yes,' muttered the Count, half to himself, 'yes, that's where he was, in Rome, yes.' Tommy looked up from the parchment. 'Go on,' said the Count.

'This is a copy of a document in the hands of my brother. He keeps his copy to force me to his will through blackmail and to hold me true to his policy of the ruin of the House of Romolue and the glorification of Toulouse.'

God! I should have missed that bit out! thought Tommy. But the Count only quivered and went a little red in the face.

'Whosoever may see this document, be he of this time, of a time decades in the future or even of centuries to come, I ask that you should give me some little fragment of sympathy for the terrible torments which I have lived through, the agony which I have suffered. My crimes cannot be forgiven on this Earth—'

'Crimes!' exclaimed the Count, no longer able to hold himself back. 'Crimes! The ruin of the House of Romolue. Is that not enough!' and then subsided.

Tommy continued, as Drogo wrote of his coming to the château, of his meeting with Eleonora, of his tormented love for her, his betrayal of Eleonora's husband, Richard, of the birth of Eloise. As the terrible confession reached its climax, the Countess gripped Eloise's hand in hers, as Tommy read of Drogo's great hatred and jealousy, of Eleonora in the aisle of the cathedral, and they could see before them Drogo, grasping in his claw-like hand the heavy crucifix, stealthily moving from behind a pillar, now behind Eleonora, and with a great blow, striking her down, her blood running on the cold stone of the aisle, of the baby rolling on the ground.

'...And I know that I killed her with it,' read Tommy.

Eloise burst into sobs of grief and rage, and the Countess rose and clasped her in her arms. The Count sat white with passion, gripping the arms of the chair, his face a mask of anger.

'That's not all,' said Tommy. 'See what Drogo has added below, later,' and he passed the parchment to the Count.

'The child grows so like her mother, that I may have to kill her too,' read out the Count.

'God! Your life's in danger, Eloise!' exclaimed the Count.

'And has been for a long time!' added the Countess.

'That's why I went after Eloise to the Abbaye, Father!'

'What's that? Did you, Thomas?'

'Yes, and maybe that's why the Bishop pursued us through the night when we fled from the Abbaye. He was after the parchment. Maybe he thought I had it on me.'

'Ha! He told me that he'd been chasing after you! The madman! But, I don't understand,' continued the Count, 'the Bishop didn't know that the parchment was gone, did he?'

'No! That's true, you're right, he didn't. In fact they still don't.'

'Good! But why was he chasing after you, then? Why is Eloise so important to him? I mean, why pursue—?'

'Remember, Drogo and the Bishop want me betrothed to Clarice, Father, just like you said before!' interrupted Tommy.

'Ah! Clarice, that little minx of a Toulouse child! Yes, yes. I was forgetting. Ah! And they see, er, that maybe...' And the Count became a little red in the face. 'Yes, well...'

'That I want to marry Eloise, Father, yes!' Eloise gave a little gulp and nodded, as Tommy grasped her hand tightly in his.

'And Drogo is crazed,' interrupted the Countess, 'he sees Eloise as Eleonora born again, and he will kill her a second time!'

As this conversation went on, Eloise looked from face to face, thinking as she listened that all that she heard was true, but that the greatest mystery of all, the great mystery of that world she had seen, with the sky lit yellow, burning lights, 'cars', this vision overshadowed everything! The truth about Thomas... somehow all else seemed pale beside it, even the death of her mother, her mother, a myth, a beautiful ghost. The Countess had shown her a tiny painting once. It was like looking in a little mirror: she was the image of her mother.

'This man must die,' Eloise heard the Count say. 'You shall have your revenge.'

He pulled himself out of his chair and began to pace the room, tension flowing from him and invading the small space.

'Damn me, that I never knew this before!' he shouted suddenly, clenching his fists.

'Please!' whispered the Countess, and Eloise buried her face in her hands.

'But this cannot remain secret for long,' said the Count in a lower voice. 'Surely Drogo will miss the parchment soon, even if he hasn't yet!'

'He may not miss the parchment, not the parchment,' replied the Countess, 'but the crucifix. It was damaged.' At this the Count raised his eyebrows. 'It was Thomas, but the point is that I've hidden it,' she went on hastily, 'in the stone bench – you know the little compartment, you remember!'

The Count looked hard at his wife.

'Yes, I remember!' he said quietly, and well he should.

He used to leave a little bunch of flowers there – violets, pansies, snowdrops, whatever he could find – for the Countess, when they first met. Barely older than Thomas and Eloise, they were, and a little smile came to his lips, and a little answering smile from the Countess. Eloise looked at them wonderingly, sharing this intimate moment, without understanding, but with a sudden sympathy.

'Yes, I remember,' repeated the Count. 'It's well hidden, then! And Drogo thinks the parchment's still inside?' The Countess nodded.

'Who else... does anyone else know about this?' asked the Count.

'Jacques, he knows,' replied the Countess.

'Jacques! You'd trust him, then?' *Before me*, he would have added.

'Yes, Jacques, he is…'

Here the Countess was suddenly quiet. This was coming too close to the truth about Thomas, if truth it was. But how could she doubt it? She had spoken to Thomas's mother, with that thing, that devil's thing!

'What is it?' demanded the Count, seeing his wife suddenly so lost in her own thoughts. 'Are you still holding something back from me?'

Tears came to the Countess's eyes as she thought of her own Thomas, lost in some other world, some strange world beyond her understanding.

But the Count mistook her tears for tears for Eleonora.

'This man must be destroyed!' he exclaimed, 'This manuscript, this parchment, this is his own death warrant; he's written his own death warrant! And all the time the Bishop knew of this, all these years…' added the Count, his voice rising in anger again… 'we will destroy them both!'

'First Drogo,' cried Eloise suddenly.

'Yes, first Drogo,' echoed Tommy, 'and we start on Sunday!' The Countess was nodding vigorously.

'Sunday?' asked the Count, 'But on Sunday we will be at mass in Toulouse Cathedral. Have you forgotten?'

'No, Father, I have not,' replied Tommy. 'We're going to use that confession, like you said. This is what I think we should do…'

Tommy began to explain, the Count nodding, forgetting he was listening to his little son, the stupid little boy of the larks in butter and the boar's head of the banquet last Sunday night, and he looked closely at Tommy as he spoke.

Is this Thomas, he asked himself, so self-assured, so grown-up?

He seemed to see his son for the first time, so full of purpose, strength even, a new man, a new… He gazed at his son, as Eloise and his wife sat hand in hand, leaning forward, attentive to every word.

As the Count looked on, he saw that on his son's forehead… *No*, he shook his head, on his forehead… The Count frowned, puzzled. Surely the scar from the boar hunt, had it really faded completely over the years? He must ask his wife. Later, of course, later. And he suddenly realised that he had almost lost the thread of what Thomas was saying.

'Sorry, my dear Thomas. Say that again. I – I was looking at you, not listening properly. Please go back to the part where…!'

But the Count at that moment could not resist walking over to Thomas and passing his hand swiftly and gently over his forehead.

Eloise started out of her chair as he did so.

'Why did you – what is it?' she said, in confusion.

'Nothing, nothing,' replied the Count. 'Go on, Thomas, my boy!'

Thomas did as he was asked, of course, and the plan unfolded before the Count.

'The players! The "circus", as you call it,' said the Count, as Tommy paused. 'Are you sure that they can be relied upon, I mean, they are just players, or perhaps they are not?' he added, and grinned. 'I think I recognise the big one, the boss, Pulchinelle, even in his mask. I think it's—'

'Sssh,' said the Countess, standing up and laying her hand in the Count's, 'do not say the name. Let them be themselves for now. Just players. Come,' she went on, 'it must be time for their performance.'

And she led the way out of the room.

Twenty-two: Punch and his Friends

s Tommy, Eloise and the Count and Countess made their way along the corridor, they could hear the clatter of many feet and noisy shouting from below.

'So there's really going to be a performance, then?' asked Tommy. 'There's really time for that?'

But before anyone could answer, he could hear from below the Emp, or Pulchinelle, bellowing, 'One, two, three!'

And then started a noise which sounded to Tommy like someone strangling a parrot, or several parrots, accompanied by a nearly human voice with a very bad cold and a fuzzy sound as if a lot of people were blowing as loud as they could through combs wrapped in newspaper.

'Ah, see! The music's started! There you are,' exclaimed the Countess.

Obviously if the real Thomas had any memory of music in 1599, he had been able to forget it, because Tommy couldn't recall hearing anything like it in his life before. It was stomach-churning, and he could feel the larks fluttering about inside him. But as the racket rose to a climax, suddenly there broke through, like a ray of sunshine, the sound of a violin, a bit scratchy at first, but playing a tune, soaring up and over the bedlam going on in the undergrowth, which sounded more and more like a large industrial vacuum cleaner, Tommy thought.

'Stop!' they could hear the Emp yell. 'Where was the hunting horn, eh? Again!'

'Oh, no!' murmured Tommy.

Even the Bristol-Avonmouth Bypass Symphony Orchestra, otherwise the school band, sounded better than this, and he giggled to himself.

As they made their way down the grand staircase, passing the chapel, they met Jacques darting up towards them.

'Ah! Monsieur le Comte,' he began. 'The Bishop, sire, the Bishop has sent Georges, sire, to search the...'

His words were lost as the call of the hunting horn pealed out and several more parrots met a horrible death below.

'The Bishop!' exclaimed the Count. 'Come in here, all of you, into the chapel, and shut the door behind you, so that we can hear ourselves think. Who let those maniacs into the house?' he added.

As they entered, the Count placed a hand on the altar where the crucifix had stood, and drumming his fingers on the cold stone of the vacant place, nodded to his wife.

Jacques looked from the Count to the Countess, and at the empty altar, his face a question mark. How would the Count react to his news?

'Well?' said the Count.

'Er, yes, sire. Well, Georges, the commander of the Bishop's men, he's down below with a couple of other guards, demanding that he be allowed to search everywhere in the château. He wants all the keys, for everywhere – for the ladies' rooms, everywhere.'

'Search for the crucifix, you mean!' said the Count.

'So, sire, you – you know something about...' began Jacques, hesitating to say too much.

'Yes,' broke in the Countess. 'He knows everything. Thomas has just read out the confession, which I have – God! – here, in my hand. Where are the Bishop's men?' she said hurriedly.

'Georges and the others; down in the kitchen, Madame. I've been trying to get them properly boozed up, but they seem wise to that.'

'Keep 'em there, whatever you do. Tell them – tell them... Oh, you know what to say! I've got to get rid of this!' She waved the confession and rushed out the chapel, straight into the arms of Georges, who had decided that he had waited in the kitchen long enough and was taking matters into his own hands.

'Madame! Excuse me!' he said, as they almost fell over one another.

The Countess went white, and losing her grip on the parchment, it fell to the step between her and Georges. Both she and Georges stared down at it, as it moved slightly in a draught of air wafting up from below. The Countess made as if to stoop down.

'No, my Lady... let me, my Lady,' said Georges, and bent quickly down, holding it for a moment, his touch quite unused to parchment, for of course he could not read a word, and then he gave it back into her trembling hands. He looked at her suspiciously, wondering why she was in such a fright.

'Excuse me,' he repeated.

Hearing a scrap of the conversation on the staircase outside, in a lucky lull in the music, the Count came quickly out of the chapel, followed by Tommy. They looked down the staircase to see the Countess, her back to the wall, clutching the parchment again, and Georges facing her. He was mumbling some further words, but these were lost in the sound of the Orchestra of the Quaking Marsh, or as Tommy named it, the Royal Cacophonic, which had started up again.

The Count ran down the staircase, shouting as he did so, 'Away with you!' His hand was on his sword, and he placed himself between Georges and the Countess, who backed up the stairs.

'How dare you threaten Madame de Romolue in this manner! Guards!' he yelled.

'Sire, you misunderstand. It was just an accident, my good Lord.'

And the Count turned to the Countess, who nodded feebly and tried a weak smile.

'Very well! Return to the kitchen. In a few moments I will interview you and discover what you want in our house. Armed men not of our household do not freely roam about the château. Go!'

Georges gave a little bow and went, meeting several of the Count's men clattering up the stairs as he made his way down – for Jacques, seeing the situation, had run down the servants' staircase and ordered them to the aid of their master.

Tommy looking down upon the scene, breathed a long sigh of relief as he saw Georges turn and leave.

'If the Countess had dropped the parchment in her fright!' he muttered to himself.

He and Eloise moved down the stairs, where the Count had placed his arm protectively around his wife.

'Come, we will hide the parchment together,' he whispered in her ear.

She shook her head. 'No, you go and attend to that brute. Let Thomas and Eloise come with me. I'll be safe now. Place guards outside my bedroom door.'

The Count nodded and a flick of his head was enough for the guards to follow the Countess, Tommy and Eloise along the corridor to her room. Within a few moments, the key was extracted from the beneath the flagstone floor of the lavatory, and the parchment was safely tucked away in the Countess's jewellery chest.

'I dropped it right in front of Georges, you know!' whispered the Countess.

'Gosh!' said Tommy, 'You don't think he had any idea what it was. He didn't get a look at it, did he?'

'Well, he picked it up and handed it me back, but of course he can't read a word!'

'What! Not read?' said Tommy. 'Oh! of course not! I – I was back…'

'Can everyone read in your time, then?' asked Eloise slowly, with wonder in her voice.

'Yeah, well, pretty well everyone, in England at any rate, I mean!'

The Countess and Eloise exchanged looks of astonishment.

'No time for that now,' said the Countess, shaking her head. 'Let's get down to the players, or everyone will be wondering where we are – including Georges and his friends!'

'Yes, I need to brief the Emp. It's great that the Count's behind us now.'

'So long as he doesn't blow up too early!' said the Countess.

'Blow up…' muttered Tommy, following Eloise and the Countess out of the room and nodding to the guards outside to accompany them. 'Yeah, that's another thing. I wonder what they're thinking of blowing up.' He was wondering about the gunpowder, of course.

Well anyway, just at that moment, what the Emp and his men were doing was blowing up a most filthy noise, the Royal Cacophonic in full flood, the reedy wail of some pipe thing and a clatter of drums, and then the hunting horn.

'Right, that's it, perfect!' bawled the Emp.

'God! I wouldn't like to hear them when they hadn't been practising,' whispered Tommy to Eloise.

She gave him a curious look. I suppose to her, this is music, thought Tommy. Wait till she hears Rap, and finds out what real music is about, and maybe Beethoven, he added as an afterthought. In a moment, they emerged from the dark hall at the foot of the great staircase into the brilliant sunlight and heat of a July afternoon in southern France.

A canopy, draped with heavy red cloth, had been arranged in front of the château. This would provide shade for the nobles, the whole contraption supported on wooden poles, held upright by guards, who stood gripping the supports and sweltering in the sun.

'Get them some wine,' said Tommy to a footman.

'Sir?' questioned the footman.

'The poor fellows holding the poles. They'll die in this heat!'

'There's more where they come from, sir,' replied the footman.

Tommy recognised the man he had seen kissing Flore in the airing cupboard the night before, and tried to scowl at him, but then couldn't help grinning.

'Just get them some wine, man!' he ordered and walked on to where Eloise was beckoning him to a place beneath the canopy.

The Count and Countess were already seated.

'Wasn't that the footman who came running out of the airing cupboard last night?' she whispered to Tommy and giggled.

But before Tommy could so much as nod, the music set off again, drowning out all thought. Everyone who worked in the château was there, plumped down on the gravel, leaning back against the stone parapets, or sitting on the steps in front of the great door. Many were nodding their heads in time to the Royal Cacophonic.

Mugs of wine were also passing freely about, and a steady stream of people went back and forth through the kitchen door, some already swaying gently. The peasants in the fields had crept as close as they could, ranged along the bank on the other side of the river, leaning on their forks and rakes, some even lying in the long grass, all work abandoned.

A holiday for them, thought Tommy, shifting uneasily in his chair. But I'm sure that I can't relax. He glanced at the Count and Countess. They still looked grim after the reading of the confession, and he could see the Count was on the edge of his chair.

He's a man of action, thought Tommy. It must be as difficult for him as for me, sitting pretending to be interested in this circus thing.

Just then, the music stopped abruptly.

'Ho, ho, ho!' bellowed Pulchinelle, adjusting his mask so that he could take an enormous swig out of his mug. 'Poooh! What muck is this?' he roared, a great jet of red wine spouting out of his mouth, watering the front row of the stalls on the château steps.

Whereupon Joncilond, or Harlequin, bounded out from where he had hidden along the wall of the château, carrying a great spoon-shaped stick, with which he madly slapped the bottoms of anyone in reach – *whack*, *whack* – and not too tenderly either.

'Ha!' cried Joncilond-Harlequin as he reached centre stage. 'We've ruined the vintage, we've done for the wine. You see,' he said, suddenly sly, as Pulchinelle stood looking into his mug, rubbing his enormous stomach, 'you see –' and he beckoned everyone closer, as if to tell a secret for their ears only – 'you see, we lined up all the horses, and put buckets under them all...'

A great groan went up from the crowd.

'What's that, he's saying?' could be heard from the spectators, for Joncilond's brother was there too.

'Ha-ha-haaaa, yes, yeaaas,' continued Harlequin. 'We lined up all the horses, gave them lots of water to drink, and...'

'*Uuuurrr!*' bawled the crowd, for they knew what was coming, many sniffing their mugs suspiciously.

'Collected all the...'

'*Piss!*' roared the crowd.

Harlequin looked surprised. 'How did you know that?' he demanded and everyone started to laugh.

The Countess and Eloise were giggling away and clapping, whilst the Count was also deep in the unfolding drama, slapping his thighs.

God, they're like children! thought Tommy, as he saw how the tension in the Count seem to have dissolved so quickly. How can they be so relaxed?

His nerves were as tight as the belt around the Emp's waist, and he found himself drumming his fingers on his knee. He looked back at the players.

'Anyway, after drinking all that,' began Harlequin, pointing his finger at Pulchinelle, 'drinking all that…'

'*Piss!*' shouted the crowd.

'He needs a doctor,' went on Harlequin.

At that, from the château steps, up sprang Jacques the Tailor, dressed in black robes – an old nun's habit – and bent half double, marched splay-footed onto the scene, with a long quill pen in his hand, pretending to scribble on an imaginary scroll of parchment.

'Live mice, with their eyes not yet opened. Swallow them whole, twice a day!' he announced loudly.

'Oh! Ah! No!' cried Pulchinelle, gripping at his throat.

'Shove a piece of cheese up your…'

'*Bottom!*' roared the crowd.

This is just like panto, thought Tommy, beginning to enjoy it, despite himself.

'Up my…' began Pulchinelle.

'*Bottom!*' roared the crowd again, and Pulchinelle danced about clutching his rear end and fell over, lying on his back and kicking his legs in the air.

'And swallow a rat!' added the doctor scuttling off to take his place among the audience again.

The orchestra blew a great blast and then the wavering sound of a violin made a little melody – something like music, thought Tommy, and Tommy could see Jacques the Tailor, otherwise the doctor, fiddling away on a violin-like thing, but with only three strings. Perhaps one was bust, thought Tommy, remembering that they should have four. Anyway as the tune wound around them, Colombina pranced delicately out from the crowd onto a little carpet, specially laid down by one of the players, did a little twirl and stopped beside the prone figure of Pulchinelle.

'Poor, poor, Pulchinelle, died of dwinking too much wine, I see,' trilled Colombina. 'Oh! Oh! Oh!' she said in sympathy, and bending down, took hold of Pulchinelle's hand.

But she was abruptly pulled to the ground on top of Pulchinelle, who grabbed hold of Colombina and seemed intent on making love to her there and then.

'Oh! Oh! Oh!' shrieked Colombina, on quite a realistic note, as they rolled about on the carpet and the crowd began to clap.

And then there marched on, very pompously, another character, strutting about and taking his stand with his legs apart and his chest puffed out.

'*Le Capitaine*. I am *Le Capitaine*,' he announced in a rich bass voice. 'It is I who win the hearts of all the ladies around here – not you, you brute,' he said, whacking Pulchinelle on his bottom with his walking stick.

'And it's me who whacks bottoms, not you!' sang out Harlequin, zooming past Le Capitaine and connecting with a well-aimed swipe.

'You'll pay for that!' screamed Pulchinelle and Le Capitaine in chorus, with Pulchinelle dragging himself off the ground, pushing Columbina away and shaking his fist in Le Capitaine's face.

Tommy noticed that Pulchinelle's tummy had slipped a fair bit, but no one seemed to care. Out of the corner of his eye, Tommy also noticed Georges and a couple of the Bishop's guards standing at the door of the kitchen. Georges was scowling, whilst the two guards were happily swigging large gulps of wine.

'I'm going to make you pay for this!' yelled Pulchinelle again.

'Pay, pay!' croaked a weaselly old voice, as a figure draped in red, with a large purse hanging down one side, came stumbling onto the scene at a half-run.

'Pan-ta-lon, Pan-ta-lon!' shouted the audience, as Pantalon, the greedy old merchant, tripped and fell flat on his face over the corner of the carpet.

Old rusty nails and pieces of brass came tumbling and clattering out of his purse.

'It's all I've got,' he moaned to the audience. 'The rest I've spent on Colombina!'

And on all fours he beat the ground with a fist and moaned again, scrabbling around trying to collect his wealth together.

Looking about, Pantalon then saw Colombina.

'What are you doing here, you naughty girl?' he said, standing up, turning towards Colombina and chucking her under the chin.

'They're fighting over me! Oooh! Isn't it exciting?' said

Colombina, backing away, ignoring Pantalon and advancing towards the nobles' canopy, jerking her thumb over her shoulder at Le Capitaine and Pulchinelle, who stood gripping each other's shoulders in mock battle.

'Oooh! It's exciting to be fought over!'

And she skipped about, did a little pirouette, got her feet all mixed up and fell on her backside, her mask and wig falling off as she did so, to cheers from the crowd.

'Gerome!' shouted a voice, but Harlequin rushed into the audience and was upon the foolish fellow who had shouted the name and the chase was on – *whack, whack*!

'Mercy!' cried the culprit.

Whack went Joncilond, as they disappeared around the corner of the château, and everyone knew not to say a word about the real identity of the players, even if they did recognise any of them.

Meanwhile the stage had cleared and the orchestra had started up again. Bending forwards in his seat, Tommy saw that Georges had disappeared, probably back into the kitchen, but he hadn't seen for sure where he'd gone. The guards had sat down on the kitchen step.

I hope that Georges isn't starting his own private search, thought Tommy. There's no one inside the château to stop him. Everyone's out here!

In his anxiety, he leant over to the Count and whispered, 'Father, I think that Georges, the Bishop's man…'

'Yes, Thomas,' replied the Count, 'I've got Jacques keeping an eye on those three, on Georges especially, don't you worry!' And Tommy nodded.

Footmen brought wine for the nobles and small almond pastries. Tommy wolfed them down. They were good, slightly crunchy. Excellent, for the larks at lunchtime had far from filled him up. The Royal Cacophonic was going full belt, and this time it was the reedy, almost human-sounding warbling voice which rose and penetrated the air.

Whee, whee, whee, it piped and then the whole orchestra rose to its feet. Forming a line, they began to snake their way through the crowd. Harlequin reappeared and began to spring around, rolling great cartwheels, bouncing in the air as if he were on springs.

At the same time, Pantalon, wearing his greasy old robe and jingling his purse came to the front of the stage in front of the nobles.

'Has anyone seen Colombina?' he shouted out, and then, behind him, onto the stage came a strange four-legged creature, back legs Colombina's, front legs, those of a footman, in black leggings.

'Brighelle, Brig-helle!' shouted the crowd.

They seemed to know the players pretty well, thought Tommy. 'Brighelle' was the name of this creature apparently. The whole thing made no sense to him. Searching his mind shared with the real Thomas, he could vaguely remember something he'd seen a few years before. Pulchinelle was obviously Punch, like in Punch and Judy! Yes of course, and the Harlequin, Joncilond, he'd seen harlequins before, or in pictures. But the whole thing was mixed up between his own mind and the memories of Thomas. Anyway, just at the moment, he was much more interested in Georges and the Bishop's guards, the confession, that horrible confession, and Eloise.

He glanced at her shyly, but his thoughts were interrupted by Pantalon who, wringing his hands in despair, shouted out right in front of him, 'Has anyone seen Colombina?'

The Cacophonic then thankfully trickled to a halt. Harlequin, meanwhile, raced around Pantalon on tiptoe, pointing his finger and mouthing, *What a fool, what a fool*!

At the same moment, the four-legged monster suddenly rose up, and a muffled yell was heard from inside.

'I'm stifled, let me out!'

In fact the heat must have been unbearable for the back legs of Brighelle. For, just as Colombina could be seen fighting her way out, half ripping her costume as she did so, one of the guards holding up the canopy fainted in the heat, or maybe the wine, and the whole thing fell on the nobles' heads.

'Idiots!' yelled the Count, as guards dragged the red cloth clear and disentangled the Countess's rather complicated hair-do.

Pulchinelle stepped forward, and bowing deeply, said, 'My most humble apologies, sire,' receiving a whack on his backside from Harlequin for his troubles.

'You ape!' shouted Pulchinelle, forgetting who he was meant to be for a moment, and Harlequin ran gibbering off on all fours.

At that moment, Jacques came hobbling up, looking worried.

'My good Count, sire,' he began. 'Georges is getting too impatient, sire. He's demanding to speak with you, sire!'

'Right! I wondered how long you could get him to hold out! I'd not forgotten about him and his crucifix,' exclaimed the Count.

'Well, he's hopping up and down, sire,' said Jacques. 'Something about being back to the Bishop with the crucifix tonight, sire, if you see what I mean!'

'Alright, alright, I'll come in and talk to him. What do you advise, Jacques?' asked the Count, as he began to walk towards the kitchen. Turning, he called back, 'Hey, Thomas, you come too! What do you advise?' repeated the Count to Jacques.

'Well, I should say, sire, that they should not be allowed to search alone, without members of the household present. That would not be proper, sire, I am sure that you agree. But a thorough search must also be allowed, so that they do not get suspicious.' He paused.

'And another thing, sire. Remember that you have no reason to think that the crucifix is especially important. I mean, just a very fine piece of work, but nothing else, of course.'

The Count nodded. Jacques was very good at this diplomatic kind of thing. Make sure that they go away satisfied, that they had every opportunity he repeated to himself…

'Ah, Georges! I thought that you would be watching the players,' said the Count, entering the kitchen with Thomas and Jacques at his heels.

'No, sir. The Bishop sent me, sir, on urgent business. He is very concerned about the crucifix, sir. Seems it has a long and important history. Even in Rome, sir, the Holy Father has expressed an interest…'

What sort of yarn has the Bishop been spinning him? said Tommy to himself.

And so the search started. Georges and the two guards went from room to room, from floor to floor, the Count, Thomas and Jacques appearing to do everything that they could to help, but feeling inwardly rather smug, since they all three of them knew exactly where the crucifix was to be found!

'Where could Louis have been able to get to, sire?' asked Georges. 'I mean hardly into the Countess's jewellery chest!'

Tommy blanched slightly at this wild but accurate guess.

'No, I'm not sure myself that I know where the key is for that!' said the Count.

'Hmmm,' said Georges. 'Louis might really have been more able to hide it outside than inside the château, don't you think?'

'Maybe in the stables,' chimed in Jacques, 'or the dairy, perhaps...'

'The wine cellars?' asked Georges.

'Locked,' said Jacques and jangled a large bunch of keys that was tied around his waist.

'Mind if we have a bit of a snoop around outside, Monsieur le Comte?'

'Of course, Georges. I am as interested as you are in finding it. Though I reckon that it's disappeared with Louis! Probably melted down by the robbers in the marsh!' He was getting good at this diplomatic stuff, telling lies, that is.

'We haven't been in here,' said one of the Bishop's soldiers, putting his hand on Tommy's door as they turned to leave.

'Well, you can go in if you like. It's my room, actually,' said Tommy.

Damn and blast it, he added to himself. Louis was holed up under Tommy's bed. If they look under there, there's going to be some explaining to do!

'No, come on,' said Georges. 'We're wasting our time in here! If you'd come running with a great bronze crucifix, covered with bits of gold which you'd just killed for, like this 'ere Louis did, you'd most like stick it somewhere, like a hole in a bridge, where the stones don't fit too well together, or something like that. Out of sight, but somewhere where you could lay your hands on it again. Come on, let's try outside.'

The Count, Tommy and Jacques had all been looking out of the window, not trusting the expression on their faces, pretending to be watching the players, who were still larking around outside, falling over each other, punching, dancing and yelling insults.

'Just a quick glance, perhaps, just to say that we've done it?' asked the soldier.

'Okay, then,' replied Georges, 'just put your head around the door.'

'Hey!' shouted the soldier excitedly, as he pushed the door open, and Tommy and the Count turned their heads, bumping into each other in their haste. 'Hey, look! There's a crucifix, a great big bronze and gold one. That's it...'

'Don't be a fool!' rasped Georges, grabbing the other by the shoulder as he started to go into the room. 'There's more than one crucifix in the house, isn't there? This one's hardly hidden, is it? You nitwit!'

All the while the Count and Tommy were staring speechless at one another. Because it *was* the crucifix! Only Jacques seemed quite relaxed, shaking his head and pulling the door closed, as Georges and his two soldiers made their way down the corridor, down the servants' staircase and out of the kitchen door.

'Jacques, one moment,' ordered the Count, speaking rather sharply. 'Just what is going on, Jacques?' he demanded, lowering his voice.

'The crucifix?' said Jacques, trying to look innocent.

'No, not the crucifix – my best hunting boots, Jacques! What do you think?' said the Count irritably.

'Mmmm, well, sire, I argued to myself, that this Georges is a right pig, but he's not dumb. He can work things out, and he did work out that the crucifix is much more likely to be stuck in some hole outside the château, sire; in a bridge, he said. Could just as well have said a bench, sire.' He lowered his voice to a whisper. 'And I thought to myself, best move it. I got the head, the head of Christ, sire, to stay on pretty firmly and then, I thought, well, if it's in the house, there's always the chance they'll find it! But, y'know, if it's absolutely obvious, then they won't find it, not if it's right in front of their noses, as you saw, sire!'

'Bit of a blooming risk, wasn't it?'

'Everything's risky, sire.'

'Phew! You might have told us,' said Tommy.

'Well, I'm sorry. But I didn't want you to get all worked up. I mean it was only at the last moment that they went in there at all!

Look, hadn't we better be getting outside to see what it is they are playing at?'

Tommy went over to the window, overlooking the front of the château, but Georges was nowhere to be seen.

'Let's have a look the other side,' said Jacques, and they went into Tommy's room.

'Don't be alarmed, it's us,' hissed Jacques, and they heard a muffled grunt from under Tommy's bed.

Pushing open his window, Tommy craned his head out to right and left.

'There they are!' he said, pointing across the bridge, and the Count and Jacques joined him at the window.

Georges and the soldiers were wandering about the geometrical garden, looking under bushes, poking at the ground here and there, slowly approaching the stone bench. They watched as first one soldier and then the other plonked themselves down on the bench.

'I'm half ratted,' said one of the Bishop's guards.

'Me, too! I'd prefer a few more mugs of wine and watching the players to this.'

'Who wouldn't?' said the other, mournfully kicking his heels against the bench. 'This is a waste of bloomin' time!'

'Hey! You two,' cried Georges, looking up from where he was poking into some bushes with his sword, 'get your butts in gear, will you? What about that bench that you're…'

Georges sprang upright.

'Look!' he shouted. 'There, where you've been kicking at it. Here,' he said, rushing up.

The soldiers looked down. Where one of them had idly kicked, the block of stone had moved, just a bit, but it was clearly loose! The Count, Tommy and Jacques watched breathlessly from the window as they tried to make out what was going on down there at the bench.

'I think they've stumbled on the hiding place. Damn me!' said the Count. 'Quick, let's get down there!'

'I'm not sure,' piped up Jacques, 'that we should show too much interest, y'know!'

'Yeah, that's true,' said Tommy, 'but perhaps I could go and see what they're doing. Inquisitive boy stuff, you know!'

The others nodded, and Tommy was quickly down beside Georges and the soldiers.

'Found something interesting, then?'

'Yes, my Lord!' exclaimed Georges. 'Looks like this stone's been moved quite recently.'

Georges had his dagger out and was prising the stone out of the bench. It was the letter *e* of *ego* in the inscription, Tommy noticed. After a moment of working the dagger back and forth, the stone swung out smoothly.

'There's a large hole here,' said Georges. 'The perfect hiding place!' He put his hand in and scrabbled about inside. 'Nothing! Damn me, nothing!' But he went on feeling about inside, all the same. 'Hey! What's this?' And he drew out a tiny fragment of metal, that glinted in the sunshine. 'Gold!' exclaimed Georges. 'Hmmm,' he said, and waggled his head.

'Interesting,' said Tommy, his self-control in overdrive.

'I reckon it could be that the crucifix was hidden here, y'know,' Georges was saying to the two soldiers, who were crouched down beside him, inspecting the little piece of gold. 'But that Louis, he came back, probably in the night, and made off with it!'

Then, turning to Tommy, he asked, 'That crucifix in your room, my Lord,' he began, and Tommy's heart leapt to his mouth, 'that one. Is it about the same size as the one we're looking for?'

'Ooh! Now you've got me,' replied Tommy, and he tried to look as though he was thinking it out. 'No! I should say the one you're looking for is probably quite a fair bit bigger, I think.'

'I'd like to show the Count this, though!' said Georges, holding up the tiny piece of gold.

'Yeah!' said Tommy. 'I think he might be pretty interested in that, actually.'

But Georges only grunted in reply. Does he know he's being taken for a ride? wondered Tommy. We'll have to watch our step!

'See if you can find anything else in there,' Georges ordered his two soldiers, and he left them fumbling around inside the bench.

'Yes,' murmured the Count, still trying to recover from the close escape, standing with Jacques beside Georges a few moments later. 'Yes, interesting. It could certainly have been the crucifix. But, y'know, gold stays bright for a long time. Could be anything, really!'

Georges looked doubtful. I mean, he thought to himself, was this family in the habit of hiding things made of gold in the garden inside the stone bench? P'raps they were. The nobles were a funny lot. He began to reckon things up. He could search longer, around the château, or he could go back to the Bishop with at least the information that the crucifix had most likely been hidden there.

'So what?' the Bishop would say.

'Well, we're a bit closer,' he would reply…

Georges was in the habit of rehearsing conversations with the Bishop. Not that it usually worked out too well. The Bishop always had a completely different way of looking at everything. This would probably be no exception. And he sighed.

'Anyone else know about the stone bench compartment?' he asked casually.

'Anyone else than who?' chipped in Jacques, and Georges gave him a thunderous look.

He'd wanted the Count to admit that he knew about it. Too late.

'Well, I mean, I suppose that…' began Georges.

The Count just shook his head in a way that could mean anything, and kicking at the gravel in the path, began to amble back towards the great door.

The performance had finished some time before. There were just a few people left in front of the château, in little groups. They were pretty drunk and, nodding and hiccuping, were trying to look respectful as the Count passed them, with Georges trailing after him.

'I think,' said the Count, turning towards Georges as he was about to enter the château, 'that you should go back and report to the Bishop what you have found. We'll see him on Sunday at mass. If anything new turns up…'

He let the sentence tail off, dismissing Georges with a sharp movement of his hand. Georges, used to the arrogant ways of the nobles, bowed, and called for his men.

His later conversation with the Bishop, if conversation it could be called, went rather worse than he had imagined that it might.

'You idiot!' de Montfort bawled, when later that night Georges reported back and told his story, showing him the tiny fragment of gold. 'You stopped looking when you had that clue in your hands. They were leading you by the nose!' Here, the Bishop threw up his hands and stamped about the room.

'You think, sire, that they know where the crucifix is, then?'

'Do you think that they know where their own backsides are?' sneered his master. 'Of course they do!' And then he paused for a moment, putting his hand to his chin.

'You didn't see any other crucifixes on your guided tour of the Château de Romolue, did you, by any chance?' asked the Bishop with a sly look on his face, holding up his index finger before Georges' eyes.

'Er, well, what makes you ask that, sire?'

'Answer my question!' shouted de Montfort. 'Did you or not?'

'Well, sire, we did just for a moment, sire, in Thomas de Romolue's room, there was a large bronze and gold crucifix...'

'*What!*' roared the Bishop.

'Yes, sire, but it was sitting right there for anyone to see as soon as you opened the door. It can't have been...' Then a sort of shiver went through him, and he repeated rather faintly, 'It can't have been...' as he saw Drogo's reward of five gold coins slip through his fingers.

Duped! He'd been duped! He began to go very red in the face.

'It's that Jacques! The Count's too dumb for this!' muttered the Bishop to himself, ignoring Georges, who was now trembling with rage.

'Shall I ride back, sire?' asked Georges through clenched teeth. 'I'll burn that place down if necessary!' he shouted suddenly, and thumped the table, spilling ink over a document on which the Bishop had been working before Georges arrived.

The Bishop looked from Georges to the document and back again.

'Get out, you clumsy oaf!' he said. 'Get out!' his voice rising.

'Don't go near that place, I tell you. It would be war. We are not prepared for that... yet! Go! Tomorrow, or Sunday, we shall see!'

With Georges out of the room, the Bishop sat down once more and leant forward at his desk, fiddling with the edge of the ink-covered document.

'And Clarice? What of Clarice de Toulouse and Thomas de Romolue?' he muttered and sat pondering the problem of their betrothal for a few quiet moments.

Just then, he was interrupted by a timid tap at the door.

'Enter,' commanded the Bishop and looking up, exploded, 'You again!'

Georges flinched at the half open door. 'Sire,' he began, hesitantly. 'Sire, I should tell you that both Thomas de Romolue and Eloise de Narbonne were at the Château de Romolue... both, er, my Lord.'

The Bishop only grunted in reply, scowled and with a wave of his hand, dismissed the man. Alone again, he drummed his fingers on the surface of his desk.

'Hmmm... Thomas and Clarice,' he muttered once more. 'That will require a gentle touch, yes... gentle,' he added and he picked up the ruined document and crunched it into a ball in his hand.

Twenty-three: Off to Toulouse

aturday broke to a sullen sky. The château seemed to crouch beneath the hot sun. Tommy felt an uneasy stillness in the house, after the noise and friendly excitement of the day before, the frenzy and fun of the show, the Royal Cacophonic and the people of Town. Today, guards were posted around the grounds, at every place where an entry could be made, in case the Bishop were to return in force after the crucifix. For, at the château, they knew that while Georges had gone away empty-handed, the Bishop would not be fooled. We seem under siege, thought Tommy. Now and then a shout could be heard from the fields where peasants were bent over their work. But that was all that broke through the haze of the day. No Bishop appeared at the head of any armed men to reclaim the crucifix.

The day wore on, the close heat sweating its way through the heavy, sticky clothes which Tommy seemed forced by custom to wear. The only movement was the occasional rustle of the trees around the château. Sometimes a faint rumble of thunder sounded in the distance. Servants, footmen and all the staff padded quietly along the corridors, voices scarcely raised above a murmur. It's as if the weight of Drogo's crimes bears heavily down on us all, Tommy mused – or more likely everyone is feeling the effects of yesterday's mighty booze-up, especially the people of Town, of whom Tommy had seen nothing all day. They had wisely hidden themselves away, Tommy found later, among the ruins of the old château, with as much bread and as many boiled eggs, onions and jugs of wine as they could beg from the kitchen.

Tommy had barely seen Eloise, either. She was under the watchful eye of the Countess, who never let her out of her sight for a moment. Does she think I am going to run off with Eloise, or what? wondered Tommy, standing in the corridor outside his room, looking out at the dark green shapes of the trim bushes stretching before the château.

'What I'd really like to do,' he whispered to himself, 'is to walk with Eloise down there, just for a bit.' But it seemed that Eloise was out of bounds to him today. He was sure that the Countess was plotting to steal her away to a nunnery, to hide her away from him, and he gave a grim little smile. 'She'll have to think twice,' he muttered to himself.

The time passed slowly, the tension gathered, like the dark thunderclouds on the horizon, and electricity was in the air, as the hour of mass on Sunday in Toulouse Cathedral came nearer. Just tomorrow! thought Tommy as Sunday mass loomed before him. He had attended many – as Thomas – but this was going to be different, pretty different. God! he added to himself, has it really been only a week since those Greek letters crawled in front of me like demented beetles across the page – 'In the time of the Emperor Augustus...' – as I stood at the lectern in the church at Romolue last Sunday? Since I came to Ellie-la-Forêt in the 21st century? Since I met Eloise? Since I read Drogo's confession? Only a week, or a year, or a minute, perhaps. Gosh, I'd like to flop in front of a TV, he suddenly thought. Not much hope of that!

There were plans to be made, though the shadows were already lengthening before Tommy, Eloise and the Count and the Countess met once more.

'At what time will the Emp and his men be leaving for Toulouse, Father?' asked Tommy; for the Count now knew who these men were – what he had suspected all along, of course.

'Why? D'you have to talk with them? You have enough to think about,' replied the Count, who disapproved of his son mixing with outlaws.

They were all sitting again in the little padded room of the Countess's. This time, Jacques was with them too.

'True,' replied Tommy, 'but I need to settle one or two, er, details with him and his men.'

Eloise nodded.

'Well, if it is necessary. We seem to be in your hands! The Emp said about the hour of sunrise. They will come to Toulouse in their costumes. No one should recognise them, I hope!'

'You are bringing many of your guards, are you not, Father? You can protect them.'

'How should I look before Robert de Toulouse, eh? "Defender of the thieves and murderers." Eh? Don't expect too much when it comes to the people of the marsh, Thomas. They are outcasts. The Church has excommunicated them. It is no sin to kill them! You know that.'

Tommy frowned and sighed.

Yes, he knew it. But he did not feel it. He had knowledge of this time, but the feelings of his own time. How would Eloise manage to live in the twenty-first century with neither one or the other? he wondered. How were they to get back, anyway? Make a break for that magical slope, down towards the marsh? Maybe.

'I need to have a bit of a talk with the people of the marsh. Now, I mean,' Tommy announced. 'There won't be time tomorrow. After that, it's bed,' he said, rising and yawning.

The Countess nodded her head. 'Get a good night's sleep,' she whispered. 'You go now, too, Eloise. I'll come with you,' she added, glancing at Tommy.

Negotiations with the Emp and his men turned out not to take very long. They were pretty well drunk, and Joncilond at least seemed to think that the play was still on, rushing about with his bum-slapper. The Emp seemed a bit subdued.

'Gathering me forces, boy, gathering me forces,' he muttered, taking a half-hearted swipe at Joncilond, as he careered past.

Tommy fell asleep in about two minutes and seemed to wake the next minute. Sunday! Tommy, so frightened of oversleeping, had set his mobile to wake him an hour before dawn, risking that the eerie peeping might be heard by his father next door to him.

The château was very much alive when Tommy appeared downstairs. Serving girls were running everywhere, a dozen or more guards in the kitchen, polishing their boots, shining their belts, oiling their moustaches, flirting with the maids.

'Quick,' said the Countess, as she met Tommy by the foot of the great staircase. 'Get into your best things. Your cathedral clothes. Flore!' she called. 'We're off in less than half an hour!'

Oh, God! Flore! said Tommy to himself. 'I'll be in your room soon, Mother. Wait for me there,' he whispered to the Countess, and she nodded.

'Are you sure that you can go through with this?' she said urgently to him.

'Nothing can stop it now,' said Tommy, taking her hands in his and forcing out a smile.

They both turned to see the Count watching them from the landing.

Nodding his head, he said, 'There's a Romolue for you! Action, action and no regrets. Keep the world in the order the Almighty has ordained! Each in his place,' he said loudly, 'each in his place!'

Tommy turned to see the Countess looking at her husband in admiration. At that moment, Flore came running towards them, tears in her eyes. She is really very pretty, thought Tommy. Damn! he exclaimed to himself.

'Jean, the footman, he – he…' she sobbed.

'No time for that nonsense,' said the Countess severely. 'Get Monsieur Thomas here dressed in cathedral clothes, Flore, and be quick about it!'

Flore nodded silently and they rushed off up the grand staircase, Flore curtseying to the Count as he came down the stairs past them, and Tommy giving him a brave grin. As they turned the corner, there was Eloise, standing on the staircase, with her head turned slightly, lost in thought. Tommy stopped suddenly, feeling himself blushing, as Flore ran on up, dropping another tiny curtsey as she went past Eloise.

'You look so… lovely!' exclaimed Tommy to Eloise, as Flore disappeared ahead of him, turning into the corridor leading to his room.

'And you look a right mess! You need to change,' replied Eloise. 'How's the Emp?' she added in a whisper.

'All ready to go. In fact, they'll be on the road by now!'

'Monsieur Thomas!' Flore called from the corridor above. 'Monsieur Thomas!'

Tommy took Eloise's hand just for a moment, and as he moved past her, brushed her cheek with a kiss.

'Naughty boy.' She smiled and ruffled his hair.

'Monsieur Thomas!' Louder this time.

Letting his fingers slowly untwine from Eloise's, Tommy moved up the staircase, and then darted away around the corner, to be greeted by the pretty little face of Flore, grinning through her tears. Tommy wondered briefly what Jean, the footman, had in fact been up to.

Just a few minutes later, Tommy was into his cathedral clothes, as the Countess called them, and in fact as he knew them as well, the stiff uncomfortable collar rubbing his neck, the narrow buckled shoes, too tight, and the silly frilly pants. Something for Gerome! If there had been any of Flore's wandering fingers, he'd had no time to notice, with the vision of Eloise before him.

And in fact he still didn't notice Flore standing in front of him, frowning and pouting. Suddenly she flung her arms around his neck and gave him a kiss, smack on the mouth. Then she stepped back, putting her hand to her lips, gave a him little grin and ran off, without a word.

'Phew!' said Tommy to himself, shaking his head. 'Bloomin' 'eck!' Then: Oh, blast! The mobile! he suddenly thought.

'Damn and damn! Flore's run off with it in my dirty trousers. The mobile's in the pocket. Oh, damn and damn and dammit!' And he rushed out into the corridor.

Where had she gone? Down the servants' staircase, or up to the top floor, perhaps? What did they do with dirty clothes? he asked himself as he ran along the corridor. He searched his memory. Not a trace of an idea about what happened to dirty clothes! Just as he reached the back staircase, Jacques came tap, tap, tapping up, as fast as he was able, obviously in a hurry too.

'Monsieur Thomas!' he said, and pressed the mobile into his hand. 'Don't let Flore distract you like that!' he added, with a wink.

'She didn't, I mean… Oh, but thanks, you're great! How did you get it back so quick?'

'No time for explanations,' Jacques cut in. 'Get along to the Countess's room. She's waiting for you. Where are you going to hide the parchment? And where's the crucifix? Still in your room? I'll go and fetch it,' he said, without waiting for an answer. 'Move it, I think. They're going to be back.'

'Where are you…?'

'Best you don't know!' answered Jacques, and motioned him off to the Countess, who had appeared at her half-opened door and was anxiously peering down the corridor towards them.

'Something wrong?' she demanded. 'And why are you clutching that devil's toy?' she added.

'Oh, gosh!' said Tommy, for he was still holding the mobile tightly in his hand. He slipped it deep in his pocket.

'Shut the door,' ordered the Countess. She had the keys to the chest ready in her hand. 'Here,' she said, a moment later. 'Take the confession!' She thrust it towards him and muttered, 'God! I hope that this is the right thing to do!'

Tommy took hold of her arm, with the parchment in his other hand, looked her full in the face and whispered, 'Can we let that madman kill Eloise? Can we?' His mouth tightened and his anger was rising.

'No! No! I know that you're right. Yet if there was a less dangerous way… But we'll do it! We must,' said the Countess. 'But afterwards, you promise, my Thomas, my Thomas, he must come back to me!' And tears came to her eyes.

'Yes!' said Tommy, 'he will. We'll get him back, I promise, he will be back here soon!'

They stood for a moment, Tommy with one hand still on the Countess's arm, and in his other, Drogo's confession. The Countess gave him the faintest of smiles.

'You know, the Count, he's going to be disappointed that you're not the real Thomas. In a way, he will be!' Her voice fell to a whisper.

Tommy shook his head, though he had the feeling that the Countess might be right, or at least partly right.

'Look! Where am I going to put the parchment?'

'In your sleeve?'

'No! It might fall out. I can't go around holding it all the time. Look I'll shove it down my trousers, like I did once before!'

The Countess smiled. 'Yes, why not! I don't suppose anyone will be looking down there, will they? After all, Flore's not coming with us…'

'Oh, for heaven's sake!' said Tommy, and dashed out of the room.

The carriage lurched along. Tommy knew that it was going to be more than two hours, cramped up in this ghastly little rattling box. But at least he had Eloise pressed up against him on one side. He'd managed that, grabbing her hand as they got in, with Maddy – Madeleine, his little sister – pulling a face as she squeezed in beside the Countess and the Count. Jasper, his young brother, trying to pick his nose without being noticed, was huddled on the other side of Eloise. He hadn't seen a thing of either Maddy or Jassy almost all the week. But he often didn't see them much, he recalled.

Jassy! Yes, that was the pet name for Jasper. Jassy, Jasper, Jasper, Jasper… Tommy closed his eyes and images swam into his mind of the Emp's palace, the hot sunlit streets of Town, squirrel stew, Eloise as a nun, of Joncilond.

'Joncilond!' said Tommy, and shook his head, coming half awake. 'Can Joncilond be kept under control today?' he muttered to himself.

The carriage gave a sudden lurch over a bad patch of road, and opening his eyes, Tommy sent Eloise a tiny smile. She stirred against him and, turning her head just a fraction, she very faintly breathed, her eyes closed, 'Thomas?' As she spoke the corner of her mouth wrinkled and a slight blush came to her cheeks.

Tommy glanced over at his adopted parents and at Maddy. They seemed sound asleep, his father's eyelids flickering slightly and his mother's head resting on the Count's shoulder. And so he dared, very slowly and carefully, to edge his hand over Eloise's and gently rub his thumb over her fingers. A little hum of pleasure escaped from Eloise and she settled more deeply into her seat. Tommy could feel her warmth as she moved beside him. Just for an instant she snuggled her nose against his neck and then let her head rest against his shoulder. Tommy looked up to make sure that the Count and Countess had noticed nothing, but they remained far away, rolling as the carriage rolled.

How can they be so relaxed? thought Tommy, as he began to run over in his mind the events of the coming hours. He frowned, and Eloise, feeling the tension in him, crooked her forefinger over his.

Yeah! We'll need to keep our fingers crossed! thought Tommy, closing his eyes once more and trying to let his thoughts disperse. He could feel the comforting pressure of his mobile deep in his trouser pocket.

Gosh! Wait till I tell Harry some of this! Tommy mused, and allowing his thoughts to stray still further, he very faintly whispered, 'So they've won the football. I wish I'd been there to see it. I wonder if Harry scored…?'

Sunlight came streaming into the carriage as the Count leant forward and let up the blind. Tommy came suddenly awake, but feeling the weight of Eloise's head on his shoulder, stiffened and remained as still as he could.

'Well,' said the Count loudly, 'we're almost there!'

This was the signal for everyone to wake up, stretch, rub their eyes, yawn and feel extremely cramped and wriggle in their seats – especially Jasper.

'*Pipi*, Mummy! I must pipi!' said Jasper.

Me too, thought Tommy, adding to himself, I'm glad that Jasper said it first!

The Count rapped on the carriage door and the carriage slowly drew to a halt.

The guards, dressed in the blue and gold of Romolue, seated high on their horses, must have had a fine view of the House of Romolue relieving itself, thought Tommy, as they climbed back into the carriage. Wisely, he kept the thought to himself; it was something his real Dad might enjoy, but not the Count, no, not the Count.

Under way again, and as the carriage turned to avoid a large hole in the road, Tommy caught a glimpse of the massive tower of the cathedral of Toulouse.

Close! They were close! How the great building dominated the city, impressing on one and all the power and wealth of the Church of Rome. *I must confront this today, head-on*, thought Tommy, clenching his fists at the thought of Drogo sheltered in the Bishop's palace – or probably huddled in the Bishop's coach on the way to the cathedral by now.

Eloise and the Countess sat stiffly upright, as they approached the main square in front of the cathedral. The Count was frowning to himself. Tommy could feel the tension rising around him. Maddy and Jassy felt it too, shifting uneasily in their seats.

'Mummy…' began Jassy.

'Ssssh!' said the Countess, and the Count gave his young son a smile, intended to reassure, but a smile so tight that Tommy felt that the carriage might burst with it, as the wooden wheels, bound with iron, ground over the rough cobbles.

The Count put his hand for an instant to his sword, which stood beside him against the seat. The carriage halted, still some way from the cathedral.

'Guards!' called the Count. 'Dismount and keep close around us!'

Then he stepped from the carriage, nodding to his family to follow, buckling on his sword as he did so.

Tommy paused an instant to adjust the manuscript of Drogo's confession inside his tights. The damned thing kept sliding down! Then he hurried out after the rest of his adopted noble family.

Twenty-four: A Fruitful Outcome

here was a great crowd outside the cathedral, standing in the shadow of the west tower. People were strangely hushed, with only a quiet murmur of conversation rising and falling. Tommy could see the carriages of Robert de Toulouse and of Bishop Henri, each surrounded by their guards, the red and white diamonds of de Montfort and the gold crosses and red coats of Toulouse.

Stalls were set up close to the cathedral, and several massive piles of fruit and vegetables stood by the west door: oranges, pears, peaches, plums, onions, cauliflowers. The voice of a small, very fat man in a leather apron rang out over the murmur of the crowd, calling the prices, praising the quality. But there were few buyers. All eyes seemed fixed on the troops of guards, red, white, blue and gold, converging towards the west door of the cathedral. The crowd drew back to make way.

Tommy, surrounded by the guards of Romolue, was looking urgently around for the people of the marsh. At last he spied them, off to one corner, half hidden by a great stone buttress, and got up in their costumes, in their disguise. For a moment, he caught a glimpse of Joncilond capering about, swinging his slapstick, but then Tommy passed out of view into the cathedral, behind the red and white of de Montfort and followed by the red coats and gold crosses of Toulouse. He gave Eloise a brief, tight smile. No words were exchanged between the noble families, and silence reigned among the dark columns of the cathedral. The heavy slow footfall of the armed men echoed within the grey stone walls, brilliant patches of coloured light shining here and there on the worn stones of the aisle, as the sun glittered through the stained glass, eerily lighting the faces of the nobles and their guards as they passed.

In front of him, Tommy could see the tall form of the Bishop, wearing his ceremonial robes, gold threads and jewels flashing in the rays of sunlight, his long gown dragging and swishing on the ground behind him. The drab form of Drogo, shoulders stooped, in a black, hooded gown, walked by his side. Each step that Tommy took seemed to him to sound like a great bell, tolling him to the ordeal ahead. And indeed, the deepest bell in the tower began to ring at that moment. At the sound of the bell, the procession halted and the Bishop turned, raising his right hand in blessing.

'*In nomine Patris, et Filii, et Spiritus Sancti...*' he began to intone, the familiar words ringing around the church.

As he ended, there followed a moment of stillness, a tense moment of quiet, but then the bell began to toll once more.

'You may take your accustomed places,' announced Bishop Henri and, still in silence, the noble families entered the pews reserved for them.

Tommy took his place to the right of the central aisle, between the Count and Countess, close to the foot of the pulpit. Louis, now Tommy's personal guard, stood close by, ready for action, as indeed were all the guards of Romolue. Eloise sat to the Countess's right, and beyond her were Maddy and Jassy, hating every minute that they were there.

The common people then began to stream into the cathedral, beginning whispered conversations as they took their places, mostly standing, but some squatting on the flagstones. The noise grew steadily as the cathedral filled.

On the left side of the aisle, Tommy could see Robert de Toulouse and his family.

Which was Clarice? he wondered. What does she look like, this girl that Drogo wants to marry me off to? He leant a little forward and cast a swift glance across the aisle. A tall pale girl with blonde hair sat beside her mother... Isabelle, he seemed to remember her name, yes, Isabelle was the mother's name. He caught a quick glimpse of Clarice's profile, if Clarice it was. A flash of blue and red light through the stained glass lit up a sharp little nose, but that was all that Tommy could make out in the gloom of the cathedral.

The guards were not admitted far forward in the church, and each family was allowed as a symbol of their power only a single soldier. For the House of Romolue, there was Louis; for Toulouse, a young man, holding a long lance; for de Montfort, Georges, the commander of the Bishop's guards, whom Tommy knew only too well. Tommy looked at the ground, not wishing to catch Georges' glance. The mass of guards was stationed at the back by the west door and spilling along the side aisles, separated from their masters by the great crowd which now filled the cathedral.

Out of the corner of his eye, Tommy could see the people of the marsh passing along the aisle to his right side, keeping well in the shadows. Tommy nodded to himself and gave the Countess a quick look. There was a grim smile on her face, and she too gave a small nod and briefly pressed Tommy's hand, Eloise sitting motionless beside her.

The Emp as Pulchinelle, Joncilond as the harlequin, Gerome as Colombina, and all the rest, they were all there, moving carefully behind the pulpit, almost out of sight, but ready to act when the time came – and that time was close approaching. Tommy could feel Drogo's manuscript pressing against his leg. But where was Drogo? The Bishop stood up and began to approach the altar.

Where is Drogo? repeated Tommy to himself, and as if reading his mind, the Countess motioned with her elbow, to the left. Drogo had moved from the Bishop's side and had taken his place in the pew of Toulouse, as if to underline their alliance: Toulouse and de Montfort against Romolue. Following Tommy's look, the Count scowled to see Drogo so close; but the closer the better, thought Tommy.

The cathedral was now brimful of people. The last note of the bell tolled and rang in the air. Time held its breath, the Bishop, with his back to the congregation, raised his hands to the altar – and now, the moment had come!

Tommy rose to his feet. Everyone tensed at this strange interruption, and a ripple of excitement passed through the congregation. The Bishop, sensing this, turned to see who had dared to interrupt the mass.

Without losing a moment, Tommy strode to the foot of the steps leading to the pulpit, and pulling open the little pulpit gate so violently that it slammed against the column that held it, ran up the steps, taking his place before the great eagle lectern where only the Bishop might ever stand.

'What is this outrage?' shouted the Bishop, and at the same moment, forgetting his injuries, Drogo jumped to his feet.

'*You!*' yelled Drogo, spit flying out of his mouth in his fury. '*You…*' he said, pointing his long bony finger at Tommy, and seeming to choke on his words.

'Guards!' shouted the Bishop, as both Robert de Toulouse and the Count de Romolue also rose from their seats.

As they did so, Louis took up his position at the gate to the pulpit, sword drawn, and the people of the marsh came running from the shadows, forming a defensive ring around the pulpit.

Tommy meanwhile was fighting to extract Drogo's confession from his tights. He'd felt it slip down his leg as he had raced up the pulpit steps. A murmuring, rising rapidly to shouts and screams, rose from the congregation. Guards were trying to push their way through, at the Bishop's command, but the side aisles were blocked, choked with people pressed up against the walls.

Tommy had his arm right down his tights by this time, and he caught Eloise's horrified look, as several young men near the front began to hoot and point at him. But at last he had the manuscript in his hand. Pulling it free, he waved it in the air.

'You recognise this?' he shouted at the top of his voice. 'Drogo, you see this!' he cried, letting the parchment roll out before him.

Looking up with wild eyes, Drogo gave a yell of horror, slamming his fists against his forehead.

'*No!*' he roared.

'Seize Thomas de Romolue!' shouted the Bishop.

'See! Father Drogo is his own accuser!' yelled the Count de Romolue, pointing at Drogo.

'Guards!' shouted the Bishop again, but to no avail.

Their way was blocked, and the people would not let them pass. What was more, the pulpit was guarded by strange creatures, whose masks and disguises looked frightening in the shadowy light of the church, as the men of the marsh paced menacingly back and forth, holding swords and axes in their hands.

'You, I accuse you!' shouted Tommy at the top of his voice, pointing at Drogo, who stood there like a statue, staring at the parchment falling from the lectern.

The Bishop strode to Drogo's side, looking up at Tommy.

'The confession,' he muttered under his breath as he saw the parchment.

In that brief moment of indecision, the Count de Romolue put up his hands and yelled, 'Silence! Let us see what Thomas de Romolue has to tell us!'

'Sacrilege in my cathedral!' shouted the Bishop, as the congregation fell quiet.

Then the large hand of the Emp closed over de Montfort's mouth, as Pulchinelle, Jacques and François bodily removed him, thrusting him under the pulpit with a gag in his mouth, where Joncilond trussed him up with a coil of rope.

This act was greeted with a great shout of approval and laughter from the congregation. Many families had suffered harshly at the hands of Bishop Henri de Montfort. They were delighted to see justice done to him at last. The noble families were shocked, but powerless to act.

Tommy leant forward over the lectern and looked down at the great sea of faces below him. The laughter and cheers of the crowd subsided as they waited expectantly.

'You! I accuse you!' shouted Tommy again, and Drogo seemed to sway under the impact of the words, grasping the edge of the pew beside him, but remaining on his feet, and staring up at his young accuser.

'Listen,' said Tommy quietly, and a hush fell upon the church, 'listen, and you will learn the true character of the family of de Montfort! Listen!' he said, almost in a whisper.

Taking the parchment in his hand, Tommy began to read:

'Written the 15th August, in the year 1585, at the command of my brother, Henri de Montfort...' At this, some muffled moaning noises could be heard from under the pulpit, silenced by a sharp kick in the ribs by Joncilond. 'Secretary to the Cardinal of Ferrara, Piero Vincenzo di Colonna,' continued Tommy, 'at the Palace of the Vatican... Signed, Drogo de Montfort. This is a copy of a document in the hands of my brother. He keeps his copy to force me to his will through blackmail…'

Tommy paused for a moment, surveying the great crowd before him, the shocked faces of the House of Toulouse, the great cathedral quiet and expectant, Drogo standing, still staring up at Tommy as if he had lost his reason.

As the story began to unfold, there were at first titters at Drogo's self-portrait of himself as a scarecrow, with his long, thin, none-too-straight nose, and then gasps and cries from the congregation as the horror of the story began to be exposed, of how the detested priest became infatuated with the beautiful Eleonora. The gasps turned to shouts for Drogo's blood as Tommy read of how Drogo arranged the murder of the messengers carrying the ransom for Eleonora's husband, Richard. Then, as the tension grew, with Drogo's vision of Eleonora appearing in this very cathedral, standing before him in this very aisle and asking, 'Would you kill me if I cannot love you?' and Drogo still standing clutching the side of the pew, still staring up at Tommy, the silence in the church was absolute.

Tommy paused, and then, his voice strained with emotion, he read on:

'I learned that Eleonora would be visiting the cathedral of Toulouse on the next Sunday, to pray for her husband, Richard… I became consumed by a great rage and hatred for this young woman, who had destroyed my life. I entered the cathedral later that Sunday evening. I took from a side chapel the great bronze crucifix which now stands in the chapel at the Château de Romolue, and, creeping stealthily up behind Eleonora, creeping out from behind a column, I slammed the crucifix down upon her head and killed her.'

At this, there came a great cry from Drogo. 'It was here, here, it was just here!' he shouted, pointing at the ground beside him, and falling to his knees, beat the flagstones with his fists.

'Kill him! Kill the monster! Don't let him escape justice!' roared the crowd, and it began to surge up around him.

But by this time several of the de Montfort guards had managed to push their way down the central aisle.

Grabbing hold of Drogo, they dragged him, half-conscious, towards the west door. The crowd parted, crushed against the columns and walls of the cathedral to avoid the drawn blades of the guards, as more of the de Montfort soldiers came to Drogo's rescue. Meanwhile, Bishop Henri was freed by Georges, as the men of the marsh made off as fast as they could.

'Stop them!' yelled the Bishop, as he pulled the filthy gag from his mouth.

He had recognised the Emp and his followers, of course. The men of the marsh were almost at the west door, the crowd scattering out of their way as best they could. But de Montfort guards were close at their heels. They came out running, followed by the guards with weapons flailing.

Hurtling past the fruit stall, the Emp yelled, 'Now!'

Then there was a mighty explosion and oranges, apples, cauliflowers, onions, peaches, plums went flying high into the air in a cloud of acrid smoke.

Fruit and vegetables rained down upon the guards and upon Drogo, who was being carried towards the Bishop's carriage. As they were about to bundle him into it, with fruit still falling about their heads, the air was shattered by a second explosion, and the Bishop's carriage disintegrated before them, the four horses bolting and dragging the wreckage after them. In the confusion that followed, the guards stood dazed and immobile, and the Emp and his followers escaped into the narrow back streets of Toulouse.

'Went up something great, eh, that pile of fruit!' said the gunpowder man, chuckling to himself, as they paused a moment to catch their breath, well beyond pursuit.

'Yeah!' he added. 'Biggest bloomin' fruit salad this side of Paris, I reckon! And the coach. I'd love to see the Bishop's face…!'

'Yeah! And did you see that fat little fella, the fruit seller, screaming blue murder?' said the Emp. 'Let's get this bloomin' mask off,' he added, tugging the great crescent shape away from his face. 'Did you see him? Ha! That's the little bastard who ratted on me all those years ago. Paid in gold, he was,' the Emp added grimly, 'paid in gold to get me strung up. Nearly got me, too, but for these good men!' He gestured towards his four courtiers, and the Emp put his hand to his throat as if he could still feel the rope around his neck.

'*Bang!*' shouted Joncilond, 'Bang, bang, bang!' And he took great swipes with the slapstick.

'Let's go,' said the Emp, and they were rapidly beyond the last houses of Toulouse, melting into the thick woods nearby, beyond the reach of the nobles and the Church, soon safe in the quaking marsh and behind the walls of Town.

In the cathedral, they had left an uproar behind them. The two massive explosions, following so fast upon the recital from the pulpit of the crimes of Drogo and his accomplice, Bishop Henri, left people staring about them in blank amazement. Then some rushed outside in search of Drogo, to a mass of pulped fruit, a pall of smoke, and four maddened horses careering around the square, pulling the Bishop's shattered coach clattering behind them. Others remained in the cathedral, advancing with shouts of hatred upon the Bishop, who retreated with his back to the pulpit, with only Georges beside him. Eloise, white in the face, gripped the Countess's hand, both standing, looking towards the west door where Drogo had been dragged out.

Tommy still stood at the lectern, grasping Drogo's confession in both hands. Robert de Toulouse and the Count de Romolue both moved towards the Bishop, and Georges drew his sword and placed himself before his master. Guards of Romolue and Toulouse pressed around them.

'Drogo!' shouted Tommy, from the pulpit, 'Get Drogo!' He then came clattering down the steps of the pulpit.

The guards of Romolue turned and followed him as, grabbing Eloise's hand, he ran down the aisle, stuffing the confession down his tights as he went. Coming out of the cathedral they could make out a group of de Montfort guards, just fifty paces in front of them.

'Drogo! There he is!' shouted Tommy, and they could see the slumped crow-black form of Drogo being thrust onto a horse.

Guards of Romolue came rushing out behind Tommy and Eloise. Immediately, bowmen of de Montfort knelt in a circle around Drogo's horse. Bows drawn, arrows ready to fly, the crowd pushing, shoving and scattering in all directions to avoid the crossfire. At that moment, the Count de Romolue emerged from the west door.

'Hold!' he shouted. 'Hold your fire! Bows down, men!' for some of his guards had already fitted arrows to their weapons.

At the Count's command, both sides lowered their bows; yet both were ready to shoot at a second's notice, and Tommy and Eloise stood directly in the line of fire. But Tommy and Eloise had eyes only for Drogo.

'We take commands only from the Bishop!' shouted a de Montfort guard.

'Then fetch the Bishop,' called the Count de Romolue, as both sides eyed each other aggressively.

Drogo now sat upright on his horse, his head covered by his black hood, his face turned away from the cathedral. One of the guards began to lead the horse away by the bridle, making a passage through the bowmen and the surrounding crowd, with his sword drawn.

'Stop them!' shouted Tommy, clenching his fists in frustration, but at that moment behind him appeared Georges, and then the Bishop, darting out of the cathedral door.

'Ride!' shouted the Bishop. 'Ride, my brother, or you will be murdered where you stand!'

At that, Drogo half turned his head, saw Tommy and Eloise, and glaring his hatred at them, suddenly found strength to spur his horse. The horse plunged, Drogo grabbing at the reins, and then took off at a gallop, Drogo's black cloak billowing out behind him. The crowd parted to avoid the flying hooves as guards of de Montfort followed him. Tommy and Eloise watched helplessly as Drogo escaped across the square, clattering over the cobbles and disappearing from view down the main street of Toulouse, leading north towards Bordeaux.

The Bishop watched him go, with a bleak look and then shouted, 'Bring me my carriage!'

'There, my Lord Henri,' said the Count de Romolue, indicating with his sword the four horses of the Bishop, steadied now, but still nervously pawing the ground, tossing their heads, wide white eyes glittering and teeth showing, their harness held tightly by the coachman, his eyes to the ground.

'My c-c-carriage!' stuttered the Bishop, putting his hand to his head, as he surveyed the few broken pieces of wood and a smashed wheel which had become entangled with the reins, lying beneath the hooves of his horses. This was all that was left of his coach, the rest just fragments of wood lying scattered about the square.

'Yes, your carriage, my Lord Henri,' repeated the Count.

The threatening crowd took this as a cue to turn upon the Bishop, whose remaining guards pushed their way through to him, with weapons drawn. Georges still stood by his side, his hand on his sword. The Bishop's guards made as if to ready their bows, as they turned to face the crowd.

'Do not shoot,' cried the Bishop, 'or we are dead men!'

As he said this, a half-pulped peach soared through the air, landing splat at his feet; a well-aimed pear caught Georges at the side of the head, and oranges, apples, plums began to fly from all directions. The Bishop and his men stood stock still.

'Do not move an inch,' he commanded.

His fine robes became splattered with pulped fruit, and plum juice ran down his face. This would long be remembered in the folk history of Toulouse, as the hated red and white diamonds of de Montfort disappeared under a mass of squashed fruit, the Bishop's men huddling to the ground as they became covered with the second great fruit salad of the day. Only the Bishop remained standing, his eyes shut, wiping peach pulp from his face with the fine linen sleeve of his robes.

'Can't you try to stop them?' he suddenly shouted in anguish to the Count de Romolue, the last words muffled by an orange catching him on the side of the mouth.

'Stop them!' he yelled again, managing to dodge a large cauliflower, which impaled itself over his shoulder on the cross brandished by St Etienne over the west door, as a further barrage landed on his men.

'Patron saint of cauliflowers,' muttered the Count, glancing up at St Etienne.

'What was that?' demanded the Bishop, but the Count just shrugged, and, turning his back on the scene, made his way over to where his family had assembled.

'Let the crowd vent their rage on this vile man, who has sentenced to death and burnt so many of their sisters and mothers or condemned their sons, husbands, brothers to hang for petty or imagined crimes,' he told himself. Henri should count himself lucky that it's fruit and not rocks that are landing on his head! The Count would willingly have thrown a few plums and peaches himself, if he had not realised, even with his poor grasp of diplomacy, that this would not do.

All the family were gathered within a shield of blue and gold of the Romolue guards. The Count strode into the circle.

'Well! My own Thomas,' he began, 'you did it! It was well done, very well done! I'm proud of you!'

The Countess took Tommy's arm and Eloise moved towards him, but just put out her hand and touched his face with her fingertips.

'But Drogo has escaped!' interrupted Tommy. 'He's escaped our revenge. He should be tried for murder and condemned. Everyone knows that he is guilty!'

'Ah, Thomas, we will catch him. Just now, he'll be safe in the Bishop's palace. But he cannot stay there for long! We will capture him yet. You'll see a scaffold for him, in this very square. You'll see it, yes – and soon, I hope,' said the Count.

Oh, God! thought Tommy. I want to see him in prison, not a public execution, for heaven's sake; but he said nothing, as he saw Eloise nodding vigorously at the Count's words.

Just then, out of the corner of his eye, standing quite close to the Romolue carriage, Tommy caught sight of a figure regarding them closely. This figure was gazing especially at Eloise. This man stood apart from the crowd, taking no part in throwing fruit at the Bishop, a figure dressed in a sailor's uniform of canvas breeches and a white shirt, a tall, handsome figure – the figure of the sailor that they had seen viewing so keenly that night the Château de Romolue, the same sailor that they had seen on the road to Romolue, singing that English sea song.

These thoughts in Tommy's mind were interrupted, because at that moment, Eloise saw him too, and gave a little start, an exclamation of surprise.

'Oh, Thomas!' she whispered, and she gripped his arm suddenly, feeling tears rising behind her eyes. 'That man…' Her voice trailed off.

For an instant, the sailor caught her gaze, and then he turned from her, a look of pain upon his face, and began to walk slowly across the square. Eloise, still holding Tommy's arm, took a step in the direction that the sailor was taking, but Tommy gently took her elbow and steadied her. She turned towards him, her eyes full of tears.

His little pang of jealousy returned. Who was this sailor who seemed such a magnet to Eloise? Eloise shook her head, and almost roughly freed her arm of Tommy's hand. But the sailor had disappeared into the crowd, and search as she might, she could not pick him out. A sigh escaped from Eloise, and the Countess turned to her.

'We must remain here, in Toulouse. Thomas, Eloise!' she announced, saying their names loudly in an effort to get their attention.

The Count nodded. 'Yes, there's some matters to tidy up here,' he said, glancing towards the Toulouse family, gathered around their carriage, nearby. Tommy and Eloise followed his look, and again the blonde head of the daughter could be seen, as she was just about to enter the family coach.

'Is that Clarice?' whispered Eloise. The Countess gave a brief nod, and a little frown passed over Eloise's face. 'And Maddy and Jassy, where will they be if you stay here?' she asked.

'Oh, they'll stay with us in Toulouse,' answered the Countess. 'You two can return to the château in the carriage.'

'Have it sent back to collect us,' added the Count.

'Of course, Father!' said Tommy, his heart leaping with delight. In the coach alone with Eloise!

'You will have guards with you, naturally,' said the Count, gesturing to his men. 'Five of you, please,' holding up the fingers of one hand. 'Step out!'

The Countess took the hands of both Tommy and Eloise and squeezed them gently, as if to say, 'You have earned some time alone together in peace!'

In just a few moments, they were in the coach, the coachman poised with whip at the ready, the guards at each corner and one in front. Tommy put his hand out of the window of the coach and pressed the Countess's hand, waving also to Maddy and Jassy. But they seemed more interested in looking at the wreckage of the Bishop's coach and kicking at the squashed fruit lying among the cobbles.

'We'll return tonight – or more likely, tomorrow,' said the Countess, and her husband inclined his head, gave the coachman a nod, and they were off.

Tommy settled back in his seat with a sigh and Eloise opposite him smiled gently. Tommy put out his hand and touched hers, and she clasped his fingers in her own. As they moved out of the square and out of sight of the cathedral, Eloise came and sat beside Tommy, and rested her head on his shoulder.

'Thomas,' she murmured, 'Oh, Thomas! Now you can tell me: what are cars?'

❧ END OF BOOK ONE ❧

In the next book...

When Tommy and Eloise find the key to making the time switch, the tale overflows into the twenty-first century. Here, Eloise, with Tommy as her guide, encounters a whole new and perplexing world, including cricket, supermarkets and more. Pursuing and pursued by Drogo, they are forced back to 1599 and a series of adventures leads them... Well, where? Read the next volume and discover for yourselves.

Printed in the United States
40906LVS00001B/7-15